Fitful Head
A Ghost Story

CJ Harter

Published in 2018 by FeedARead.com Publishing

A CIP catalogue record for this title is available from the British Library.

Cover design by Mike Martin

www.redherringcg.com

For Harry,

life without whom I cannot imagine

Chapter 1

They're eating breakfast, Richard with the children and Isobel, her bodied self. She's watching them. Can smell the toast, the coffee, see the light bouncing off the jug of juice, the crumbs around Ben's plate, hear background radio from the kitchen, Terry Wogan. What she can't do is touch. She hasn't tried but knows this absolutely. There are rules.

The children's ages flow, it seems. Ben, at once, all his years. His bright new teeth: seven. Excited and loud: ten. Embarrassed high-deep voice: twelve. He's all there.

Melissa's toddler-chubby face on her etiolated nine-year-old body. Her teenage hair uncurled, radiant.

Richard, in her favourite blue-green shirt he never wears, leans across and pinches a sugar puff from Melissa's bowl. "Oi!" She smacks the back of his hand with her spoon.

They laugh.

All of them.

She, Isobel, laughs with them, only she's unheard. She aches for them. Sun streams through the window. This isn't home: their dining room's never sunny. The light flares Richard's hair. He looks up at her. At *her.* That smile: beautiful, healthy, sane.

A white halo.

The last supper.

She pulls back, like a cameraman seeking the wide view, or a woman desperate to obliterate it. She's drawn out to the pink-slashed dawn. Her children are never up at this hour. Now she's outside the cottage, she recognises it. Their holidays at Sumburgh.

Light, friends, music. Cliff walks, boat trips, puffins, whales… they float before her. Or she floats by them?

She's walking on the cliff. Steep grassy climbs, slippy with dew. A Shetland sea fret fogs out sheer drops. Chill, sound-blotting. Except for the ripping cries of fulmars soaring, the guttural thrum of razorbills huddled on the rocks far below. Eerie, otherworldly.

Fitful Head.

Crack-crack! Beyond the smothering gauze, she can't see. Spins around, aware of the cliff-close drop. A firework? Richard leans across and pinches a rice crispy from Melissa's bowl. He snatches: snap. They laugh: crackle. She smacks: pop. Run. Run! She knows this. She's on her belly. Presses her face into the scratching grass. Draws her arms up to protect her head. Please don't kill me. The children! Where are they? They were here just a moment ago. Weren't they? Why can't she remember?

Lie still.

But the children!

Play dead.

Crack! Stuttering, unbodied, dragging death closer, closer. Richard! Don't go, don't leave me. He saunters across the sun-blind road, smiling at her over his shoulder. Bleaching away. Silly Bel, I *have* to go. She scrambles to her feet, starts to run.

It grabs from behind, it always does. Sly. The blue-black arm clamps her shoulders, crushes her chest. The ground falls away.

Eyes shoot open.

The cuckoo clock sang out with that irritating woodland echo. Isobel Hickey had survived another night. Her relief felt almost like happiness. Until she remembered. Her border terrier sighed and snuggled closer into her warmth. She took her phone from the stack of books that served as her bedside table and peered at it: 07:00. A civilised time to rise, for a change. She felt giddy and… something else. She struggled to identify the sensation. Was it hope?

She sat up, swung her legs to the floor, feeling creakier than she should at forty-two, pressed her hands into her lower back and stretched. Brodie copied her, stretched front legs first, then the back. She tickled his ear. He yawned, emitting a tiny yowl that sounded more cat than dog. She ran a hand through her unmanageable hair. It needed a damn good cut. She wound some of it around her finger, shocked yet again to see the bands of grey threading through her chestnut. You should do something about that, Ursula kept telling her. She reached for the ratty dressing gown the dog had been sleeping on at the bottom of the bed and shrugged it on. It was too big, an old one of Richard's.

The bubble of hope burst with a cold splat. She held the sleeve to her nose and breathed in. It smelled of dog. Nothing else. The temptation to curl up and drag the duvet over her head again almost swallowed her, but she pulled on the two pairs of woollen walking socks she'd left on the floor the night before. The red pen-knife lay on the book pile, inviting, but she resisted and headed downstairs for coffee.

The kids would be stirring soon. She had the quiet to herself for half an hour, tops. She stepped into the wellies by the back door and took her coffee outside. The garden was tiny, no more than a yard, but it wasn't overlooked like The Elms. She watched the fields and small wood beyond the new low fence emerge with the dawn, glad she'd done away with the six-foot monstrosity that had been here when they moved in. Why would you want to block a view like that? It was the only good thing about this house.

A sudden outpouring of birdsong thrilled her: the thrush on the tree by the back gate. He'd been there every day this week, singing even before light. She listened to the silences between his liquid calls. Soon she'd hear neighbours clattering pans and crockery as they made breakfast. It reminded her of camping. It felt temporary, everything felt temporary; the tiny house, the view, as if she was on holiday or dreaming. But the proximity of people comforted her. She didn't have to like them, just needed them near. Like a buffalo standing back to back with its herd.

Against danger.

"Mum, what are you doing out there? It's freezing. Come inside." Melissa stood at the back door, tousled and beautiful.

Isobel smiled. Wasn't that *her* line?

Chapter 2

Nights at Beauview were usually easier than days, but this last shift had been a bitch. Still dark when Isobel got home at seven. She pushed the front door closed behind her and examined the backs of her hands. All night she'd had the feeling her skin was thinning. She called softly to Brodie, heard him jump off Melissa's bed. He peered round the top of the stairs.

"Come on, lad. Let's go for a walk."

He ran to get his lead while she left a note for Melissa and Ben. They would be up and gone by the time she got back. Then she could fall into bed, a contented, well-exercised dog by her side, and sleep until they were home.

She pinned the note to the fridge door with her *Have we no wine here?* magnet. They hadn't. If they had, she'd have drunk it for breakfast. The reminder, *FEED THE DOG*, she'd left last night in the magnetic Scrabble letters, now read *FEED THE GOD*. Melissa.

She grabbed her thick fleece and walking boots.

The sun was rising through the trees as she left the car. She'd promised Ben she wouldn't walk at Pennington Flash in darkness, because of the doggers, but they weren't interested in her. And she liked losing herself in the flat, empty black before dawn. She zipped up her coat, pulled on her woolly hat.

She reached the golf course and let Brodie off the lead. He lingered briefly, sniffing bushes, leaving his mark. Then he shot ahead, knowing the way. No golfers yet. He disappeared into a cloud of mist that lay across the grass. She called him back. No road noise. No birds. Through cold-scented mist, thick here, the little copse in the middle of the course... that first tree looked like a crucifix or a ... or a man, with his arms outstretched. She stopped: something had moved over there. She peered through filmy air, glanced over her shoulder. No one about, but eyes on her. She should turn back. The haze lifted momentarily, and she let out her breath.

It's just the tree, you idiot!

Giving the copse a wide berth, she left the golf course path, and took a rougher one alongside the brook. Brodie ran on. Vapour clung to the water. She was walking on clouds. She loved having the place to herself on days like this. Even when Richard was around, she'd choose to walk the dog alone in the early morning, to revel in this peace.

The pain hit her. She clutched her stomach, tasted that hot tang of grief at the back of her mouth. How could she have wasted all those opportunities to hold his hand? To talk with him? She'd thought they had forever.

Stop it now.

She turned away from the brook and entered a tunnel of trees. The new sun hadn't reached here yet, and she could barely make out Brodie through the gloom. His rough black and tan coat blended into the dun path. She called him. He trotted back then veered off into the scrub, distracted by a new scent. If the mist stuck to the canal, the tow path would be lovely.

Brodie growled.

He came to her, then stood still, staring ahead along the path. Snarling. Trees rustled. She strained to see through semi-darkness. A shadow rushed at her. She threw up her arms. The blackbird broke cover in a flurry, scolding, as startled as she was. She put a hand to her throat, laughed.

Brodie stopped growling, but stared ahead still. She followed his gaze. So dim, so quiet, she couldn't be sure... a darker shadow sliced from the murk, reached toward her. Her heart pounded.

A man, just a regular man, emerged on the path. Another dog walker? She tried to make out if she knew him. She bent to put Brodie on the lead until she could check the other dog, but he backed off.

"Hey, boy. What's up?"

He gave her a baleful look and slunk into the bushes. She couldn't see the other dog. Maybe he wasn't walking a dog? But then the man looked back and called: "Zag!"

She relaxed. He was nearly level with her now, holding a lead.

"Morning! One word from me and he does exactly as he pleases."

She smiled. "Mine's the same. Your dog's called Zag? That's what my husband wanted to call-"

But he didn't pause to chat. He simply raised a hand and walked on. As he passed close to her, she caught a hint of his aftershave. *Aramis*: warm, comforting, manly.

She called Brodie. He followed her via his own circuitous route through the trees.

She climbed the steps to the towpath. Dips in the slope between the canal and the Flash preserved the recent snow. In the lingering mist, they floated like little islands in the clouds.

She'd been the first out on last week's snow. Beautiful, the moon still high, glinting off fresh white. The air had smelt cold and clean, and she'd breathed deeply to chill the back of her throat, like she used to do as a kid. She'd followed the footprints of a hare, weaving on the path until they disappeared into the undergrowth. Then she'd picked up fox spoor and something that looked like a cat's. She'd tramped along making her own marks, snow crunching with each step. Brodie had run ahead leaving scamper tracks not much bigger than the cat's. She saw all sorts of bird trails, too. A privileged view of all the wild creatures' private lives.

But then there had been those other footprints. How come she'd forgotten those?

She'd done her 'there and back again' walk that morning a week ago, because she hadn't much time before work. When she returned to the East Bay path, she'd been pleased to see hers and the animals' were still the only tracks. She amused herself trying to walk in her own footsteps, looking back to see what the new marks looked like. But she could hardly feel her nose, and the cold was beginning to bite through her clothes. She strode on.

And that was when she saw the other set of prints.

She'd paused, disappointed she no longer had this crystalline wonderland to herself. Someone had walked alongside her earlier footsteps. It looked like she'd been walking with someone in big boots. And then… but how could that be? She walked closer, keeping her eyes on the new trail. She was right. The larger footmarks didn't diverge off the path; they simply ended whilst hers strode on towards her. As if whoever made them had evaporated mid-stride. She stared down at those last two prints, going over the route she'd taken, trying to account for them. Brodie scrabbled at her leg.

"Sorry, lad. Are you getting cold, too?"

She walked into the oncoming double tracks. Strange. Even stranger when, a hundred metres or so further on, those larger prints disappeared. Again, no footsteps joining hers from the edge of the path. They started abruptly, mid-stride. Someone had gone to a lot of trouble to create that effect. Someone out there was thinking about her, trying to amuse her. Or scare her.

She'd cut short the walk, pushing through an overgrown path back to the car. If there were any more of those footprints, she didn't want to see them.

Chapter 3

Back on mornings, Isobel pushed the tea trolley through to the main lounge. This job always fell to her, being unqualified. Her arms ached. She could barely summon the energy. She needed some decent sleep, but rarely got more than two or three hours before strange dreams woke her.

Bloody hell: Tamzin said they'd fixed this damn trolley.

She kicked the twisted wheel into place and pushed.

Reading didn't work, nor did hot milk. Sometimes she dozed off again only to be woken a couple of hours later. She hadn't even been aware of her peace of mind until it was gone. Now she had to learn to live without that, too.

"Good morning, Florrie. Here's a cup of tea for you. Florrie?" She bent and stroked the old lady's hand. "Sorry to wake you, sweetie. Let me help you with this. We need to keep your fluids up, don't we?" Florrie stirred and opened unrefreshed eyes.

I know exactly how you feel, love.

"Here you go. Have a sip for me. That's it. Well done! You coped with that better this morning, didn't you?" She dabbed Florrie's chin with a tissue and stroked her cheek. The old woman smiled up at her. "I'll leave the cup there. Can you reach? That's it. See you in a little while, Florrie."

She had to manoeuvre the trolley back and forth to get the wheels aligned.

Useless piece of...

She pushed it through to the sun lounge, bracing herself for Ernest's groping, pinching fingers. You had to be light on your feet in this job. Not easy on so little sleep.

Julie, the manager, followed her into the lounge: "Isobel, when you've done with drinks, can you go up to Dorothy, please? I've phoned her son. They're setting off now, but it'll be a few hours before they arrive. So we need to make sure she's not left alone."

"Of course. Poor Dorothy."

"We knew it was coming, but it's never easy, is it?" Julie turned away. "Peter, you old flirt! You are incorrigible." She strode across the room, briskly pulled up the old gentleman's trousers, fastened them and gently directed him back to his chair.

Isobel smiled. She liked working with a manager who wasn't afraid to get stuck in.

When she finished the drinks round, she nipped down to the kitchen to grab a coffee. Sam, the chef, pushed a plate of delicious-smelling home-made biscuits across the counter to her.

She took one. Still warm. "Ta. I'll take it up with me."

"Going up to Dorothy? Give her my love."

"Will do."

She ate the biscuit on the way upstairs. She wiped stray crumbs from the corners of her mouth, tapped on the door and stepped in. Birgitta sat by the bed, stroking Dorothy's arm and singing softly to her in Slovenian.

Isobel glanced at the chart. "Shall we change her now, Birgitta? Save you coming back in half an hour?"

"Okey dokey."

They worked gently, neither of them reacting to the diaper's feeble stench, finally slipping the base sheet from under Dorothy and replacing it with a fresh one. Isobel was shocked by how much weight she seemed to have lost since yesterday. She'd stopped swallowing now which was why Julie had called the family. As they worked, she spoke quietly to Dorothy, explaining what they were doing. She was far advanced in Alzheimer's and seemed not to have understood the spoken word this last couple of months, but maybe compassionate handling and a kind voice still carried meaning for the poor woman.

Birgitta tucked in the final corner. "There you go. All clean and beautiful again." She swept the hair from Dorothy's forehead and bent to kiss it. "See you later, sweetheart. Isobel's here to sit with you now." She smiled and closed the door quietly behind her.

Isobel looked about the room for any jobs needing doing. Everything was in order, of course. Scent of parma violets hung heavy on the air. Birgitta must have anointed Dorothy earlier. There was a delicate bottle of it on the dressing table.

Walls full of photos. She saw that a lot with Alzheimer's, families desperate to have their loved one recognise them.

She settled into the chair by the bed and took Dorothy's hand.

"Brian and Cynthia are on their way, Dorothy. They'll be here very soon. So you just relax, sweetie."

She squeezed the bony hand, felt papery skin through cool clamminess of near-death. She leaned across to the bedside cabinet for her milky coffee. Only lukewarm now, but she sipped it anyway. It would stave off her hunger pangs and she enjoyed not having to rush it. They were at the top of the house. The room large and light. Quiet. Big horse chestnuts, still wintry-bare at the windows on two sides, blew about vigorously. It hadn't been especially windy when she arrived at work, but now it was building to a silent gale. She felt she was on a ship; the trees' swaying created an illusion of motion, while the peace in the room seemed to launch them from the rest of the house.

She jolted. She'd nodded off. The cup was on the floor. Good job she'd finished the coffee. But something was wrong. Dorothy writhed in the bed, throwing her head from side to side, moaning. Isobel pressed the call button. She stroked Dorothy's face. "It's all right, sweetie. I'm here."

Lisa knocked and entered. "How is she?"

"Think she needs a top up on the morphine." As well as Alzheimer's, Dorothy had cancer. Hard to say which of the two was killing her. "Can you tell Sheila? And could you bring up some moisture swabs, please? Oh, and some Vaseline?" Dorothy's lips were dry and cracked.

A couple of minutes later, Sheila, the duty nurse, came in. She put swabs and Vaseline on the cabinet, checked Dorothy's pulse, and swiftly administered the morphine patch.

"That should make her more comfortable. Call me if she doesn't settle. Are you ok, Isobel? You look very pale."

"Tired, that's all."

Sheila gave her an appraising look and she felt she came up short. "Make sure you start getting some proper rest, if you don't want it to be more than that."

"Yes ma'am."

"I'm serious, Isobel. You need to take better care of yourself. Don't think I haven't noticed you losing weight. You'll end up being no use to anyone."

Dorothy let out a little, unassuming moan, relieving her of the need to reply. Instead she said: "All right, Dorothy. You'll soon feel better."

She got busy moisturising the old lady's parched lips and mouth.

"I'll leave you to it. Call if you need me." Sheila closed the door.

Isobel sat down. The heat in the room was sending her to sleep again. She looked around for something to do. A pile of *Hello!* magazines on the little couch by the TV. She went over and picked them up. She settled by the bed and flicked through, reading aloud any bits of gossip that might once have interested Dorothy.

Eventually, Isobel's head nodded. She glanced at the watch pinned to her violet-vile tunic. She'd been up here nearly two hours. Someone would probably come to relieve her soon.

A strange sensation prickled her scalp. She looked up: Dorothy was staring at her with bright, feverish eyes. Feverish, but not unseeing. She was looking at her intently. Recognising her, *knowing* her. But that wasn't possible, she was well past knowing anyone. Dorothy's mouth worked, but no sound came out. Of course not. She had last spoken soon after Isobel started working here six months ago. Nevertheless, she was trying to speak now. Her lips moved. If Isobel hadn't just moistened them, they would have cracked as she struggled to form words. She raised her arm from the sheet; a feeble but definite movement.

What the hell…?

"It's all right, Dorothy. Relax. You don't need to do anything. Try to sleep."

But Dorothy struggled to lift her arm higher, and Isobel watched, fascinated. The hand dropped, rather than was placed, onto the one with which Isobel gripped the raised bedside. She tried not to flinch. Where had all this energy come from?

Dear God. Dorothy was lifting her head from the pillow now. Still working her mouth and staring at Isobel. She wanted to say something. Isobel bent, placed her ear close to Dorothy's mouth. Sharp gasps creaked from dried-up lungs. Isobel smelled sour death on her breath and fought not to recoil.

"He says: 'be happy'."

"What?" Isobel snapped upright. "Dorothy, what did you say?"

Dorothy's head fell back on the pillow. A faint smile played on her lips as she closed her mouth. She drew in a breath with huge effort. A pause. Isobel waited. The frail chest rose again. And a third time. But no breath was released.

Recognition faded from bright grey eyes. Then life faded from them.

She was gone.

Isobel looked down at the withered hand still placed on her own on the bedrail. What had just happened? Hardly daring to look at the face now, she picked up the hand carefully and replaced it on the sheet. She backed away, watching that dead mouth.

What in God's name just happened?

She pressed the call button.

When the family arrived, Isobel escorted them upstairs. She hated this part the most. As she withdrew, the daughter stopped her.

"How was she at the end?"

"Peaceful. Comfortable and free from pain." Trite, but what the daughter needed to hear.

"Did she ask for us? Did she miss us?" This well-groomed, professional-looking woman was about to fall apart.

"She thought I was you. She called me Cynthia. I stroked her hair when she said that. She thought you were here with her."

The daughter broke down. "Thank you for being here. I was so afraid she'd be all alone, that she'd be frightened. I can't tell you…" Her brother took her in his arms, his eyes full of unshed tears and mouthed "Thank you" over her shoulder.

Isobel nodded, went to leave. But Cynthia wasn't finished with her.

"Did she say anything else?"

"Oh Cynth, you know." Her brother struggled with his tears.

"I know. I just wondered."

Before she could stop herself, Isobel said: "She did. Just before she slipped away, she spoke." The brother looked at her, eyes sharp.

Be careful.

"I … I was very surprised."

"What did she say?" Cynthia's expensive mascara wasn't waterproof.

Isobel looked at the brother. He was angry, but what could she do? His mother *had* spoken.

"She said: 'He says: be happy'."

"'He says: be happy'?" Cynthia looked askance at her brother. "What could she mean?"

"Cynth, she was confused. The dementia. She couldn't really speak."

"But this lady says she did."

"I was shocked. I…" The son didn't believe her. She should have kept quiet. But Cynthia wasn't letting it go.

"'He says: be happy'... Oh, I see! She meant Dad, Brian. She was with Dad. Wasn't she?" She cried harder.

"I suppose she was." Brian was crying with her now.

"I'll leave you to…" He nodded, gave Isobel a tight smile.

She closed the door behind her and leaned back on it, trying to forget that reedy, half-dead voice.

Chapter 4

Friday night, and Ben was stuck at home while Davis had the lads round at his for a few beers. Davis' mum let them use their garage. Pool table, darts, and Nathe would bring his usual cheese. It'd be cold enough to freeze your bollocks off tonight but it'd be a laugh, and they'd probably go up Leigh later. But not Ben. Oh, no. Because he was mum-sitting. When he'd agreed with Melissa they needed to keep an eye on Mum, he hadn't realised the sly witch would manoeuvre him into first patrol. Turned out she *had* to see Daniel to*night*, because Daniel's *dad* would be back next *week* and then there'd be *no way* Daniel would be allowed out, *ever.* Where the dad was back from she didn't divulge. Prison, probably.

He flopped on the bed and scrolled through his ipod. He needed to filter through blue space, and that called for Tangerine Dream. Not something he could ever admit to his mates. Music he'd caught off his dad. He rolled onto his back, gazed at the damp stain on the ceiling. Maybe he should paint over that. Maybe he could do the whole room. Or even the whole house. Mum would never get around to it, no matter how much she moaned about the living room wallpaper. And he was the man of the house now. Auntie Sula was always banging on about that. Melissa was right, though. Mum had been acting weird... more weird… recently. Like something must've happened at work the other day, because she was proper freaked when she got home. But could they keep an eye on her 24/7 like this? Maybe he should talk to Auntie Sula? Or Belinda? Belinda was less likely to interfere, more likely to spend time with Mum, and that'd be him off the hook. Sorted. Nice one.

Was that Mum? He pulled out his ear bud.

"Ben! Come quick!"

The dog was barking like mad. Ben took the stairs four at a time. Flew, basically.

The front door was open, and she stood looking out, getting herself all worked up again. "I heard a noise. I thought it was - And look. *Look!*"

Three pushbikes piled up in the tiny front garden, the wheels on the top one still spinning. Ben looked up the street, and down. No one. She was squeezing his arm, shaking.

"Let's go in. It's freezing out here." He steered her back inside.

"We can't just leave them there."

He didn't see why not, but she was already on the phone.

"Who are you calling?"

"The police."

"What? Mum, wait -"

Too late. She was already through.

The person at the other end was clearly unimpressed.

"But they're on my property. Someone has been in my garden and dumped them. And I don't want them here. They could be stolen." He gestured for her to give him the phone, but she turned her back to him and said: "I'm on my own here. I lost my husband." Yeah, but not like *yesterday.* "And I don't know what to do… Thank you, yes. Bye."

"Mum, they could do you for wasting police time."

"What else am I supposed to do? They're sending someone when they get a free half-hour, so."

"On a Friday night, that'll be sometime never."

She peeped through the curtain. "They're still there. Where did they come from, Ben?"

"Someone's dumped them. Not rocket science."

She was getting all het up. "Who would do that? Why?"

"It's not crime of the centu -"

Loud bang on the door. Brodie went berserk. It was the cops, three of them. Mum looked embarrassed and apologised for taking up their time.

"No worries, love. Lucky we were passing with the van when we got the call."

"And *you* don't know anything about this, mate?" one of them asked Ben.

"No idea. Sorry."

"So probably nicked and dumped. Been some muggings up Leigh by kids on bikes. Might be that. We'll sling them in the back of the van and get them out of your way."

As they drove off, Ben twigged: "Did Daniel and his mates come on bikes?"

"Daniel? No. I..." She coloured up again. "You don't think...? No, he was on his own."

"Only Melissa said something about meeting up with friends?"

"He wasn't dressed like he'd biked it."

He wanted to get back to his music, but sat with her while she watched TV. Dad smiled his infectious smile from the massive framed photo over the fireplace, like he was about to wink at him. Ben tried smiling back, but that made him feel like shit. He hadn't seen his dad for... jeez, nineteen months now. How could that be right? It was nuts. Mum shouldn't have put these photos back up when they moved. Supposed to be a fresh start, according to Auntie Sula. The pictures kept Dad close, though, which was good. Or was it? Didn't help in the end, did it? He was dead. Nothing could change that.

"Ben? You ok, love?"

She'd switched off the TV, but he could tell she didn't want him disappearing upstairs again. As long as she kept off girlfriends, he didn't mind.

She nearly cacked herself when the cuckoo clock struck ten. Stared at it like she'd never seen it before, like it wasn't her who'd kicked off when Melissa said she didn't want it up there.

Shouts. Laughter. Melissa burst in, trailing Daniel and three randomers. "Mum, call the police! The bikes've been robbed!"

"But you didn't tell me. How was I to know?"

"Mum, what've you done?" Melissa put her hands on her hips, all arsy.

Mum tried to get mum-ish. "The police came. They've taken them away."

"You called the *cops*? Why would you *do* that?"

"I thought they'd been dumped."

"But they knocked to tell you. " Melissa turned to the lads. "You did *knock*, didn't you? You *knob*heads! How was *she* supposed to know? Well, you'd better piss off and find your bikes, hadn't you? Go on."

She flapped her hands to shoo them, like they were geese or something, and Daniel let her do it, sad bastard. "I'd better go with them, Liss."

"Yes, you better had. You didn't tell me you had idiots for brothers."

"See you, then. I'll call you?"

"Whatevs." She closed the door on him.

Proper bitch, but Ben laughed, anyway.

"Melissa, love. I'm so sorry. I didn't -"

"Forget it." Melissa started to laugh. "You should have seen their faces. They're *such* Neanderthals. I don't know why he brought them. It wasn't to impress *me* with his witty, intelligent family, that's for sure. Completely ruined the night. They'll not be coming again. And I'm beginning to see *him* in a whole new light."

"Oh now, Melissa, don't be mean."

Mum liked Daniel, despite him coming from Westleigh.

Melissa tossed her hair in that irritating way: "Anyone want toast?"

Not predictable at all.

Chapter 5

Isobel couldn't believe it was almost March. She was still getting over Christmas with all its hideousness. Was it always going to be this hard? As she walked, the sun rose and bright sunshine filled a cloudless sky. The air smelt of warming earth. In the tunnel of trees, she looked up. She knew it was beautiful - luminous green, closely-furled leaves against clear azure - she just couldn't make herself feel it. Her head ached from so much bright colour.

She ought to learn to identify the trees. They'd been going to. Richard bought books. But they'd remained unread, because then he decided he was into bird-watching, and so he'd bought binoculars. Loads of them. She couldn't look at that stuff now.

The strong, low-angled sunlight strobed through branches and dazzled her. Shadows of thin trunks striped the path like prison bars.

The dog scampered up the steps to the canal without being told. When she reached the towpath, he ran ahead, barking: she was not alone. A man stood on the footbridge. At first, she couldn't tell which way he faced - all in black, like a silhouette - but soon she saw he had his back to her. He leant on the rail, weight on his left leg, shoulders slightly hunched. Kind of pensive, like he'd been there a while. Like he was waiting. He held something in his right hand. It looked like a lead, but she couldn't see a dog. Maybe he was looking for it. From up there he'd have a good view down the bank to the water and across the other way towards Westleigh. He didn't *seem* to be looking, though. Stories of a flasher came back to her. Brodie barked louder. But the man didn't react, didn't move at all.

She drew level with the bridge: it was the guy she'd seen before. Brodie quietened, and sloped off down the bank.

"Morning!"

He didn't reply. He didn't even look at her. A bit rude. She walked on. Maybe he was wearing earphones. When she turned to call Brodie, the man was watching her. She walked faster, a tickle between her shoulder blades. Why did he stare like that? She couldn't resist: she glanced back. He hadn't moved. *Was* he watching her? Perhaps he was looking for the heron over at the winding hole. But she hadn't noticed any binoculars, or a camera. She walked faster. Bit stupid to come up here by herself. Anything could happen. Like that time with those idiots on motorbikes. That could have turned nasty, and there'd not been a soul about. She patted the phone in her back pocket, suppressed a sudden mad urge to run.

Jill rounded the bend ahead with her elderly spaniels and strode towards her, every inch the brisk countrywoman. If she'd been toting a barrel-broken shot-gun, Isobel wouldn't have been surprised. Would've been relieved, even, because Jill was tough but she was seventy, at least, and the spaniels didn't have a full mouth of teeth between them. Brodie charged out of the long grass to greet them.

"Not seen you for ages, Jill." The spaniels twined about her legs. She bent to stroke them. "Where's my Milly?"

Jill's face seemed to collapse a little before she pulled it back under control. "I've not seen you since, have I? And you've not heard? She's gone, Isobel, I'm sad to say. She died. It'll be two weeks on Thursday."

Not Milly, so full of life and mischief. How much more could she take? "I'm so sorry, I didn't know."

Jill nodded. "It's sad, there's no denying. I miss the old girl dreadfully. But it was quick and peaceful. No vet or anything of that sort. She simply curled up after her tea and slipped away. Just as if she'd fallen asleep. If only we could all go that way, eh? What's this? Now then, love. Don't take on." She patted Isobel's arm. "She was an old girl. It's to be expected."

Isobel wiped a sleeve across her eyes. "I'm sorry. This is so silly. But she was such a sweet little thing. God, you must think I'm soft in the head." She rummaged in her pocket for a tissue.

Jill handed her a clean, pressed handkerchief. "Nothing of the sort. Everyone loved our Milly. These two are lost without her."

Isobel blew her nose.

"Better?"

“Thank you. I’ll let you have this back.” She shoved the hanky into her pocket.

“No rush, love.” Jill peered at her. Isobel looked away. “You need to get some decent sleep, young lady. Still working at the rest home? You’re not looking at all well, if you don’t mind me saying.” After another long look, she said: “Well then. I’d best be making tracks. Come on, you lot. Bye for now.”

She strode off with a wave. Isobel turned to watch her go. The man on the bridge seemed to hold her gaze a moment. Then he moved to the far-side steps, and the bridge was empty.

When Isobel and Brodie got home, muddy and tired, Melissa was still eating breakfast.

“Free period first thing”, she muttered into her cornflakes.

Isobel grabbed the dog’s towel to rub him down. “Free s*tudy* period, Melissa. Not free lie-in.”

“Whatever.”

“Has Ben gone?”

“Yep.” Melissa laughed. “You should’ve seen what he was wearing. He’s such a loser.”

Isobel laughed, too. Her life would never be completely hopeless while she had the kids. She went to the sink: Ben had left his dirty breakfast pots on the side. Melissa scraped back her chair, brought over her dish and cup, put them next to Ben’s and kissed her cheek.

“Thanks, Mum. You’re a star. Oh, by the way, Phyllis knocked to say they’re coming on Saturday, and thanks for inviting them.” She reached to stroke a gentle finger across Isobel’s eyelashes. “Have you been crying again? Come here.”

Isobel snuggled into her warm hug.

Chapter 6

The front door hit the radiator with a resounding bang. Richard had been to the pub again. He couldn't seem to face his family without a drink in him these days. But he said he was under so much strain, it helped him unwind, switch off before he got home. Isobel always found a hot shower worked for her, and told him so.

Richard stood in the doorway to the kitchen, a hand behind his back. "Your work's not the same, love. The pressures are different."

"How?"

"You're not dealing with other people's money."

She reached in the fridge for a bottle of beer. "Merely their lives. Trivial, I know."

He raised his free hand, refusing the beer. "I'm not saying your work's not important. It's much more important than mine, let's face it. But mine's full on, you know?"

She did know. He had targets to meet. Penalties if he failed. No safe salary, like her. His income all commission and rewards. She understood. He could never relax, never switch off, every social event, every new acquaintance, a potential earning opportunity. For him, the line between work and play was forever blurred. If he took the kids to school, he'd be jubilant at teatime that he'd convinced one of the mums to sell through him. He'd sulk after the theatre if friends refused to discuss mortgage arrangements with him. Even at the pub, supposed to be unwinding, he'd be working the room, full of bonhomie, getting to know who had money troubles, who'd recently got a pay rise, who had a baby on the way, who might be the next to up- or down-size.

She was throwing together a quick feta salad to have with couscous, but he wanted to talk, and it must be serious because he'd turned down that beer.

"Are you ok, Rich?"

He laughed, whipped a bottle of champagne from behind his back and slammed it on the counter in front of her. Steam from the couscous condensed on the glass.

"I thought you wouldn't reach that target for another week or so? With the Lowndes' sale?"

"All on track for the end of the week."

She wiped her hands on a tea towel and picked up the bottle. "So what's this?"

"A celebration. Ask me. Go on!"

She sighed. "A celebration of what?"

"Of - no, wait. Where're the kids? I want to tell you all together."

Damn. He'd get them all hyped up about some trip of a lifetime, only for another office to pip them to it. Like he did with New York. After that, Richard had promised never to mention incentives to the children. Isobel would be the one to tell them should a holiday ever become a reality.

He laughed again, pulled her to him, tapped the end of her nose with a finger. “Stop worrying. It’s ok, trust me.”

She let him run upstairs, shouting the kids to come down.

She heard Ben shout back: “I’m on the bog!”

“He’s always on the bog, Daddy. And he’ll stink it out.”

Melissa and Richard came downstairs hand in hand.

“Don’t say ‘bog’, Melissa. It’s not nice.”

“I didn’t say it, he did.”

“She’s right, Bel.”

Melissa gave her a sly look. It would be great if, just once in a while, he’d back her up.

Eventually, he had them all lined up on the living room sofa. He paced in that agitated way she’d noticed a lot recently, then stopped and faced them, his smile showing off beautiful white teeth. Good teeth and a clean, new car being the secrets of selling. Success breeds success, yada, yada.

“Ok, folks. Here’s the thing. My grandad’s brother Tom died.”

Melissa looked at her, unsure how to react.

“Oh, Richard. That’s sad. I didn’t know your granddad had a brother.”

“Neither did I!” He started pacing again. “Got a call from a solicitor in… Bromsgrove, I think he said. Old Tom had no children, no family except me. Us. Isobel, I’m his heir. He left me everything.” He stopped pacing. “And he had a lot to leave.”

Isobel’s mouth went dry. “How much?”

"The house he lived in. Rental properties, too. Some've still got tenants so…Land in Birmingham city centre. And savings and investments of over a million."

"Jesus Christ!"

"Ben, that's enough."

"No, he's right, Bel. Sweet Jesus Christ!"

Richard danced about. Melissa jumped into his open arms. The dog yapped. Ben grabbed his dad's waist, and they conga-ed out of the room and back, then pranced around the sofa.

Could this really be happening? There had to be a catch.

She watched them caper, not liking the febrile shine in Richard's eyes. Not liking it one bit. "Should I open that champagne, then?"

Chapter 7

That bloody nuisance of a cuckoo clock was striking seven as Isobel finally walked through the door. She hated the thing. It jarred with the clean lines, the minimalist look she was trying to achieve in this grand new house. Maybe it should meet with a nasty accident? She threw her keys on the hall table, dropped her briefcase and kicked off her heels. Brodie skittered along the polished floor to greet her.

"Hello, lad. Get down. You'll ladder my tights." She bent to scratch his ears. He squeaked with pleasure. "I'm home, if anyone's interested."

"Kitchen!"

The three of them were crowded round the fridge, heads together, a beautiful auburn rainbow from Richard's strawberry blond, through Melissa's vibrant copper to Ben's more muted chestnut. Like a hairdresser's colour board. Love for them fired in her, and the day's aggravations receded. There was a lot of laughter.

"This looks fun."

Richard came and wrapped his arms around her, kissed the top of her head. "Good day?"
"Not really. You?"
"Excellent."
"Glad one of us is having a good time."
"Isobel, don't be like that. Come and see. We're getting super-organised."
He took her hand and led her to the big, red fridge.
"Voila! We have Scrabble letters. For the fridge! Now we can leave each other messages, make shopping lists. You can boss me about in Scrabble format. They're magnetic."
"Really? I thought they were hanging on for dear life with their tiny little fingers."
Ben laughed. "Good one, Mum."
"Isobel, are you hungry? Grumpy usually means hungry."
"I'm tired, Richard. I've had five urgent hospital discharges to find care for out of zero extra staff, and three carers call in sick. If I have to listen to another social worker bleat about bed-blocking, I'll - sorry, that's work. Yes, I'm hungry. I don't suppose you've had time to cook with all this Scrabble revolution going on."
"It so happens you're wrong there, my grumpy pumpkin."
The children laughed and quickly spelled *GRUMPY PUMKIN* on the fridge. Very educational.
"Put the kettle on, Rich. I'm going for a shower."
She hauled herself up the unnecessarily big staircase, and headed for her opulent en-suite. More and more, recently, she felt like the outsider,

excluded from this game of living the lottery-winner life.

This house wasn't home. The other day she'd driven straight past on autopilot and ended up almost pulling onto the drive at Abbey Road before she remembered. The new owners had got rid of the venetian blinds.

She reached into the shower and turned on the tap.

What had possessed her to agree to all this?

Chapter 8

It hadn't felt like home, not at first, but Isobel had soon learned to love The Elms with all its excesses. After all, home wasn't a place, it was family.

Could she ever feel at home again, now her family was broken? The blue-flowered wallpaper sinewed and choked the heather tweed sofa and armchair, so cosy in the pearly morning room of The Elms, so out of place here at Bodden Street. But she was determined to keep them; the wallpaper would have to go. She'd already had to sell the larger chesterfield and its armchairs from The Elms' living room. The smaller one now crouched here in the kitchen corner behind a cheap Ikea dining table Ursula bought to replace the gorgeous long oak table Isobel and Richard had so loved entertaining at. Once-glossy leather sickened against pallid walls painted the barely-blue of a cold, foggy day.

Soapy water cooled. She hurried to get the washing up finished, her searching eyes on the woods across the field. She picked up the next plate. It was cold, like it had just come out of the freezer. She glanced across at the fridge, accusing, foolish. That was when she noticed her breath expelling as little clouds. She turned quickly, sensing someone behind her. Nothing. She pressed her back to the sink, solid, certain.

No one.

But so cold. And sudden fear, strong, real.

A movement. Across the room, on the table. She looked from the sides of her eyes, not daring to move her head. A squelch. She'd left a knife on the table, stuck in the butter. The knife wobbled. Or was that her sideways glance quivering? The knife clattered to the table. She started. That wasn't her eyesight. A scrape. The knife was sliding to the table edge, gaining momentum. Still, she daren't look straight at it. Not until it flew at her. She ducked. It hit the cooker hood, fell at her feet. Didn't bounce or clangour, simply lost energy. Waited to be picked up. She looked from it to the cooker hood to the table. Had it overbalanced, fallen off? Could it have slid across the lino? She gripped the edge of the sink behind her. She needed solid as her legs threatened to collapse under her. The cooker hood had a big dent at head height. That hadn't been there before. The room swayed. She held on tight, her fingers numbed by refrigerated steel.

Whatever's here with me is not on my side.

Her breath puffed in gasps. A tendril of hair fell across her face and danced in the rushes of air.

Then the breathing mist was gone and the washing-up water warm, almost hot. She bent, picked up the knife, and washed it.

Chapter 9

Isobel finally agreed after Melissa and Belinda ganged up on her. She hated parties, so this was a housewarming get-together, and a small one at that. She closed the fridge door with her bum, her hands full of wine bottles. The bloody thing still rocked despite the cardboard she'd shoved under it. She eased her heel from her shoe for a moment's relief. She hadn't dressed up in ages.

"Can I help you with those, Mrs H?" Daniel took the wine from her.

"Thanks, love." A nice enough boy. Bit skinny, starved-looking even, but handsome with gentle, watchful eyes. Thank goodness Melissa had some continuity in her life right now. Just a shame about his family. Richard wouldn't have given him house room. "There's more pizza in the oven. Make sure you get some."

"I will. Like your dress, Mrs H. That colour suits you." He smiled, and carried the bottles through to the living room.

She smoothed the tight-fitting, turquoise cocktail dress over her hips.

"Hands off, Flirty Gerty!" Melissa emerged from the bathroom. "You go entertain your guests. *I'll* put the pizza out. Is Ben coming to this thing?"

"This is not a thing, Melissa. This is a get-together."

"Whatever. D'you think he'll bring the girl?"

"If he does, you behave yourself."

"Might. Might not."

Isobel set a bowl of Greek salad on the table, breathed in the scent of fresh basil. She started cutting bread, and called: "There's more pizza here if anyone wants it!"

Bill, from across the road, came through. "Isobel, love, you've put on a grand spread for us."

She sidled round the table away from him. "Do get stuck in, Bill. It all needs eating."

"I will that. Don't need telling twice."

At last, Ben put in an appearance. "You know what Dad always said -"

Melissa butted in: "There's only two kinds of people in this house -"

"The quick and the hungry!" they shouted together.

Isobel offered her cheek for Ben's kiss. "Finally! So where's Eamee?"

"Talking to Auntie Ursula."

"O-oh." Melissa put on a posh accent. "And what GCSEs did you study, if I might enquire? And where have you applied to university? Oh, not Oxbridge? How *very* disappointing."

"Good point well made, Squirt. I'd best go rescue her." Ben grabbed a piece of bread and headed back to the living room.

Bill spoke through a spray of quiche: "Fine-looking woman, your sister."

"I suppose she is, Bill. Thank you." Isobel giggled with Melissa as he waddled off with his fully-laden plate.

Belinda swept into the kitchen, glass in hand, resplendent in a flowing red dress that paled her blonde hair to white. Isobel would never have guessed the queen of tight jeans owned such a get-up. "So this is where the fun is! Can I give you a hand, Melissa? You go mingle, Iz. Bill'll be missing you." She winked.

"Mustn't keep him waiting, I guess." Isobel picked an olive from the salad: "That pizza just needs slicing."

She'd only invited immediate neighbours but the cramped living room thrummed with life. Bill filled a lot of space. His wife, Phyllis, didn't. Little old Maud had toddled the few doors down, and perched in the corner, clutching her sherry. Isobel was surprised Joe Jessop next door had accepted her invitation. He kept very much to himself. He was chatting with Ursula, but kept glancing at the door. According to Belinda, who worked from home as a free-lance researcher so was professionally nosy and well-placed to know everyone's business, he'd been widowed young and never looked at another woman since. But he could hardly ignore Belinda tonight. Not in that dress.

The clock struck nine.

"Oh, how charming! A real cuckoo clock." Maud smiled. "You don't see them often nowadays."

"They brought it back from Heidelberg a few years ago. Not to everyone's taste, naturally." Ursula sniffed.

Ben made an eye-poking gesture behind his aunt's back. Isobel frowned and shook her head.

Maud said: "I think it's absolutely charming. So musical."

"It has a certain whimsy about it, if you go in for that sort of thing."

"Auntie, would you like another drink?"

"Thank you, Ben. You're a good boy. I've been chatting with your young lady. Come here, Eamee."

The poor girl trying to blend into the wall by the stairs was strikingly tall and slender with high cheek bones and large glasses that accentuated her big brown eyes.

Ursula blustered on: "Eamee tells me she's thinking of dropping her A-level courses to work at *The* Asda." She made speech marks with her fingers. "That can't be right, can it? I mean, even if she needs a summer job, you have a Sainsbury's in Leigh now, don't you?"

"Eamee, I'm Isobel. It's lovely to meet you, at last. D'you want to give me a hand in the kitchen?"

Eamee's gratitude was palpable. "Yes, please."

Isobel took her hand and led her through the arch. "Sorry about Ben's auntie. She's a bit old-fashioned."

Eamee laughed, a little shy. "No, she's boss."

Ben followed them. "You don't have to be polite, Eamee. We know what she's like." He threw an arm around her shoulder and hugged her. "So, what do you think?" he asked Isobel.

"I think we'll get on fine, don't you, Eamee?"

Melissa stuffed pizza in her mouth and said something unintelligible.

"Nice, Squirt. Way to show me up."

Melissa laughed. She showed Ben a mouthful of chewed food and made a performance of swallowing it: "I *said:* You were in Mrs Litman's class at Lowton High. I remember you spell your name weird."

She handed Eamee a plate and took one herself. They set to filling them, gossiping about mutual friends.

Ben shrugged at Isobel and sauntered back through to the living room. She followed him into the heat radiating off so many bodies in too little space. Should she open a window? But the evening seemed to be going well. Belinda had managed to manoeuvre Joe Jessop into a corner. She twirled her long hair, as she listened intently to him, and now he didn't seem so interested in the front door. Daniel, bless him, was playing host to Bill and Phyllis, listening to pros and cons of petrol versus electric lawnmowers. Ursula now sat by Maud, regaling her with a history of the cuckoo clock. Who knew she was the expert? Though it shouldn't surprise her, as she was an expert in everything else.

That's not fair. Where would you be now without Ursula?

She still thought about that awful day…

Miss Read held Isobel's hand tightly and led her into the office. It smelled funny: not chalky like the rest of the school. It smelled of old people. A big desk with a big chair behind it. A smaller chair in front with Ursula sitting in it. Isobel wanted to run to her, she hadn't seen her for weeks, but Miss Read still held tight to her hand. So she gave her a little wave instead. Ursula waved back, but didn't smile. Then Isobel noticed two other people standing to one side, like they were trying to hide. They had uniforms on. Policemen. Well, a policeman and a police lady. Isobel glanced up at Miss Read. What had she done wrong? She tried to think. She'd called Jezza Thorpe a fucking bastard the other day and he said he'd tell on her, but they wouldn't call the police for that, would they? Ursula's hair was messy. She looked scared. She looked at Isobel like she was trying to get a secret message into her head without anyone else hearing it. But Isobel didn't get it, and then Ursula started to cry and held her arms out to her, and then it all started happening and everyone started telling her things and they could never ever take those things back.

Ursula said: "Come here, Izzy."

Miss Read let go of her hand. Why was everyone looking at her? She walked over to Ursula. "What are you doing here? Has university finished? Mum's supposed to be picking me up today." Ursula pulled her close, hugged her and cried into her hair. "What's up? What's the matter? Sula, tell me!" She looked around the four grown-up faces. The fear in them hit her hard. "What's happened? Where's Mum? I want Mum. I want my Mum!" She was shouting at the head mistress, Miss Benian, and the policeman, but she couldn't help it. "Where *is* she?"

Miss Read stepped forward. "Isobel, sit here." She glanced at the policeman who rushed to place another chair next to Ursula. Isobel sat. Miss Read knelt in front of her. A big chunky necklace, all red, blue and green. Miss Read liked chunky jewellery. "Your sister's got something to tell you. You'll have to be really brave. You're a brave girl, aren't you?" Isobel nodded. Was she? She didn't know. "It's about your parents."

The room seemed to tip. Just like that ride at Blackpool. She looked at Ursula. Everyone else, even Miss Read, seemed to fade and sink back. All she could see now was Ursula's terrified face.

"Go on, love." A hand touched Ursula's shoulder. She jolted like it was an electric shock.

"Izzy… Mum and Dad've had an accident. Driving to work. There was an accident. A lorry - they died. They both died."

Ursula's face disappeared in a muzz of tears. "Mum? You mean *Mum*? But she brought me to school. She was here just before. Then she was going to take Daddy to work. He's a doctor. He works at the hospital. So he can't be... It can't be Mum. It can't be *our* Mum, Sula." She grabbed Ursula's hand. "It's not *our* Mum. It's ok, Sula." They'd made a mistake. She turned to the police lady. "My Mum dropped me off this morning, so she's ok. She's not - died. Her car's a red car. It's a - what is it, Sula? It's a Uno, isn't it? Tell her!" Ursula winced. Isobel was squeezing too tight. She let go.

The police lady knelt beside Miss Read. She had blond hair in a bun at the back. She was pretty. "Sweetheart. There was an accident this morning. Your Mum was driving your Dad to work, after she dropped you here. They were in the red Uno. A lorry had a puncture and the driver, he lost control and crashed into their car. And they died. I'm so sorry."

Ursula was properly crying now. "Izzy, do you understand?"

"But… but…"

"What, darling?" This was Miss Read.

"Who's going to look after me? Sula, who's going to take care of us? I haven't got the door key! What about Tess? She's locked in! She'll be frightened. She doesn't know!"

"I've got a key, Iz. We'll go home and see to Tess. We'll go now, ok?"

"Will Mum and Dad be there?"

"No, we just said. They won't be. They can't… We won't see them again."

"But maybe after a while?" Isobel knew this was stupid, but her brain wouldn't let her think such a bad thing. Ursula looked so sad, she had to try to make her brain work properly. "They died. Really dead?" Ursula nodded. "So *we'll* have to look after Tess now?"

"Yes."

"But who'll look after me?" The biggest lump she'd ever felt rose in her throat, but she didn't want to cry. Not yet, because she had to sort this out. "Can we still go home?"

"Of course we can. It's our house. We'll go now." Ursula brushed away tears. "Izzy, you mustn't worry, because *I'll* look after you, ok? We'll look after each other. And Tess. I promise."

Isobel was gazing at Ursula, and it took her a moment to register that everyone had stopped talking. They stared at the clock. It was striking again. Surely an hour hadn't passed? She glanced at her watch: coming up to nine thirty. But the cuckoo clock only marked the hour. She looked around for Ben. Had he been messing with it? He couldn't leave anything alone. But he was gawping along with the guests, because the clock wasn't cuckooing anymore, it was rasping. She shivered. It had grated out at least ten choked retches now, and it kept going.

"Mum, it's stuck. Make it stop. It's gross. Sounds like a dirty old man."

Ursula snapped: "That's enough, Melissa, thank you."

The party atmosphere was draining fast, but Isobel couldn't speak. And she couldn't turn away. She could only watch the cuckoo burst from its door and cough, burst and cough.

Joe Jessop stood before the clock and tilted his head to one side. "Can you make that out? Can you hear that?"

Belinda sidled over to him. "Oh, yes… Listen."

The room became still, except for the cuckoo's obscene croaks.

"Oh dear." Maud put a hand to her throat. "What is it saying?"

"*Saying?* It's not *saying* anything. Don't be ridiculous." But even Ursula didn't seem so sure.

The rasps rattled on. The cuckoo was not going to stop. It must be Maud putting the thought into Isobel's head, it had to be, but it did sound like the clock was speaking, like it was trying to tell her something, and it wouldn't stop until she got the message. Crazy, but she strained to hear its rough, choked words. She moved nearer. Her guests parted to let her through. Joe stepped aside. And there it was: "List-en, list-en, list-en." The voice of a mortally ill man.

And then a plank in reason broke

"Ben, take the battery out. Now! We mustn't let him in!"

Ben lurched forward, took the clock from the wall. He almost dropped it in his hurry to shut the thing up. Silence. Isobel looked around at the others.

"Well, I'll be damned." Bill scratched his head, like a puzzled cartoon character. The others stood about, clearly not sure how to react.

She tried to sound upbeat. "Gosh, how strange. Sorry about that. And they say German manufacture is second to none. Who's for another drink?"

"Actually, I think I shall make a move now, Isobel. It's …" Maud glanced at where the clock had been. "Late."

"Of course. Ben, would you and Eamee walk Maud up the road?"

"Oh please, don't trouble …"

Joe Jessop spoke up. "I'll walk you home, Maud. See you settled in."

Belinda stepped forward: "Shall I keep you company?"

"I don't think we'll come to much mischief going all of twenty yards." He held his arm out to Maud and she took it, looking relieved.

"I suppose we should make a move too, Bill. It's getting late." Phyllis clung to her husband's arm. Was she shaking? Oh, lord. Some party.

The neighbours shuffled out with thanks for a lovely evening and nervous glances at the clock which Ben had balanced face down on the mantelpiece.

"Bugger. I thought he'd be walking *me* home. I got posh coffee in, specially." Belinda winked at the kids, took Isobel's arm, and hustled her through to the kitchen. "What the hell was that about? What's got into you, Iz?"

"What? I -"

Belinda looked into her eyes. "You need your bed, honey. Don't wash up now. We'll do it in the morning. Upstairs with you."

She chivvied her back to the living room. "I'm off. Leave the mess, kids. We can handle the wreckage between us tomorrow. Get your mum to bed now."

Isobel saw a look pass between her and Ursula.

"Shall I see you across the road, Belinda?"

"Don't be soft, Ben. He's a sweetie." She said this to Eamee. "You're a lucky girl. I'll love you and leave you." Isobel returned her hug. "And what is it they say on the telly? Don't have nightmares?" She laughed. "I'd get rid of that thing if I were you." She let herself out.

"Yes, Mum. Let's throw it away. That was well creepy." Melissa looked at the clock with dislike.

"We can't throw it away. It's your Dad's."

"He doesn't want it now, does he?" Ben sounded weary, and older than he should: "I'll sling it in the shed, and have a proper look at it tomorrow."

Ursula picked up some glasses, took them to the kitchen. Isobel wanted to sleep for a week, but she dutifully gathered scattered plates and placed them by the sink. Ursula ran water.

"You put too much on that boy, Isobel."

What was she supposed to say to that?

Chapter 10

"Darling, I know this is hard." Ursula squeezed Isobel's hands. "Sshh, I know."

She let her cry it out on her beloved leather chesterfield, the dog in her lap, surrounded by huge, framed photos of Richard smiling and laughing at her from every wall.

Eventually, Ursula said: "Let's sit at the table. Then I can show you the figures, hmm?"

Isobel allowed herself to be led into the dining room.

"That's it, sweetheart. Sit here." Ursula pulled out a chair. "Gosh, it's going dark already. It'll soon be the shortest day."

Isobel stirred from her stupor. "The children'll be home soon."

"Ben's got football. Melissa's going to Bernadette's. We need to do this, Isobel. We can't keep putting it off."

She *had* been trying to postpone this, to make excuses. She didn't know what Sula had discovered but it couldn't possibly be good news.

Richard had been spending too much for far too long. And now he'd gone and left her with the mess.

Ursula took a deep breath. "This is quite complex, so stop me if you don't understand. Toby has been marvellous, helping me get a plan together."

Toby. Even the thought of him, short, tubby like a teddy bear, rolling about on her summer lawn, play-fighting with Richard and the kids, calmed Isobel. He'd been meeting with Ursula. The two of them would turn up unannounced and closet themselves in Richard's study for hours at a time. She hadn't given it much thought until he'd urged her to go through the bureau. He said it was full of personal papers, photos, diaries. She supposed she'd get around to it sometime, but the idea of doing it now made her feel jolty, unstable; that stepping-off-a-cliff sensation. It was simply good to have Toby around, more friend than family solicitor. He loved his food so she enjoyed cooking for him. The times he stayed for tea were the closest to normal they ever got these days.

"Isobel, are you listening?"

Ursula went through the figures but Isobel couldn't summon up interest. Not until Ursula put it simply: "Richard hadn't been paying the mortgage on this place, my love. He'd spent most of the capital, you see, so he started holding back payments on the house."

A great tit landed on the twiggy berberis outside the window. Isobel had wanted to buy outright from the sale of the inherited properties. When Richard said he'd rather take out a mortgage, she argued for a less extravagant house. One they could afford a mortgage on...

"You daft egg, we can afford this. More than. We could even move to Cheshire, if you like. There's some amazing properties in Alderley Edge. All the footballers live there. It's you who wants to stick around here, Bel." He flicked through the TV guide, his leg swinging over the sofa arm.

"Our friends are here, the children's friends. The school, everything. You're the one who wanted to raise a family here, close to where you were brought up, remember? We've made our life here, Richard. If you'd wanted to live in Cheshire you should have said so long ago. We could have. You know that. We could have lived in our house in Hale."

"And have Ursula living with us?"

"It was her house, too."

"Exactly."

"But we didn't have to turf her out."

Richard's leg stopped swinging. "We didn't throw her out. She bought the flat with her share, didn't she? And, anyway, now we can help her more, financially, if you want to."

"Yes, but my point is we dragged her all the way over here to be near us, and now you want to move back down there."

"I've said we'll stay, haven't I? But we need somewhere that fits our new…"

"Station in life?" She smiled. This inheritance was going to his head.

"Our changed fortunes."

"How very Dickensian."

"You may mock." He tossed the magazine aside. "But what's the point in having money if you don't live like you have it?"

Richard's idea of living like he had money had got them into this muddle.

"How long had he not been paying?"

"Eighteen months. And, of course, it's not been paid since he… these last five months while we've been trying to sort out the mess." Oh, god, that meant they'd only ever paid six months' mortgage. "I really don't know why you allowed him to handle the mortgage when you knew how hopeless he was."

"He... I… he needed it. You don't understand, Sula. His confidence, his self-respect was so fragile, I couldn't keep undermining him."

Ursula didn't look convinced. "I wish you'd told me at the time you were leaving it to him. Toby thinks he must have been gambling. Still, it's done now. There's no way around it, the house will have to go back to the mortgage lender. I'm sorry. Don't panic, though. We've come up with a plan."

Isobel couldn't listen to this. She fled to the garden. Colourless, bedded down for winter, but come spring all her bulbs would bring it to life. Would she still be here to see them? She wrapped her arms around herself. Tears cooled her cheeks. She'd come to so love this ridiculous house and now it was all slipping away. She wiped her eyes, and went back inside.

Ursula sat at the dining table still, surrounded by documents. She looked over her glasses. "Better? As I say, darling, we can't put this off much longer."

Isobel pulled up a chair and placed her elbows on the table. "Fire away."

Ursula gave her a stern look, then started explaining. Isobel tried to concentrate, though the great tit distracted her with its acrobatics. But she tuned right back in when Ursula said: "You can use money from the children's trust funds. They're safe. Toby saw to that. Not all of it, obviously. We'll find you somewhere modest."

Richard bounded through the front door, slung his new leather briefcase on the hall chair and stood in the kitchen doorway. "You'll never guess what I've done!"

Isobel was washing up and took advantage of her turned back to compose herself. "Go on, surprise me." She dried her hands, and faced him with a smile.

"In there," he gestured to the briefcase, "are details of two trust funds. Count them, two! One for Ben, one for Melissa. £100,000 each to be held in trust until their twenty-first birthdays. How mental is that!"

"Richard, oh my god, that's fantastic. Thank you!" She launched into his arms and he staggered back, laughing.

"The boy done good, then? Toby said you'd be made up."

They kissed. When he put her back on her feet, she said: "I didn't know you were even thinking about this. I can't believe it. I'm so proud of you, Rich."

He pushed a wisp of hair from her face: "I want you all to be safe. I know I'm not always Mr Reliable. I can be a bit unpredictable sometimes, I know that, Bel. But I do try, and I know where my responsibilities lie. And…" his eyes slid from hers, "if I'm ever not here to support you guys, I want you to be ok."

"But why wouldn't you be? Richard, did you go to the GP? What did he say?"

"When have I had time, with all this high-finance wheeler-dealing?" He kissed her forehead. "Shall we tell the sprogs?" He shouted up the stairs. "Kids, daddy's home!"

"But how can we do that? We can't touch it. That's the point of a trust, isn't it?"

Ursula took off her glasses, rubbed her eyes. "Toby says it's do-able. You'll need to discuss it with Ben and Melissa, naturally. We believe you can get a nice terrace round here for no more than £80,000 or so, possibly less. That's £40,000 from each fund which leaves them both with plenty. And they'll own the house, of course. So that's an investment for them."

A nice terrace. Wasn't that an oxymoron?

Chapter 11

Isobel shambled into the kitchen, wrapped in Richard's dressing-gown, and stood in the middle of the room, trying to see through the cloud that fogged her mind. She'd dreamed, she knew that much, and she'd come down because there was something she had to do, had to prevent.

a drum kept beating beating

She looked at her hands. Paper thin, transparent, but still there.

She needed to eat, or go back to bed. But she couldn't do either. Too weak, too insubstantial. She sank to her knees. Brodie came and licked her hands. He tried to climb on her lap, but she pushed him away. Chill seeped from the lino through the dressing gown, and she was glad. She struggled to her feet, dragged herself to the back porch and switched off the heating. She slid to the floor, her back to the cold bathroom wall, and stared into the dark. The dog pawed her. She was fading, her essence draining.

Brodie barked at her.

"Quiet. You'll wake everyone."

He barked louder.

"All *right*. We'll go out. Just shut the hell up."

He barked until she struggled to her feet, then he chivvied at her heels, like a bloody sheepdog. Someone had changed her message on the cheap-and-nasty fridge: *PUT BIN OUT* to *BUT NIP OUT.* She felt a smile warm her failing face.

Thank God for the kids.

Fog. The new sun trickled through mist. Grass remained frosted where its warmth couldn't reach. She walked along the canal, chatted with a couple on a narrowboat they'd called Hope. They were up early to watch the sun rise over the water. They'd recently retired, full of their new adventure. Away from them, loneliness wrapped her like the fog. She wandered onto the grassy hill that used to be slag heaps, and sat on a bench overlooking the Flash. Damp wisps floated over the water. Tears welled, and she let them. Brodie looked up at her, head cocked to one side. He jumped on the bench and nuzzled her, leaned in to her. She stroked him.

"Look at me. What will people think, eh?" She blew her nose. "Who gives a flying fuck, anyway?"

She sobbed, loud and unrestrained. But soon her propriety - or was it her inhibition? - kicked in. She wiped her eyes, sniffed back tears, and drew in a lungful of cold, wet air.

"Right, get yourself together. You've got a dog to walk."

Brodie jumped down and ran. She followed slowly, eyes hot and sore. He disappeared round a bend into the fog. A man's voice: "Hello there, Brodie!"

Who's that?

Brodie reappeared, running back to her at full pelt. She bent to greet him, but he ran straight past into the hill's long grass. There he stopped and watched her. She peered into the grey. A shaft of sun broke through the blanket from behind her and lit the sea of mist ahead, turning it gold. Out of this emerged a figure: tall, all in black.

The guy she'd seen before by the canal, the one who'd lost his dog.

"Still not found him, then?" she said, needing to fill the closing silence between them.

He stopped before her, looked her over as if trying to recall who she was. Or trying to learn every detail of her. "He's wandered off, like he does, down by the water. He'll come back when he's ready. Filthy and wet, no doubt."

"What is he? What breed?"

"Short-coated retriever. You know, the black ones?"

"They love water, don't they?"

"Bred for it, and don't I know it." He turned back the way he'd come and shouted: "Zag!"

"Zag? Really? We were going to call -"

"If you see him, give me a shout? I'll be out here for hours, otherwise."

"Sure. What should I shout?"

"Thanks." He looked at her too closely. Could he see she'd been crying?

He didn't move, so she walked on. She called Brodie and he came after her, zigzagging through the overgrown meadow. He'd never lost that crazy weaving run, driven by his tail wagging, propeller-like. Twice now she'd tried to tell that guy they'd thought of naming Brodie Zag. She wouldn't bother again. He clearly wasn't into small talk. He also didn't seem to want to tell her his name. A bit weird when she had the definite impression he liked her.

Chapter 12

Isobel felt a little better today, stronger, more solid.

She was making coffee when she heard the post arrive. She always had to race Brodie to it if she was in. When she was out, he never touched it. One of those baskets over the letterbox would solve the problem, but she'd never get round to fitting one. A single postcard on the doormat: an unfamiliar thrill of interest. Who did she know who was away right now? She picked it up. Picture of a cathedral. A cathedral she knew: Sagrada Familia in Barcelona. Rather than drop it, her first instinct, she turned it over. A large, confident hand declared in turquoise: "Thinking of you all, Marcus and Lil", with a huge kiss cross. She flung the postcard across the room. Brodie dived on it and ripped it to pieces in seconds.

Good lad.

They'd known Lily and Marcus for years. They were close, or so she'd thought until a few moments ago. She didn't even know they were in

Barcelona. But, then, they wouldn't tell her, would they? So why had they sent the bloody card? She fought Brodie for the shreds, strode out the back, opened the bin and pushed them under the remains of last night's tea.

She washed her hands, then flopped at the kitchen table. Two more friends gone.

"Marcus, please don't shout me down."

Lily's cheeks flushed. Isobel rose to open a window.

Marcus, large and ruddy like a farmer, despite being a pharmaceutical sales rep, exchanged a look with Richard. "I can't let you get away with that, my love. The Anglican church is corrupt to the core."

What was it they said? Never discuss religion or politics? A perfect hostess would steer the conversation to safer waters, but why waste a good argument? Before she could open her mouth, Richard chipped in: "You never used to be a god-botherer, Lily."

Lily laughed, reddening more. "I simply feel there has to be more to this life."

"Why?" Richard wasn't aggressive, merely curious. He leaned forward, elbows on the table and fixed Lily with his big blue eyes. So not curious, flirting, because he knew Lily liked it, and because he enjoyed it, too.

But Lily wasn't to be deflected: "Because nothing makes sense if there's no God. What's it all for, otherwise?"

Marcus snorted. "Nothing makes sense if there *is* a God, you mean."

"No I don't, Marcus. Don't put words in my mouth, please."

A marital spat loomed. The perfect hostess really must intervene now, so she blurted: "I used to believe."

Richard sat back. "Isobel! You *promised* never to disclose that in public."

Marcus laughed his big bear roar.

She batted Richard's arm: "Give over, you."

Lily smiled. "Really, Iz? I never knew that."

Isobel nodded. "It's why we got married. It didn't feel right starting a family without approval."

"You're joking! You two?" Marcus looked askance at Richard.

"It's true, mate. She was adamant. Changed her tune since, like. I was happy living over the brush."

Isobel pinched his ear, playful but satisfyingly hard.

"Ow! That's not very Christian!"

She got up to pour more wine. "I find the whole faith issue fascinating."

"Let me, love." Richard took the bottle from her. He poured large glasses all round.

Isobel resumed her seat. "I mean, what is it that makes you believe, Lily, while Marcus scoffs at the whole idea? You've been together, what, fifteen years? Plenty of time for you to absorb each other's opinions. We do on most things, don't we?"

"Who does?" Marcus showed polite interest, but his heart wasn't in it. She knew his plentiful thoughts on "gobby women".

"Us. Couples. After a while, we think the same way about lots of things. Politics, for instance. I wonder why the same doesn't go for religion. Faith doesn't seem to rub off. You either have it, or you don't."

Richard quaffed his red. "Ah, but you said you *used* to believe. You had it, then lost it."

"Well spotted, my man." Marcus tipped his glass to Richard. How much had he drunk? He could be a pain with too many in him.

"That's just it, love. Because I thought I believed once, I can see now that I never did believe at all, not really." She sounded pretty far gone herself. *Never mind, press on.* "And I wanted so badly to believe. I wanted to belong with the believers."

Marcus roared again: "Don't tell me you wanted to be a nun?"

"No, I get you, Bel. You needed the support, the love."

"The church I went to as a teenager, it was Baptist, all happy-clappy, electric guitars, good-looking minister, young congregation. That's what attracted me. I believed in *them* and mistook that for faith in God, I guess."

"So how did you find out you had no faith?" Lily asked.

Heat rose up Isobel's neck. "I asked God to help me, and he didn't. Simple"

"But there are lots of reasons why a prayer doesn't appear to be answered."

Isobel didn't like Lily's patronising tone: "Like because there's no one there to answer it?"

"Like because it's answered in a way you're not expecting."

Richard warmed to the debate. "Good! Give us a for instance, Lil."

"If you pray for a problem to be taken off your hands, He might decide not to do that, but to make you strong enough to bear the problem, instead."

"Sounds plausible. What d'you say, Bel?" He winked at Marcus.

"No one answered my prayer. I was talking to an empty room. No one made me stronger. I did that for myself."

Lily gave her a condescending smile.

"I did, though!"

Richard reached out, stroked Isobel's cheek. "We believe you, love."

She brushed him away: "This is my point. The same event, right? But two people see it differently. Lily sees a prayer answered, against all evidence, because she has faith. I knew my prayers went unanswered because I had no faith. Don't you see?"

None of them did, going by their patient expressions.

"Prayers are always answered. We've simply to understand what form the answer takes," Lily said.

"Bel?" Richard seemed to fancy himself as David Dimbleby.

"What if it's not the *answered prayer* that confirms faith, but *faith* that confirms the prayer is answered?" Why were they being so dense? "Ok, here's what I think: faith is genetic. Like red hair or green eyes."

"Genetic? I like it!" Marcus said, looking like he really didn't.

"Why don't Lily and I agree? Because we're hard-wired not to."

"Women hard-wired to disagree. You heard it here first, folks." Richard high-fived Marcus.

"Funny guy. You're not listening, as usual. When it comes to faith, we can't choose. I couldn't. You either believe or you don't."

"So…" Marcus helped himself to more wine. "I don't believe because I'm genetically indisposed to, not because religion is the world's biggest confidence trick?"

Isobel caught Lily's puzzled look: "I'm not saying your faith's not genuine, Lil. Of course it is. I'm saying *I* can't believe because I don't have the gene."

"So where do I fit into all this?" Richard reached for the last bread roll. "I've never really thought about faith."

"That's because you don't have the gene."

"So I'm condemned to hell for all eternity?"

"Don't be soft."

Lily bridled. "It's not that. It's because you haven't yet faced something in your life where you've needed to turn to God."

"Steady on, Lil." Marcus said. "That's a little presumptuous."

"And what Isobel's saying isn't? We find Him when we need Him."

"If that was the case, don't you think I'd have found him when I was orphaned at the age of ten?"

Isobel pushed her chair back, and started clearing the main course.

Lily stood too. "Let me help you."

"I've got it, thanks."

"I'm sorry, Iz. I didn't ... I'd forgotten -"

"Sit down, and stop digging, woman," Marcus said through the side of his mouth.

"Doesn't matter. Anyone for syllabub?"

Isobel carried the stack of plates to the sink. Usually she enjoyed eating in the kitchen. Now she wished she'd put them in the dining room. She wanted them all to go away and leave her alone. She heard Richard say, in response to Lily's whispered question: "Give her a minute. She'll be fine."

He said it loud enough for Isobel to hear the instruction. He didn't want any falling out. Neither did she. She'd had too much to drink, that's all.

"Lily, would you come and give me a hand, please?"

Richard's radiant smile warmed her.

Dreary blue kitchen walls reasserted themselves, and she felt the wrench back to her present reality like a physical burn in the pit of her stomach. She shifted on the hard kitchen chair to relieve the numbness in her backside.

She was no longer alone. Melissa hugged her from behind. "You're shivering. How long have you been sat like this?"

Isobel reached for her coffee cup. Milk congealing on top of it.

Melissa put a hand out to stop her. "That's stone cold, Mum. I'll make you another."

Isobel looked at the clock. Gone four. Surely she hadn't sat here all day? Brodie scratched at the back door. She stood, stiff, creaky, and nearly toppled over. Melissa grabbed her arm, and held her around the waist. "You need to lie down. Come on, upstairs."

Isobel lay on the bed, stroking Brodie's head. The lowering sun pressed on closed curtains, spitting shafts through the gap. She heard Maud and Joe Jessop exchanging pleasantries outside in the street. A car pulled up, and its engine died. That donkey brayed again in the distance. Inside, Melissa nattered on her phone, and the dog snored. Isobel tried to sleep, but her mind pulled to its magnet…

"So, it's all genetics? Faith, belief in an afterlife, the whole shebang?"

Richard pulled off a sock with a flourish, and threw it over his shoulder.

Isobel laughed, and pulled the duvet up under her chin, deliciously warm.

He divested the other sock the same way and started on a none-too-sexy striptease. "D'you want me? You do, don't ya? What woman could resist this?" He swayed his hips, thrust his pelvis in her face, practically. "You're gagging for me!"

"Ew!" She pushed her face into the pillow to stifle her giggles. "The kids'll hear you. Shush."

"Let them hear." He started on a bizarre war dance, lumbering from one foot to the other. "They should know they have a sex-god for a father. It'll make them *proud*." *Proud* turned into a Tarzan call to which he beat his chest.

Ben banged on the door. "Oi, Casanova! You're impressing no one. Give it a rest."

Richard dived into bed beside her. "Shit, I thought he was going to come in!"

She laughed so much she could barely breathe. "And you in all your glory."

He lifted the duvet and peered below. "He's cured that for the time being. How old is that boy, anyway? Fourteen going on forty?" He pulled her to him. "So, no afterlife?"

She snuggled into him, cocooned in Aramis. "I don't know. Maybe there is for people with the faith gene."

"The Faith Gene. Sounds like a book. You should write it."

"Someone's probably already done it."

"Maybe." He stroked her hair. She kissed his chest. Under the aftershave, he smelt of soap and warm skin.

"It would be nice to have the faith gene, though, don't you think, Rich? I wish I had it."

"Why? If you despise religion, why would you want to believe?"

"I don't despise it. All that love and friendship. All that certainty. That would be nice."

"And an afterlife. That would be nice."

She raised her head: "What is it with you and the afterlife, all of a sudden?"

"Everlasting life. The death of death. What's not to like?"

"Plenty. One life's enough for me. The secret is to make the most of it."

"If it was on offer, though, life after death, you wouldn't turn it down?"

"But it's not. Not unless you have the gene. And even then, surely having faith in an afterlife doesn't make it real."

"You're a hard woman, Isobel." He sounded sleepy. "I'd have liked an afterlife."

"So we'll have to make the most of the here and now, won't we?"

She trailed her hand down to his belly button, but he was already asleep, snoring softly.

She woke to darkness. Brodie snoring. She was alone with no hope of a future, let alone an afterlife.

Chapter 13

Bernard, full of the usual banter, cool sunshine feeding his good humour. He adored his scruffy mongrels, Clegg and Kipper. Loved putting them through their paces for an appreciative audience. Well in his seventies, slight, frail, with robin eyes, he brought out Isobel's competitive nature. After all, Brodie had his own repertoire of tricks to show off. They made each other laugh with their one-upmanship and she was always pleased when he phoned to suggest meeting at the Flash. He'd be tickled to know what Belinda called her dog-walking friends: the GeeGees, Geriatric Gigolos.

"That's my lot for today. Come on, lads. Let's get our stuff packed up. Fetch!" His dogs darted off to pick up the scattered toys. He nodded towards the golf course. "Don't walk that way, Isobel. There's been a bloke hanging about the last few minutes, watching us." She looked around. "He's gone now. Only, they still haven't caught that flasher."

"It's probably someone dazzled by our dog-handling prowess."

"Of course! Why did I not think of that? Seriously, keep your eyes open and your mouth shut."

"Yes, boss."

"I'd best be off. I'm late already."

He said this every time. A widower, he spent most of his day walking the dogs. He'd stop off now at MacDonalds on the bypass, pick up a coffee and a Big Mac, then head up to Borsdane Wood to walk some more. It got him through life, and good for him.

She wandered on, crushed by the desolation of being alone again. A man stepped out from a little-used path to her left. She gasped.

Zag's owner.

"Sorry." A disarming smile. "Thought you'd heard me coming."

"I was miles away. We've been talking about - and I thought - never mind."

"How are you today?"

"Fine, thanks. You?"

"And how's little Brodie?" He bent and held a hand out. Brodie backed off. "Is he shy?"

"Not usually."

"What is it with me and dogs? Can't even keep my own under control. I thought he'd gone in there." He gestured back the way he'd come. "Have you seen him?"

"I've not been looking. I was chatting on the field so he may have snuck past us."

"I bet he's buggered off to the burger van again. I'll head over there." He made no move to leave. He looked at her in that concentrated way she noticed before. "Are you feeling better? I saw you crying the other day."

"I must get going." She strode on, face burning, his eyes boring into her back. "Come on, Brodie!" The little sod appeared from the undergrowth.

On the path ahead, she saw Lawrence limping along with his old white bull terrier, Griff. She called to him, and put on a spurt to catch up.

"What number's *1 Xtra* on this?"

Ben leaned on the kitchen counter, fiddling with Isobel's new digital radio. She scowled at him. He was waiting for his tea. Football tonight, but he hadn't thought to feed himself. Why do that when he could wait for Mum to come home from a bitch of a shift wiping backsides and cleaning up sick? Isobel grabbed the frying pan and slammed the cupboard door. He'd have to make do with eggs, beans and microwave chips. Except she knew this wasn't making do for him. It was his favourite meal. No doubt Melissa would want something different when she got in from netball practice. One day she might surprise them. Tell them to make their own sodding teas. Ursula was always saying she spoiled them. She did. They were more than capable of cooking their own meals. They had done, before. But now she had this constant dread, this feeling that something bad might happen if she failed in her motherly duties. Stupid.

"Don't mess up my settings, please. It took me ages to work them out. Leave it on Radio Manchester."

"Really?"

"*Yes*, really."

He pressed the button a couple of times, and found a Mancunian accent, the drive-time presenter: "After the news, we have the second in our series *Ghouls, Ghosts and the Unexplained*, and here's a heads-up if you live anywhere near the East Lancs Road at Haydock. You won't want to miss tonight's episode, believe you me."

Monster Mash came on. "That's just down the road. Ghosts in Haydock… spooky!"

"You don't want to believe everything you hear." She cracked two eggs into the frying pan. "This'll be ready in a sec. Can you set the table, please? I'll eat with you. Lissa's not in 'til later."

"But let's listen. It'll be cool. '

As the song neared its end, they sat with full plates before them.

The music faded: "Tonight, we hear from Peter Pensby, a retired postman from Golborne, a man not usually given to flights of fancy. It'll be up to you to decide what you make of him and his strange tale. Before Peter joins us, we'd best warn parents this item may be unsuitable for our younger listeners. Remember you can text us on the usual number or Tweet, if that's your thing. We want to hear from *you*. All right, if you're sitting comfortably, here's Peter's story."

Another voice, older: "Last winter I were driving along the East Lancs towards Liverpool. Me and the wife, Doreen."

Ben laughed. "There's always a Doreen."

"Your eggs are going cold." Isobel picked up her fork.

"…to her sister's in Rainford. We stopped at Haydock island lights. The set by the motorway bridge. It was late, about ten, as I recall. Proper dark night, and a cold one. Felt like we might get some snow. Not much traffic, but there was a couple of cars in front of us so we were under the bridge when we pulled up. No streetlights under there. All of a sudden, this man appears. I didn't see where he come from. Hadn't been paying attention, you know how it is, but I suppose he must've been hiding in the shadows under the bridge. He stands in front of the car. At first, we couldn't see his face. He was tall, and he was right in front of us. Then he bends down to look at us. At least, I think he were looking at us. He had one of them hoodies on. A dark one. The wife reckons it were green." Isobel shifted in her seat, stole a glance at Ben, then at the door to the porch where Richard's old parka still hung. "They notice clothes, don't they, women? Had it pulled down over his face, the top half anyway, so we couldn't see his eyes. Looked proper rough, he did. Well, it gave us a turn, I don't mind saying. He was right there. Very close. Doreen tells me to lock the doors, and I don't need telling twice. The lights went green, and the cars in front pulled away, but this bloke stood there. Wouldn't move. I beeped the horn, but he wouldn't shift. Except to lean down more, and put his hands on the bonnet. It's a little Micra, my Doreen's car, so not much of a bonnet."

"Ben, do we have to -"

"Shush. It's good."

"...cracking little car. Anyway, he leans forward like he's trying to see in through the windscreen, his face right up close to the glass. The lights changed to red again, and he stood his ground, peering in at us. Only we couldn't see his face properly for that hood he were wearing. Then Doreen screamed. He's bleeding, she says. And so he was. Blood dripping all down the windscreen, onto the bonnet. It seemed to be coming from his face. I unlocked the door, but Doreen grabbed my arm. Don't get out, she says. But he's hurt, I says. The lights changed to green again. Couple of cars beeped me as they passed, but no blighter stopped. He needs help, I says. You're not getting out of this car, she says. She can really dig her heels in when she wants, our Doreen. So I sat there. And he stood leaning on my ruddy bonnet, bleeding all over it, looking in at us. And his head, it swayed like a …like I don't know what. Like he couldn't hold it still."

"Hey, Mum, you're spilling your tea."

Isobel gripped the mug that had slipped in her loosened grasp. She placed it carefully on the table, then put her hands in her lap to hide their tremor. Ben appeared not to notice and tucked into his chips with gusto.

The guy was still talking. "It were proper creepy. Doreen leaned across me and locked the doors again. Lights went to red. I'm beginning to feel like a right idiot. Can't stay here all night, I'm thinking. Don't want blood all over the car. So I revved the engine a bit. It sounded louder than I meant with being under the bridge. And - this is the strangest bit - suddenly he were gone. Vanished. Like he were never there. Lights went green. Quick. Go, before he comes back, says Doreen. She's crying now, and it takes a lot to ruffle her. I were in a right state, myself, by this time. Let the clutch out too fast. Stalled it. I wouldn't mind, but I've been driving fifty years or more. Be sharp, he might come back, says Doreen. I'm thinking, I'll be all the sharper if you stop your nagging, woman, but I didn't say anything. I got it started again, and cut straight across the junction into the petrol station. Good thing there were nothing coming the other way because I didn't even look. I needed to get to where there were lights and other folk. My hands were shaking that badly, and Doreen were right upset. Anyway, we couldn't turn up at her sister's with blood all over the car, could we? Never hear the end of it. So I pulled up to the jet wash. There were a bloke filling his motorbike. He came over, asked if everything was ok, only he'd seen us waiting at the lights through all those changes, and wondered what were up. Thought we'd stalled, he did. Thought there was something wrong with the car. Said he were about to come over when I started moving again. He never mentioned the bloke in the hoodie. Never mentioned him. And you know why, don't you? He didn't see him, that's why. Only we saw him. And you'll not believe this, but when I got out to wash the car, the blood was gone. What d'you make of that? Any road up, we didn't tell anyone about it. Not likely. This sort of thing's best kept under your hat. So we kept quiet, oh, a good few weeks, until I overheard a conversation in my local, the Hare and Hounds. I couldn't believe it, a man telling the exact same story. Same junction, same dark green hoodie, same time of night. And same car. You'll not credit this - we both had Micras. And not only that, both our Micras are pale blue. Well, of course I introduced myself. He's a plumber, Phil Rigby. Sound fella. Anyway, we put our heads together, asked around and, believe it or not, we've tracked down four more drivers who've been stopped by the hooded man in the last six months. And that's not the only thing we have in common: we all have blue Micras."

Ben switched off the radio. "Blinkin' 'eck, Mum. I wouldn't drive that way again if I were you." He grinned, mouth full, and pointed his fork at her. "Haven't I been saying you should get rid of the Micra? It's getting old, and that baby blue's way too girlie if I'm going to learn in it. The Audi A1's much cooler."

Isobel pushed her plate away.

Chapter 14

Isobel needed to be here on the hill for the eclipse, in all this silence. Strange lustre, glow-washed. Not dawn not dusk, high-swung sun. Steel-soft light. Shadowed beauty.

Air-chilled cheeks, full-frozen breath. She filled with frail hope, tried to ignore the knot in her stomach every time she thought about Zag's owner. What *was* that? Anticipation? Dread? Both, she suspected.

She bumped into Sylvia with her little mongrel, Fliss, and they sat on the grass together, watching the black shadow pass across a watery sun. No birds sang. Even the dogs settled, seeming to respect the oddness of the light. And then she saw him, away down the slope, strolling by the water's edge. He wouldn't join her, not with Sylvia here, she was certain, but he waved. Then he pointed upward. Not all the birds had stopped singing. A single skylark spiralled higher, higher toward the misbehaving sun, its fluid song coiling around it.

Why does a skylark do that?

Richard would have known.

"I knew I'd put you somewhere safe."

Isobel pulled out the cardboard box from under her bed. She hadn't looked under here since she moved in. A thick layer of fluffy dust covered the closed flaps. She wiped it away with her sleeve. Dust scratched the back of her throat. She opened the box and lifted a small pocket book from the pile of bird books nestled with several pairs of binoculars. Richard hadn't found a pair that exactly suited him; something about the optical ratio thingummy. She doubted it helped that he only tried each one out for five minutes in the Trafford Centre before bestowing them on the children and dashing back to the shop for more. Ben told her later the shop assistant had offered to swap them but he'd wanted to keep them all. She'd been working that day. She had to ensure an income he couldn't touch.

She stared at the book. Remembered when he bought it for her at Leighton Moss Reserve. That had been a good day, a calm day. She caressed the cover. A painting of a chaffinch on the front, a kingfisher on the back. She lifted it to her nose. It smelt dustily of neglect, lack of love, death. She couldn't open it.

A shock of sudden pain took her breath away.

Richard, please don't leave me alone anymore. I can't bear it.

She shook her head. She should be used to the feel of her heart breaking, after nearly two years.

kept beating beating til I thought my mind was going numb

Still she couldn't open the book. In a flurry, she dropped it in the box, closed the lid and shoved it back under the bed.

She must have knelt there for ages. When sounds of life downstairs drifted up, her feet were already numb. She clambered from the floor, pins and needles fizzing through her calves. The children would be wanting their tea.

Chapter 15

She's walking the tow path. Day's breaking. Mist hangs on the canal and down across the dip to the Flash. Silence broken only by harsh heron cries.

She walks. It feels like floating. She knows it's cold, but she can't feel it. Movement above. Three cormorants fly over the canal towards the fog-draped lake. Her feet seem hardly to touch the ground. They move freely. Shoeless.

Wings slap, flap, splash as the cormorants hit the water. She shivers and surveys her body. She's naked. The mist is cold now, raw and wet against her skin, but it feels good, invigorating. What if she should meet someone? So, let them see.

Mist is everywhere. Thickening. Silent and still. She strains to see. Something moves out there. She makes out a figure through the murk. Distant. Receding or approaching? It draws closer, ebbs away, pulls close, fades back. Pulsing with her heartbeat. She wants to call to it. To him. She moves to meet him. Something about his walk, his body's sway... She yearns for him to see her, to acknowledge her. She wants to be real. She wants to feel his touch.

She walks faster. She's certain now he's moving towards her, yet he comes no closer.

Hurry, she wants to cry, *hurry, there's not much time!*

Her side-sight catches movement. Another shadow in the mist rises up the slope, like smoke. Now he walks as an ordinary man. She knows that walk. This second man is nearer. He moves inexorably.

A stirring to her right. A third figure looms on the opposite bank. He walks with her, water-blocked, matching her progress. Hungry eyes eating her. She likes it.

She knows him. Them. She thinks she does.

Is it you?

Before the words leave her lips they're upon her, all three of him. They're so close she feels their freezing breath. Close-cold, they almost touch her. Tall and powerful, they force in. Their hands stroke the air, inches from her aching skin. She lives at last. They want her. They need her. She presses into their touch, burning to be held, longing to lose herself in them.

But her desire shifts with the fog as the left figure, *sinister*, touches. She shrinks back, folds arms across her breasts. The right shadow, *dexterous*, lifts a cold dead hand to her bare back. Her hot skin crawls and freezes, but she dares not move away. The first figure, the true man, spreads his arms, pushes the others aside. Not roughly but with authority. They fall back and stand a way off, watching her. They're greedy.

She is ravenous.

The true man stands before her, but she can't see his face. A dark cowl obscures his features.

Is it you? Her voice barely a whisper. *Don't leave me. I'm nothing without you.*

She unfolds her arms, reaches for his face, wants to push back the hood, but dares not.

She feels him look down at her, imagines cornflower-blue eyes. A river of molten gold to speed her from her cold, dead life.

The hood slips back. A black void where the face should be. Blood gushes from the vacant space, spills cold over her, rushes into her mouth, red and wet and drowning.

Chapter 16

Isobel could still change her mind. She didn't have to go through with it. She glanced in the rear-view mirror, smoothed her hair in the weak glow of the Micra's interior light. So many other cars, so late at night. She hadn't known what to wear. A skirt would be easiest, she supposed, when she dared imagine. But nothing nice. Nothing she'd want to wear again. She could back out. Still time. She didn't have to stay.

"You know this isn't a right good place to park, Bel."

They'd pulled into the little tree-hidden car park at the Flash.

Isobel yanked the handbrake, checked her hair in the mirror. "Why?"

"What are all these blokes doing with their newspapers, eh?"

"Come on, Brodie. Out you get."

Richard closed the passenger door. "See. They're all looking. Can't resist a cut of prime beef." He flexed his biceps, pulled up his collar. She marvelled at how his hair always made it look like the sun was shining even on a dull day like this.

"I should have left you at home." She tucked her arm through his, and they fell into stride along the muddy trail. The dog trotted ahead.

Two men approached, one in a smart suit and shiny shoes, quite unsuitable for the rough track. The other dressed in shorts and tracksuit top, like he was about to play squash. They both avoided eye contact with her.

"Morning!" Richard called. They hurried on. "Bloody brazen as you like. But then, maybe they're after an audience."

"What are you on about?"

"Isobel, does nothing strike you as odd about those two?" He tapped her head. "Hello? Anybody home?"

She stepped back. "Don't, Richard."

"Doggers. Sex in the shrubbery? Preferably with strangers watching?" He thrust his hips in a crude gesture.

"But isn't it a bit cold?"

He roared with laughter. "I expect they work up some friction."

"Oh, you. I see a lot of men walking here. I wondered why they didn't have dogs."

He hugged her. "You're a cracker. Brodie, get out of them bushes. I'm not coming in after you."

A few big drops of rain.

"Let's call it a day, Bel. It's chucking it down."

"It's specking. And the dog's not had long enough."

"But I have."

"Don't whine. It's not attractive. You're worse than the kids."

He thrust his hands in his pockets - he had on that tatty old khaki parka - jutted out his bottom lip, and scuffed the stony path.

"Will you give over?" But she laughed, he looked so like Ben. "Let's walk as far as the bridge. Then we can cut back along the top path."

"But I'm wetter than an otter's pocket, here."

"You poor thing. Besides, we haven't talked any of it through, yet. That's why we took the day off, remember, to get our heads round what we need to do?"

"We can't talk in this." He pulled his hood over his head so she could barely see his face. He looked like the one they kept killing in *Southpark*.

"Richard, you can't keep putting this off. We need to decide what we're going to do."

"You make it sound like a problem. Isobel, we're rich. What part of that don't you understand? We can afford to give up work. Both of us. Do all those things we talked about. Travel. Buy a yacht. Learn to drive it. Sail the kids around the world. Australia." He flung out his arms. "Isn't it amazing?"

"But how long does this kind of money last? How do we invest for the kids' future? How do we get the best price on those properties, the land? And what about the sitting tenants?"

Richard pointed up and down the length of his body. "Estate agent?"

"Not for much longer, if you get your way."

"Relax, Isobel. This is a good thing for us."

"So why doesn't it feel like it?"

"Because you're a miserable bitch who doesn't know how to have a good time? Joke! I'm joking."

Maybe he was right and she was over-reacting. But ever since he heard about the inheritance, he'd been behaving strangely. And it made her nervous.

Back at the car, Richard pointed. "Can you see them now?"

Several vehicles with lone men reading newspapers. She had noticed that before, now he drew her attention to it. She'd always assumed they were on a lunch break. "How do they know to meet here?"

He shrugged. "Websites. Blogs. Dirty bastards. They should get a room."

She'd promised Richard, that day, she wouldn't park here again. In exchange, he'd sat down and focused on their finances. She'd left most of the arranging to him. Big mistake.

She waited in the dark, gazing into the woods, not sure what would happen next. Then it dawned on her: she'd parked the wrong way round, should be facing into the car park. She pulled out slowly, turned and reversed back into her spot. She'd declared her intentions now.

A guy in a car across from her shook out his paper, pretended not to watch. She opened the glove compartment and took out the condoms; she hadn't completely lost her mind. Back then, she'd felt sorry for these pathetic excuses for men. It had all seemed so sordid, so degrading. Now though, she understood their desperate need to connect and be seen, to feel a solid part of the world, to be held, to matter, even for a single moment.

She allowed the man to catch her eye.

What the hell was she doing?

She switched on the ignition, flicked on her headlights. Another car opposite flashed its lights.

Oh, shit.

Its driver's door opened.

Is that a Jag? Surely not.

The man got out.

Don't you dare come near me.

She checked the door-lock. He stood by his car, waiting. He squinted into the glare of her headlights and covered his eyes, a signal for her to switch them off.

She didn't.

He waited.

She threw the Micra into gear, yanked the steering wheel, squealed past him. In the rear-view, she saw him stagger back. She drove too fast toward home, trying to stifle her conviction that, any moment, an unseen hand would grab her collar and drag her back. She shrugged, wriggled to dislodge the feeling. Turned onto a darkened industrial estate. Pulled over, switched off the engine. Her face in the mirror shadowed. She leaned across to the glove compartment.

She pulled up her right sleeve, sat back, braced herself against the seat. The light was poor, even under this streetlamp. She flicked on the interior light. The skin of her inner wrist looked a sickly mustard colour. She traced the lines of delicate veins with a gentle finger. They were green in this light: alien. She opened the red pen-knife, ran a finger along its edge. She'd sharpened it, sterilised it over the stove. But that was days ago. She hadn't really intended to… she never did.

She pushed up her sleeve further, exposing the neat purple welt just below the crease of her inner elbow. She'd been careful, hygienic. It had healed well. She pressed the raised, outraged scar. Not even tender now, it gave no satisfaction.

She searched the glove compartment again, and retrieved a pack of tissues. She rolled the entire contents into a neat, fat wad, and dropped it in her lap. Placed the pen-knife blade across her arm, an inch below the scar. Braced again, bit her lip, and pushed the blade into her flesh. The bite, the burn, the pain. Release: immediate, cleansing, freeing. She let her head fall back on the seat-rest, hot tears stinging her eyes. She needed more, looked down at her work. Blood, that's what she needed to see, but the shocked skin held back. She drew the blade along the incision's pink maw, digging, deepening, lengthening it to match the other cut. No need for it to look a mess.

Smell of warm metal, and now the blood. Black. Beautiful. Hot. Hot. Purifying. Tension and fear ebbed out with the blood. No longer part of her.

She was clean.

Until next time.

She breathed evenly. Relived the sharp, the stab, the relief. Then she placed the knife in the coin tray, picked up the tissue wad and pressed it to the incision. Dull, gnawing ache deep under her insulted skin.

It was enough, for now.

She retrieved the condoms from the foot well, wound down her window and threw them out.

Chapter 17

Isobel headed down the slope towards the water. A man sat on the bench, his back to her, looking out over the Flash. He turned to her. Zag's owner. She felt an absurd rush of pleasure. As Brodie trotted past, the man bent to stroke him.

"Careful! He's filthy." She needn't have bothered: Brodie sidestepped him and headed down to the little beach without a backward glance.

She drew level with the bench. "Bloody foxes."

"He's not rolled in it?"

"And rubbed it behind his ears."

He laughed, deep, pleasing.

"Is Zag down there, too?"

"He was. I think he's wandered off somewhere."

He must trust his dog. She couldn't be so laissez-faire.

"Brodie needs a good swim to get some of it off. I'm not having him in the car in that state. What do foxes eat, anyway, to make their shit smell like that?" He laughed again, and she tingled. "Smells kind of fishy, doesn't it? I've heard you can neutralise it by rubbing tomato ketchup into the fur. But then he'd be a hotdog. Do foxes eat fish? I'll have to try tomato ketchup. I wonder how it works?"

Do shut up, Isobel. He doesn't want to hear this.

"The joys of dog-owning, eh?"

"I wouldn't be without him, though."

"Of course not. He's a nice-looking terrier. Pedigree?"

"If you believe the piece of paper that came with him. To me, he's a little varmint." From the beach, hidden by bushy scrub, the sound of ducks quacking, lots of splashing. "Always showing me up. He never catches them, he doesn't even try. No killer instinct. He just likes to scatter them. Not a typical Border Terrier." The man looked up at her, attentive, squinting against the sun behind her. "I wanted a spaniel, but Richard, he had to have a Border. He was right, though. He's made a great family dog. Friendly, but protective, you know? He never used to growl even, but he's a great little guard dog since -"

You're doing it again.

The man watched her.

"I'd better go see what he's up to."

He stayed her with a gesture, as if he would take her hand in his, but somehow he didn't make contact.

"That's an unusual ring. Eye-catching."

She placed her right hand over her left. Her wedding ring, the pale gold of her father's thick wedding band overlaid and bound with a twirling thread of darker gold from her mother's. Ursula's wedding gift to them.

"It's nothing." She pulled away though she wasn't held.

She picked her way to the little littered beach and called Brodie out of the water. Just in time as an angry swan bore down on him. He scrambled ashore, and shook all over her trousers. Great. Now she'd smell of fox shit, too. The little sod looked pleased with himself. He loved to share his goodies.

Like that time in Shetland.

The children loved the strange St. Ninian's beach surrounded by sea. Intense hot day.

"It's so beautiful. I can't believe we're still in Britain." Isobel lay back, hitched up her teeshirt to expose her midriff, and gazed into infinite blue sky.

Richard lay beside her. "We're almost not. Doesn't even feel like we're in Scotland."

He stretched, lithe, brown, healthy. "What've you got there, boy?"

"Rich, don't encourage him." She squinted through her sunglasses.

"Whatever it is, he's bringing it over." Richard jumped to his feet.

The children were off building sandcastles, but came running. "He's got a seagull! It's dead!"

"Brodie, no!"

Too late. He charged into her, dropped the carcass on the rug, shook sandy water all over them and rolled on his trophy.

Isobel jumped away from the soggy, rotten thing. "Do something! Get it off the rug!"

Richard laughed so hard he was useless. Melissa tried to chase the dog away, but he ducked between her legs. He was having that bird.

"Ben, help!"

Ben grabbed a banana from the picnic basket. "Imagine being here in a storm. There'd be no escape."

"Ben!"

He shrugged. "Come on, Brodster, with me!" He took off, waving the banana, along the sand-spit towards the little island it tethered to the mainland. The dog raced after him.

Picnic curtailed, they drove to see puffins.

Richard got out of the car. "Smell that peat."

He teased and jostled Ben as they walked by Gord Farm with its peat sods neatly stacked by the path. They argued about who could lift the most. Melissa linked Isobel's arm and Brodie, still stinking, trotted beside them.

Richard had studied the map with her last night, after they'd settled the children. Still light in the tent at eleven, the Simmer Dim just a few days away. She'd got the guidebook out. "It says here Fitful Head is Old Norse for Ward Hill, so it's going to be steep. The cliffs are high, Rich. The views'll be amazing, and there might be puffins, but are you sure you'll be ok?"

"The kids'll love it. It'll be fun."

She should have got that in writing.

He was quiet on the walk up the approach. It wasn't as steep as she'd expected, the tarmac path easy underfoot, but he hung back. She walked on with the children.

"Can you hear the sea yet?" Trying to catch that elusive moment when the wild silence of the cliff's shoulder gave way to the roar of waves smashing below.

Melissa rushed forward. "I can! Here. You have to come right here." She jumped on the spot. "I found it, you didn't." Ben strode over and shoved her.

"Ben, stop that!"

"What's up, love? He's only playing."

"I told you I didn't want to come this way."

"Richard, you didn't."

Melissa tugged his hand. "Come on, Dad, you'll be fine. I'll look after you."

Richard shot a *see what you've done?* glance at Isobel. "Thank you, Melly, but I'm here to look after *you*! Wahaha!" He swept her up, threw her over his shoulder in a fireman's lift. Her shrill laughter competed with the cries of breeding birds.

"Watch it, Dad. You don't want to drop her over the edge."

Richard put her down and gripped her hand. "Ben, get back from there! It could be loose, unsafe. There might be overhangs."

"Oh, Richard, give over. You'll give them a complex." But she put the dog on the lead. She walked close to the edge, breathed deeply: salt air and guano. Fulmars and gulls circled below her. Nearer, puffins waddled at entrances to grassy burrows. The steep turfed slope gave way to majestic cliffs, dotted with nesting birds. From far beneath wafted cries of razorbills and shags. She couldn't see them for spray. She felt the precipice's magnetic pull, and stepped back.

"Puffins!" Melissa struggled to get her hand back.

"Careful now, Mellymoo. Not too close."

But she rushed to Ben's side.

"Isobel, for fuck's sake, get them away from there."

"Enough with the language, please." To Melissa, she said: "Come and stand with me, sweetheart. You're making Daddy nervous."

He shot her another filthy look.

"Dad, seriously, come closer. It's a brilliant view."

"I can see plenty from here, thanks, son."

Ben shrugged, and raised his binoculars.

"Isobel! She's too close to the edge. Grab her!"

"Hold my hand, Melissa." She gave the dog lead to Richard and went to stand with the kids. "Ben, it says on the map there's a cave down there called The Thief's House. How cool is that?"

"Moderately."

"Lissa, look. Can you see those puffins? That one's just popped out of his burrow, see?"

"Oh, yes! He's like a funny little old man. Like he's tried putting eye shadow on but he's not very good at it."

Ben lowered his binoculars. "Ha! That one did a massive shit out of his burrow. Projectile poo."

Melissa shrieked with laughter. "Let me see!"

He put the strap over Melissa's head and helped her focus in on the bird. Isobel let go of her hand.

Richard came up behind them. "You have to keep hold of her, Bel. It's dangerous." He looked down and took a step back. "Jesus Christ, why did I agree to this?"

Melissa lowered the binoculars. "Daddy, are you ok?"

"I'm fine, sweetie. Just a bit dizzy."

She went back to puffin-watching. “Too much dirty beer last night. I heard you both.”

He put a hand on Isobel’s shoulder. “Let’s go. It’s getting windy.”

“In a while. The kids are -”

“You do know if I die up here I’m going to come back and haunt you?”

Ben laughed. “But, Dad, you won’t die up here.”

“That’s good to know.”

“No, you’ll die down there.” Ben made a diving motion with his arm. “Splat!”

Melissa let the binoculars fall. “Raspberry jam!”

“You’d only need a tiny coffin. Jam jar would do, probably, d’you reckon, Liss?”

Isobel chewed her lip to disguise a smile.

“Bel, I have to go.”

He stomped off to stand a good fifteen metres back, hands in pockets, shoulders hunched. Maybe she was unreasonable expecting him to enjoy this. If you’re scared of heights, spectacular rock formations probably don’t impress. Still, they’d always said they shouldn’t pass on their stupid hang-ups to the children. She’d kept her fear of spiders from them; so well that Melissa would pick one up to show her, and she’d have to remain calm while she opened the door to let her Attenborough mini-me release her charge into the wild. If she could quell her revulsion at that, why couldn’t Richard make some effort now? He caught her eye, gave an apologetic shrug. Maybe he *was* trying. More reason to be wary of a high cliff than a house spider.

“Come on kids, your dad’s waiting. Let’s go find another beach.”

“Can we go back to the tombola beach?”

She smiled. "It's a tombol*o*, Lissa. St Ninian's all right with you, Rich?"

"Anywhere but bloody Fitful Head."

Isobel had been standing too close to the water. The wind was stronger now and little waves lapped over her boots. She looked down at her cold hands. Her wedding ring wasn't on her finger. It was biting into her tightly-closed fist. She didn't remember taking it off. She thrust it into her pocket, zipped it shut and opened her palm. An angry circle imprinted on white skin.

"Come on, Brodie."

When they emerged from the little beach, the man had gone. She tried not to acknowledge her disappointment, and picked up a good pace to keep warm. She walked back the long way between the new hotel and the brook. Sometimes kingfishers darted blue along the water course here. Today, though, something else drew her eye to the scrub on the other bank: a sense of something shifting like Bigfoot in the trees.

Chapter 18

Friday was Isobel's regular 'get smashed on single malt' night with Belinda. Tonight, they were experimenting with a way-too-smoky Jura.

Isobel pondered Belinda over the rim of her second glass. "I was -" She cleared her throat. "Can you hear me ok? Am I faint?"

"I hear you fine. Go on."

"I was watching a spider in the garden the other day. It was sunny, so I sat out. I thought it might make me feel better." Her own dry laugh depressed her.

"Good." Belinda nodded, smiled, trying to encourage her, bless her. "And did it?"

"I took a book and a coffee outside. It was nice. The sun, the birds. And I saw a spider, a little spider, crawling along the arm of the chair. Busy, like it had somewhere to be, scurrying along. And I could have, I nearly, I could have snuffed it out." She pressed her thumb into the sofa-arm, hard. "I didn't, of course I didn't. But I might have. I might have done it accidentally, even. Maybe I did. Or maybe I sat on its sister. Maybe I wiped out its whole family."

Belinda leaned forward, squeezed her hand. "It was only a spider, honey."

"But it wasn't, though. It was like all of us."

Belinda sat back and held up her glass, warding her off. "I don't get you."

Isobel hardly wanted to put it into words, but if she didn't she'd burst from the pressure of keeping it in. "I don't know, it's a feeling, like when you say 'I'm going to get that back bedroom cleared out one of these days', or 'I'm going to stick with this job for another twelve months, then…' You know?"

"Tell me."

"Well, you can't, can you? You can't decide. Deciding doesn't make it so. You can't plan. It's not in your hands. We're deluding ourselves. There *are* no plans, because…" Why was she even trying to explain? It made no difference.

"I'm listening. How d'you mean?"

"Those plans, *any* plans, they aren't real. They only exist in the future. And there *is* no future. We think we control our lives. God, we're so arrogant, Blin. We plan, we scheme, we dream even, but the place where those things exist, the future, *that* doesn't exist."

"I see."

"Do you? Really? I can see in your eyes, you don't believe it. We're sitting here now, drinking, talking, *living*. And we think this is what we are. We feel we're solid, we're *here*. We so believe we're here to stay, and we're not. We can be gone," she snapped her fingers, "like that. Alive, not alive. In a moment. Less than a moment.

Everything that's me will be gone in less than a moment."

A door slammed upstairs.

Belinda jumped, then laughed: "I thought the kids were out?"

"I must have left a window open."

She hadn't.

The dog, sprawled in front of the fire, grumbled in his sleep.

Belinda swirled her glass. "I get how you're feeling, after all that's happened. And you're right, I'm sure you are. Life is fragile. But we can't live our lives like that. We can't hold that at the forefront of our minds, not all the time." She gazed into her amber drink. "Or maybe we should. Maybe this is what people mean when they say live in the moment? Because it could be your last, so make it count?"

"Or don't, because what's the point? If we have no control, no autonomy, why bother? Why try to live to the full? What does that even mean? Nothing. We have nothing. We *are* nothing."

"No, I'm not having that. It's simply not true, Iz. Look, you've lost so much, yes, I know that. But you still *have* so much. More than a lot of people."

Isobel's laugh came out as a sneer this time, quite unlike the joy-filled laughter she sometimes thought she heard in the empty dark.

Belinda bridled. "I mean it. What about Ben and Melissa? They're your future, surely?"

"But they're not mine to keep. I can't protect them. I could lose them just as easily. Don't you see how simple it is to lose everything you love, everything that's solid in your life, that holds you up, makes you real?"

“I guess I don’t feel it because it hasn’t happened to me. But wouldn’t it be impossible to bear, to live life that way? It’d be like constantly perching on the edge of your seat. Never sitting back to relax.”

That was it, exactly.

“Oh, Iz.” Belinda put down her glass, knelt before her, took both her hands. “You poor thing. No wonder you’re going loopy.”

“Hey, Mrs!”

Belinda hugged her, then held her at arm’s length: “Do you still want to talk, or are we done with the Friday night philosophy? Can we get whisky-wazzed now?”

Isobel laughed. It sounded like pebbles clattering in a brutal surf. She pretended to move on.

But she didn’t. She wouldn’t. She couldn’t.

Chapter 19

Isobel pulled into the canal bridge car park, turned off the engine and sat there. The hurt look on Ben's face when she pushed him away. She'd never seen that green sweatshirt before. He'd caught her off guard: with the hood up, he looked like…

She got the dog out of the car.

But he shouldn't have phoned Belinda. There was no need, she was fine. Blin was bound to tell Ursula, and now they'd all be watching her. Poor Ben, she must have frightened him, shrieking like that. She should apologise to Melissa, too: she saw it all.

Her fragile little family, falling apart. She was pulling it to pieces. She felt for her wedding ring on the chain about her neck. Raised her face to the gentle, cooling rain.

Brodie yanked the lead.

She'd keep to the hill this morning. Fewer people.

A breeze chased away wisps of cloud, left the sky startling blue. Sun spilled a silver pool onto softly-moving water. She stopped to absorb it. Skylarks soared skyward, pouring out their rending song. Ducks bickered. A small flock of Canada geese landed on the water with inelegant skids. A thrush gave voice from a stumpy tree.

"Morning."

She flinched.

He was standing right behind her. How did he get so close without her hearing?

He stepped back. "I've done it again. Frightened you."

"No. Yes. I didn't hear you."

"*He* did." Zag's owner pointed up the hill. Her wonderful guard dog was well away, glowering at them.

"He'll come back when he's ready."

The man fell into step beside her. She felt his presence almost as if he'd put an arm about her. No sign of Zag.

"How have you been, Bel?" She stared at him. "Sorry, too familiar? I had a friend once, called her Bel. Comes naturally to me."

"No one calls me that. I'm usually Isobel. I prefer Isobel."

"Isobel it is, then." He gave a little salute.

"You've never told me your name."

"Look at him!"

Yes, he was definitely avoiding giving his name. But why?

Fifty metres away, Brodie paced from side to side as if held by an invisible fence, like he wanted to get back to her, but couldn't. He barked so hard his front paws left the ground at every woof.

She patted her leg. "Come on, then! What's stopping you?" The dog sat, watched her, all plaintive. "Mad thing."

They walked on. She glanced back. Brodie followed in a parallel line behind that imaginary barrier.

The man asked about her work. He asked about her friends, the children. She chatted on. He had that same knack as Richard's golfing buddy, David, a journalist. David would put you at ease, get you to talk freely, make you feel you were the most enthralling person in the room - Hang on, could this man be a reporter? Was that his game? She'd been approached by tabloids and magazines when they returned from Barcelona. They'd offered a lot of money for her "story". Ursula had beaten them all off. But why would they be interested now, after so long? No, she was being paranoid. He was a kind, friendly person, that's all. He was maybe even a bit lonely, like her.

She stole a look at his face. Strong chin, bit of stubble, gentle eyes. He had his dog lead slung around his neck. It didn't look like a lead, though. More like a -

"See!" He pointed up. A bird of prey dropped from the sky. Surely it hit the ground? But, no, it rose swiftly, a small creature in its talons.

Isobel gasped. "Sparrowhawk!"

"Peregrine. Bigger, more powerful than a sparrowhawk. That was lucky. You don't see one of those every day." He smiled. Eyes locked in the wind-whipped peace, they listened to the awful, victorious screeching, and lesser, hopeless squeals, as the falcon flew into the trees to feed.

She shuddered.

"Cold?"

"Poor thing. Would it be a mouse?"

"Maybe. Or perhaps a young bird? The skylarks are nesting."

"It's too sad. So sudden, so random. But beautiful, somehow… I don't know."

"A privilege to witness."

"I guess so. I've got loads of books at home about birds. And binoculars. I should bring them out with me."

"Absolutely. Why not? Nothing more restful than bird-watching."

She looked for Brodie. He still kept to that parallel path of his. She chatted on as they followed the track around the country park. The man laughed at her attempts at humour, asked sensible questions. But mostly, he listened. She hadn't felt this relaxed for ages. Eventually, they reached the track back to the car. She looked at her phone: they'd been walking for over an hour.

"I'm heading this way."

"I'm over in the big car park. I bet Zag's had a tray of chips off the burger man by now. I've asked him not to feed the little bugger, but what can you do?"

She lifted her hand in a foolish wave. "See you soon."

"Hope so." His smile radiant, teeth white.

As she turned to go, he held out his arm as if he would lay a hand on her shoulder, but didn't touch her.

"Be happy, Bel."

"What?" Dorothy's dying mouth...

"Take care."

"No, you said -"

“I said take care.” His eyes steady. “Is that Zag I can hear? I’d better get off or he’ll wreak havoc with the geese.”

She couldn’t hear a dog. She put a hand out to stop him. He leaned away from her touch. Ever so slightly. “But why did you say that? *Be happy*?”

“Are you all right?”

He made no move to leave her, his eyes concerned. Blue, like cornflowers. Like…

He wasn’t what he seemed.

“Brodie, come on!”

The dog fell in by her side. She didn’t look back. She knew he would be gone.

Chapter 20

"What're you doing?"

Isobel jumped. "Bloody hell, Richard. You frightened me."

He came in: his study, after all. "You said you'd never step foot in here again after you cleaned it up last time. See, no prodigal plates, no mould-infested mugs. The boy done good, yes?"

She'd thrown a proper tantrum that day.

"I was looking at these." She held out the sheaf of credit card statements.

"You've been going through my stuff?" He snatched them from her, and slung them on the open bureau. "Don't do that."

"It's not your stuff, it's ours. *Our* debt, Richard, not yours. I'm the one who's working. They'll come after *me* for it, don't you get that? What the hell are you thinking? This isn't Monopoly money, it's our lives you're playing with, the children's future. Don't you care?" Was that a sneer? "Don't you dare turn your back on me. We need to sort this mess out. I'm talking to you."

He came back, smiled, indulgent. "You're not talking, you're nagging, and you're doing it in a very loud voice. If you've finished, if you're prepared to talk adult to adult -"

"*Me* talk like an adult? Richard, can you even hear yourself?"

He pushed up close, his breath hot. "I don't need this constant barrage of questions. Can't you give it a rest, love?" She flinched, and tried to disguise it by folding her arms. But he'd seen. "I'm sorry. That wasn't respectful. Not like me at all, eh?" He tried the cheeky grin, then turned it off. "Do we have to argue all the time? Can't I come home once in a while and not get the Spanish Inquisition?" He raised his hands. "Mea culpa, ok? Friends?" He held out his arms, a grand gesture.

She shrank from him. "I don't know if I can do this anymore." She pressed her lips together, tried to concentrate on the garden through the window.

"I'm sorry." His voice softened. "Please, Bel, believe me. I didn't mean to upset you."

His hand on her shoulder. She dipped away from it. "I know you don't mean to, but all this…" She gestured at the desk. "I can't keep clearing up after you, Richard. It's too much. I've had enough."

His arms wrapped around her, pulled her into a gentle embrace. He was so warm, so big and warm and strong. She pulled away. That was the problem right there: he wasn't strong. Not his fault: this thing, this illness. So she had to be the strong one, and it was wearing her down. She'd only ever wanted two children. Now it felt like she had three.

"Don't say that, Bel."

God, she didn't say that out loud?

He went on: “It’ll be all right, I promise. I’ll change. I need to get my head sorted, I know that, and I will. I’ll see the doctor again. I’ll go back on the meds-”

She turned on him. “You’ve come off your meds? Richard, you can’t do that!”

He backed off, started shuffling papers around his bureau. “I was feeling better.”

“You idiot. Why didn’t you tell me? How can I help you if you won’t tell me anything? Make another appointment. I’m coming with you.”

“I’ll see him, it’s fine.”

“But I want -”

“I’ll handle it.”

“So nothing’ll change. We’ll carry on like this until you get yourself into really serious trouble, into something I can’t dig you out of. And you’ll drag us down with you. Richard, you’ve got children, responsibilities. You can’t keep living like there’s no tomorrow.” Of course! How could she have been so blind? “That’s it, isn’t it? You don’t actually *want* a tomorrow.”

“Bel…”

“That’s how you’re behaving. I come home and dread what I’m going to find. Why d’you think I arranged for the kids to go to the homework club after school?”

“You’re kidding me. You don’t seriously think-”

“I won’t have them come home and find you…Oh, god. I don’t know. You’re really messing with my head, you know that, don’t you?”

“I don’t mean to.”

“I can’t live like this.” She dropped into the leather wing chair, put her face in her hands, blocked out the light. Her head banged. "I can't do this anymore."

The cuckoo clock ticked. She thought he'd slipped out, run away again, but he said: "Give me another chance. I'll go back on the medication, all of it. I'll see the psychiatrist, get something stronger. I'll keep on it, I promise, Bel. Please don't give up on me. If you give up on me, I'll have nothing to get better for. You're my whole life, you and Ben and Melissa. I need you, Bel."

And there it was: he needed her. That's what their relationship had turned into. But maybe she didn't need him, didn't even want him anymore. Look at him: thick, tousled hair stark and dull, fevered blue eyes pleading with her, bruised circles beneath them.

But what had need and want got to do with it? She loved him more than she ever had, in spite of his unreliability, his weakness, or because of it, she didn't know, and at this moment she couldn't make herself care.

She stood. "I'm going to make a start on tea."

That bureau crouched in the corner of her bedroom now. She'd moved it from The Elms, untouched inside. She still couldn't face opening it. Ursula had sifted through it when she and Toby were making sense of the finances, but Isobel had never plucked up the courage.

She ran an experimental finger along the polished oak grain. It left a clean trail through thick dust. She rubbed the dark grey smudge on her jeans. This house was shrouded in dust. Ursula had told her ages ago to look through the remaining papers,

Richard's personal stuff. But she couldn't. She stepped back. She just couldn't.

Toby had phoned for a chat. She liked that he kept an eye on her. He asked what she'd found in that mess of personal items. She evaded the question, ashamed she hadn't been curious enough to find out.

But she daren't open the bureau.

She slipped a finger under the desk flap, then slid her hand behind and flicked it. It slammed open. She jumped back. A pungent smell of pencil shavings billowed out. The desk was crammed with piles of paper, stacks of notebooks.

What is *all this?*

She closed it. It wouldn't shut fully now, as if the papers had taken a deep breath and were pushing to get out. She opened the three drawers; more notebooks, some loose photos. She'd start with the desk top. She pulled out a notebook. Plain navy blue A5, from WH Smith. A white label on the front, in Richard's hand: *January 2011*. The same month he inherited.

How long had he been keeping a diary?

Brodie lay on her bed snoring, though his eyes never left her. She sat next to him, placed the notebook on her knee, unopened. It was a grenade. She daren't touch it.

But what was the worst that could happen? She grabbed her pillow, propped it against the bedhead, and made herself comfortable. The dog curled up on her lap. She opened the book at random.

Richard's urgent, heavy scrawl. Black fountain pen. Heading: *5th January*. Before they came into the money. Did he write this each day? She flicked through. It seemed so. All those times she thought he was sleeping, lying exhausted or simply staring at the ceiling, he must have been doing this. Feverish activity she knew nothing about. She began to read. It flowed more like a short story than a spontaneous diary entry: he'd put some work into crafting it.

Another shit day. Here's how it goes.

It's happening again, the slipping. Screen won't sit still. Jumping all over the buggering place. Everything's shattering, pixelating. Like looking through cut glass, or a... crystal. Yes, a crystal. Shit, I've got to go. If I don't go now, I'll not be able to drive.

"I'm sloping off early, guys and gals. Poets' Day, am I right?"

Don't engage. Grab your jacket: car keys are in it. Don't be distracted. Aim for the door. Try to walk straight, man. They'll think you're drunk. They do, they think you're pissed. Look at them gawping. Tossers. When have I had chance to get a drink today, you morons? Chained to that bloody desk and phone since nine. Maybe they know I'm sober. Better they think I'm pissed. Don't fumble the door. Reach for the handle. Careful, now! Shit, I look like a spastic.

"See you, then. Have a great weekend, one and all."

There, think I got away with it. When did it rain? Wanker! Bastard aimed right for that puddle. There's the car, where I left it, across the road and up a bit. Never thought I'd be glad it's yellow. I can pick it out, yellow.

Keys. Here they are. Come on, now. Concentrate. Two hands, that's better. Think I've scratched the paint. Sod it: I need to get home. Isobel will know what to do. She'll find my meds. Oops, no! Don't mention meds to Isobel. Verboten. Meds! Hickey, you fool, you've got them on you. In my pocket. No, not there. Trousers? Somewhere... Shit, that one nearly had my wing mirror off.

"What part of yellow can't you see, moron?"

Got them! Back pocket. Knew I had them. Promised the doc I'd keep them with me at all times. Like a good little soldier. Anything to take them with? Hate dry-swallowing. Nothing in the glove compartment. Must be a bottle of water somewhere? Isobel and Melissa are forever necking the stuff. Hang on, I've got that miniature. No, better to swallow them dry, don't mix them. What the hell. Sugar the pill. That's it. Now sit back. Try to relax. What were those breathing exercises? Hippy shit. Deep breaths, that'll do.

Why's Janice watching? Yeah, you don't like that, do you? That's it, scuttle off, silly bitch. Eh up, she's brought in the big guns. Sid's rubber-necking now. Have it out, or keep it out, mate. Yeah, jog on. The light's gone off. They're locking up early. Like I said: Poets' Day. I didn't tell them they could knock off, though. There'll be words on Monday. What's that? Bastard phone. Where did I put it? Sid. Bloody old woman. Don't need that grief.

He's at the window again. Thinks I can't see him. Little wave. Hiya, yeah, off you go. Ok, good. It's kicking in. Vision's calming down. Should be good to go. Should be ok. Would be good to go if these drums would stop. My head, Jesus! Need to wait a while. Can't go home like this, can't go home like, can't go home, can't go, can't. Sleep a while.

Sleep it off, it'll be fine. Tip the seat back, have a nap. Need some sleep then I'll be fine. I can go home.

Then it goes like this.

"Wake up, Richard! Can you hear me?"

Isobel. You know, she'd tell you her hair's brown, chestnut, she says. But it's not. It's not now, anyway. It's flaring red, blazing. Even though it's dark out there. And those eyes, oh my.

I say: "Isobel, hi! What are you doing here?"

She's banging on the glass with the flat of her hand. Her wedding ring's tap, tap, tapping. Where's the window button? Need to turn on the ignition. There we go.

"Hi, Bel. I was just on my way home."

And she says: "Move over." Like that. "I'm driving."

Tell you what, Sid had better die this weekend. If he doesn't, he's going to wish he had.

She closed the diary.

You bastard. If you could write it down like this, you should have shown me.

She flung the book across the room. It hit the yawning bureau, and fell to the floor.

Chapter 21

Rain. Isobel pulled up her hood over the bush hat, so the brim peeped out like a visor. She didn't want to wash her hair before work. No time. Stupid o'clock, just getting light. She had less than an hour. She let the dog off the lead, and stood a moment looking out over stippled grey water.

St George's Day. Shakespeare's birthday. Another day without Richard. She squeezed the keys in her pocket until they bit into her skin.

How could he do this to me? I told him not to go. I told him.

She pulled the keys out, examined the marks in her palm. No blood.

She skirted the edge of the Flash, keeping the woods to her right, scanning the water for birds. The dog snuffled somewhere ahead. She could bring along a pair of Richard's binoculars, but that would mean opening the box again. Perhaps she should get rid of it.

Swans, Canada geese, couple of grebes, loads of ducks. She stopped to watch them. A golden-headed grebe dived then emerged seconds later, silver thrashing in its mouth.

You and me both, little fish.

Other birds cruised over and the fish was swallowed in a couple of gulps.

Movement in the trees close to the path. Still dark in the undergrowth, but something there, more solidly black than its surroundings. And close. She clutched her keys in a spiky knuckleduster. Did it move? It was big. A dog? A big dog. She glanced round for Brodie.

It moved again. Nearer? Her heart thumped. She held her breath. Something pale in the darkness. Oh god, a face! A man's face. Looking directly at her through the branches. It didn't move. What should she do? He was so close. Only feet away.

Don't look. Pretend you haven't seen. Keep walking.

She felt in her pocket for her phone.

And suddenly he was there beside her. He'd emerged without apparent effort, or even movement.

"Zag! Where are you, you useless hound? Oh, hello there."

"What the -? What the hell were you doing in there?" She was shouting.

"Hey!" He put his hands out, placating, soothing. "It's only me. I've lost Zag. I'm looking for him."

She gulped for air. "In the bushes?"

"Isobel, you're shaking."

"What were you doing in there, you pervert!"

"I was…That's where he goes. You know he's done it before."

"No, you were watching me. I saw you."

"I was looking for Zag, but I've frightened you, I can see."

He hadn't been searching. He'd been crouching in the bushes, waiting for her, watching her. Always appearing when she didn't expect it, always looking for his damn dog.

Those kind blue eyes, no shadow of guilt. She wanted to get away, to run. Instead, she tucked a strand of wet hair behind her ear. She was buggered if she'd give him the satisfaction of seeing her rattled.

"I've got to get to work."

"Isobel, don't go. Not like this."

He reached out to her, but she shrank back, straightened her hood and turned to go.

"Bel, please!"

She rounded on him, fierce. "Do *not* call me that! Piss off and leave me alone!" She flourished her key knuckleduster. He didn't even step back. "I'm warning you, you'd better not follow me."

"I won't. It's me. You're safe, Isobel."

He was the flasher, had to be.

"You'd better piss off quick, because I'm calling the police. Don't think I won't."

He stood his ground.

"Brodie, come!" The dog appeared at her feet. She hated herself for the way she scurried, feeling that creep's eyes in her back.

When she glanced over her shoulder, he'd gone.

Chapter 22

"Come *on*, Iz! You're not going to change my mind by dragging your feet."

Isobel shouted: "I'm coming. Keep your hair on."

She'd been so absorbed in sorting through the bird-watching box, she'd lost track of time. The lightweight binoculars and single pocket-book she'd decided to keep lay on the dressing table for her next walk. The box, still full of binoculars and a dozen hardly-used books, sat by the door ready for the guy from the ornithological society. He ran a kids' bird-watching club at weekends, apparently. She checked her lipstick in the mirror.

And there it was again, that weird fading sensation. For a moment, all she saw were her blood-red lips. Like the Cheshire Cat's grin... or Dracula's bride. She wasn't behind them. She was gone. Nothing.

Then it passed, and she was all there. She blinked rapidly. Perhaps she needed her eyes checking.

She ran a hand down the lacy sleeve of her new dress, double-checking the scars weren't visible.

No more bare arms for her. She wobbled down the stairs in her heels, trying to hold her skirt down as it hitched up indecently, and clinging desperately to her fragile good mood. Why did they need to get all dolled up? Belinda was already outside, standing on the doorstep.

She whistled when she saw Isobel. "Don't you scrub up well?"

"I thank you." Isobel did a mock curtsey, immediately regretting it as she turned her ankle on those crazy heels. "I can't walk to the pub in these."

"Course you can. Link with me."

She locked the door, dropped the keys in her bag. Belinda was on the pavement, itching to be off. Isobel turned to join her but saw she'd left the light on. "Bugger. Just a sec."

"Come on, will you? It's cold."

She fumbled for the keys, unlocked the door, reached in and flicked the light switch. She locked up and started to turn away, only to see the light back on.

But I just switched that off.

"Isobel, I'm going with or without you." Belinda half way down the street, warbling: "*With or without yo-uuu.*"

Been pre-drinking all on her lonesome, then. Isobel looked in at the window. The bright overhead bulb flooded the living room with harsh, shadowless light. Brodie lay unperturbed on the sofa. He gave her a lazy glance, then closed his eyes.

Sod it. What harm can it do, anyway?

She tottered to the pavement. "Wait for me!"

and I dropped down and down

The bar was packed, noisy. They grabbed two leather armchairs close to the door. They attracted attention as soon as they walked in. Belinda wallowed in it.

"What's the harm, Iz? We're young, free and single." Isobel grimaced. "We are, though! You've got to start getting out there."

"Out where?"

"You know. *Here*. Dating. Men. You can't live like a nun forever."

"Nice." Isobel sipped her wine to hide sudden tears threatening to spill.

Belinda placed a hand over hers. "Don't go getting upset, honey. I want you to enjoy life again, that's all. It's been two years."

"It'll be two years in July."

"But don't you miss company? You know, sex? Come on, you must do! I don't think I could go two years without. And it doesn't have to be serious. You wouldn't be replacing... All I'm saying is, if you don't get out and about, you're never going to meet someone."

Isobel sat back, folded her arms. "I'm here, aren't I?"

"And you're ignoring that bloke who keeps smiling at you."

Isobel blushed. Blin had her back to the bar: how could she see? Inbuilt radar. Run on witchcraft, no doubt.

The guy, who had indeed been trying to catch her eye, was fifty at least, and could never be accused of gym membership. Belinda looked over her shoulder at him, and he raised his glass to them. She giggled.

"Stop it, Blin. I don't want to talk to him."

"What, because he's … a little mature?" Isobel spluttered into her drink, "Or because he doesn't look like George Clooney?"

"If you must know, yes, of course I miss… physical relations."

"Bless. You're so quaint, Iz."

"But I've…" She leaned in. "I've only ever been with Richard. I wouldn't know where to start."

"Sweetie, there's only one model. They've all got the same buttons and knobs."

"He's coming over."

She sank deep into her seat, hunching her shoulders.

"Iz, you idiot. Sit up!"

"Evening, ladies. You're looking very lovely tonight. I'm surprised your husbands dare let you out." Isobel could smell beer on his breath, mixed with something oniony. She wouldn't want to see that pot belly naked. "I'd like to buy you both a drink, if I may?"

"That's very sweet, but -"

Belinda butted in: "A Chardonnay for me, please, and my gorgeous friend is on Pinot Grigio."

"No, really, not for me, thanks. I'm just leaving, so…"

The man looked offended. "Not on my account, I hope?"

"No, my husband will be wondering…"

"Ah, I see. Message received and understood. Sorry to have disturbed you, ladies."

If he'd been wearing a hat, he would have tipped it. He moved on.

"Isobel! All he wanted to do was buy us a drink."

"I'll get these in, then."

When she came back, Belinda made space for the fresh glasses. "So tell me about this one you've been seeing. This guy with the dog at the Flash."

"Oh, him."

"Don't 'Oh, him' me, lady. You fancy him."

"I don't!"

"Why are you blushing, then?"

"I'm not!" She was. "He's, he *was* just a nice man. Friendly, that's all."

Belinda didn't seem to notice the past tense. "Nice? Friendly? I can't work with these. I need more." She leaned forward, tucked her hair behind her ear. "Come on." She made an impatient beckoning gesture.

Isobel sighed. Belinda had actually seen him the other week when she'd come for a walk. On the hill, he'd strode across their path fifty yards ahead, hurrying down towards the water. She'd realised how much he'd been slowing his pace for her on their walks together when she saw him at full speed like that. He covered the rough ground fast. Too fast? She'd nudged Belinda and whispered: "That's him!"

"Who?"

"Zag's owner, shush. Morning!"

He hadn't so much as broken stride, moving like a missile. He looked neither left nor right. But he wasn't far ahead of them: he must have heard.

Belinda had looked about her. "Where is he, then? Let me at him."

He disappeared over the shoulder of the hill. He must have been after Zag. When they reached the point where he crossed in front of them, there was a single wet footprint. Why had Belinda pretended not to see him?

"Look, I'd rather not discuss him."
"Oh, really?"
"What do you want to know?"
"Whatever you think's important." Isobel opened her mouth to reply. "*Except* nice and friendly."
"I've only met him a few times."
"And every time, you've come home and told me about it."
"Have I?" Belinda widened her eyes at her. "Ok." Isobel *had* enjoyed talking about him. "He's tall. Quite slim. Very dark hair. Short, close-cropped. Not shaved, though. It's kind of velvety, *looks* kind of velvety, I mean." She drank some wine. "Well, you've seen. He wears black."
"Eyes?"
"Blue."
"You didn't even have to think about that, you hussy!"
"They're like Richard's, so."
"Oh, *are* they now?"
Isobel blustered on. "I'm a noticer of eyes. Don't read anything into it. Old Bernard's got dark brown eyes, if you're interested."
"Stick with Mr Tall Dark and Handsome. He *is* handsome, I take it? What *is* his name?"
"I don't know. It's never come up," she lied.
"You're seriously out of practice, Iz. You can't bed someone if you don't even know their name. That would be plain slutty."
"I'm not going to *bed* him, Little Miss Mills and Boon."
"Not with that attitude, you're not! So tell me what you like about him. Apart from his all-round gorgeousness."

She could simply tell her about the other morning, about how he'd turned out to be a creep and she was an idiot, and that would be an end to it. But she didn't want to say that. She didn't even want to think it. Since when had this guy become so important to her? "Isn't that enough?"

"Pure lust, then? Lust is good. Lust is great. A relationship can't go far without it."

"He was just a nice man I chatted to when I was walking the dog."

Again, Belinda ignored the past tense. "So he's one of your Geriatric Gigolos."

Isobel laughed. "No…" She drew the word out.

"So…" Belinda drew that word out.

"Ok, I liked him. All right? Satisfied?"

"Hurray!" Belinda clapped her hands. "More drinks, I think. Then we'll get down to detail." She skipped off to the bar. Isobel watched her shimmy her way to the front of the crush, thanking and bestowing smiles as she went. A few moments later, she emerged with two large glasses of wine. "These are courtesy of the guys at the end of the bar." She placed the drinks on the table and wiggled her fingers at two rugby-looking blokes who raised their glasses to her. Isobel sighed. "What? They offered. It'd be rude to decline. They're cute, both of them."

"In a two-year-old kind of a way, yes."

Belinda looked over at them again. "Too young?"

"Definitely."

"Hmm. We'll see." She undid a button on her silk blouse as she gazed across at her prey. She was so unselfconscious about this, Isobel wasn't even sure she was aware she'd done it. "Anyway, you were telling me about Mr Blue Eyes."

"What else is there to say?"

"Stop being coy. Why do you like him so much?"

Isobel tried not to meet the older rugby player's eye. "He was kind. He listened. He was easy to talk to. He was, I don't know, good company."

"He sounds lovely, Iz."

"I don't know."

"What don't you know?" When Isobel didn't answer, she pressed her: "What's not to like?"

"Nothing. I just…"

"Go on."

"There's something about him. He's a bit…" She'd nearly said 'rapey'. She didn't want to think that about him. She really didn't. "He's a bit strange. Intense. Kind of proprietorial? Like he thinks we have more of a relationship than we actually do. Like he knows me."

"Like a stalker? He's not going to turn into some sort of bunny boiler, is he?"

Belinda was joking, of course, but Isobel felt spiders crawling up and down her back.

Chapter 23

Belinda had been promising for ages to get up early and join her for a dog-walk, but Isobel was surprised when she phoned and said: "Give me five minutes. I'll come over."

Eight o'clock on Sunday morning didn't usually exist for Belinda. Especially a Sunday morning after the Saturday night they'd just had.

But twenty minutes later, they were bowling along towards Liverpool.

"You cynic. I love the great outdoors. What's at Crosby, then? Where *is* Crosby?"

When they pulled up at the marina, the dog barked to be let out.

"Bloody hell, Iz, it's freezing." Belinda hugged her Barbour knock-off.

"Don't be so nesh, woman. It's a bit windy, is all."

"A bit?" She pretended to lean into the gale.

"Give over. Let's get moving or we *will* get cold."

They linked arms and strode out. Brodie darted ahead.

They reached the promenade. Off-shore wind farm in full sail, sun glinting off its blades. A ferry crossed before it, about to enter the docks. To their left, wind turbines beyond the dock wall thrummed into whistling gusts. Tide was out. They had the whole sun-bright expanse of beach.

Isobel breathed in salty-seaweed air and led the way down to firmer sand.

"Look at that guy. What's he doing? He's walking into the sea, the idiot." Belinda stopped, her mouth open.

Isobel laughed. "Have you never seen them before?"

"Who?"

"The statues. They've been on telly. See, all along the beach."

Belinda laughed. "But they're so realistic." She ran to the nearest iron man submerged to his thighs in sand. The dog danced about her. She waved like a windmill. "Come and see. They've got willies!"

Isobel cringed, looked around. As she drew level with Belinda's statue, Brodie cocked his leg on it.

"Stop that."

"He's showing it who's boss. They're cool. Are they all the same?"

"Cast from the sculptor's own body, apparently. Antony Gormley? There's an information board. I'll show you later."

Belinda took her arm, hugged it close. "There's something about them. They seem so sad."

They gazed at the scattered crowd. Sea- flayed faces, supplicating hands, unflinching vulnerability. Swallowed slowly by the turning tide, they wouldn't fall back to safety. Soon they'd be in over their heads.

"Iz, are you ok?" Belinda squeezed her arm. "Let's keep walking. It's too nice a day to be getting all maudlin."

Isobel allowed herself to be led into the whipping wind.

"Did I tell you about the research I've been doing for my mad Victorian author?" Belinda had to raise her voice above the bluster. "She wants an undetectable murder method."

"Sounds like a challenge."

"It's interesting. I do love my job, sometimes."

"What've you come up with? Brodie, leave it!" He was eating something gross. "Come here, you little sod. Sorry. Go on."

"Arsenic. Slow poison in tiny amounts. But I know that's been done. Seen it on TV. So how about this? In Victorian times, arsenic had all sorts of household uses. They even put it in wallpaper. Some historians say a lot of folk died through slow poison in their home environment. They think it could be why so many women suffered from hysteria, back then. I guess they were the ones stuck in the parlour, poor cows."

"Nasty."

"But a pretty good plot device for a murder mystery."

"Absolutely."

"She's going to love it, and when she loves my work, she pays really well."

"Great."

"It got me wondering about *your* wallpaper. You're always complaining it's out to get you."

"I mentioned it *once*."

Belinda trotted to keep up. "Whatever, it might be worth getting it checked out?"

"Don't be daft. It's not that old."

"It's not like any print *I've* ever seen. Oh, by the way, I've got something you could try, if you wanted."

"For the wallpaper?"

"Something to help keep your ... these moods at bay."

Oh, here we go. This is why she wanted to come. "What moods?"

"To help keep you a bit more mellow."

"Mellow? What is this, the sixties?"

"Ok."

"I don't need anything."

"Ok."

"I didn't like that spliff. It got me all paranoid, you know that. Didn't help at all."

"I still think you could do with something. You weren't right last night at the pub, I could tell. And it's not healthy, you coming here on your own, thinking about…"

Isobel stopped. "Thinking about what?"

"You know what. I don't want to say it."

Isobel strode on. "Give it a rest, Blin."

Belinda struggled to keep up. *Short-arse.*

"It's not pot I'm talking about, it's tablets."

"You're joking. I've got my job to think about, and the kids."

Brodie arrived in a skid of wet sand, dropped a stick at Isobel's feet. She picked it up and flung it. He tore after it, barking.

"They're not pills, Iz. Not like that. They're prescription tablets. My Gran's. When I was clearing the flat, I found loads of packs of pills she hadn't taken. I reckon she was stockpiling them, you know, for a rainy day?"

"Belinda, that's so sad."

"Always practical, our Gran. I looked them up. Some are pain relief for her arthritis, and also there's her diabetes medication. She should have been taking those. Could have been what finished her off, come to think of it. Anyway, there's beta-blockers, too."

"For her heart?"

"I guess so. But they're also prescribed for anxiety, apparently. They calm you down. I heard this programme a while ago on Radio 4? Don't look at me like that. I do listen to Radio 4. Turns out classical musicians, violinists and that, pop a beta-blocker right before a performance. Stops their hands trembling."

"Brodie, with me! And?"

"I've tried them. They work. They help relax you. Stop you feeling antsy."

"I've never felt antsy in my life. What does antsy even mean?"

"Stressed. Anxious. If you take one when you're feeling that way, it can help. Want to try?"

She should say no. She could lose her job.

She looked out at the perpetually drowning iron men.

Chapter 24

So much for sodding Spring. Mud-soaked and wind-lashed. Isobel would have to bath the dog before work when all she wanted was a hot shower, warm bed and to sleep forever. She put him on the lead to cross the lane. As she unlocked the car, he snarled: it was him, Zag's owner. The dog strained and snapped at him. Bloody hell, he was coming over.

"Brodie, enough!" She pulled back on the lead. The dog sat, looking anything but acquiescent.

The man stopped several yards away, watching him.

Not so cocky now.

"Keep away. I've never seen him this het up." She stepped behind Brodie and he stood again, his hackles raised. She wiped a drip of rain from the end of her nose.

"I wanted to apologise for the other day. I obviously scared you. When I thought about it afterwards, I realised how odd it must have seemed. Especially with it being dark. I was looking for the dog and I went in further than I realised." He stepped forward. Brodie growled. The man stopped. Rain ran from his hair. "It must have looked like I was lurking."

He *was* lurking. "I've got to go."

"Please, I'm sorry I frightened you. It's the last thing I meant to do."

"So what exactly *did* you mean to do?" Nobody about. Shouldn't talk to him. She tightened her grip on the lead. Brodie pulled, head thrust forward, teeth bared.

"Nothing. The last thing I want to do is frighten you, that's all I mean." He shrugged. "Zag ran into the wood and I followed him." Rain streamed down his face. He wasn't wearing a coat. He never wore a coat.

"Do I look like an idiot?" Brodie started barking. She lengthened the lead. The man retreated. "We both know what you were doing. But, hey, you don't have to explain to me." She opened the car door. The dog barked all the more.

"I do, though. I thought we were -"

"What? You thought we were what, exactly?" She shouted over the dog.

He spread his arms, palms forward. "Friends. I'd never hurt you, you do know that?" He raised his hands to the dog lead slung around his neck, pulled on it, stretched it. It was rubbery, and there was a chrome disc... He saw her looking and hid it behind his back. "That's all I wanted to say. Just, sorry for… you know. And I hope we can still be friends?"

She glared at him, chin up. He mustn't see she was scared. He started walking backwards. Brodie brought the barking down to a rumble.

"Please don't be afraid of me. That would be really sad. Thanks for listening. You need to go and get dry. And I've left Zag in the car, so I'd better…" He gestured towards the other car park.

"Yeah, right." There *was* no dog, no Zag. He was like a creepy old guy offering sweets to children, and she'd been suckered. "Don't let me keep you." He walked to the footbridge over the stream and disappeared from view. Brodie lunged after him, snatching her arm. "Hey you, quiet down."

She watched to check he didn't come back, then knelt beside the dog, her trousers clinging cold to her legs. "Who's a good boy? Yes, you are!"

She leaned back to avoid Brodie's kisses, remembering another time he'd had to defend her.

Saturday afternoon. They were off to the Trafford Centre. Madness. Isobel hated the crowds, the slow shuffle of restricted strides. And she dreaded Melissa's pester power egged on by Richard in spending mode. Ben, wise child, had excused himself. His friend, Ernie, had the new X Box: no contest. Still, it was a family outing of sorts. They hadn't had one in a while. Richard had not been in the mood.

"Come *on*, Bel. You said ten minutes."

He had a cheek, the time he spent preening. She took a last look at herself in the bedroom mirror, and headed downstairs.

"Hey, that's nice, Mum."

Isobel paused on the stairs. High praise from her little fashion fascist. The coat was pre-loved. She'd spotted it in a Culcheth charity shop window. All paisley brocade in deep greens, blues, purples with gold threaded through. It pinched in at the waist, flattered her figure. One good thing about this overblown staircase: it was great for sweeping down.

Melissa looked her up and down. "Very posh. Bernadette's mum's got one a bit like it."

The seal of approval.

Richard came to the bottom of the stairs. "You can't go like that."

"Don't you like it? I know it's secondhand, but it's never been worn. Still had the original tag on. It's a name. Can't remember…" She held her collar and twisted round to try to see the label.

"You can't wear those boots with that bag."

Not this again. "What d'you think of the coat?" She attempted a half-twirl on the stair.

"Change them, yeah?"

"We're late already."

"Change them."

Melissa slipped out of view into the kitchen.

"Don't talk to me like that, please." She tried to step past him, but he blocked her.

"I mean it."

"What is your problem?"

"I haven't got a problem. You're the one with the problem. You can't go out wearing brown boots with a black bag."

"Why on earth not?"

"Just change the boots, Isobel. Or bring a brown bag. I'm not fussed."

"Oh, really?"

Brodie trotted through from the living room and stood between them, looking up at Richard.

"Bring that new bag I bought you. The Mulberry one. You haven't used it yet."

Because she'd returned it. Got back the £650 he'd paid for it. She could never carry around a bag that cost more than anything she'd ever put in it.

"Richard, this is only a problem in your eyes. No one else'll notice."

"I will. You can't wear brown leather boots with a black leather bag. They don't go. You look a mess."

"Thanks a lot." She stood her ground.

"Change it, or we don't go."

"Fine, stay home if you want. Melissa and I are going, whatever." She moved to pass him, but he grabbed her arm. The dog growled.

"You're going nowhere dressed like that."

She looked at his hand squeezing her upper arm. "I have black bags and brown boots. That's it."

"You have that new brown bag I gave you." His face was close to hers. She saw realisation dawn. "You didn't! Say you didn't. Did you take it back?"

"It was way too expensive."

"It was a gift."

"That we can't afford."

He pushed her. She fell on her backside, hitting the stair hard. Brodie growled louder and curled back his lips. "You cow, you're always trying to undermine me, make me feel small."

"Richard, please, I'm not. But you spend too much, you know you do. We've talked about it."

He leaned forward, his face right in hers now. "*You've* talked about it. You never bloody stop. We have money. We're rolling in money. I want you to look like we have money. You need to loosen up, for fuck's sake, have some fun." She closed her eyes against the spray of spit. But Brodie'd had enough. He launched at Richard from the stairs. Richard put his arms up, releasing her, and dodged back to avoid a bite to his neck.

"Brodie! Enough!" The dog immediately sat at her feet, still growling and glaring at Richard.

"You bitch. You'd better get that dog under control, or I will." He walked out of the front door, slammed it behind him.

She was shaking. Sweat trickled down her back. She patted Brodie and whispered: "Good boy."

It felt like a betrayal.

Isobel closed the front door, leaned back on it. She was cold and wet and needed a bath. She called the dog through to the kitchen. He jumped on top of his crate. She towelled him down, her hands still shaking.

"That's a good boy. Did that weirdo frighten you? He scared the shit out of me. That's it: you're done."

He jumped down, and curled up in her tweed armchair in the living room. She ran upstairs for fresh clothes. When she came down, he was fast asleep.

Oh, for a dog's life.

She ran the bath with lots of bergamot bubbles, eased herself into the heat, lay back and tried not to think about Zag's owner. She examined the artex ceiling. That would have to go, along with this avocado suite. Steam rose. She drifted.

The water cooled, but she was too relaxed to move just yet. She ran a finger along the plastic bath rim. So cheap and tacky. She hated that the bathroom was downstairs in this poorly-built extension. She'd found slug trails in here. She'd love to get an architect to draw up plans for a loft conversion. She pictured light flooding through the stairwell, from huge windows in the roof, to brighten the whole house, her big white bed up there in the sun-filled space. She'd have a stunning en-suite. Her room now would be a family bathroom. And she'd demolish this eyesore to create a bigger garden with maybe a window wall dividing it from the kitchen…

Brodie scratched at the door.

"Come in, then, it's open."

Who was she kidding? She'd been here ten months already and hadn't even had the gumption to paint over this awful sickly blue that clashed so horribly with the avocado.

She was beginning to wrinkle. She pulled the plug and stood. At least her towels were quality. She wrapped herself in the plum bath sheet that she imagined still smelled of The Elms. Who would be bathing in her beautiful en-suite now? Had that awful woman been the buyer's wife, or something else? They'd better not rip out that perfect wet room. It had been her favourite part of the house. She stepped onto the plum bath mat. Her toes snuggled into John Lewis gorgeousness. Brodie scratched again.

"Stop it!"

She sat on the toilet. "I'm trying to have a wee, here. Will you stop? You'll scratch the paint. Just push, idiot."

He stopped. His shadow flitted in the gap under the door, pacing to and fro. His claws tip-tapped on the porch's cheap lino: something else she was dying to change when funds allowed. He padded back and forth, guarding. Sweet. That bloody man had rattled him. The shadow stopped. He scratched again.

"I said, come in!" She leaned forward but couldn't quite reach the door handle. "It's not shut, you daft hound."

He gave up. She couldn't see his shadow now.

She washed her hands, and started to clean her teeth. Then stopped, her mouth full of toothpaste.

Didn't I close the kitchen door?

She dropped her toothbrush. It clattered, too loud, into the sink. She drew her towel tighter. If the door was closed, how had he got into the porch? And why hadn't he come through the open door to the bathroom?

She hesitated, her hand on the door handle. What was she afraid of? Seeing her own dog?

Man up, woman.

But what if it's not -?

Enough!

She opened the door. Darkness. Because the kitchen door *was* closed. She turned on the porch light. No Brodie. She turned off the light, pushed the bathroom door closed again, and looked at the gap under it. No light shone through. And yet she'd seen the shadow of his legs. But how could she have? There was no light to cast a shadow. She crept into the porch and pushed the kitchen door: it was securely shut. Brodie couldn't have opened it - she shuddered - *and closed it again*, unaided. She and Brodie were not alone in the house. She gathered the towel to her chest, pushed damp hair from her eyes, steeled herself and turned the kitchen door handle. Ever so carefully. She peeped around the door. “Brodie?” Her voice, a hoarse whisper, creeped her out.

She stepped, tentative, to the arch.

Brodie was asleep in the armchair, exactly where she’d left him.

Chapter 25

A warm, muggy morning. Isobel had already dispensed with her fleece, tied it around her waist. She strode along, gazing up at grey sky through overhanging branches, trying to recognise birdsong. She could tell the robins all right. They were easy because she always saw them. But how did thrushes differ from blackbirds? And there was a tumbling little song she'd love to pin down. She should get one of those phone apps.

She wandered on. That bloody man. She glanced over her shoulder. The way he'd behaved, how he'd tried to justify himself. He'd no damn right. Pretending to walk a dog to cosy up to her. What a creep. And yet he'd seemed so attractive. Anyway, it was over, whatever it had been. He'd gone.

She ducked through the hedge. An elliptic path ran the field's length between bypass and old railway line. The dog liked to jump about in the long grass. But when they reached the field Brodie sniffed, puzzled. It had been mown, the path barely visible in a wide expanse of pallid green. Here and there, the grass yellowed as if sun-splashed though the day was flat and dull.

They walked on until Brodie stopped and growled. He cowered behind her, peering between her legs.

The man stood on the far side of the field. All in black, like a silhouette, watching. Was he waiting for her? A rebellious thrill of excitement gripped her.

He's a pervert, remember.

She raised her hand, uncertain. What if he didn't wave back? But he did, and strode towards her. Her excitement was swamped by something else, cold, rising from deep in her belly. Dread? He had not been there when she arrived on the field, she was sure. Did he come into being only when she looked for him? Who in hell was he?

"How are you two this fine morning?" He called across the closing gap, pleased to see them, like their last two meetings never happened.

He can't have forgotten?

Brodie backed away.

"One look at me and he's off! I could take offence."

He laughed, loud. And somehow inviting, familiar.

She looked around for Brodie. The little bugger had scuttled off. Away over the field, he sat watching them.

"I saw him with a young man the other day. Your son? He's a good-looking lad. Very tall. Like his dad, I expect? That must be a comfort."

"I'm sorry?"

"And your daughter? Who's she like?"

Isobel glared at him.

"I guess it's hard for you all."

"What do you know about me?"

He smiled. "Some."

"Who told you?"

This isn't right. Who is *this man?*

"You know how everyone talks."

Bloody Bernard. And Nick at the burger van, always pulling customers in with gossip.

He must have finally caught her look, because he said: "I'm sorry. It's not my business. I shouldn't intrude. I like you, that's all."

He likes me?

All at once, she was back in the school yard playing kiss chase.

And, like an idiot, she fell into step.

"I don't want to talk about - "

"Absolutely. No problem."

They walked on. She watched him surreptitiously from under her fringe. His clear blue gaze fixed straight ahead. At the edge of the field, she called the dog. He watched her, insolent.

"Come on, you little sod!"

The man laughed again, deep and appreciative.

"I'll get off, then."

No excuses about finding Zag this time.

He disappeared round the corner. He hadn't mentioned Zag, but he still carried that strange rubber lead about his neck.

"Brodie, I'm warning you." And there he was, at her feet, wagging his tail. "What is the matter with you? You're doing my head in." She bent to stroke him. He jumped up, ecstatic, almost as frantic as that day, it seemed like yesterday, when…

When she got in from the office and he charged at her, desperate for attention.

"Hello boy." He ran to the kitchen and scrabbled at the back door. She let him in the garden. He'd clearly not been out all day. She walked back through piles of unwashed clothes in the utility room to the kitchen. The washing up wasn't done, either. No sign of the children. She headed upstairs. The bedroom door was half-open. She paused on the threshold, took a deep breath and peered into its gloom. Richard was in bed, very still. She listened, heard him breathing, and let out her own. She turned on the overhead light. He lay on his back, staring at the ceiling. Didn't react to the sudden brightness.

"Hi, love. Are you not feeling so good?" She picked up his clothes, and slung them on the little wooden chair. His eyes didn't flicker. "Richard? I'm home." Nothing. "Have you eaten?"

She sat on the bed next to him, brushed his fringe to one side and felt his forehead. This was going on too long. She couldn't remember a low like this. She always meant to mark them on the calendar, to keep a diary so she'd have evidence, some way of showing him how much he still needed help. The trouble was to identify the start. One day he'd be fine; well, not fine, but happy enough, enjoying life. The next, he'd be slightly adrift, irritable maybe. But he'd still be out and about shopping, going to the cinema, the pub, spending. Then gradually he'd quieten, become subdued until, before she knew it, he'd dropped into a depression like this. She let him down every time it happened. She wanted to ignore the problem when he was all right. Despite the spending, he was easy to live with, fun to be around. He engaged with the kids, loved her: the model family man. She always, always allowed herself to believe he was better, until he became convinced of it too, and came off his meds. Talk about co-dependency.

"Did you manage to do the shopping? No?" She stroked his cheek. "Never mind. I'll go and see what there is for tea. There might be a pizza in the freezer. Will that do?" He stared at the ceiling. "Have the kids been in touch?" They wouldn't; what would be the point? It had become their routine to stay away until she phoned to say she was home. It was unspoken, this avoidance of their present-absent father. She didn't blame them: she'd avoid him too, if she could, when he was like this. The dog barked. She'd left him outside. She straightened the duvet over Richard and went downstairs.

She was washing up, having put the washer on, fed the kids, and fed and walked the dog. She'd scraped Richard's uneaten pizza into the bin. Too tired to shop tonight, she'd curl up with a glass of wine and read some more "Jane Eyre"; if she didn't fall asleep first.

"Let me do that." He came up behind and put his arms around her, his strong manicured hands over her soapy ones. He kissed her neck, nuzzled in, and she leant into the warm tickle of his breath. He whispered: "Sorry."

Why did he have to do this: blank her one moment, get all lovey-dovey the next? She wanted to scream at him to stop messing with her head, but she turned in his embrace, held wet hands up between them. Suds trickled down her arms.

"How're you feeling?" He shrugged. "Had your tablets?"

"Been sleeping. I'll take them now."

"And then why don't you have a soak in the bath?"

He let go of her. His arms dropped to his sides. "Yeh." His voice colourless. "Right. Sorry."

"No, I didn't mean I don't want to..." She bit her lip. He turned away to the cupboard where he kept the medication since she'd insisted on supervising it. It now came in blister packs, prepared by the pharmacist, after the last accident with them. As well as the drugs for hypomania and depression (the names of which she'd had to google to find out what they did), he was on something to help him sleep. She'd looked that up, too.

She rinsed a glass, filled it with water, passed it to him.

"Thanks."

She resumed washing-up. "The kids have been in and gone out again. Ben's gone swimming with Davis and that new lad, Nathan, is it? Melissa's over at Bernadette's. Oh, she got the part, by the way. She was up against that Carrie Barrett so she's thrilled to-" She twirled round to lean her back against the sink and tell him all about it, but he'd wandered down the hall to the stairs.

She swallowed back that familiar bitter taste. What *was* that? Anger, hurt, sadness? Or fear?

"Are you all right, my dear?"

An old gentleman with a brown cocker spaniel stood over her. She was kneeling on the damp ground, hugging herself, rocking like an imbecile. Brodie was running frantic circles around her, whining. She had no recollection of having sat down. Was she finally losing it?

He gently took her elbow, and helped her to her feet.

Chapter 26

Isobel woke with a start. She'd dreamed of ice. Swimming in a sea of icebergs, conscious of great masses beneath. Chilled. Small wonder she was dreaming cold things; the room was freezing.

So cold, in May?

She got out of bed, reached down a wool blanket from the wardrobe shelf, pressed it to her nose. They'd bought it in Shetland. More a picnic blanket than for sleeping under, a bit rough, but it would do. She spread it carefully over her side of the bed and climbed back in. Gradually she warmed, but now she couldn't fall asleep. The dream was still with her. Made her think of Iceland, before the children, when Richard was healthy. When they were happy.

They were so excited to be in this astounding country, changing, growing, before their eyes. The lava field landscapes so alien, empty, they felt they'd travelled to the ends of the earth. And yet, in the city, young people from all over the world greeted them and they danced through the night, fuelled by water and ecstasy.

They booked a day trip from Reykjavik to visit waterfalls.

“Look, Richard! You can see it, straight ahead. There, see?” The guide book said it wasn’t that high, but still it was visible from a couple of miles away across meadows richly greened by volcanic ash.

“I see it. Wow!”

The tour guide, Valur, who was also their driver on this mini-bus full of young world adventurers, confirmed: “Ahead, you see Seljalandsfoss. That’s where we are heading, friends. We’ll stay an hour or so. You can explore the waterfall, the meadows and there’s a small shop at the car park where you can buy Icelandic sweaters. Very reasonable price. Put on your waterproofs. I know we have a beautiful day here today but you can walk behind the fall and there’s not so dry.”

They had, of course, walked behind the fall. Cave-like, wet-mossy under the great overhang. Crashing water formed a violent curtain between them and vibrant grass lowland stretching south to the sea. They danced in slippery pools on the ledge, laughed and hugged, drunk on the energy fizzing around them. They arrived back at the bus soaked and cold, like the rest of the passengers. Valur put the heating on and the van steamed up. Isobel rubbed her window constantly, frantic not to miss any of the breathtaking views of glaciers. Richard fell asleep. They’d been clubbing until five that morning. They hadn’t bothered going back to the hostel, but grabbed breakfast at the old harbour and went straight to meet the bus.

"Next stop, Skogafoss. If you like Seljalandsfoss, you will love Skogafoss. This is a longer stop. There are walks to the top of the waterfall and there's a cafe also where we can eat. I ask you please not to embark on the longer walks from the top. They go into the interior and I'm afraid we don't have time today."

A flutter of laughter. They'd all heard stories of the interior, attainable only in the summer months. She and Richard had hooked up with some American guys a few days earlier who'd just returned from trekking there. It sounded amazing.

Her first view was of a cloud nestled in a depression in the cliff. As the road curved, she saw it wasn't cloud but spray from a huge waterfall which gradually revealed itself.

"Thirty metres high," Valur informed them. They pulled up at the car park. Everyone scrambled to be first out. Valur shouted: "See you in the café, later. Have fun, my friends."

They approached the fall along the pebbly shore of the river it fed. Already, at the car park half a mile away, the noise was tremendous. Sun beat down but the air was cold and full of moisture. The other passengers headed for steep steps up the cliff that led to a viewing platform overhanging the fall. She followed Richard along the riverbank and into the cloud of spray.

He clicked away on his cheap camera.

"Stand right there. That's it. Beautiful. You look gorgeous all wet like that."

He yelled over the roar. She struck silly modelling poses, feeling glamorous despite the borrowed, damp-smelling blue waterproofs clinging to her.

"Oh, Richard, look!"

The sun slid from behind a cloud and suddenly the air was filled with rainbows. They ran on towards the fall, holding hands, laughing and slipping.

"I've got to get this." Richard started snapping again. A rainbow formed before them, and as they watched, the two ends glissaded round to meet each other, forming a complete circle at their feet.

"Rich, this is the end of the rainbow. Let's look for the pot of gold!"

She pranced and twirled, her arms spread wide, face up to the spray. She burst into tears with the pure joy of it.

"You soft sod. Come here."

He lifted her and spun her around until they were both giddy and staggering.

"Come on!"

"You're going to break the camera. It's too wet."

He shoved it in his already sodden pocket. "Come *on*!"

"We can't get closer!"

"Don't you want to know how it feels?"

He ran ahead, a shadow inside dense spray at the bottom of the fall. She ran after him, scared and exhilarated. He stopped at the water's edge. They could go no further. They stood side by side, heads tilted back until they were dizzy, gazing up into falling, roaring white, high as a skyscraper. A few steps more and they'd be crushed, battered by the weight of it. Drenched to the skin with spritzy, invigorating spray, she'd never been so happy. Alone in a world of dancing rainbows.

"Come here, you."

He grabbed her by the waist and pulled her. Rainbows played about his hair, wet-dark, plastered to his face. He pushed her gently until cold wet rock jabbed into her back. She wriggled to avoid a jutting stone. He pressed against her, groaned. They kissed. Heat coursed through her. They held their tongues out to the spray, laughing, and then they kissed the sweet water from each other. They licked one another's faces, couldn't get enough of the fresh, clean mountain taste. That energy in the air! It fizzed, buzzed like a pylon, but lighter, freer. She tingled, thrilled. He tugged at her waterproofs, trying to get at her.

She laughed. "We can't. Someone'll see."

His voice rough and hot in her ear: "No one's coming this far in."

"What if they can see us from up there?" She could hardly get the words out. Breathless, she tried to push her hand down the front of his jeans. The heavy wet denim pinched her skin, and she pushed harder until she found what she was searching for. Hot down there. Probably steaming. They could've seen it if they weren't already enveloped in spray.

"You and me, Bel. We go beyond this world. You're mine for all time."

He found her trouser zip. She let him.

They skipped lunch, missed climbing to the top of the fall and had time only to grab a hot chocolate which they drank out on the verandah, soaking in the views. The café owner surveyed them, aghast, as they dripped inside, clothes clinging askew, to use the toilets. When they climbed aboard the bus, the last to get on, there were whistles and one of the lads slapped Richard on the back. She hugged herself, happy and embarrassed. Ignored the other girls' sidelong glances. Richard couldn't wipe the biggest grin from his face. He wrapped his arms about her, rested his head on hers and fell asleep.

Chapter 27

"We'll get pissed wet through if we stand here much longer." Bernard called his dogs over. He stowed the toys back in his rucksack. "Are you staying out, Isobel?"

"For a bit. Got my hood."

"I'll be seeing you then, love. Don't get too wet, now."

He loped off with a wave, the dogs glued to his heels. She called Brodie back. He bounded to her, pleased not to be leaving with the others.

She zipped her waterproof and put up the hood, in readiness. Only mid-morning, but the sky to the west was a low, twilit grey. The forecast had threatened monsoon-like rain and, further south, high winds. So far, no wind here but it looked like they were right about the rain. She walked on past the frog pond where the first giant drops plopped into the water. In moments she was drenched, but she pressed on, head down. The deluge stopped as abruptly as it had started. She pulled the dripping fabric of her all-weather trousers away from her thighs, and shook it. Brodie sat before her, so wet he seemed half his normal size. She laughed at his pathetic little face.

"Let's get moving. We'll soon dry off."

He shook himself half-heartedly. Warming, watery sunshine filtered through the darkness, but those heavy clouds weren't shifting. They'd be soaked again before they got home. Still, she wanted to stay out. Melissa would have a fit when she saw the state of them both. She was doing the weekly clean, for which Isobel paid her handsomely. Melissa enjoyed housework, inexplicably, and wouldn't appreciate wet, muddy feet on her clean floors.

Isobel walked on. Not a soul about. She liked the rain.

She headed for the hill. Zag's owner might show up if no one else was around. She should stop calling him that. He must have a name.

She walked, hood up, head down, the dog close at heel. The only sounds the skylarks spiralling, the rustle of her hair in the hood, her boots' crunch. A sheet of sunlight escaped the cloud. Steam rose from the path. Fresh smell of wet-warming soil. She stopped, flung back her hood. Did she really hear that? There it was again: a cuckoo. She froze: and again it called. A fleeting, untrustworthy dart of happiness.

She stayed a few moments to gaze across the water at the field of scarecrows on the opposite shore. What was in that field that needed so much protection? As far as she could tell, it was a grass paddock. Horses grazed there. One crude bird-scarer close to the shore had an arm raised as if to throw a stone at her. Or was it beckoning? "Come on in. The water's lovely."

She shivered: “Let’s go.”

She walked back through the tunnel of trees where it was dark as dusk. Brodie lagged behind to eat something vile. She walked on briskly. He might leave it and follow her. But he didn’t, so she turned to scold him.

Birdsong loud now, and sharp: something had changed. She whirled around, dizzy. Trees pressed in on her, too green, too heavy. Air vibrated. Blackbirds and robins screamed their warning, and everywhere she saw bright green caterpillars hanging from branches by ghostly threads.

He was standing at the edge of the trees about hundred metres ahead.

Motionless, he watched her.

She called to him: “What do you want with me?”

Could he hear? He gave no indication.

She started towards him. “Who *are* you?”

She broke into a jog. And he did a strange thing: he raised his right hand, mechanically, like a robot. A simple gesture, warning her to stay away, or was it a farewell? It felt like neither. More like a blessing, a benediction. She slowed to a walk. He stood with his hand raised, watching her. Sunlight flooded through the trees behind him. She shaded her eyes against the dazzle. The next moment a cloud covered the sun, and all was dull once more.

He was gone.

The rain slammed down.

Chapter 28

Isobel closed the fridge door: *DOG VET.*

Damnation!

She glanced at the clock.

"Come on Brodie, we've got to go." He didn't come. She found him curled up on the sofa. He'd been lacklustre for days. Even when she produced the lead, he didn't react.

Out at the car: "Yoohoo, Isobel! A word?"

"Bit of a hurry, Phyllis. I'm late already."

"I won't keep you. I wanted to check everything's all right."

She scurried across the road to Isobel's car.

Isobel lifted the dog onto the back seat. Phyllis never usually asked after her family. It was always: "*Please don't leave your bins out. Please tell your daughter not to let the dog urinate outside my gate. Can you ask your sister to park elsewhere?*"

Now she was standing uncomfortably close. "Only I've seen him a few times."

Isobel stood with her back to the car, arms folded. “Who?”

“The doctor who’s been calling.”

“What doctor?” She didn’t have time for this.

“I’m sorry, dear. Perhaps I shouldn’t have said anything. Bill told me to mind my own business.” Phyllis backed away. “Only I thought if someone’s ill, if you need anything, well, you know where we are.”

“I’ve no idea what you’re talking about. There’s been no doctor here.”

“I’m sorry. I’m a nosy old lady. I’ll be off and leave you -”

“Phyllis, I’ve not had a doctor visiting.”

“I’ve seen him, dear. But it’s your business. I won’t pry.” She turned to go.

Brodie scratched at the car window, wagged his tail limply. Isobel had to get going or she’d miss that appointment.

“Wait up! Tell me what you’ve seen.”

Phyllis came back, all confidential. “He’s not from our surgery. But he’s well turned out, smart suit and so on. And he carries an old-style doctor’s bag.”

Something wrong with Ben or Melissa? They were old enough now to see the GP on their own, if they chose.

But do GPs even do home visits anymore?

“When did he call? I mustn’t have been in.”

There was something in the look Phyllis gave her then that she couldn’t shake off, later. “But you let him in, dear. Or someone did.”

“When?”

"Well…" Phyllis seemed reluctant to be involved now. "He's been every day for the last week or so. I thought you knew."

"But who answered the door?"

"I thought it was you. But now I think, I've not seen who's at the door. It opens a crack and he slips in, d'you see? He was here this morning, of course, early. About seven, wasn't it?"

"But I've been in all morning. No one's been here today."

Again, that look. "Oh, I see. I must…" She gestured across to her own house. "See you anon."

She scuttled away.

Isobel got in the car. A strange image flashed before her: a man, tall, dressed in black, glances over his shoulder straight at her as the front door opens a crack. Then he slips in.

She shuddered, looked back at the dog. Coarse coat dull, standing stiffly, head lowered, he seemed in pain. She switched on the engine.

She was home again an hour later. The vet couldn't account for Brodie being off his food, but prescribed expensive antibiotics, anyway.

She was putting the kettle on when the phone rang. Belinda.

"Can I come round? I know you've got work, but I won't keep you. We need to talk."

"Sounds serious?"

"Not over the phone, chick."

She knocked on the door a couple of minutes later.

"Come in. It's open." Isobel called from the kitchen. "Coffee?"

"A quick one." Belinda sat at the table. "I've just had Phyllis round, all upset."

"Can that woman not mind her own business?"

"The thing is, she's right. I've seen him, too."

"This mysterious 'doctor'?" Isobel made sarcastic quotes with her fingers.

Belinda didn't smile. "He looks like one."

"Why didn't you say anything before? Anyway, I was in this morning when he's supposed to have called."

She passed Belinda a coffee and sat opposite her.

"I saw him yesterday. About half eleven? I thought it was funny, because I knew you were all out. I was surprised when someone let him in."

"But we *were* all out. Who answered the door?"

Had the kids come home early?

"Couldn't see. They only open it a little so he can slip in."

Slip in: that's what Phyllis had said. Isobel didn't like that present tense one little bit. "How many times *have* you seen him?"

"Three or four over this past week. I'm sorry, hon, I should have said something, but I was waiting for you to bring it up."

"I didn't know anything about it. The kids haven't said. One of them must be ill, really ill, do you think? A GP wouldn't visit unless…but wouldn't the surgery tell me? I know Ben's old enough now, but Melissa's only fifteen. They should've told me."

"You were in the other day, weren't you? Your car was there. When he called on Tuesday? You were because you'd just got back from your walk. I was relieved. I'd begun to think you didn't know, what with all the secrecy."

"Secrecy?"

"You know: the door only opening a crack, and him glancing over his shoulder like he does." Her eyes flitted towards the front door. She lowered her voice. "Like he's checking who might be watching?"

"But Blin, nobody *came* to the door on Tuesday."

Isobel called in sick. She had to be here when the children got home.

They arrived together. Ben's bus must have been early. They strolled up the street, chatting and laughing. Love for them welled up, fierce and hot. She stroked Brodie as he perched on the windowsill, watching with her.

How could she not have known one of them was ill? It was down to her now to keep them safe.

Barcelona loomed: she forced it back.

Ben, a foot taller than his sister, almost a man, looked ever more like his dad. Even the way he stooped slightly to listen to Melissa was Richard. Melissa looked up at him, laughed at some joke and nudged him into the gutter. The sun emerged from a cloud, set her hair aflame. She was still laughing. Her full sensual lips were Richard's, but her eyes, pure, almost grass-green, were all Isobel.

Melissa saw her at the window and waved. Brodie leapt from the sill and ran to greet them. As they came in, he jumped up, licked their hands.

"Hey, Cutie, I missed you, too! Mum, what are you doing home? I thought it was my turn to make tea. Are you ok?" Melissa hugged her.

"I swapped shifts with Karen so she can go to the dentist tomorrow."

Ben thumped upstairs three at a time.

"Ben, I need to talk to you."
"Need a crap."
"Then you're heading the wrong way. Again!"
He about-turned. "I knew that. Just testing."
Isobel followed Melissa into the kitchen. "I want to talk to you too, love."
Melissa put bread slices in the toaster. "What d'you want me for?"
"Wait for Ben. I want to talk to you both."
Melissa searched the fridge. "Where's that frigging Nutella gone again?" She slammed the door. "How did you get on at the vet?"
"They said he's fine, but we're to take him back if we're still worried."
"Poor baby." Melissa bent to stroke Brodie, who hadn't left her side since she walked in. "Bet it's in *his* room again. If he's been sticking his fingers in it, I'll…Ben! Go get that Nutella. Now!"
Few people would dare cross her daughter in full flight like this. Isobel hoped, for Ben's sake, it wasn't still in his room.
"Don't laugh, Mum. It's all right for you. You don't like Nutella." Melissa grimaced. "You don't know where his fingers have been."
So Melissa was her usual self. She didn't seem to be hiding anything. She stalked out of the kitchen, and headed upstairs. "If I find it in your room, you're dead meat!"
Ben shouted from the bathroom: "Mum, stop her!" He emerged, still fastening his trousers: "You'd better not be in my room, Ginger Ninja!"
He charged upstairs. Isobel listened to their easy bickering while her lemon and ginger tea brewed. When it sounded like the argument was escalating, she yelled: "Downstairs, both of you!"

Ben swerved through the arch, holding the Nutella jar aloft, Melissa close behind, trying to snatch it from him.

Isobel intervened: "If that ends up on the floor, Brodie'll have it, and it won't be good for him. Put it down please, Ben."

He pranced about: "Can you reach? Can you? Here it is. Oops, too slow. Up it goes again."

"Ben, please!" She hadn't meant to shout but she was fading again and they weren't listening. She couldn't afford to shrivel. Not right now. "Come and sit down, the pair of you."

Ben put the jar on the counter and sat. Melissa pulled up her chair close to Isobel. "Sorry, Mum. Have you got a headache, again?"

"No, love. I'm fine, but I need to ask you something." She had their attention. "Which one of you's been skipping off?"

Confrontational, but it was out now. They looked at each other. Surprised?

"One of you's been home while I've been at work this last week."

Melissa snorted. "Not that nosy old bid across the road? She doesn't like me."

"Belinda thinks she's seen you, too."

Ben sighed. "*Thinks?*"

"She's seen the front door open."

It sounded daft now she said it out loud.

"If she saw us open the door, she must have seen us."

Melissa's eyes widened. "Mum, has someone been in the house?"

"No, silly, nothing like that." Isobel hadn't thought this through. "Are you ok, though? Have either of you been feeling ill?"

They exchanged a look. She should have talked to them separately. If one of them was ill, they wouldn't say in front of the other.

"Melissa, will you go and make a start on your homework, please?" She went without a word. A little too eagerly? "No, Ben. I've not finished with you."

He sat down again. "I haven't missed college. I can't afford to, you know that. What did they say?"

"I haven't spoken to them."

"Why not? They'll tell you I haven't missed any days."

He got up.

"Ben, wait. Have you seen a doctor recently?"

He hesitated in the archway. "You look really tired. Why don't you go and have a bath? Me and Liss'll get tea ready."

More than tired, she was pathetic, useless. She crossed her arms on the table, dropped her head onto them. She heard Ben go upstairs, quieter this time.

Chapter 29

Thick fog. Isobel ran for a while, but suddenly feared she might collide with something, some*one* unseen. She slowed to a damp, chilled walk, her thin waterproof jacket inadequate. She should have worn a fleece. She should make up her mind before she came out: running or walking? She should, she should. Incapable of making even the simplest decisions. Not at work: there, she was competent, good at her job. But at home she was a wreck. Look at the mess she'd made of that with the kids yesterday. She put her hand to the tension in the side of her neck, shook her shoulders, tipped her head from side to side. Her neck creaked painfully.

And creak across my soul with those same boots of lead again

The trouble was she had no one to talk to anymore, no one to plan with, to share with. And she put too much on the children, especially Ben. She couldn't help it. She wasn't self-sufficient like Ursula. Even Belinda made a better go of life.

She looked back for the dog.

"Come on, lad. Let's not be out all day."

She waited. Eventually he trotted out of the fog, tail wagging, not a care in the world. He was the only thing keeping her sane right now. Ben disagreed: he thought she'd already tipped over that edge. He didn't say it, but last night he'd suggested she see the GP again. Only she didn't want to revisit all that. If she went back, he'd prescribe antidepressants again, and what was the point? They hadn't worked last time. They couldn't cure this. Nothing could cure this.

"But it's been nearly two years, Mum."

She'd tried to explain how that was no time at all, but, to a seventeen-year-old, it was an eternity. To her too, in the middle of the night.

She held out a treat for the dog. He trotted straight past her and into the trees by the water's edge where he merged once again with the fog. She could have come out later, given it chance to clear, as she wasn't working today. But she clung to her routines as lifebelts in a stormy sea. She zipped up her coat and walked faster.

"Brodie, with me!"

When she reached the path that led away from the Flash towards home, she stopped. Where was he? She looked back. The path receded into a grey blankness. Bloody dog could be anywhere.

"Brodie!"

She heard a faint yap. Was that him?

"Come on, lad!"

Another bark, a bit louder. What was he doing?

"Here, boy!"

Again, he replied to her call. Why didn't he come? He wasn't stuck, trapped somewhere? Shit, he might have gone down a fox hole. Border terriers did that. She'd heard the horror stories. She ran back the way she'd come.

No sign of him. She waited, called. Another couple of short, urgent barks, dampened by the fog, but he didn't come. Still she waited. She was about to phone Belinda for help when she heard another muffled bark.

"Brodie, you little sod. Come on, now!"

She listened. Scrabbling sounds. Was he digging? Maybe he *had* found a hole. She hesitated: wait and risk him disappearing down a burrow, or go in after him and get cut up in the undergrowth? She pictured Melissa's face if she came home without him.

"You are one dead dog when I get hold of you."

She plunged into the bushes. Her foot snared in a low-trailing briar. She lost balance, almost fell, clutched a flimsy branch for support.

"Ow!"

A bramble, it punctured her thumb with many tiny spikes.

Broken branches at eye level. Rich smell of sap. Twigs snapped underfoot on spongy ground. Something yanked her backwards. She grabbed her neck. A branch had caught in her coat collar, scraped her skin. She pulled herself free. Blackberries, rampant green, scratched her shin right through her trousers. Hot sting.

She pushed on through, stumbled over another booby-trap hiding in undergrowth: what the hell? A blanket. Cheap acrylic, like Melissa's old leopard-print one in Brodie's bed. Covered in dirt, leaves, twigs, its camouflage pattern green and brown. She picked it up by a corner. Wet through.

Was this what he was after? It stank of pond and shit. She dropped it, wiped her hand on her trousers.

That's not fox.

Anglers, probably. It wouldn't be the first time Brodie had returned covered in shit; some of those guys had appalling habits.

"Brodie, here. Now!"

Another yap. She spotted him a few metres away in a little clearing.

He ran to her, all excited, then straight back to the - what was it? A heap of clothes? Not in bags or anything. Just clothes. Huddled under a tree. Not strewn. Kind of arranged. A trainer. No, two trainers at the edge of the heap. Jeans. Something grey. A breeze rustled the trees and the smell hit her, sickly-sweet, rotten. The mossy ground undulated. She gagged.

"Here, boy." An inarticulate croak.

Brodie sat next to the heap. No, this couldn't be happening: he *leaned* into it. Like he did with Melissa on the sofa when he wanted a cuddle. The pile was about the size of Melissa, and he was snuggling into it.

Oh Jesus, he's trying to warm it.

It wasn't clothes. Not only clothes. She edged closer, afraid to disturb it.

"Are you ok?" She whispered, like an idiot.

A hand, awful blue-grey turning to black, lay swollen on the ground, still holding an empty bottle of Bell's whisky. Isobel's dad used to drink that. She crouched, too close. It slouched against a tree, had slipped to one side. Long fair hair poked from under a pulled-up hoodie. Pink trainers. A young girl. She daren't look at the face.

Ok, use your training. Ascertain life signs. CPR. Call the police.

Quick glance at the face. Half-open clouded eyes. Grotesque swollen tongue pushed out of the vomit-crusted mouth. Defiant.

Isobel shrank back.

Not like the newly-dead. Changed. Discoloured. Swollen. No longer human. But about the same age as Melissa, and so cold and wet.

Cover her. Get her warm.

But the blanket was soaking wet. Isobel took off her coat and leaned forward to lay it over the body. But she couldn't make herself touch it. She put the coat aside. She shouldn't touch anything. She must get help. She could do nothing for her. It was all too late.

"It's all right, sweetheart. I'm here. You're not alone now. I won't leave you."

She reached out to touch the dead hand, but couldn't. Brodie did it for her. He started to lick, and the putty-like skin peeled under his tongue. She retched. Grabbed his collar and tried to stand. Her legs wouldn't hold her. She ended up on the ground too close to that dead hand.

She scrambled backwards. Brodie jumped up at her. She pushed him away. He whimpered, slunk back to the body. She fumbled in her pocket for the lead.

"Come with me."

She dragged him back through the brambles and dropped down on the path, shivering violently. She'd left her coat, and she'd said she wouldn't leave her, but she couldn't go back in there, she'd never feel clean again. That black hand, the whisky bottle...When she was little, her dad had taught her to pour a finger of Bell's whisky for him. Did this girl's dad drink it, too? Those poor parents. She had to get help. She had to tell someone.

She pulled her phone from her pocket and dialled 999.

Chapter 30

That night the dreams become nightmares.

Lorraine Road, so she must be four or five, but she's Alice after she's swallowed the *Eat Me* cake, grown impossibly big. Unwieldy, liable to break things. She's in the Jacksons' house looking out of Colin's bedroom window. She's played here lots, but now the bed seems small. Airfix models hanging from the ceiling, Battle of Britain, tiny, defenceless. She bashes one with her big high head. Colin isn't here but the room smells of him: mud and warm baked beans.

Is he hiding somewhere?

Perhaps she's supposed to go looking. But she's afraid. She's all alone. She wants to go home. Home is across the way, shiny black front door and daffodils. She yearns to be family-wrapped. They'll be having tea. She can smell the cheese and onion pie Mummy was making earlier. Her mouth waters.

So what's stopping me?

She clambers down: she's been sitting on the window ledge. But before she can turn to go, *she's* there, in the street below: the rabbit-faced woman. She speeds past on her bicycle with the basket on the front. She looks up at Isobel as she flies by. Grins with her rabbit mouth and her rabbit teeth.

Get across the road before she makes it round the block. Quick!

She's outside the house, running down the drive, but she's Alice-shrunk. Her little legs, pumping, burning, can't cover the ground. It's not fair; she doesn't remember taking the *Drink Me* potion. Stupid dream. It doesn't follow the rules...

She stirs and almost wakes, but feels herself pulled, drawn back under…

There she is again, the rabbit-faced woman, zipping past on her basket bicycle, rabbit-grinning. Slimy, inside-slipping fear of spiders and frogs and all cold-creeping creatures. She can't touch the rabbit-faced woman. She's dead-cold and pulseless. Cruel, unhuman.

And soundless. No whirring wheels, no smattering grit. She leaves no marks, she makes no din as she laps the block. Like a film looped to torment.

I want to go home. Please, I want my tea.

She puts out a foot to cross the road, but falls back as the rabbit-faced woman whips past, a blur except for that whiskered face that won't let her go. Again, she puts out her foot. Snatches it back. Wind from the faster-faster rabbit-faced woman lifts her Alice-band hair.

She must get across this road.

Mummy will be angry. Tea will be cold.

Why don't they come? Why don't they see she's trapped?

She steps out. Falls back. But now it isn't the rabbit-faced woman staring at her with mad triumphant amber eyes: it's Richard.

Richard in his running gear, power-running past, his legs a cartoon blur.

Richard, come back! Help me.

He makes it round the block in no time, running faster than possible, blocking her, grinning his rabbit teeth. He disappears from her left vision, instantly back in her right. Racing by, elusive, grinning like Alice's cat.

She's trapped, and he won't help her. He won't protect her. He doesn't want to. He flies, unreachable, untouchable, exhilarated. He doesn't care.

He's not human.

She stands at the curb, little and lost.

He won't let her come home.

She wakes in darkness, tangled hot in her duvet, pillow wet with tears.

Chapter 31

A knock, loud, assertive.

Not him?

Isobel peeped through the arch. In the frosted glass of the front door, a dark figure shimmered. She cowered.

"Mrs Hickey? PC Dyson."

Do get a grip.

She opened the door.

"I phoned a few minutes ago?"

"Come in." She looked beyond him. "On your own?"

He stepped inside. "We don't always roam in packs. It's not like the telly."

He smiled, warm and kind.

"Sit yourself down. Can I get you a coffee? Or tea?"

He was tall and broad: exactly the size you want in your local bobby. He made the sofa look tiny. "Coffee would be great, thanks. Milk, no sugar?"

When she brought the drinks through, he got out his notebook and a form to fill in.

"I've got notes on what you told the attending officers yesterday, but we need to formalise your statement for the coroner. Is that all right?" She nodded. "So, let's see." He looked at his notebook. "It was about 8am when you found the body. Could you talk me through it? Start with the weather. Tell me about that. It was foggy, yeah?"

He wrote as she talked, but watched her too, his grey eyes compassionate. She'd been dreading this, but telling it felt like a relief, like helping the girl, or at least her poor family.

"Would you like to pause there, Mrs Hickey? Have a glass of water?"

"No, I'll be ok. It's just…it was horrible finding her there, all cold and alone like that."

He nodded. "Must have been a proper shock. It's something you never get used to, even in our line of work."

"I guess you deal with this sort of thing a lot."

"Someone's got to." A scraping noise from the kitchen. "What's that?"

The dog lay asleep at her feet.

"D'you have another dog? Sounds like he wants to come in."

"I've only the one."

"Can you hear that? That scratching? Sounds like *someone* wants to come in. Is there anyone else in the house?"

"It's nothing."

"Maybe I should take a quick look."

"No! It's fine. Really."

PC Dyson was about to say more but was cut off by a hollow clang from the kitchen. "What the -?"

He was in there before she could stand up.

She followed him. Bread bin on the floor, contents scattered. Canisters of pasta, tea, coffee, lined up neatly on the edge of the counter, ready to dive off.

He bent to gather the bread, tapped the bin with his knuckle. "You wouldn't think this could make a din like that. D'you have a cat?"

"No. Why?"

"Cats sometimes do that. Push stuff." He muttered almost to himself, scanning the room. He strode to the back door, tried the handle. Locked, the key in the hole as usual. "No one else in. Who lives here with you?"

"My children, but they're at school, college."

He checked the window. "Has anything like this happened before?"

"Like this? I don't know."

"Is anything else disturbed in here?"

She looked about her. Everything looked as it should. Except… were the fridge letters all messed up like that earlier? Hadn't there been a message? Usually there was. "It looks fine. I don't know how that happened. Maybe I…"

He pushed the bread bin and canisters back against the wall. "That should do it." But he didn't sound convinced, and gave the kitchen another sweep. "Where were we?"

She led him back to their seats. The dog hadn't budged, snoozing by her chair.

"Is he deaf, the little fella?"

"No, he..."

"Funny all that clatter didn't rouse him." He watched the dog, looking thoughtful. Then he said: "I need you to read through the statement and sign it for me, please. We can change anything I've got wrong, no problem. While you're doing that, you don't mind if I take a quick look round? Just want to make sure everything's in order."

"Please, you needn't bother."

"Two ticks." He stomped upstairs. She listened to him rooting about. He opened each bedroom door and presumably looked around before gently closing it. He rattled the bolt on the loft hatch, then trotted back down. "Nothing to report."

She held out the statement. "Shall I sign?"

"If you're happy with it."

He took it from her and gave her a card.

"You can contact me on this number if you have any questions. The coroner's office'll be in touch if they need more information, but don't worry, you'll be offered support if that happens. It looks straightforward so I think it's unlikely, as it stands."

He went to the door, hesitated. "Mrs Hickey, I've seen something like this before." He nodded his head at the kitchen. "There are people who can help, if you need it. It's not my business, but if you want me to put you in touch with someone, ever, phone me on that number, yeah?"

He stepped out into sunshine, and strode off down the road.

She watched him go.

"People who can help"?

Isobel saw Phyllis at her living room window, and waved. Phyllis retreated into shadow.

That's right; keep your nose out.

Isobel went inside, found her bag and took out her purse. She tucked his card in with her bank card. She dropped the purse back into her bag, and something red caught her eye. The pen-knife. She lifted it carefully from the bag, turned it over in her hand.

Relief. Release.

She'd told herself she wouldn't do it again. Wasn't healthy. Maybe not, but it felt good. Afterwards, she'd feel in control again...for a while, at least.

She switched on a gas ring on the stove, opened the blade and held it over the heat. She glanced over her shoulder at the bread bin and canisters. They remained where PC Dyson had placed them. For now.

One little cut. Not deep this time. Just a scratch was all she needed.

The phone rang.

Shit. Ignore it.

But what if it was Melissa, or Ben? She switched off the gas, and picked up the phone.

"Hi, hon. How did it go? He wasn't with you long. Meet me at my car. I'm taking you to Bents for lunch. No buts."

The glass-ceilinged café buzzed with conversation. Isobel sorely needed the normality, away from that damn house.

"I'm treating us to those immense meringues." Belinda held up a hand. "Resistance is futile. They've got strawberries and blueberries on top, look, so that's two of your five-a-day right there."

They ordered big cappuccinos, too.

"Do they know who the poor girl is yet?"

"Can we talk about something else?"

"I'm sorry. It's been horrible for you, and here's me going on."

Isobel placed her cup on its saucer, trying not to let it rattle. "I will want to talk about it some time, I think. Just -"

Belinda touched her hand. "Just not right now. I get it."

Isobel picked at her meringue, removed some of the thick cream, placed it on the side of the plate.

Belinda ate hers with gusto. "What are these?" She picked up a fruit. "I always want to call them syphilis, but that can't be right."

Isobel smiled: "Dope. Physalis. Chinese lanterns."

Belinda pointed a fork at her. "Made you laugh. So, with all this going on, did you get chance to talk to Ben and Melissa about you-know-who?"

"We're not in Hogwarts, Blin. They don't know anything about it. Or say they don't."

"You don't believe them?"

"He's not coming to see me, so it must be one of them." *Unless he's not a doctor, at all.*

Belinda licked milky froth from her spoon. "What if he's not a doctor?"

Isobel stared at her. "You said he was."

"He looks like one, but why would the kids deny it, if he was? He carries that bag, and now I'm wondering what's in it. If they haven't been seeing a *doctor*, maybe they've been seeing someone else? I mean, why is he so secretive?"

Isobel sat back, sun on her face. Then she got it. "What, like *drugs*, you mean?" Belinda shrugged. "Not my two. They're straight, to the point of boring." Richard's mean phrase popped out before she could restrain it. "They wouldn't."

"You're right, they're good kids. And whoever heard of drug dealers making house calls?"

Isobel had. But that was a whole other story.

Belinda went on: "I keep going over it, how he appears without me seeing him arrive, the way he sways his head like that." She shuddered.

"Sways his head?"

"It's weird. Bit like a polar bear in a zoo."

Another mental image Isobel could do without. "He's probably got the wrong house. We've not been there that long. Maybe he's after the previous tenants."

Belinda had this way, sometimes, of fixing you with a long stare like she was reading your mind, or trying to get you to read hers. She did it now. "I've never seen a car. I don't see him walk up the road. He's always there at the door when I notice him."

Isobel wanted to change the subject but a fearful fascination was growing in her. "So?"

"There's something not right about this whole thing." Belinda chewed her lip. "I can't stop going over it. I'm even dreaming about him. The more I think about it, the odder it gets. I'm sorry, I shouldn't say this, I know. Joe said not to. He says you've got to live there. But that's it, isn't it? You've got to live there, so you *should* know."

Heat drained from the sun. Chatter around them receded. Isobel had been alone with all this so long, too long. "Know what?"

"It's all wrong. All those times I've seen him, they've been the same, except -"

"Yes, you said. The same routine every time."

"Not the same routine, Iz. The exact same thing, apart from -" She glanced at the next table, lowered her voice: "It's like I'm watching the same piece of film over and over. Apart from his eyes. They're mean, like he wants to hurt someone. And they weren't, not to begin with. When I first saw him, they were kind, calm, like…"

"A doctor's."

"Yes."

"But how can you see his eyes when he's all the way across the road? Are you making this up? Is he even real, Belinda?"

"This whole thing's too weird. He is real, but he's not *right*. I can't explain." She retreated into her coffee.

Isobel moved pieces of meringue about the plate with her fork.

Belinda put her cup down with a clatter. "Ok, it's got to be said. We know he's called when you've been in, yet you haven't seen or heard him, right? So maybe he isn't…completely there."

Isobel sighed: what took her so long? "You mean like a ghost?"

Belinda's usually soft brown eyes blazed. "Do you want to find out?"

Chapter 32

Isobel tapped on the door. No reply. In her head, she knew there could be no doctor but, in her heart, Belinda's theory about drugs wouldn't stop niggling. She knocked harder. "Ben? Can I come in?"

He opened up. "Sure."

He'd changed out of his cycling gear into jeans and a faded Nirvana teeshirt she'd been trying to throw out for ages. He stood back to let her into his small, too-tidy room. Since Richard, he'd become so self-disciplined, as if he'd joined the army. He was listening to Led Zep; one of his dad's albums. He turned the music down.

"We haven't had a chat for a while." She picked up the Storm Trooper from his desk, and smiled.

"So what was that we were doing at teatime?" He flopped on his bed. "Come on, Ma. Out with it."

She sat beside him. "You know this doctor Belinda's been on about?"

"Not this again. Did you phone college, like I said?"

"Of course I did. They confirmed you haven't skipped off. But listen, Ben. Now she thinks he may not be a doctor."

"More a figment of her under-utilised imagination? What d'you want me to say?"

"Is there anyone who'd come looking for you at the house?"

"Like who?"

"I don't know. You'd tell me if you were in trouble, wouldn't you? You know you can talk to me."

"Oh, so he's police now?"

"No!" *Was* he*?* "You don't have to hide anything. If you were in trouble, if you owed money to... someone, for... something, you'd talk to me?"

"I get it. You think it's drugs. D'you think I'm stupid enough to get into that shit after everything that happened with Dad?"

That came at her like a slap in the face. "What do you know about that?"

"Nothing. Just stuff they said at school."

She stood. "Who said? You know *nothing* about it." She was shouting but couldn't stop herself.

"Some older kids. Ages ago. They knew people who - never mind."

"But I do mind, Ben. You don't know. You don't understand what it was like for him."

"Jesus, don't try to defend him."

She clasped her hands to stop them shaking. "How dare you! Don't you judge him. You can't possibly know."

"Ok, Mum, you're right. I don't know anything."

He stood, tried to put his arm around her. She shook it off. "Please don't get involved with those people. I couldn't bear it."

"I'm not, I promise."

Did she believe him? Surely he wouldn't lie to her face, not her Ben. "Get back to your music, love. Don't stay up late. Do you want a drink? I was going to do some hot milk for Lissa."

"Hot chocolate?"

"As long as you-"

"Remember to brush my teeth, I know."

She turned to go. Melissa stood in the door. How long had she been there?

"That noise has started again in the roof above my bed."

"Lissa, I told you, it's only birds, those starlings we were watching, remember? Looking for a place to nest. They've got in under the slates."

"But it's really loud."

They escorted her back to her room. Clothes and magazines scattered over every surface, tights hanging from the wardrobe doors. A mobile number scrawled in red lipstick across the full-length mirror. Fruity perfumes clashed and caught at the back of Isobel's throat.

"Jeez! Smells like a tart's boudoir in here."

"Ben, that's enough."

"Listen." Melissa's eyes shone, owl-like.

Loud scratching from the ceiling. That didn't sound like starlings. More like a dog scratching at a door, hard, persistent.

God, not rats?

"That's not birds." Ben sounded impressed.

Melissa's eyes widened.

"Shush, Ben. Of course it's birds."

The scratching continued, brazen. How had Melissa been able to sleep with this going on? "How long's it been happening, sweetheart?"

"A few days. Since before we saw the starlings."

"It is a bit noisy. Tell you what: I'll phone someone tomorrow and get them to remove the nest."

"They won't hurt them, will they?"

If it was rats, Isobel certainly hoped so. "Of course not, sweetie. Now get into bed."

Ben fetched the old kayak paddle he kept propped in his room. "Shut up, you little buggers! We're trying to sleep down here!" He rapped on the ceiling, three sharp taps. The scratching stopped.

"Thanks, Ben. Now get some sleep, Liss-"

Scrape, scrape, scrape. Louder this time. Like a reply.

"Whoa!" Ben stepped back.

"Mum, I don't like it. I want Dad."

"It's all right, love. Really, it's just birds. Look, why don't you sleep with me tonight, and I'll get it sorted out in the morning, I promise."

Ben raised an eyebrow. She shook her head. Melissa grabbed her pillow, and Isobel ushered her out.

On the landing, she checked the loft hatch bolt.

Chapter 33

Even at half-term, it fell to Isobel to walk the dog. The kids were still in bed. She didn't mind. She needed to get out. Brodie trotted to heel as she strode across the hill. She never tired of these views. A breeze rippled expanses of water into black velvet pleats while elsewhere remained glassy, reflecting the sky. Like a mirror with age-spots. She wandered along, throwing the ball. She'd last seen Zag's owner nearly two weeks ago. She hadn't understood, at the time, the finality of that strange salute. A creeping sense of dread made her walk faster.

She bumped into Bernard, sitting at one of Nick's rickety tables at the burger van. He sported ill-fitting sunglasses, and had his head thrown back, apparently sunbathing. His dogs, as usual, ignored Brodie's enthusiastic greeting.

"Hello, crazy mutt." He appeared to have blagged a coffee yet again. He never carried cash, *much like our own dear Queen,* he was fond of saying, and Nick wasn't as tough as his weathered, chain-smoking exterior suggested.

"Nick, he'll put you out of business if you let him."

"I'll have you know, young woman, Nick draws many clients from my patronage, isn't that so? My very presence at this establishment gives it the mark of distinction. I'm a respected pillar of this here community."

Nick snorted. "Pillock, more like."

Bernard aped offence to make Isobel laugh.

Nick nodded at his coffee. "So that's on the tab, then, is it?"

"*Tab*, my man?" Bernard laughed. "Course it's on the tab. I'll settle up with you tomorrow. Want one, Isobel?"

"Not today, thanks. I'll have to be getting back for work."

Nick wiped his counter, and leaned over it to look at Brodie. "Not had this little 'un hanging around here so much lately."

"I'm wise to him. I've had enough of running around after him, so he's on the lead anywhere near here, now."

There'd been a couple of near-misses with cars by the burger van. Brodie lost all sense in his relentless pursuit of dropped chips. Nick had grabbed him more than once before he came to harm.

"Don't suppose either of you have seen a tall guy about the place? Always wears black?"

"Oh aye. Is this the one you dumped me for?" Bernard winked at Nick. "The one with the black retriever?"

"He hasn't got a dog."

"I thought you said he couldn't control his dog? Isn't that the fella?"

"Yes, but turns out he - I was mistaken."

Why had she even mentioned him?

"Isobel? You all right, love? Nick's saying, what does this chap look like?"

Why couldn't they drop it? "He's tall."

"Good-looker?"

She didn't appreciate Bernard's sly wink.

"You'd know him if you saw him. He's smart."

"Not a scruff, like me, then?"

Bernard, always out with his dogs, big khaki anorak, muddy walking boots. She looked at her own grubby jacket with its ripped sleeve, her grime-smeared trousers and mud-caked boots. The dog-walkers all dressed more or less like scarecrows. When they bumped into one another at the supermarket, it was always: "Didn't recognise you with your clothes on."

But not Zag's owner; he wasn't like them.

He was all wrong.

"He wears black." It had been only a fortnight but she couldn't picture his face. "He always wears black. Black shirt, black tie." *That can't be right.* "Black suit."

"Blimey. Sounds like a bouncer." Nick went back to wiping the counter.

Bernard laughed. "A suit? Who walks their dog round here in a suit?"

Who indeed?

But, she realised now, he'd worn it every time she met him. Looming out of the cold dark in a black suit. Sitting on a bench, warm sunshine, black suit. Emerging from wet undergrowth in a black suit. And shiny black shoes. Even the other day, when he'd waved and disappeared into the light...

How had she not seen?

"It'll ruin in no time. How does he cope with your Brodie jumping up like he does?"

Brodie never had jumped up at him. Brodie had never been near him except that time when they argued, and then he'd been on the lead, unable to get away.

"He must stand out. I'll keep an eye open for him. I'll let you know if - "

She needed to picture his face. She'd told Belinda he had blue eyes. And his hair was dark, surely? Wet and plastered to his face that day. Or was it blond? His face a featureless blank. All she could see was a black suit.

And why had she assumed he had a dog? Because he carried a lead, and if you carry a lead... *But didn't he* tell *me he had a dog?*

"Hey, Isobel, what's up? We're only having a bit of fun. Don't walk away like that."

He did carry a lead. Even after she knew there was no dog. A strange lead: black, shining rubber that forked at one end. And wasn't there some chrome to it? He held it always in his left hand. No. Not always. Sometimes he wore it slung around his neck. And then it didn't look like a lead, at all.

Chapter 34

Late Saturday evening. Ben was out with Eamee, Melissa in her room, reading. Isobel sipped a second glass of red in front of the TV. Meaningless images moved across the screen. It had been a long week.

This dreadful blue wallpaper, tendril-twiney, could drive you mad. In someone else's house she could like it, possibly, but here it might pounce and choke her. She'd get rid as soon as she managed to get some cash together. Her eyelids drooped. The TV sound weaved in and out of tune.

"Mum! Mum!" Melissa, terrified.

Isobel leapt from the sofa, ran upstairs, the dog ahead of her, barking, and burst into Melissa's room. She was huddled on the bed, white, shivering, knees drawn up under her chin.

"Mummy!" She raised her arm, pointed over Isobel's shoulder.

Isobel spun round in panic: "Who is it?" No one.

"Up there." Melissa whispered: "Listen."

"Oh, Lissa. Not this again."

Overhead, scraping, shunting as if someone was moving a heavy box. Isobel's scalp crawled. Something hit the ceiling. They both jumped.

"And look at that."Melissa pointed again. In the corner of the ceiling, by the door, was a tiny round hole. It looked like it had been drilled.

"Is that what you were trying to tell me earlier?"

Belinda had phoned and Isobel shooed Melissa away when she'd tried to interrupt the conversation.

"It was there when I came home tonight."

"Are you sure, Melissa? This hole is new?"

"Look. You can see where the ceiling's fallen down."

A little pile of plaster dust on the floor under the hole. That was definitely new.

Bang, bang, bang!

Oh God, the loft hatch!

She clutched Melissa, pulled her close.

More scrapes, shuffles. They followed their progress across the ceiling. Then the hatch banged again. Echoed. The bolt rattled.

"Mum!" Melissa's voice tiny, choked. "Can it get in?"

"Stay here."

"Don't leave me!"

"Don't move, d'you understand? Brodie, stay with Lissa." He jumped on the bed and stood in front of his charge, facing the door, fur bristling. No one was getting past him. "I'll be back in a minute. Do *not* move, ok?"

She ran onto the landing, pulled the bedroom door shut behind her. The hatch had shifted in its frame despite the heavy padlock she'd had fitted the day the pest-control guy found nothing up there. A draught came through the gap, but the lock still held.

Bang! The hatch slammed back into place with a dead echo. She cowered. The dog barked.

It's trying to get in. You have to do *something. Think!*

"Melissa, stay put!" She ran downstairs, outside and next door to Joe Jessop's. His car was there, thank god.

"Joe, Joe!" She hammered on his door.

"Hi, Isobel." His hair stuck up. The pinkish imprint of a cushion corner marked his cheek. "You ok?"

"Something - someone in my loft, quick, I've left Melissa on her own." *Oh my God, you idiot!* "Quick, I need you." She grabbed his hand and pulled him unresisting into the street. "Oh, your feet!" But he was already running through her front door.

At the top of the stairs, they paused to listen. Nothing. Melissa came to her door, Brodie in her arms.

"Hello, you. Can you still hear them?" Joe kept his voice low. Melissa, wide-eyed, shook her head. "Where's the key for this padlock?"

"Here." Isobel kept it on her key ring.

"We've had this before. Kids in the loft space. They're all connected, the lofts. There's gaps in each house divide. Only small, like, but big enough. Stupid design. You can get right from one end of the terrace to the other, up there."

"You're joking."

"I'm not. We had it a few years back. Them at 68 was burgled by a kid who was friends with their next door neighbours' son. That's why most of us keep the hatches bolted shut. Bet I know who it is this time, an' all. I've had my suspicions for a bit, and Maud's been worried, lately. I'll take a quick look, but sounds like he's scarpered."

"Who?"

"I don't have proof so best not get too excited. Can you get me a torch?"

While he was up there, Isobel climbed on a chair, stuffed kitchen paper in the hole in Melissa's ceiling, then stuck a large sticking plaster over it.

"That'll do for now to stop any draughts. How does it look?

"Like a plaster on my ceiling."

"I'll get it repaired, don't worry. It'll be good as new."

"Nothing here is good as new, Mum."

Joe dropped down from the hatch. "Nah, he's gone. Little shit. I think you should report this, Isobel. And keep that hatch padlocked, all right?"

"Thank you, Joe. You're a star."

Burglars, she could cope with.

Chapter 35

Ben shovelled cereal into his mouth, workman-like. His fringe flopped forward, obscuring his eyes, watching her watching him. He put down his spoon. "I'm worried about you, Mum."

She attempted a laugh. "Why?"

He sat back, and for a moment looked so much like his dad it took her breath away. She leaned against the counter.

"There you go. Stuff like this. The way your moods change so fast. The way you keep crying."

"I'm not crying." She brushed her cheek.

"You are, Mum. I'm not stupid. I know you're thinking about Dad. You look at me and think of him. It's a pain. Why can't you just see me?"

"Of course I think about him. Don't you?"

"He's not coming back. You know that, right?"

"Don't be silly. Obviously I know that, but -"

"But *nothing*. I hear you talking to him when you think we're asleep. I hear you laughing like you used to when he acted the clown. He's not coming back. It'll be two years next month, and we need to get on with our lives, me and Lissa, even if you don't want to. Mrs Doyle says -"

"Mrs Doyle?"

"The counsellor at college. I told you. She says it might help to write to him, write down anything we want to say to him. I've been trying it over the holiday. Maybe you could give it a go?"

She sat opposite him. "Who's looking after who here?"

He smiled Richard's smile. "We're in this together, aren't we? All for one, and one for all?"

She watched him finish his cereal. When he got up to rinse his bowl he said, his back to her, "Mrs Doyle wonders if you worrying about our health is to do with what happened to Dad, if it's made you stop trusting."

"Stop trusting?"

"You know. The universe, life, whatever."

So he was discussing *her* in these cosy little chats with Mrs Doyle. The cuckoo clock started striking eight.

"You'd better get a move on." She went to the stairs. "Lissa! You're late!"

Ben came through and stared at the clock.

"And things like this. You had to put it up as soon as we moved in, and you got it fixed when it broke, even though Lissa really hates it."

She hadn't told them the repairer insisted it was in perfect working order. "But it's our clock."

"It's *Dad's* clock."

"We chose it together."

"I was there, remember? Dad chose it. You didn't want one, but he dragged us all round Heidelberg. He had to have a genuine Black Forest cuckoo clock." He laughed. "It's so naff."

She smiled. "I know. It's your Dad all over, isn't it?"

"But that's why … I mean, look at these photos. That big one of him. You know Dad'd freak if he saw that?"

"He won't though, will he?"

Had Ursula put him up to this? Because she hated those enlargements: *"Do we have to endure him watching us all the time?"*

"That's not the point, Mum. You brought all his stuff here. Bodden Street was supposed to be a fresh start."

Ursula had said exactly the same.

"It's *my* stuff, ok? When you get your own place, you can decorate it however the hell you like. Now go and get your things together. You'll be late."

When they'd gone, she sat in the living room, staring at Richard. His wide blue-horizon eyes gazed down at her, mockingly full of life. The dog jumped into her chilled lap and curled up like a cat. She stroked him. God, this house was cold. You'd think it was December, not June. The sun didn't even try to reach inside, but she couldn't be bothered to get up and fetch a sweater.

The phone rang, rousing her from stupor. She looked at the clock. Almost ten thirty. She tipped Brodie off her knee and creaked to the kitchen.

"Hello?"

Belinda, whispering: "He's here, Isobel." Spidery footsteps up her spine. "Iz?" The familiar musical voice compressed to a hiss. "He's at your door now. Can you see him?"

Isobel didn't want to look.

"Wait a sec." She peeped round the arch. No shadow at the door. She let out her breath. "He's gone."

"He's standing right at your door now." Belinda sucked in her breath. "He just looked at me. I think he saw me." Ragged breathing.

"No one's there. Are you making this up? Why are you doing this?"

A clatter down the line. "Jesus!" That wasn't a whisper.

"Blin? Are you all right?"

Sound of scraping. "The ironing board fell over. Just a sec." More muffled movements. "Scared the shit out of me. Oh - he's gone!"

"He was never there. You're frightening me now." Isobel peered round the arch again. "Is that what you want, to scare me? Is that why you're doing this? Have I offended you, is that it? Have I done something wrong? Why are you making up all this weird shit? I thought you were my friend."

"I'm coming over."

When Belinda banged on the door, Isobel was still clutching the phone. Belinda's silhouette in the frosted glass was solid, definite. There.

"It's me, Iz. Open the door."

Isobel's legs tingled, leaden. She hobbled over, turned the key and stood back.

The door flew open, hit the wall. "Oh my God, Isobel, look at you! You need to sit down."

Belinda hustled her into the kitchen and plonked her on a chair. "You're freezing, honey."

She took off her own cardigan and wrapped it around Isobel's shoulders, then pulled up a chair and sat next to her. "I *am* your friend, you know that, right? Why's it so cold in here?"

She got up again, returned with the woollen throw from the sofa, and wrapped Isobel in it. Then she produced a crumpled tissue and dabbed Isobel's cheeks. "This is mad. We need to think. We've established you can't see him at the door. I saw him. You didn't. We need coffee."

She made it quickly, brought the mugs over, spilled the contents of both as she set them down.

Isobel picked up her drink, wrapped her hands around it, but couldn't swallow. She put it down. "He wasn't there. I'd have seen him through the glass, like I saw you just now."

Belinda drummed her fingers on the table. "There must be an explanation, something we're missing." She continued to drum. The clock ticked. "I did some research a while ago for a strange guy who was looking into... never mind what he was looking into. D'you think it could be like I said before, some kind of film? What if me and the others, we're seeing a film of something that's happened before, like a recording, but you can't see it from inside this house?"

Isobel glared at her.

"I don't know, do I? I'm only trying to make sense of it." Belinda took her hand, squeezed it. "I *am* your friend, Iz. I'd never try to hurt you, you do know that? And it's not just me. Phyllis and Bill have seen him, too, and Maud. Drink up. You need to get warm." She paced the kitchen, repeatedly going to the arch, peeking at the front door. She looked really scared.

"Blin, I didn't mean what I said before. It's just I can't get my head around this." Isobel slammed her mug down, spilling the coffee.

"I get that. It's all so wrong. But don't think about it now. You need to rest."

That wasn't all she needed. She couldn't go on like this. She had to get help: professional help.

Chapter 36

Dr Malcolm's room stank of cigars. Did he have the cheek to smoke in here or did the smell travel with him to work? He leaned back in his big leather chair, appraising her over his rimless glasses.

"So, Isobel, here's what I'm going to suggest. Start the medication again at the dosage you were on before - hear me out - and I'll refer you to our practice counsellor. Let's say six sessions in the first instance. How does that sound?"

"Like you're humouring me."

"Not at all. It's important you resume the antidepressants. They'll help you get on an even keel if you give them a chance, but it takes time, and -", he held up a hand, "I don't, in all honesty, believe the medication was responsible for your experiences."

She folded her arms. "Then what is?"

"I'm not entirely sure, to be frank, but you should have consulted me before coming off them.

Withdrawal can have its side-effects, too. I'm sure I explained that when I first prescribed them."

He looked at her over his glasses again. He tapped his keyboard, printed off a prescription, signed it and pushed it across the desk to her. She didn't pick it up.

"I'm suggesting the counselling to help you develop coping strategies, to better manage these…experiences. But talking therapy works best alongside appropriate medication. If you won't take the antidepressants, I can't refer you for counselling. There'd be no point."

She picked up the prescription.

"Good." He scribbled a note. "Now give this to Joan on Reception. She'll get you booked in. Come back and see me in two months. Or before if you feel you need to, of course."

He was on his feet, offering his hand.

"Thank you." She scurried out and handed over the scrawled note to the practice manager.

"Good grief, does he never listen? I explained only this morning the counsellor's booked out for the next three months."

"Three months?" Tears sprang up, hot and stinging. "But that's too long."

"Don't worry, dear. I've made an arrangement with some private practitioners, one of whom will be more than happy to take you on. Why so glum? In some practices, the waiting time for counselling is six months. I think we do rather well here, wouldn't you say?"

Isobel glanced behind at the busy waiting area. "Does counselling work, do you think, for people in my situation?"

"I'm sure Doctor wouldn't refer you if it wasn't going to work, now would he? Here's the list. You see there are a couple who are very local. The others slightly further afield, but all come highly recommended. Let us know who you decide to go with so we can arrange the necessaries."

Isobel took the list. "I'm not sure how to choose."

"I'm sorry, dear? Do speak up."

"I don't know what I need to ask them."

"I'm sure they're all highly competent." The receptionist looked past her to the growing line of waiting patients. "Now, if that's all?"

"Thank you." Isobel walked to the exit, careful not to catch anyone's eye.

At home, she smoothed the list on the kitchen counter. Did she really need counselling? She hadn't expected old Dr Malcolm to hold with that kind of thing, and she'd managed the past two years without it.

If you don't want his help, why did you see him?

Four women, two men. She picked up a pen and crossed out the men. Two women in Leigh, one in Wigan. Too close. One in Knutsford. She circled that name. Then she picked up the list, screwed it into a tight ball and threw it in the bin.

Chapter 37

Isobel walked with Brodie across the hill. He ran off down to the water. No one else about. She'd never felt so utterly alone. Could not see a way forward, a way out of this horrific... God, she didn't even have a name for what was happening to her. Friends couldn't help her and neither could family, so why would strangers be able to?

The sun cast a shadow ahead. Why such a long shadow so near mid-summer? It had rained, and now it was muggy and sweaty despite a lively breeze off the water. She tied her waterproof around her waist, giving her silhouette exaggerated swaying hips. She seemed to strut and sashay, her shadow impossibly hour-glass and slinky, giving the lie to the reality that she was hauling her reluctant carcass about for exercise it didn't want.

The breeze picked up, blew hair into her face, rushed in her ears. She heard footsteps in the wind and turned. No one. She walked on, swinging her arms in the cooler air. And then… And then something happened to her shadow. Its arms merged with the shade of her body. A moment before, her back had been warm but now she felt clammy, chilled, as if someone had walked up close behind and blotted out the sun. She slowed, mesmerised, as she watched her shadow legs merge into the solid oblong mass of her silhouette. She stopped. She could no longer make out her hair or the coat about her hips, only a long rectangle of black. The shadow darkened, darkened, until she could no longer see the grass beneath it.

But that wasn't possible.

A warm sigh close to her ear.

She spun around. No one. Completely alone. Her heart hammered.

Then, as she watched, her shadow widened along its length, sprawling black, like ink spilled on blotting paper.

This can't be real. You're dreaming.

Fear rose in her throat. Intense heat beat down, as the shadow broke apart, like a cell splitting under a microscope. She gasped: now there were two of them. Two human forms. Not the same. The new shade not her replica, but taller, heavier. Male. She felt breath at her neck, whipped around again. Nothing but the hint of a sigh on the breeze. She turned in panic to face the two shadows.

But she was singular once more.

Alone, again.

She didn't go back to the Flash for a week. Poor Brodie made do with short road walks, but he was desperate to be off the lead so she relented and faced her fear. It would be fine. She just wouldn't go up on the hill.

"Hello, Isobel. Not seen you to talk to for a bit."

Bernard, togged up in his old anorak despite the hot sun, looked pleased to see her.

"Not seen you, either. Where've you been?"

"Coming out later. Feeling my age."

"Give over."

"I'm seventy-five, don't forget. I find I need my beauty sleep." He wiped a hand across his nose. "I was beginning to think you were avoiding me, love, after last time when you buggered off like that. And then you didn't let on the other day, so I thought I'd offended you. Wasn't sure how, but you seemed angry with me."

"I wasn't angry. I'm sorry you thought that. If I'd known, I'd've rung you."

Bernard nodded. "I've been away for a few days. Did I tell you?"

They fell into step as he recounted his latest camping trip. She let the stories flow over her, simply enjoying his company. The dogs chased one another up ahead. Sun warmed her back. Tension drained from her shoulders. She lengthened her stride to Bernard's easy gait. He wasn't for slowing down any time soon.

"…saw you with him the other day. That chap with the errant dog."

She stopped. "Where?"

"You were walking together. I gave you a shout, but you didn't let on. That's why I thought you were narked with me. Either that or you were too engrossed." He winked at her.

"When did you see him... us?"

Bernard looked alarmed. "Are you all right, love?"

"When, though?"

"It would be, let's see, it was the day I went into Manchester, so it must have been Tuesday."

Today was Monday. She hadn't seen Zag's owner for weeks. "Can't have been me, Bernard."

"You're hard to mistake, love."

"Then it was probably Fred with me."

"Do me a favour! Fred's nearly as old as me. No, he was young, like you. Tall, in black, like you said. Carrying a lead. First time I've seen him."

Brodie jumped up at her, impatient to be on the move again.

"Where were we when you saw us?"

"Walking across the hill. I was down by the little beach where these two swim. I did call to you, but you were in a world of your own, the pair of you. Good for you, I say."

"But -"

"Eh, you don't have to explain. You're young and beautiful. You shouldn't be alone."

"You don't understand -"

"You're a free agent. It's nobody's business but yours."

She was too tired to argue, and besides, she didn't want to say the words out loud.

"I'm heading back now. Got work."

"All right, love. Hope to see you sooner than later."

He raised a hand in farewell and took off at a good pace. She turned towards home.

Last Tuesday.

Battalions of spiders swarmed her spine. Brodie trotted in close to her heel.

Last Tuesday was when her shadow split.

Chapter 38

Ben adjusted his rucksack on his shoulder as he walked up Bodden Street, glad he'd ignored Nathan's fooling so he could hit the library at lunchtime. He'd kick back tonight. Maybe watch some more of *The Wire*. That creepy, smelly kid, Carl Hare, was sitting on his front doorstep, eating something sloppy from a bowl. Ben gave him the finger and kept walking.

He heard Mum and Melissa rowing before he even opened the front gate. What now? He didn't have to go in; he could turn around, walk away. He pushed the door open. As soon as he dropped his bag, Brodie leapt into his arms, scrabbling at his shoulders trying to gain purchase.

"What the...! Hey, mate, calm down. You're ok."

But Brodie absolutely wasn't, he was trembling, eyes so wide the whites showed.

They were in the kitchen, screaming over each other so he couldn't make out the words. He held Brodie tight in his arms, and strode in. They were facing off across the table, arms waving, mouths contorting. Mum was crying and, shit, so was Melissa.

"What's going on?"

They didn't look at him, didn't even pause for breath.

Mum slammed her hand on the table: "Stop lying to me, Melissa!"

"You're a nutter, you are! You're a fucking -"

"Don't you dare speak to me like that!"

Ben had to do something before they started throwing things: "Enough!"

Melissa whipped around: "Where've you *been*? She's lost it, Ben. We've got to get help. Oh, Brodie?"

She took the dog, then stood behind Ben like she needed protecting. Surely not from Mum?

Mum saw it, too. She shrivelled like a burst crisp packet and hung her head.

"Mum?" He went to her, but she backed away. He held out his hands. She shook her head, face bright red, tears and snot all over it. She wouldn't look at him, so he turned to Melissa: "What's going on?"

"She's the one doing crazy shit." Melissa stabbed a finger at Mum. "And then she says *I'm* lying! Ask *her*."

"I'm asking you."

"She's trying to frighten me -"

"I'm not, Melissa. Oh, please, I'm not, sweetheart." Mum's voice sounded small, strangled.

"I came in from school, right, and she was on the floor."

Ben turned to Mum. "Are you alright? Did you fall?"

"She was *crawling*, Ben."

"No, I... I was just -" Mum's voice came out as a cracked whisper.

"She was crawling around in there," Melissa nodded toward the living room, "like... like that witchy woman in *The Ring*. I thought she'd had a stroke or something, but she hadn't. And she wouldn't stop. She just kept crawling, like she couldn't hear me, like she didn't even know I was there. And Brodie was terrified, trying to get away from her, scratching to get in his crate, but he couldn't. The door was closed."

"No, it wasn't like that. I -"

"He's scared shitless. Look at him." Melissa buried her face in Brodie's fur. Ben saw the raised hackles.

He turned back to Mum. She looked so small, so old, all hunched with her arms folded tight. As scared as Brodie. "Come here."

"Don't Ben, don't touch her!"

He gave Mum a big hug, rocked her. *Crawling?*

She could barely speak for crying: "I'm sorry, I don't know what happened. Lissa says I... I wasn't, I didn't. I don't think I..."

He stroked her hair. "Shh. Doesn't matter now. I'm here. We're ok. We're all ok, aren't we? Melissa?" He gave her a look.

"No."

She turned away, cradling Brodie. He heard her run upstairs.

Chapter 39

Isobel worried about Ben. She'd understood when he refused to leave them alone in the house that weekend Joe Jessop checked the loft. But that had been almost a month ago, and he was still sleeping on the landing in front of Melissa's door. He ate most of his meals up there too, passing the time on his iPad or reading. He couldn't be getting much sleep. She'd tried to persuade him that Joe must have scared off the intruder, but he had his father's stubborn streak, and took his role as man of the house too seriously. He kept the loft hatch unbolted when he was "on lookout", despite her protests. He wanted to be free to climb up there fast. Element of surprise. Don't tell the police, he'd said. Not yet. Let's wait until we have proof. She couldn't judge which of them knew better anymore, so she'd waited.

When she got in from walking the dog, Ben was already home and at his station. He must have bunked off early. She sat on the top stair to chat. He sprawled on his sleeping bag, playing some game on the tablet. The screen blued his face. It was beginning to smell like his room up here.

"What d'you fancy for tea?"

"Pasta?"

"Spinach, mascarpone?"

"Sounds great." He hadn't yet dragged his gaze from the game.

"Ben, you in?" Melissa's heavy school bag thudded to the living room floor.

"On the landing." Melissa clumped upstairs. Isobel knew she would have gone straight back out if Ben hadn't been home. They'd spent no time alone together since... since -

"Move, Mum. What is this, a meeting of the mothers' union?" Ben raised his palm, still not looking up. Melissa hi-fived him. "Yo bro. How's it hangin'?"

"None of yours."

She laughed, went in her room, slammed the door.

"Lissa, what time d'you want -?"

Ben was on his feet. A resounding bump, then heavy scuffles from above. He put his finger to his lips *sh!* and waved her to Melissa's room.

"What are you going to -?"

"Sh." He jumped onto the landing banister rail, punched the loft hatch open, grabbed the hatch-frame sides and boosted himself up into the dark.

"Ben!" A weak light flailed. An almighty crash.

"I've got you, you little fucker."

A face thrust through the hole, young, eyes wide, mouth gaping. It wasn't Ben.

"Don't let him hurt me!"

"Got him, Mum! He was trying to open up that hole, dirty little perv."

The head jerked, emitted a muffled *ooph.*

"Ben, don't hurt him."

"You're going to die, you little shit."

"Help me, lady! I didn't mean to -"

Melissa burst onto the landing. "Carl Hare, ohmygod, you paedo! Wait 'til everyone at school hears about this."

Melissa's laugh had something vicious in it. Isobel had to take control before this turned into *Lord Of The Flies.*

"Ben, you help him down, right now. Do *not* drop him, do you hear? Melissa, help me."

But she stood back. "Paedo-o! Paedo-o!"

"Melissa!"

"Come on then, sicko. Come to Auntie Lissa." She stood with her arms out ready to catch him.

"For goodness sake." Isobel reached up and grabbed the boy's proffered arm. How the hell was she going to do this without hurting him? But he'd chosen to go up there. He should have thought about how he'd get down. She braced against the banister and held his weight as he slithered through the hole. A controlled fall. Ben must have been holding his leg. He landed heavily on the top stairs. Melissa pounced, slapped him hard about the head. He brought his hands up to his ears and cowered. Ben sprang down, grabbed his scruff, dragged him downstairs. The boy's head thwacked against the wall.

"Keep your eyes forward, dickhead. You don't get to look at my sister." Ben wrenched the boy's arm and frogmarched him into the kitchen.

Where did he learn to do that?

She and Melissa followed. Ben sat him on a chair and menaced him. The kid started to cry. He could be the same age as Melissa. Slight, with a dirty patina to his skin, he looked like he lived rough.

"So you know him, Lissa?"

"It's Carl. One of them scummy Hares at the end terrace. Their mum's the one you said has a voice like a constipated cow. He's in my class, and ohmygod, he is *never* going to live this down!" She made a *watching you* gesture, fingers pointing first at her eyes then his. Isobel pitied him, then.

"Would you like to explain what you were doing in my loft, please?"

"Go on." Ben cuffed the back of his head.

"Ben, that's enough, thank you. Carl?"

He wiped his nose on his sleeve. "Looking for summat."

"In my loft?"

"Didn't know it was your loft, did I?"

Ben pressed in on him. "Cheeky little shit."

He shrank back.

"You knew it wasn't yours, though."

"Just a loft, in'nt it? What's it to you? You don't go up there. And you can get through. There's nowt stopping you. You should have blocked it up if you didn't want people in. What d'you expect? Stupid bitch."

He hit the floor, nose bleeding, before Isobel registered Ben's punch. Melissa lunged, kicked him in the belly.

"That's enough!" Isobel glared at them. "Get up! Come on, you're fine." She pulled him up by his arm. He was so light, frail. "Here, wipe your nose." She gave him some kitchen roll. "Do you think it's a good idea to insult me on top of everything?"

He looked at the floor, shook his head. Then he said quietly: "*He* knew I was going in there. He saw me."

"I'm sorry?"

He jerked his head at Ben, but didn't dare look at him. "Him. He's been up there, too. Tried to scare me, didn't yer? Think you're so hard."

"Ben, what's he talking about?"

"No idea."

The lad turned on him. "You're a dirty liar! It was *you* shat me up that day. I saw you creeping about. Didn't know it was you, then. Thought it was a… Tried to jump down through your hatch but you'd soddin' bolted it."

That godawful banging.

"Thought it was a what, Carl?"

"Nowt. It were dark, weren't it." He hung his head, but she saw fear flash in his eye.

"Tell your mum that if I ever catch you in my loft again, or hear you've been in anyone else's, I'll report you to the police. And if you go *any*where near my daughter -"

Melissa snorted. "Like to see him try. His life is so *over*."

Isobel believed her. "Ben, walk him to his door, but lay off him."

"Come on, shit-for-brains. Let's take you home to mummy." The boy let himself be prodded out of the house.

Melissa followed "Paedo-o! Paedo-o!"

"Melissa Hickey, come here *right* now. Make a start on those onions."

Isobel turned to her laptop on the counter. She needed a builder who could start work first thing in the morning.

Head back, Isobel closed her eyes. Muted voices drowned in warm running water. Firm, intelligent fingers made waves across her scalp. This alone was worth the money. To seep out of herself, to stray into bodiless nothing. This warm, red-black blank. Nothing could touch her here. She was out of reach, didn't have to ask herself who, or what, she was hiding from. She was lost, safe. Murmured conversation, dryers' drone, drifting thoughts. She let them move on through, leave no mark. No use to her. Not here.

"How's that little dog of yours? He's such a cutie. I've seen you passing with him."

Shepherd's crook of meaningless chatter yanked her back into this wretched body, this miserable existence.

Today was Tuesday. Tomorrow might be Wednesday, but who cared? Then Thursday, Friday. Until it wasn't. Until it stopped without warning.

Hands pressed her shoulders, instructing her to sit up. But what was the point?

This was the point, sitting here with her in Costa. Melissa. And Ben. They kept her going. Whenever she fantasised about the least painful way to end this, she always imagined who might find her. And it was Melissa's face she pictured every time. No way out that way.

Noisy chatter. Fragrant coffee. Chill from full-blast air-con. Tables full of dirty crockery, spilled sugar. Melissa found somewhere by the window. Isobel quickly tidied the mess and placed the used cups on the next table.

"I like it. It's darker than I expected. Your red bits have gone. But, yeah, it's nice. You'll need to wash all that off round your hair line, though."

"Does it look a mess?" Isobel luxuriated in Melissa's attention. She seemed finally to have forgiven her for that...episode.

"It's fine. Probably, it's just me because I'm so close?" Melissa placed her lips around the straw, voluptuous, unselfconscious, and sucked up her milkshake. "What's your hot chocolate like?"

"Hot, chocolatey."

Melissa smiled, gave her a thumbs-up and took the straw back in her mouth.

"Did you get the top you were after?"

Melissa bridled: "No! You won't believe this. They sold out! I asked him last weekend, I asked if he had many left. And he said yes, loads. But now he's sold out. Bloody liar."

"Melissa!"

"Well, he is. I'd have bought it then if I'd known, and now I haven't got anything to wear tonight, and Carrie's going to be so, *oh poor you. Didn't you wear that at Jane's party? Oh but, sorry, I keep forgetting, you're a single-parent family, aren't you?*" She twined her neck, dipped her head from side to side in imitation of her nemesis.

Isobel laughed.

"But she will, Mum."

"There must be another top?"

"This is Leigh we're talking about, Mother."

"What about the Trafford Centre?"

"And how do I get there?"

"Call me old-fashioned, but I've heard they run things called buses?"

"Ha ha." Melissa pulled out her phone and started texting.

Isobel folded her arms: "Don't mind me."

Melissa held up a hand: *hang on a sec*. Isobel sat back, sipped her chocolate and watched her daughter's thumbs move deftly about the keypad. Melissa paused and laughed, then keyed some more.

"Melissa, hello?"

"Sorry. Nearly finished. Let me just... There!" She laughed again.

"What was that all about?"

"Nothing." She put the phone back into her trouser pocket. Isobel raised an eyebrow in her special *this is your mother, don't mess with me* way. "Ok, but you won't like it."

"Try me."

"I've been boiling Carl Hare's bunny."

"Melissa, do you even know what that means?"

"It's what Ben says."

"What have you done, young lady?"

"Snapchat!"

God, not another thing she had to get her head around.

"Isn't that the photos one?" There'd been something about it on *Woman's Hour*. "Where kids are doing nude selfies?"

"Get you, Mum."

"But I didn't know you were on that. I thought it was just Facebook and Twitter."

"They're for oldies like you."

"Hey!"

"Well, they are. Boring! Snapchat's a laugh."

"You don't do those selfies, do you?"

"Gross, Mum!"

Isobel wasn't reassured. "So, what've you done to Carl Hare?"

"Just sent all my friends those photos. And all *his* friends."

"What photos? How can you send them to *his* friends?" She'd have to open a Snapchat account herself now, to check it out.

"The ones I took when he was hanging out of the loft. When Ben dragged him downstairs."

"I didn't know you'd taken pictures. For goodness sake, you can't send those to people!"

"Too late." Melissa sipped her drink, unconcerned. In fact, pleased with herself.

"But that's the one where photos disappear after a few seconds, right?"

"Usually."

"Usually?"

"Bernie photoed the photos and Instagramed them. And turns out so did Pippa and Grace. And, before you start on me, so did Ben."

"So, what are you saying? Those photos are all over social media?"

"Pretty much. See, boiled his bunny."

"But that was -" A girl came over to clear the table next to them. Isobel lowered her voice: "That was in our house."

"I *know*. That's the *point*?"

"Oh, Melissa."

"Do you despair of me, Mother?"

"Don't call me Mother. I not only despair of you: I disown you."

Melissa laughed, leaned across the table and planted a milkshake kiss on her cheek.

"You could borrow that coral top of mine? The one you said you liked?"

"God, Mum, I'm not *that* desperate."

"None taken."

"No, I mean, it's nice, on *you*, but…"

"Ok, you can stop digging."

"I'll go to Bernie's to get ready. She'll have something. Or her mum will."

Chapter 40

Isobel was trying to forget the strange doctor, and that whole weird episode, but Belinda wasn't making it easy. She'd tried to video him on her phone, apparently. The usual routine: he'd appeared at the door, waited, glanced over his shoulder and knocked. Belinda was sure she'd got him. When the door opened, she told Isobel, she was so busy trying to see who answered, she hadn't realised she'd pressed pause. And when she tried to play back the footage, she couldn't find it on her phone. She thought this strange and meaningful. Isobel thought she'd deleted it by accident.

Belinda had another go when he turned up again. She knew Isobel was home this time but decided not to disturb her. Hadn't wanted to "stress her out", she said. She'd held her phone to the window ready to film but could see only Isobel's front door on her screen. The camera didn't pick up the doctor across the road. She lowered it and looked through the window: there he was. She looked back at the phone screen: Isobel's front door, no caller. She filmed anyway. Sure enough, all she managed to capture was a perfect sequence of nothing happening at Isobel's front door.

"He doesn't want to be filmed."

"Maybe you need lessons with that new phone."

So Belinda came up with another plan...

Isobel was baking, listening to Jeremy Vine's lunchtime radio show while the kitchen filled with scents of vanilla and warm butter. This was as close to happy as she ever came now. She'd made banana bread for Ben and a Victoria sandwich for Richard, before she remembered. How could she have forgotten? Maybe she was as crazy as Melissa thought. Now, she was beating egg whites for Melissa's lemon meringue. On the radio, politicians discussed changes to GP hours and bemoaned the demise of home visits. She whisked, briskly. They had no idea what older people had to deal with. But beyond a perfunctory spurt of irritation, she no longer cared about the state of the nation. The whites were forming peaks. Maybe she should phone in and tell Jeremy about her own mysterious home-visiting service? That might liven up the conversation. She smiled at her weak bravado and gave the whites a final whip.

She almost dropped the bowl when the phone rang. She stared at it, knew who it would be. She went to the arch: no one at the front door. She turned off the radio, picked up the phone.

Belinda, whispering: "He's here."

"Oh no he isn't." Isobel tried to sound calm, reassuring.

"We know how this goes. He's still there. Should we try it? We need to be quick, if we're going to do it."

"But I can't see him."

"You know he's there. If he knocks…"

Isobel pushed back her hair with a sticky hand. She'd only been playing at happy, after all. This was her reality. "Ok, I'll do it, but do *not* leave me. You stay on this phone whatever happens, d'you hear me?"

"I will. Like we agreed."

"I'm going to the door." Her legs leaked strength. She wasn't sure how she got to be standing directly in front of it. "I'm -" She swallowed. "I'm here. Still can't see him."

That sinister whisper again: "He's there. Wait where you are. You'll be fine. I'll come over straightaway, remember."

And do what?

Fast, shallow breathing down the line. Did *she* sound like that to Belinda? She needed the loo.

Think of something else.

What jam should she put in the Victoria sponge? She had strawberry and some apricot. Richard always preferred strawberry. Damn! She'd left the flan case in the oven -

"He's knocking. Can you hear him?" The cuckoo clock ticked. "Isobel?"

She didn't recognise her own voice, taut and high: "No one's knocking."

Blood thundered in her ears. The air thrummed, displaced, shifting.

Is that him trying to get in?

"Isobel, say it now, while he's still knocking."

Her tongue stuck to the roof of her mouth. She swallowed hard. "Come in."

"Louder!"

"Come in, come in!" A percussive crash over the phone, then silence. "Belinda?" A voice, muffled. "I can't hear you! Belinda?"

More indistinct speech, then clarity. "…how the hell it did that. It's come right off the wall - Oh, shit."

"What happened?"

"He's gone."

"Where?"

"I didn't see. The cupboard fell -"

"But did he...? Did the door open? Belinda, did he come in?"

"I didn't see. Oh God, what have we done?"

Isobel let her arm drop, still holding the phone. The living room had changed, dark, hostile. The wallpaper's blue vines threatened to choke. Eyes on her. She whipped around.

He's in here with me.

How could she have been so stupid? She couldn't protect the children if she'd let this thing in.

God, oh god.

The clock ticked, steadying, familiar. She took a deep breath.

Listen to yourself. What just happened, anyway? Exactly nothing. This is Belinda's problem, not yours. She's the one who needs help.

She retreated backwards into the kitchen to switch off the oven, her eyes glued to that front door.

The cuckoo clock pecked at her nerves. In the dim light of a single lamp, the wallpaper glowered, hid secrets. She poured herself another shaky glass of merlot. The kids had gone to bed, but she couldn't settle, didn't dare go up, couldn't bear to not know what might be happening down here.

Brodie, quiet, watchful, followed her to and from the kitchen.

"You feel it, too, don't you, lad?" Her voice too loud in the pregnant night.

She sat in the armchair by the unlit fire. Brodie jumped onto her lap, but wouldn't lie down. He circled, then stood rigid, his down-turned tail to her, eyes fixed on the front door.

She whispered: "Relax, little one. Snuggle down." Still, he stared. "Stop it now, Brodie."

She watched the front door. Why hadn't she got around to putting up a curtain across it? The frosted windows stared back, black-blank. She stroked the dog's rough coat with firm, rhythmic sweeps. Eventually, she let her head rest back, closed her eyes, dozed.

She didn't so much hear his growl as feel it, an almost imperceptible rumble. She sat up. A ridge of fur slowly rose all down Brodie's back. His tense feet pressed hard into her thighs, his head thrust forward.

"What is it?"

Then she felt it, too.

A tingle, a less-than vibration in the air, and for a moment, only a moment, she felt with helpless, paralysing fear, her flesh dissolve, her life-force disperse. For an instant, she was everywhere. And nowhere.

Then Brodie shook himself, jumped from her knee and trotted off to bed.

Chapter 41

After work, turning onto Bodden Street, Isobel tamped down a treacherous sense of dread. No one should feel this way coming home. She drove slowly between double-parked cars, and tried to feel glad. She was looking forward to opening a bottle of wine and starting a new novel tonight. But could she ever relax again in that house, knowing she'd invited in a... what, exactly? Nothing had happened. It was all in Belinda's imagination.

You keep telling yourself that.

Who was that in the road? She slowed. Yvonne Hare from number fifty: big, with poorly-dyed, close-cropped hair and tracksuit sleeves pushed up her meaty tattooed arms. She waved Isobel to a stop.

Keep calm now.

Isobel wound down her window.

"You want to be careful what you say, you do." A nicotine-stained finger jabbed at her face.

She recoiled: "I'm sorry?"

Yvonne bent to the window: "You've not been here five minutes. Who d'you think you are, making accusations like that?" Saliva gathered at the corners of her mouth. Isobel leaned back further.

Yvonne towered next to her. Instinctively, to protect her personal space, Isobel thrust her hand out of the window. Yvonne faltered. "I'm Isobel. I don't think we've met properly, have we?"

The handshake was fleeting, sticky, but diffused the attack, and Yvonne's awkwardness was almost comical: "Oh, yeah. I'm Yvonne. Live at the end house."

Isobel looked down at her lap. Yvonne squatted by the window, her breath hot, ketchupy. "Well, I expect you'll be wanting your tea."

The woman was an idiot. Had she forgotten how this little chat started? "There *was* something, Yvonne, while I've got you. Did you know Carl's been going into your loft and using it to get through to everyone else's? Did he tell you we'd caught him up in mine the other day?"

"He - I - you -"

"Because if he does it again, I've told him I'll report him to the police. Did he tell you that? Did he tell you he'd drilled a hole in my daughter's bedroom ceiling? No? He didn't mention he was a peeping tom? Did he not mention the criminal damage to my property? What exactly *did* he tell you, Yvonne, to make you stop me in the street like this and yell at me like a fishwife?"

Yvonne stood up. "This is what I'm saying." Her ample belly wobbled with every bellowed word. "You think you can come here, all of five minutes and you're making accusations left, right and centre."

Isobel opened the car door. Yvonne shuffled back onto the pavement in her stained pink slippers. Isobel got out, and faced her. "Just to be clear, it's not an accusation, it's a fact. I suggest you keep your son under control, and out of my house. Does that sound reasonable?"

"Oh, threats now, is it?" Yvonne threw back her head, shouted for the whole street to hear. "Who the fuck are you, anyway? Think you're something, do you?" She started doing that Bollywood head wobble. "With your nice car and your posh accent." Isobel had only ever seen teenage girls do that. "Think you can move in and click your fingers, and we'll all jump."

"I'm not threatening you, Yvonne. I'm trying to talk to you about your son's criminal behaviour. If I was his mum, I'd want to make sure he doesn't get into any more trouble."

"Yeah, well you're not his fucking mum, are you, so keep your fat face out of my business."

"I'm not doing this." Isobel got back in the car, started the engine.

"That's it. Walk away. Don't like it, do you? You dish it out, but you can't take it, can you?"

A finger poked through the window again, too close to her. She pressed the window winder. The hand snatched back. She pulled away. In the rear-view mirror, Yvonne postured and shouted, but kept by her own door. Isobel manoeuvred into a spot right outside the house for once, and waited for Yvonne to go in.

Maud limped down the street to the car. Isobel wound down the window.

"What a racket! Has that woman no shame? Are you all right, dear? You mustn't take this to heart. We're not all like that round here. She's an awful woman, horrible family. They've been moved around all the council estates, you know. No one will tolerate them so the council rented that house and landed them on us. Frankly, I think it's a disgrace. I've spoken to our councillor about it. Oh, listen to that carry on. And the language! Joe Jessop told me all about you finding her boy in our lofts. I've suspected something of the sort for a long time. Strange noises, and so forth. I can't possibly get up there, so I've been rather at his mercy. But no longer, thanks to you, dear. Ignore her. Hold your head high, go in your house and get your tea."

She was right, of course. Isobel got out of the car. Yvonne promptly dashed through her own front door. Isobel walked Maud back to her gate. "You're very kind. It's good to know I have some lovely neighbours."

Maud squeezed her hand in both of hers. "And don't you forget that, dear."

Isobel flung her car keys on the bookshelf. The dog greeted her. She bent to scratch his ear.

"Has anyone thought to give you your tea?"

Music blared from Ben's room. Nothing from Melissa's. She could be watching TV with her earphones in or maybe she wasn't back yet. Isobel hoped they hadn't heard that shouting match.

"Ben, will you move this jacket? I won't tell you again!"

She scooped up the parka from the sofa where he'd flung it and took it to the back porch to hang it up. She paused as she hooked it over her waterproof, smoothed its wrinkles, pulled the sleeve straight. She switched on the light. It was Richard's old parka. She held it to her nose, breathed in Richard's faint scent: Aramis, woodsmoke, warmth, excitement.

Sudden yearning stole her breath. The black hole she tried so hard to keep closed, yawned open and she teetered on its edge. She hugged the coat tight, ran upstairs and burst into Ben's room. "Who said you could wear your Dad's coat?"

"Don't we knock anymore, Mother?"

"Don't 'mother' me! Who said you could wear this?"

"I didn't." He put down his pen, sat back from the desk. "That's Dad's, isn't it?"

"You left it strewn on the sofa. How dare you!"

His patient gaze was insufferable. "You were supposed to be getting rid of that stuff."

"It's not *stuff*. And that doesn't give you the right to go and help yourself!"

"I didn't."

"Don't lie to me, Ben. It was on the back of the sofa."

"You keep it in the porch with our coats, so it's hardly out-of-bounds. But *I've* never worn it. Why would I? Have you asked Melissa? Maybe Dan didn't bring a coat. Maybe she lent it him. *That's* mine." He pointed to his donkey jacket, arranged carefully on the bed. "And besides, I don't *strew*. You know this."

She should slap his smart-arse mouth. "I want to know who's had this coat."

"It wasn't me."

She slammed the door behind her, strode to her own room, placed the parka on a hanger, smoothed the suits and shirts around it, and closed the wardrobe door.

She lay on the bed, turned on her side and curled up as tight as she could.

Chapter 42

Richard paced the bedroom. "You have to read it, Bel."

"I've got to finish this first." She held up her book. "Get in, Rich. Stop faffing about. You're distracting me."

Reluctantly, he climbed into bed but sat ramrod-straight. "It's amazing. It proves it."

She put aside her novel, took off her glasses, switched off the lamp. "Snuggle down, then." She drew him to her and they lay entwined. "That's better. Now, tell me."

"*The Third Man Factor*. It has a subtitle. Can't remember. Hang on." He switched on his lamp.

"Oh, Richard."

He leaned out of bed and scooped the book from under it. "*The Third Man Factor: Surviving The Impossible*. Stories about guys in extreme conditions, climbers, sailors, explorers, like, and they all report the presence of an extra man when they're up against it. When they're facing death, you know? They get this sense there's someone with them that they can't quite see. Like he's there at the corner of their eye but when they look straight at him, he's not." Richard raked a hand through his already messy hair, and opened the book. "Shackleton, you know Ernest Shackleton, the arctic explorer? Even he wrote about it in his journal, so it's not new. It's spooky, but kind of comforting, too. They say this presence, this Third Man, helped them through, that they would have given up if he hadn't appeared. They were near death and the Third Man saved them."

"Wow."

"I know. What more proof do you need of an afterlife? If this Third Man exists, he has to come from somewhere, right? Like a guardian angel?"

"Guess I'll have to read it. It's late. Let's get some sleep."

"It's obvious. Don't be so fucking dense!"

"Richard, please, you'll wake the children."

"But this proves you're wrong. What else could it be?"

"Any number of things." She could so do without this, tonight. She'd had a tough day. A sudden death this morning, then tricky negotiations with the union. She didn't need Richard going off on one. "Love, please keep your voice down."

He whispered: "This better?"

"Thank you. So, these people were all in danger? Could it not be stress or fear, or oxygen deprivation, even, if they're in the mountains?"

"The book talks about all that. But there's more to it. Much more. In different situations across all these years, they have this same experience! And you said there's no life after death."

"When did I say that?"

"When we had Marcus and Lil over. You rammed it down our throats."

"Is that what this is about? We were drinking, remember. And I didn't say that, exactly. I said I don't *believe* in life after death. I don't have the faith gene. If you want to believe, go right ahead."

"But that won't work. You have to believe, too."

She laughed. "Why?"

"It's no good me believing on my own. *Think*, woman. If you're not looking, you'll never see me."

"Is that how it works?"

"Don't laugh at me, Isobel." He threw back the duvet, jumped out of bed. "I'm trying to work this out." He looked haggard in the lamplight.

"What are you on about?"

"I don't want to leave you and the kids. I want to do right by you. But you know how I am. You know, don't you?"

She sat up. "Has the doctor said something?"

"It's just a feeling I may not have long."

"Don't say that. Don't even think it."

He sat next to her, grabbed her hands. "But d'you understand why it's so important?"

She snatched them back. "I want you in this life, not the next. You'd better not do anything stupid, Richard Hickey. I'd never forgive you."

"Would I? Don't be daft. But everlasting life." He started to pace again. "That would be a solution."

"Stop talking like that. You're scaring me."

He wasn't listening, muttering to himself: "To be together forever. Guardian angel. A family for always, without all this -" He flung out his arm.

"Come on, love. Things aren't so bad, surely?"

"Don't patronise me. Superior bitch!" He punched the wardrobe door. She flinched. "I can't stand it when you laugh at me."

"I'm not laughing. I just can't keep up with you."

"So read the book. We could be together forever."

Right now, forever with him sounded like the worst kind of hell. "You're shouting again. Did you take your asenapine?"

"Never mind my fucking meds. I need a clear head. I've got to work this out. It's down to me, do you not understand that?"

"Mum?" Melissa, outside the door.

"It's all right, sweetie, I'm coming." Isobel got out of bed, and said to Richard in a low voice: "I'll bring your meds. Take them, or you're sleeping in the spare room."

Chapter 43

They flung their gaily-coloured plastic bags on the sofa. Isobel didn't want to think about how much she'd spent. Her purse bled money whenever she entered the Trafford Centre's hallowed portals in Melissa's company. But they'd had fun, and they both sorely needed that.

Melissa flopped next to her shopping. "I'm knackered. Stick the kettle on, Mum."

"What did your last one die of? I drove. *You* stick the kettle on."

"In a minute." It was always in a minute with Melissa. Isobel could hear her own mother's voice: *If you want something doing...*

This time the parka hung neatly across the back of a kitchen chair - her heart surged with hope - *as if he'd just* ... She squeezed the hope to nothing in a practised, merciless grip. Ben was trying to force her hand, to make her get rid of his father's things. Couldn't he see what it did to her? She stroked the coat, left it where it was, filled the kettle.

"Mum, come and look at this! Quick, before he stops."

Isobel went to the arch: "What?"

"Look at him. What's he doing that for?"

Brodie was sitting back on his haunches, fronts paws raised, begging, head on one side, ears pricked. Expectant. So cute. Hang on, though: he wasn't doing it for Melissa, lounging on the sofa, he was facing the empty armchair by the fire. Come to think of it, he'd been sitting in that same spot when they came in.

Melissa tried to get his attention: "Brodie! Come here, little one!"

He didn't budge. The armchair had his rapt attention. Isobel had never seen him hold that position so long. He didn't even wobble.

She grabbed a handful of kibble from the plastic bin under the counter. "Here, Brodie. What's this?" Only when she knelt next to him did he so much as glance at her, but still he kept up the pose for the armchair. "Here you are, you daft dog. You can stop now."

She prodded him. He dropped to a sit, nibbled the treats from her outstretched hand. But he kept glancing at the chair, as if seeking permission.

Melissa lost interest: "Let's check out what we bought. Did you get those jeans?"

"They didn't seem to fit right." Isobel rose, stiffly.

Brodie jumped onto Melissa's lap, as if nothing had happened.

Isobel went to brew the tea, but stopped in the archway: the parka that had hung securely on the chair-back a moment ago lay spread-eagled on the floor. Arranged, like a crucifix.

She scooped it up and hung it in the porch, out of her sight.

That night, rain built to a spectacular thunderstorm. Afterwards, the air hung still and hot. And wrong. Isobel sat up with Melissa until the storm passed, and now she couldn't sleep, but lay on her back, the duvet pushed down to her waist. So sticky. She'd already discarded her teeshirt. She flung her arms wide. The window was open, and the door, to try to create a breeze. She'd have to buy a fan, because she couldn't sleep like this…

She's at school, Well Green Juniors: Yellow Classroom. The best classroom, everyone says. Yellow walls, yellow cupboards, yellow floor. Like the sun's shining indoors. She's wearing a yellow and white striped dress. That's wrong: the uniform was blue and white. Her desk is by the window: it's raining. She hears rumbles far away.

A rap on the door. The headmistress walks in and stares, her eyes as big as saucers behind her thick glasses. Hair growing out of her chin.

"Miss Read, would you ask Mr Kenyon to supervise your class, please? Then come along with Isobel, if you will."

Isobel adores her teacher. She's beautiful and clever and funny. Now Isobel catches her look of alarm, and she's afraid.

Miss Benian has spit at the corners of her mouth. "Come with me, child."

Isobel doesn't want to, she wants to turn and run the other way as fast as she can. The corridors are quiet and empty. She feels naughty just being here.

The headmistress's heels tap-tap on the silence. Isobel follows, mesmerised by the woolly grey backside swaying before her.

A friendly cow, all grey and white.

Now she's in the headmistress's office. She's never been in here before. As Miss Benian holds the door wide for her, Miss Read catches up with them, takes her hand, squeezes it. She whispers something Isobel wants to hear as *Porridge* but knows really is *Courage.*

She steps off a cliff, the fulmars and the guillemots. She's falling, falling…

She jolted awake, her face wet with tears. Lost and hopeless as her ten-year-old self. She turned to Richard: when would she learn? Pulled the duvet around her shoulders, despite the heat, rolled onto her side, cried herself to exhaustion.

She must have been dozing when the duvet tugged away from her. She pulled it back.

"Brodie, stop it."

She patted the bed beside her. The dog in his usual spot curled tightly against her, snoring. The duvet twitched again. She pulled it up to cover her head, gripped its corner.

She was relaxing back into sleep when it snatched from her grasp with a violent yank. She lay exposed, her eyes tight shut.

"Please, you can't come in. You don't belong here. I'm sorry."

Did she say this aloud or only in her head?

The duvet landed on her, gentle, cool, like it had floated down from the ceiling. She felt it tucked about her shoulders as if by a loving hand.

She snuggled into it - a distant peal of woman’s laughter - and sank into fitful slumber.

Chapter 44

Isobel tilted her face to the same sun, intense, punishing, that had watched Richard die this day two years ago. She tried to feel his presence in its heat, in her heart. A grasshopper chirruped in the tall weeds by the back gate, terribly polite and English. Barcelona, too visceral, slipped from her grasp. Still she stood, her thinning skin victim to the noon-day rays, clinging to that gossamer thread of connection, conjuring him beside her, sun-worshipper.

Ursula had taken Ben and Melissa to mark the anniversary at the ... at the ... She couldn't make herself even think about that alien place where strong, healthy, living Richard had never been. She folded her arms across her chest, hugged herself. Broke out in goosebumps.

Maybe she should go back in, tackle that bureau again. A more productive way to get close to him, and if she could clear some of his things, she might start to accept. Ursula thought so. Ben did, too. She'd needed Richard close, his clothes, his music, but she wasn't being fair on the kids, she saw that now. They needed to move on.

She entered the cool, damp-smelling dark of the kitchen like she was sliding into an algae-slicked pool. Brodie padded after her, faithful, reluctant. She paused in the living room to gaze at the giant photos of happy times: Richard embracing her in a low dip during their wedding dance, Richard nose to nose with the dog, Richard playing footie with Ben, Richard cuddling Melissa, Richard kissing her cheek, Richard alone, head-shot, full-face, laughing eyes, big grin. Beautiful, full of life.

And yet, dead.

She dragged herself upstairs. Across her room the bureau crouched, daring her to empty it, to disempower it. She pulled up a chair, sat and opened out the desk flap. The diaries fell forward in a pencil-scented avalanche of bad feeling. No desire to read more of them. She'd box them up and... she wasn't sure what. For now, she swept them to one side. Some tumbled to the floor. She left them where they fell. At the back of the bureau, pigeon holes full of papers, and a stack of drawers. She pulled the top one. It resisted. She pulled again. It came loose with a jerk and fell out, scattering paper clips everywhere. She rummaged through its contents: rubber bands, drawing pins, too many stamps for a man who only ever emailed, a strip of passport photos. She slipped those in the back pocket of her jeans. She lined up the drawer with its slots, then saw what had jammed it. The drawer below contained paperback books, and one had got wedged. She pulled it out: bent and badly dog-eared. She tried to force it back into shape, looked more closely. A poetry collection. *Her* collection of Emily Dickinson. She picked up the other volume: Thomas Hardy's poems. Both had been lost in the move to The Elms. She sat back, smoothed the covers, tried to remember Richard ever mentioning poetry, other than to ridicule it. When *Poetry Please* came on Radio 4, he'd make her switch it off. "Sundays are depressing enough without all that dreary navel-gazing." She opened the Dickinson at a bookmarked page:

Tell all the truth but tell it slant –

She unfolded the paper that served as bookmark. Two sheets of blue notepaper with printed letterhead in elegant curling font: "Richard Hickey Esq." and the Elms address. She smiled: he was ridiculous. On the first, a drawing in black ink. A gnarled old tree, one side all leaved in black. On the other, its branches empty as winter. From those naked boughs flew black shapes, could be leaves, or crows, or - she peered closer – goblins? Were they fleeing or... or gathering? A simple sketch but full of - *oozing* menace. Was it Richard's? Had he drawn it? Was this inside his head all those hours he'd stared at the ceiling? She turned it face down on the desk, pressed her hand on it, as if the creatures might escape.

She shook her head, picked up the second sheet -

What was that?

A noise downstairs.

"Hello?" It had sounded like something being dropped. Louder: "Ben? Lissa?"

Nothing.

Brodie lay on the bed, unperturbed, nose on paws, watching her.

It was nothing.

The second sheet had the same black ink, Richard's hand. Tears started to her eyes. She brushed them away, no time for that. Richard's hand, but untidy, rushed. She could feel his panic rising...

I've got to get this down. It's not right, can't be right. This isn't illness, not the bipolar, this is - I don't know what, but it's scaring the shit out of me.

Black dog. Grey cloud. No. Hot, fiery, burning into me. Coming in. Getting inside me. Invading. Out to get me.

Jesus, reading this back I sound like a nutter. Maybe I am, but here's the thing. I'm used to thinking crazy shit when I'm high, Superman, indestructible, all that, and when I'm down, worthless tosser not fit to breathe my kids' air. But this is not that. It's mad thoughts, cruel dreams, ugly violence, stench of rotten decay. Death.

And where would I have got the name from? Deofol. What the fuck's that about? And how do I know how to spell it? Never seen it written down. Only ever hear it. But he says so.

Not supposed to be writing this, won't like it, trying to stop me, but good to be my own man again, even for a moment, even if I pay. Which I will. Hide this, and I might get away with it. Needed saying anyhow, anyway, anywhere, anywise. Scratch.

She clutched the paper, tension pulling through her fingers, wrist, up, up into her neck. This was dangerous. It was dirty. She scooped up the drawing and started ripping both sheets into tiny pieces until she had a pile of hideous confetti on the desk before her. She could see the minute black creatures, separated, liberated, escaping on their little life rafts... She needed matches, a lighter. She got up, staggered, knocked her chair over. Brodie leapt off the bed. *Kitchen cupboard.* She ran downstairs, the dog close behind. And stopped short.

Something had changed. The living room was different.

Brodie whined.

All the pictures, each framed photo of Richard, every one, blanked her. They had turned to face the wall.

Chapter 45

Wigan was shit as usual. Why had he bothered? This summer break had better start improving soon. Ben drew a sad face in condensation on the bus window. Was it ever going to stop raining? He wanted to suggest they go camping now Melissa was breaking up, too. They hadn't used the tent since Dad…But Mum wouldn't agree to it in this weather. No way.

"Hey, your sister's waiting for you." Davis hammered on the window with the flat of his hand.

"Leave it out."

"She might miss us."

"The bus will stop. I'll get off. She'll see me." Ben rang the bell, and swung out of his seat. "Laters."

Davis had his nose to the window, pulling faces at Melissa. Pathetic. Ben ran downstairs. Melissa waved. What now?

He jumped off. "Yo, Squirt."

"Yo, yourself."

Her sparkling repartee needed work. She thrust her arm through his and held tight when he tried to pull away. He glanced up at Davis, still gurning. She always showed him up in front of his mates. Funny how they didn't seem to mind her hanging around.

She was piss-wet through. "How long have you been here?"

She shrugged.

"You could go home, you know. It's fine."

"It's not fine. And it's not home."

As she still clung to him, he fell into step with her. "It's all the home we've got now, so you'd better get used to it."

"I don't like it. It doesn't want me there."

He snatched his arm back. "Will you stop with all this?"

She stood there, limp and forlorn. "But it doesn't."

"What doesn't?"

"I don't know. The thing Mum's scared of. You know what I mean, Ben. Don't you pretend you don't."

She looked so lost and small he took her hand and looped it back through his arm. They walked on slowly. Rain eased and sun threw out a few pathetic rays.

"It's just a house, Liss. An old house. It creaks and stuff, is all."

"And does it move coats around? Mess with the TV? It even freaks the dog out." Her voice rose to a squeak.

"Brodie's just mad."

"He wasn't before we moved to Bodden Street. He was ok at The Elms. We were all ok at the Elms. Even Mum."

Ben wasn't so sure about that. "We'll not go straight home. Let's go to the Flash. I'll buy you an ice-cream to celebrate end of term."

"A flake and everything on?"

"Don't push your luck, Squirt."

She squeezed his arm, touched her head to his shoulder. He shrugged her off. "Give over."

They turned onto Sandy Lane, cut through the farm and wandered across the hill. The sun actually came out.

"So any hijinks?" Last year, when he'd finished at Lowton High, there'd been carnage.

"They threatened us in assembly this morning. Pain of death. No flour. No foam. They cancelled the buses after what happened last time. Loads of kids had to walk home."

"How sad."

Melissa picked flowers as they strolled. She shook the rain off, then twined them in her hair behind her ears.

"Do I look like Titania?"

"If Titania looks like a tosser, yeah."

"Fuck off."

"Fuck off, yourself."

No one about except an old guy calling for his dog away up the hill. Ben ran down to the water's edge.

"Hey, wait!"

"Come on, Squirt!" He looked over his shoulder. Her bright hair streamed, flowers spraying out in all directions. A burst of pride, he'd die rather than share with her. The old guy watched, too. What was he doing out here, anyway, in that suit? Perv.

Ben beat her easily to the water. Typical girl.

He picked up a handful of grit and started throwing it into the lake, piece by piece. She caught up and slumped, hands on knees. Exaggerating. She must be fit, otherwise why was she on the netball team? Her hair fell forward like a sheet of copper. It looked ok on her, but he was mighty relieved he'd dodged that bullet. Ginger Ninja was no way to live. He found a flat stone, skimmed it.

"You're shit at that."

He let the rest of the gravel fall, brushed his hands together. "You'll not be wanting that ice-cream, then."

"Sorr-ee." She made a little sing-song of it.

"Seriously, Lissa, what d'you think's going on at Bodden Street?"

"So you *do* think something's wrong."

She didn't look pleased to be right. If anything, she looked a bit too pale. "I didn't say that. But *if* something's not right, what d'you think it is?"

She hoicked up her tight skirt and knelt. Bloody hell, you could see her knickers!

"Mum'd kill you if she saw you like that, showing off all your assets."

The only person about was that guy, watching them still. Ben threw him a V. Dirty old git. He got the message, but strolled off all leisurely, trying to save face. Wanker.

"God, you're an old woman sometimes." Melissa tossed her head, because she knew it irritated him, little cat, but she did wiggle her skirt down. "I think it's Mum."

Shit. If she'd said it was a ghost, he could have ridiculed and reassured her. "Mum?"

"She's gone mad with grief. Like Ophelia."

"Don't hold back, will you?"

"Don't pretend you don't think it's her."

"She's not gone mad, idiot."

"Then what *has* she gone? Because she's gone *something* these last few weeks. She's gone *somewhere*." The squeak had come back. "I know you don't believe me but she was actually *crawling* round the living room that day."

"She's tired, Lissa. She works too hard. She doesn't sleep. And -"

"And she sees things. She hears things. She hides stuff and then accuses *me*. And did you hear her laughing the other night? She's like the frigging madwoman in the attic."

He didn't want to think about that laughing. "She doesn't accuse you. Don't be so melodramatic."

"It feels like she's blaming me all the time."

"That's you being paranoid."

"You know it's not. She does it to you, too. What about that smelly old coat? You didn't take it out of her wardrobe, did you?" He shook his head. "Well, then, neither did I, so she must have."

He liked her cold logic. He hoped it was true. "Let's walk. The ice-cream van'll be gone if we don't get a move on." He strode on fast so she'd have to run to keep up. Should he tell her what he suspected? Would it make her feel better about Mum? He wished Dad was here to tell him what to do. "It could have been Mum, but I don't think it was."

She trotted at his side. "Why, though?"

"Because of the music."

"But that's her, too."
"I don't think so."
"She's got Dad's cds locked up in that wardrobe, you know."
"But where was it coming from?"
He slowed so she could walk at her own pace.
"But if it's not Mum, then who is it?"
A good question. "Maybe we should go stay with Auntie Sula for a bit. She wants us to. Just until we know it's…"
"Safe?"
Melissa clutched his hand. He squeezed. It was up to him now to look after them, but he couldn't take care of Mum until Melissa was out of harm's way.

Chapter 46

They'd lost two residents to norovirus today. A charming gentleman who'd moved in with his Elvis impersonations only weeks before. And Florrie. Poor dementing Florrie who couldn't understand what was happening to her. She'd lain tiny in her bed, gripping Isobel's hand, frightened, pale eyes pleading for relief.

They'd been locked down for a week now. Such a bad outbreak unusual during summer months, government statisticians assured them. Staff were falling prey, too, so she'd been working extended shifts. She'd even worked on her birthday. Not that it mattered: she had nothing better to do.

Glad to get outside, breathe clean midnight air. She gazed at the stars, the Plough, clear and crisp. She should have finished at eight. All she wanted now was to throw her clothes in the wash and stand under a hot shower. After that, she might feel like eating.

She got in the Micra. The kids would be in bed by now. Too late for the takeaway she promised them to celebrate the start of school holidays. She'd snatched a minute to text that she'd be late.

She pulled out onto Slag Lane, and put her foot down. She'd be home in less than five minutes. Unlit road, black night, alone, untethered, in danger of floating off the tarmac into the stars. She wound down the window, breathed in fast-flowing air. She'd better not be coming down with that bloody virus. A single streetlamp marked her turn.

She checked her mirror, slowed, and entered Byrom Lane.

What the hell's that?

She peered through the windscreen. Something in the dark lane ahead. Shit, not something: some*one,* standing in the road, blocking her way. She slammed on her brakes.

What's he doing?

She couldn't see his face. He was like shadow. Hooded. She stopped only metres from him. He didn't move. Just stood there, watching her. *Hooded.* She locked the doors. Still, he didn't move. She found reverse, let the clutch out. And stalled.

Shit.

She fumbled with the key. Glanced up. He was coming, striding towards her. She couldn't turn the bloody key. He was nearly on her.

Then she recognised that heavyset body.

Yvonne. For Christ's sake.

Isobel shouted out of the window. "What're you doing in the road? Have you got a death wish, or what?"

Yvonne stopped, still blocking the way, and stared at her.

Is that supposed to be intimidating? The woman's a joke.

Isobel could turn around, go the long way home. She could, but why should she? She wanted a shower and she wanted her bed. She started the engine, rolled forward, slowly. The stupid cow lumbered out of her path, and stood to one side staring at her, pig-eyed, fists like hams.

Keep driving.

She must have been waiting for her.

Leave it.

Isobel eased past and called out: "What's your problem?"

Yvonne sprung into animation as if a switch had been flicked in her back. She waddled after the car. "*My* problem? Your little bitch of a daughter, that's my problem. Spiteful little slag, bullying my Carl. Making his life a misery." Isobel slid on up the road, slow, slow. The window down, she could still hear. "You'd better sort her out, or someone'll do it for you. Shut her mouth before someone shuts it for her, you get me?"

Yvonne stood in the road again, yelling more threats, obscenities.

Isobel stopped the car. She'd started breathing too fast. Panting, almost. Untethered. Strange. Sweaty hands tingling: were they hers? Her eyes seemed to retreat inside her skull until she peered out through a blood tunnel.

Is this what they mean by "seeing red"? Isobel, you need to calm down.

Car slammed into reverse.

Wait!

Foot down. Knuckles white, pulsating. Screaming engine. Pulsing blood. Red. Elation.

Rear-view target, mouth agape. Red. Almost on her. Screaming red. Grip the wheel. Brace.

Yvonne hurled herself aside, disappeared from view.

Isobel stamped on the brake. Car pulled sharply to the left. Did a one eighty degree turn. Stars span. She skidded to a stop. All quiet. Still alive, but her head banged, so she rested it on the wheel. Then Yvonne was sweating at her door.

Isobel lifted her head. "I've had a long day. I'm not in the mood for this. Don't threaten my kids, if you want to keep a roof over your head."

Yvonne lunged at her through the open window. "You could've killed me. You tried to kill me, you bitch."

She grabbed the back of Isobel's collar, twisted it. Another hand tightened around her throat, nails clawed her neck. She tried to pull free.

This is not how you die, Isobel.

First gear. The car sprang forward. Flesh and bone hit the window frame with a meaty thud. Yvonne emitted an "oomph", released her grip. Isobel swung the car around, accelerated away. In the mirror, Yvonne sat in the dark road, clutching an arm, yelling. Isobel stopped. She should help her. But then the stream of invective reached her. She slid into reverse again.

Just drive. You're almost home.

then a plank in reason broke

She could do it. She wanted to. She wanted to hear that sound of flesh on metal again. She wanted to shut that fat mouth up. No one would blame her. Yvonne had threatened her daughter. Her son burgled their home. She was a worthless piece of shit. Isobel reversed, too fast, aiming at the heap in the road. Engine screamed.

Bel, no! Richard, right beside her.

She braked. The car slewed again, rammed the hedge, threw her into the seat belt.

Adrenaline fizzed through her veins, but something like sanity seeped in with it. She got out, shot a cursory glance at the pile of pathetic humanity blubbing on the road, surveyed the car for damage, got back in, checked her mascara in the mirror and drove home.

Chapter 47

Ben needed someone else's take on this, and, tragically, that someone had to be Davis, because the others would laugh in his face. Davis, however, watched *Most Haunted* from behind a cushion and researched "true facts" about *Insidious*. Ben would have preferred to run it all by Ernie. Ernie was older, knew stuff. He was clever, sharp. But Ernie had turned into a wanker after Dad died. Like death was contagious. Tosser. Like it was an embarrassment to have died that way. Fuck him. No one was going to make him ashamed of his dad.

Mum was on a night shift, and he persuaded Melissa to stay over at Bernadette's. That cost him a girlie-shit dvd and a massive bag of popcorn. Oh, and the vodka. Mum better not find out about *that*.

Davis arrived half an hour late, laden with library books and a pack of tarot cards.

"What's all this shit?" Ben picked up one of the books: *Ghost Hunting: True Stories of Unexplained Phenomena*. Another, *Ghost Hunting: Understanding Orbs*.

"Do I detect a theme?"

They sat at the kitchen table. Davis emptied out the tarot cards and spread them face down in a rough circle. "We're trying to make contact, yeah?"

"How?"

"With these." He tapped the cards.

"Don't you need letters and shit, to spell messages out?"

Davis looked at his cards. "Yeah, you need Ouija boards."

"And yet you've brought tarot cards."

"Is this not what they use? I thought these was... Ouija cards."

"Div."

Davis gawped. "Bollocks. These cost me ten quid."

Ben would have done better to consult with the dog, definitely the second most intelligent being in the room. "You have no idea what to do with those, do you?"

Davis picked one up, turned it over. A skeleton with a horrible grimace, wielding a scythe. "That can't be good."

"You think?"

"Waste not, want not. I'm going to ask them if there's any dead people here. Lights."

Ben sighed and turned off the big light. Dark out now, except for next door's yard light throwing dim yellow through the window.

Davis cleared his throat. "I feel right daft."

"There's a reason for that."

"Ok, let's do it." He laughed, but sounded nervous. "Why's it so cold in here? Are you scared, Hick?"

"Are you?"

"I asked first."

Davis was right: it *had* gone cold. "No."

"Yeah, me neither." He swirled the cards around the table, swaying as he did it.

"What the frig is that about, Davis?"

"It's what they do."

"Do they?" Ben was trying for sarcasm, but this felt weird. He didn't like that sick glow from outside, the strange shadows it made. "Tell me you're not going to say," he put on a spooky voice: "Is there anybody there?"

"I don't need to now."

Davis stared at him, owl-eyed. Did *he* look that frightened? Fast losing any shred of cred he'd ever had, here. "What a shit-for-brains idea. Can't even remember what I was hoping to achieve. I've got Stella. Want some?"

"Sound." Davis quickly gathered up the tarot cards.

Ben turned the light back on. The kitchen returned to normal. He suppressed a sigh of relief, and went to open the fridge.

He stopped.

Mum had left herself reminders on the door. *MINT* and *LEMONS*. He'd changed them to *MENTION*. Not bad. Then Melissa had found *MOISTEN* which he had to admit was also seven letters. Tonight, while he was waiting for Davis, he'd changed it to *MOMENTS* which was no better, but would nark her.

Only now it read *INSOLENT*. Eight letters.

Chapter 48

"At least they'll never get old. We'll never have to spoon-feed them and wipe their arses." Ursula, consumed by violent sobs, dabbed her tears. Isobel tried not laugh at the word "arses" on her sister's prim lips.

They did this every year, though when Isobel was younger, alcohol didn't have the starring role they gave it these days. They'd gradually made more of an occasion of it until the anniversary of their parents' deaths had become what it was now: an all-night binge. Ursula always arranged it, booked the hotel.

This year, she'd brought the trip forward by a month to get the room she wanted in a swish Ambleside B&B. Or at least that's what she said. But when had Ursula ever been bothered about luxuries? No, this was a conspiracy to impose rest on Isobel. They'd all been clucking around like demented chickens recently.

Isobel bought booze on the road up, and they smuggled it past their attentive host. They ate early at her favourite, *Fellini's*. Now they were back at their room and into their third bottle of savvy b.

Isobel sighed. "But I would have liked to do that for them."

Ursula snorted. "I wouldn't."

"I would've done it, Sula, don't worry." Isobel reached across the king-size bed, on which they lolled, to pat her shoulder. "You wouldn't have had to do anything."

"Really? That's so sweet."

They caught each other's eye, and set off laughing. Cackling.

"Ssh. What time is it?" Isobel found her phone: 02:02. "Look at that. A palimpsest. Is that what I mean? No, wait a sec. A palimdrome, that's it."

"Pal*in*drome. And it's not. But it *is* late."

"Oh, shush-tush with your grammar, lady."

"Should we call it a day? We're getting up early, remember."

How can she sink so much wine, and still be the voice of reason?

However, Ursula showed no signs of moving. "I miss them every day."

"Me, too. Every hour."

"I miss them every minute."

"Every second."

"Ah-ah. Every milli-second."

"Oh, Sula, what's smaller? Nano! Every nano-second."

"That's a lot of missing."

Isobel lay back and rested her head on Ursula's shoulder. Ursula stroked her hair: "Do you still think about that day? I hope I did right by you, Izzy. I tried my best."

Isobel sat up. "You've always looked after me. What you gave up for me, I'll never be able to make that up to you."

Ursula smiled. "You have done, silly." She propped her pillow on the headboard. "Are we finishing that bottle?" She poured two generous glasses. "After these, we should settle down. We've got Loughrigg tomorrow, don't forget."

"Do we have to?"

"Stop whining. And there's something we need to talk about."

Ursula woke her at eight: "We don't want to miss the best of the day."

When she swept open the curtains, Isobel blotted out the light with her pillow. "Are you actually human?" She heard the shower running and tried to snatch a few more precious moments. She was hauled back by: "I'm going down for breakfast. I'll meet you in the sitting room in half an hour. Make sure you're ready for walking."

The door closed, not quietly.

After the initial hung-over struggle up the first rise, Isobel was glad she'd allowed herself to be bullied into this. A cloudless morning, bright with high August sunshine. She paused to look back over Windermere. A gentle breeze stroked her cheeks. Birds sang. Sheep baaed.

She trotted to catch up. "You wanted to talk."

Ursula strode on, apparently hangover-free. It wasn't fair: alcohol seemed only ever to make her sentimental. And even that never lasted long.

"Can't we slow down a bit?"

"You wanted lunch at *Zeff's* before we head home."

"Yes, but -"

"Well, then." She slowed enough for Isobel to walk at her side. "Ben phoned me again this week. He's worried about you. Especially after what happened with that horrid woman."

Not this again. "I've told him not to be. It wasn't like Yvonne says."

"He's worried about Melissa, too. He seems to think she's frightened."

"Frightened of what?" Isobel felt a catch in her throat. She'd been trying so hard to protect them both.

Ursula stopped. She pressed a hand to the small of her back, stretched. "Lord, you can see for miles from here."

"Frightened of what, Sula?"

Ursula reached for Isobel's hand. "There's no gentle way to say this, love. She's frightened of you."

After all the strange, inexplicable events at Bodden Street, and before, Isobel was not expecting this. She turned away. "That's a horrible thing to say." Windermere blurred before her. "She can't be. She's not afraid of me. I'm her mum."

"Shall we sit?" Ursula pointed to some lichen-covered boulders.

"She isn't afraid of me."

"All right. This is clearly a surprise to you. They haven't talked to you about it, at all?"

"Of course not, because it's not true." Isobel's neck felt hot as she remembered how Melissa had found her on the floor that day.

"Come sit with me."

"Not until you tell me what you've been saying to my kids."

Ursula looked taken aback. "Isobel, calm down. There's no need to shout."

"I *won't* calm down. What have you all been saying behind my back?"

"Please. We can't discuss this if you keep yelling at me. Come."

Ursula brushed a boulder and sat. So precise, so bloody pernickety. "Have you any idea why Ben might have said it?"

"I don't believe you. He wouldn't say that."

"Why would I lie about something like this? I know it must be hard to hear, but -"

"You think you can just *sit* there and accuse me of - of -"

"I'm accusing you of nothing. I'm worried about you. And the children. This is precisely what frightens them. These unpredictable mood swings."

Isobel stood over Ursula, pleased to see her cower a little. "You think I'm a bad mother. That's it, isn't it? Just *say* it! You think I can't cope. You want the kids with you. Don't think I don't know what you're up to. You've always wanted them, but you can't have them. They're mine, not yours."

"Morning!" An older couple strode from behind the last rise and paused to greet them.

Cool as anything, Ursula said: "Morning. Glorious, isn't it?"

"Going to be a hot one." The man was ready to chat, but his wife glanced at Isobel and urged him on, with a smile at them and a hand on his arm. "Must press on. Good morning, ladies."

Isobel watched them go. "You have no idea what's happening, Sula, so don't you judge me." She gripped her wrist to stop her hands shaking.

Ursula stood. "So *tell* me. I want to help you, but I can't if you won't talk to me. I know something's wrong. Ever since you moved, you've been behaving strangely. And now Melissa's having to deal with that wretched boy at school, and everything that's being said about you, and she's frightened. She says you're 'acting weird.'" She sighed. "Isobel, she wants to stay with me for a while. Just until you feel better."

"What? No, she doesn't. Why? She can't. She's got school."

Ursula reached to smooth a lock of hair from Isobel's face. "Just until you're feeling better."

Isobel pulled away. "Don't patronise me. I'm not a child. If this was happening to you, I'd like to see you cope with it!"

Ursula closed the space between them and put an arm around her shoulder. Isobel let her, all fight evaporated.

"What *is* happening? All *I* know is my kind, caring sister is behaving desperately out of character. She's angry all the time, not sleeping and now she's tried to run a woman down in her car, for goodness sake!"

How could Isobel explain? She let Ursula lead her gently back to the boulder. "Do you remember the cuckoo clock?" Ursula sat next to her, nodded. "Remember the housewarming when the clock went mad?"

"I remember it broke, yes."

"It didn't break. It started chiming out of time and the cuckoo went wrong. Remember?"

"Yes, that's what I mean."

"And it started making that awful noise, and saying -"

"*Saying?* Isobel, it broke."

"It said something. Didn't you hear it? I thought everyone did. They were all in such a big hurry to leave, after."

"They left because you got so upset, love. You practically screamed at Ben to take the thing down."

"It said: 'Listen'. Just 'Listen'. That's all."

Ursula picked at a loose thread on her sleeve. "If the clock said that, why did you insist on putting it back up when Ben wanted to throw it out? When Melissa's so scared of it?"

"Because it's Richard's."

Isobel cried now more than she had last night. No wistfulness, no nostalgia, no pleasure of shared grief. Raw, wrecking sobs, while the sun beat down.

Ursula held her, rocked her, but still she felt forsaken. Dread descended on her, deep and despairing, thick as porridge and bitter.

Chapter 49

Isobel had woken with the remnants of yesterday's hangover: nagging headache, sandpaper tongue.

"Seen my keys?" She didn't have time for this. They weren't on the hook Ben had installed by the front door because she kept losing her keys. They weren't on the bookshelf where she usually dumped them.

Melissa ambled downstairs, yawning. "Lost them again? Have you looked in the pot?"

"Why would I put them in the pot?"

"That's where they were last time." She sloped into the kitchen.

Isobel followed. "But I didn't put them there last time."

"That's where you found them."

"Yes, so one of you put them there."

"Not me."

Isobel opened a high cupboard. Melissa stretched across her and grabbed the sugar puffs.

"Don't mind me, love."

Isobel reached down the key pot, tipped it out on the counter. All sorts of odds and sods: elastic bands, shoe laces, sachets of sugar. And keys: window keys, shed keys, keys that no longer fitted anything she owned. She picked out a set with a cuddly toy fob. They belonged to the kids' long-gone electric scooters. She dropped them back in the pot, and selected a ring of tiny assorted keys. No idea what they belonged to. Must be Richard's. She'd carefully packed this pot, complete with contents, and brought it from The Elms. She'd placed it in a carton with a load of mugs when Ursula, who'd been chucking stuff out with a brutality that made her head spin, wasn't looking. Once it was established in its cupboard here, she couldn't face sorting through it.

An old-fashioned silver car key: Richard's TR5, now languishing in Ursula's garage. She should think about selling it. A hard lump rose in her throat.

Melissa put a gentle arm around her and squeezed. "Oh, there they are!" She picked Isobel's car keys from the motley pile. "Told you!"

"Melissa, are you unhappy with me going to work? Because we can talk about it if you are. You don't have to do all this to get my attention. Only it needs to stop. I can't keep letting them down like this. I'm forever late."

Melissa pulled away, stared at her, wary as a cat: "What are you talking about? *I* don't mind you working." Then she laughed, without amusement. "That's funny. Me and Ben thought you were hiding them because *you* don't want to go to work."

"I haven't been hiding them."

"Then who has, Mum? There *is* no one else. I wish you'd stop going *on* about it. You're being really weird, you know that? I told everyone I didn't believe it about Carl's mum, you would never do that, even if she *is* an ugly, evil bitch, but now..." Isobel reached out to her. "Don't touch me. You're doing my head in."

She ran out.

Isobel trailed her upstairs and tapped on her door. She could hear her crying. She knocked again. "Lissa?"

She entered and sat on the bed. Melissa lay, face buried in the duvet. She said something but it disappeared into the pillow.

"I can't hear you, sweetheart."

She lifted her head and yelled: "I said, *go away*!" Her face red, smeared with tears.

"Please, Melissa. Talk to me."

She sat up, glared at her. "I'm sick of it, ok? I'm sick of this horrible house, I'm sick of the Neanderthal neighbours, I'm sick of being scared all the time. I just want to look forward to coming home like a *normal* person." Isobel tried to brush the hair from her eyes but she pulled back. "And I'm sick of *you*. You're acting like a freak. Why did you do that to Yvonne? You could have *killed* her. You know they call you Psycho Lady? And I'm Psycho's Spawn. You're supposed to take care of us, not -" She grabbed the pillow, pressed it to her face, and let out a horrible groan. Or was it a scream? She let the pillow fall. "Not torture us."

"Lissa!"

"'Who's moved that coat?' " She mimicked her, cruelly, through her tears. "'Who hid my keys?' And what did you do to that *horrible* clock? And *then* you go and put it back up! Why are you doing it, Mum? Auntie Sula says we should be patient. She told us to be kind to you. She says you're missing Dad. I mean, like we're *not*? He*llo*? She said things'd get better, but they haven't. It's the holidays and I have to find places to go, because I never want to be at home anymore, because I don't know what you'll", she tapped her own head, "dream up next." She struggled to get the words out though tears and snot. "I don't want to live here anymore. I don't like this house. I want my Dad." She shuddered with sobs, but shrank away when Isobel tried to hug her.

"Melissa, please, I had no idea you felt this way."

"Yeah, well, you do now." She calmed as suddenly as she'd flared. "I'm phoning Auntie to come and get me. She said I could stay with her if it got too much."

"If what got too much?"

"You, Mum. If *you* got too much." She jumped off the bed. "I've got to pack." She held the door open.

"Melissa -"

"Please, Mum. You're late, remember? Just go to work."

"Hello!" Isobel pushed the front door open with her hip, her arms laden with shopping. The dog rushed to greet her. "Hello, lad. Is it safe to come in?"

She staggered to the kitchen and swung the bags up onto the counter. More in the boot but they could wait. She opened the fridge for juice. Banging headache. No break all day. Eight hours with hardly anything to eat or drink: it wasn't on.

And then she'd done the big shop straight from work, which hadn't helped. But she wanted to make a special tea, after this morning. Cheese and onion pie, Melissa's favourite.

"Kids?"

Silence.

She suppressed a crazy feeling that the house was watching to see what she'd do next.

Did Ben say he'd be out? He might have. She unpacked washing powder and put it on the table. Next to a note. A sheet torn from her shopping pad, Ben's writing, boxy and bold. She didn't want to read it.

Hi Mum

Hope you had a good shift. I've fed Brodie.

Melissa and me are going to stay at Auntie Sula's for a bit. We've packed some stuff so we've got everything we need, don't worry. Melissa's still upset. You had a row, I guess? But she'll be fine. Auntie's fine with it too. She'll call you.

I guess you won't be surprised. Melissa says she tried to tell you. All this crazy stuff is getting to her. And me.

I tried to think what Dad would tell me to do. Remember what he used to say? "Always look after your little sister." So I have to go with her. But I'm worried about you, too. I didn't want to leave you on your own, not with you the way you are, but I'm a right coward. I can't stay. There's something in this house, isn't there? Something not right. I know you feel it, too.

If you need me, call me. I will come.

I'm sorry.

Love Ben xx

Isobel put the note back on the table. Nothing from Melissa. Not even a kiss. She'd always known how to hurt her mum.

The kettle was warm, so they'd not been gone long. If she'd come straight home, she might have caught them. She wrapped her hands around it. Would it be warm when she got in ever again?

She left it unfilled, cooling, and sat at the table, the note before her. She smoothed the paper, longing to feel Melissa's silken hair under her hand. When had she last hugged her? When had she last even properly *looked* at her? She tried to stand, but her weight dragged her back into the seat. They didn't trust her, her own children. How long had they wanted to get away from her?

not with you the way you are

How long had they been afraid of her?

Hollow sickness in her stomach. She read the note over and over. They'd warned her, both of them in their different ways. Why hadn't she listened?

She'd failed them.

Chapter 50

Sky intense blue, sliced by vapour trails. Air warm, stifling. Isobel had imagined hordes of people out here on the hill in late evening sunshine, so she'd declined Belinda's first invitation. But that wasn't really why she was avoiding her. Eight weeks since she'd shouted "Come in", and still they hadn't spoken about the doctor. Maybe he'd stopped calling, but she didn't want that confirming because then she'd have to wonder why, she'd have to acknowledge her fear that he'd already gained entry. She presumed Belinda had heard about her road rage, like everyone else, but she didn't want to talk about that, either. And the kids leaving last week: she couldn't go there. But Blin was hard to deflect so here they were, sprawled on a picnic rug, sipping Pinot Grigio Blush. The Flash mirrored blue. A buzzard soared overhead, its sharp cry languid in the heat. Not another soul about.

"Drink up before it gets warm. I've got some red."

"I'm not getting wrecked."

Belinda snorted, raised her glass. "You're out with me now, lady. Get it down your neck."

They talked about Belinda's new research client. A widower, looking into his dead wife's genealogy. She'd developed the predictable crush, but seemed uncharacteristically keen to change the subject.

"So. Are you going to tell me what *actually* happened?"

"I do like your toe nails, Blin."

"Ah, thanks, hon." Belinda wore sparkly flipflops and wiggled her toes to show off the shimmering turquoise varnish. "Yours are lovely, too."

Isobel had kicked off her trainers, exposing more demure coral nails.

Belinda reached forward to pick a grass blade from between her toes. She flicked it away.

"Did you do what Yvonne says you did?"

Isobel thrust out her glass. "Have we no wine here?"

Belinda topped it up, slopping some. "Oops! So, spill."

"What did you hear?"

"Which version d'you want? The Hare kids are going round calling you Psycho, telling everyone to keep out of your way, you're a jealous mum-murderer. Yvonne's telling anyone who'll listen that you broke her arm, you tried to mow her down in your car. She's walking along, minding her own business when she hears you in your vicious little Micra screaming onto the pavement behind her. Lucky for her, she's got the reflexes of a gazelle, and she dived out of your murderous path. That's the general gist."

Isobel slurped her wine.
Belinda coaxed: "But her arm *is* broken."
Isobel slurped some more.
Belinda persisted: "I wouldn't put it past that Ricky twat she has living there to have done that to her."
Isobel examined her nail varnish.
"Come on, Iz. Which part of all that is true?"
She could lie. Belinda would believe her. "Most of it."
"You're kidding! *Isobel*?"
"She wasn't on the pavement. She stood in the road, waiting for me, threatening Melissa, effing and jeffing. You know what she's like. I drove past but she carried on, nasty, horrible threats, and she was in the road behind me and I just - I lost it." Isobel swallowed hard. "I reversed the car back at her. Really fast, but thank god, thank *god*, she's nimbler than she looks. She jumped out of the way." Isobel risked a glance at Belinda, but her hair had flopped forward, screening her face. "Say something."
Belinda's voice was tight. "What about her arm?"
"I don't know. She... I... she grabbed me. I had the window down. She grabbed me here." She put a hand to her throat. "And squeezed. She's so strong. I panicked, put my foot down. She still had hold of me. She must have ... *I* must have... I didn't mean to hurt her. Not then."
"Bloody hell, Iz."
"Yes."
Belinda fiddled with a flipflop, wouldn't look at her. "What did it feel like? When you aimed at her?"

Isobel slugged the wine. She'd felt like someone, some*thing* else, not herself, but she wasn't about to tell Belinda that. "It felt good. In that moment, the adrenaline, I wanted to shut her up, I wanted to kill her, and I could, and it felt amazing."

A skylark took fright, spiralled its musical ascent. Belinda watched it. "Don't tell anyone else that, Iz."

"No."

"She can't have told the police. You'd have been questioned."

"Do you think she will?"

"She's told everyone else. But maybe she's a better mother than we give her credit for. Maybe she thinks if she goes to the police you'll tell them what Carl did."

"I wondered about that. I feel so ashamed now. Should *I* tell them what I did?"

Belinda put down her glass. It tipped on the bumpy ground. Wine trickled away through the grass. "Absolutely not! Are you mad? Promise me, Isobel Hickey, under no circumstances are you to talk about this to anyone else, ever, d'you hear me?"

"But -"

"No buts. Drink."

Discussion over. Was Isobel really going to get off so lightly? Surely, there'd be consequences.

But, for now, the sun shone and she was with her best friend. She lay back, closed her sun-warmed eyelids. Skylarks spun out their song, exquisite and sad. Bless her, Belinda had tried so hard not to be shocked. And she hadn't believed the rumours. Isobel wished she deserved her faith. She listened to her rummaging in the picnic basket.

"There's a corkscrew in here somewhere. Voila!" Isobel turned her head and opened one eye as Belinda uncorked the red wine. "Sit up. Try this. The bloke in Morrison's said we'd like it. He's so keen to find out how much, I gave him my number."

"Have you no shame?"

"I'm forty one, Iz. Can't afford shame. But enough about me. Tell me, apart from trying to get yourself featured on *Crimewatch*, how's it been going?"

"Really, are you ok with that? Because, you know, it's serious stuff."

Belinda burst out laughing. "That's got to be understatement of the century, lady. I'll drink to that." They clinked glasses, losing precious wine in the process. Then Belinda became solemn and took her hand. "You're under so much pressure, Iz. You need to start taking care of yourself, honey. But as for what you told me, it's forgotten. Never to be mentioned again by *either* of us, ok?"

Isobel nodded. Her voice cracked: "Thank you."

Belinda smiled gently. "But I do need to ask you about the haunting."

"The *what*?"

"I'm not an idiot, babes. I've seen him, remember. We need to face it. And there's more you're not telling me. There has to be. You wouldn't have done what you did to Yvonne, otherwise. You've been avoiding me, and now the kids have moved out, so it must be bad." Isobel couldn't meet her eye. "Iz, you mustn't be embarrassed. You've done nothing wrong."

She bit her lip. "No?"

"You didn't choose this."

"It's not... I don't... they thought... " Isobel sighed. "I don't know what to do."

"It's crazy shit, that's why."

"Yes. Completely crazy shit." A cooler breeze rushed up from the water. Isobel shivered.

Belinda reached out and stroked her arm. "Has anything happened since the kids left?"

and mourners to and fro kept treading treading

Isobel shook her head.

Belinda gave her a look that said she didn't believe her. "What d'you make of the video on Melissa's Facebook page?"

"I don't have her on Facebook. She doesn't want me stalking her."

Belinda pulled out her mobile. "She's posted a film she made on her phone a few weeks ago. You need to see it."

A skylark, pinprick, circled in the blue. Bodden Street felt far away. In this clean open air, Isobel could think and be free. She didn't want to unleash the madness here. "Can we watch it back at yours?"

"You're right. Easier to view on the laptop. When you've seen, it might give you a way in with her? Maybe she's changing her mind."

"Changing her mind?"

"Iz, I know she blames you for what's happening."

How the hell does she know that?

Belinda held up her hands, defensive. "They talked to me. And I'm sorry, I should have told you, but they asked me not to. What could I do? They needed to talk to someone." She shrugged. "So."

"They could have talked to *me*."

“I know that, but they’re all mixed up. Don’t be angry, hon. I’m on your side, always.” She leaned across, squeezed her leg.

Isobel shifted out of her grasp. “I didn’t know there *were* sides.”

“Sure, no sides. Just different points of view, I guess. Drink.”

She refilled Isobel’s glass.

An hour to walk home in the dark, torches forgotten, grappling the picnic basket between them. Moonlight glinted off smooth tarmac as they trudged up silent, empty Bodden Street. They turned onto Belinda’s path and she fumbled her key into the lock.

Isobel put her finger to her lips: “Shush, you’ll wake the whole street.”

“I am shushing. It’s this key.”

When they were both inside, Belinda slammed the door, tripped and half-fell against it. “Gosh, how much have we drunk? We need coffee.”

Isobel headed for the kitchen. “I’ll do it. You fire up your laptop.”

She peered into gloamy shadows. An ironing board falling over, a cupboard crashing to the floor. Right here, in this room.

Where’s the damn light switch?

She found it, and flooded the space with stark florescence.

Bad things can’t happen with the lights on, right?

She hurried to make strong black instant, spooked by the kettle’s clatter. She placed mugs on a tray with glasses of water, and tottered into the living room, holding the tray rigid before her, squeezing her shoulder blades tight against the cold finger drawing down her back.

Belinda sat at her disorganised desk, silhouetted against the computer screen. She'd switched on a desk lamp whose drab sweep of light served only to intensify the surrounding dark. Isobel picked her way across the room, sidestepping coffee table and footstools, to put the tray down next to her. The screen glowed sickly on Belinda's dead-seeming face. Isobel recoiled.

"Here we go." Belinda said. "She put it up last night. She says she posted it because Brodie's being cute, and she's missing him. But then her friends started commenting they could see something strange." Belinda vacated the chair for Isobel, watched over her shoulder. Her breath tickled Isobel's neck, sending shivers down it. "It's a bit grainy. Watch carefully. It's very quick. And get ready, hon, because this shat me up when I first saw it."

"If I can cope with that house, I think I can watch a Facebook video." Isobel pressed play.

Her living room, strangling blue, dog lying before unlit fire. TV on. She couldn't make out the programme. Greenish-grey haze of movement, that's all. Melissa's slippered feet in the bottom of the shot. She must have been lying on the sofa, filming. Brodie stood up, sudden, alert. On the audio, Ben's voice: "There he goes. Told you! Seven forty eight." Melissa: "Shush, you'll put him off." The shot flicked to the cuckoo clock and back to the dog, too fast to read the time. Brodie approached the empty fireside armchair, stared at it. "Brodie!" Melissa called in a whisper. Ben whispered, too: "Leave him." Brodie ignored them, fixed on the armchair. Then he did it. What she'd seen him do before. He sat up and begged. He held the awkward position, balancing, staring at the chair, as if someone was sitting there. And, as she thought this, suddenly there *was* someone in the chair. A dark figure. For a moment, less than a moment, a man in black sat ramrod straight in her armchair. Then he was gone. Brodie flopped.

Isobel looked up at Belinda, pale in the gloom. "What the…?"

She restarted the film. When the figure appeared she paused it, but too late. Fleeting, yet horribly real. She played it again.

The kids whispered. They didn't react to the man's abrupt appearance. They chattered on. They hadn't seen him.

She kept playing it. Try as she might, she could not freeze the frame containing the intruder, and she needed to see him up close. Because she knew him.

Belinda pulled up a chair next to her and said, gently: "You know who it is, don't you?"

Isobel sipped some water.

Belinda persisted: "It looks a lot like the doctor."

Chapter 51

Isobel had come all this way to Bolton, and seen nothing she liked enough to try on. She wandered into the craft market in the old church. Musty, chilled air greeted her. Didn't there used to be a little tea room here? But it wasn't how she remembered. Fewer stalls, more flea market than craft. Smell of dust and neglect. No tea room, either. She wandered about, paused to browse jewellery, ran her fingers over some black beads.

"Real Whitby jet that, love. Try it on if you want." The guy slouched in a canvas chair.

She smiled, shook her head, walked on.

She hadn't slept after watching the video. It felt like more than she could take. How could she protect herself and her family against something that shouldn't exist outside her own crazy imagination? She'd let him in, and she might never dare sleep again.

She tripped on the curled edge of an old carpet.

"Steady, sister." A hand cupped her elbow.

A man, fifties, bald, with blue eyes and direct gaze. "Well, you've found me. Come on in."

Before she could reply, he drew her into a curtain-covered alcove in the church wall.

"Come in and welcome. I'm Eldred. You sought comfort and rest, and here you'll find them." He swept the curtain closed, plunging them into semi-darkness.

"Oh, I..."

"One moment." He shuffled about the small space, turned on a floral, tasselled standard light and an orange lava lamp. Both looked sourced from the flea market, as did the curtain. In their dim glow, she made out a small stone altar table. The lava lamp stood on it. This was an old side chapel.

"But I only came in for -"

"And you've found it. Sit." A rickety table covered with another faded green curtain. Two chairs faced each other across it. Tarot cards and pebbles lay next to one of those tacky graveside eternal flames.

"No, I'm really not interested in this sort of thing. Sorry." The man smiled, all blue eyes and serenity. "I don't go in for…" He nodded, attentive. She *could* do with sitting down for a few minutes. The space was small, low-ceilinged, cave-like. With the curtain pulled to, it felt private, cosy, even. "Oh, all right. Just for a minute, then. How much do you charge?" Eldred held up his hands. He didn't want to talk money. "But I don't know how much to offer."

"I'll only accept what you feel you can afford."

"I don't know. £10?"

"Whatever you feel you can afford. Sit." His voice soft, designed to reassure, but slick: she'd soon parted with that tenner. She'd never done anything like this before, but she had nothing left to lose.

Eldred sat opposite. He switched on the grave light. It lit his eyes, iridescent blue. Everything around him faded as she stared into those eyes. He was close. She wanted to push back her chair, but that would be rude. He didn't look away. People walked to and fro outside the curtain, only feet from them. She was perfectly safe. What would he make of her? What kind of claptrap would he try? Was he assessing her, thinking exactly the same?

"You have beautiful eyes, little sister. A beautiful soul."

Little sister? "Thank you."

"First I'd like to ask you about yourself. You're feeling a little better now, I think?"

"Yes. Thank you."

"Such distress in those soulful eyes. It hurts my heart to see it." He made a gesture from his heart to hers. Now she did sit back.

"I think distress is maybe a bit -"

"Where were you born?"

Shouldn't he be telling her that? "Altrincham."

"Where do you live now?"

"Leigh. Well, near there. Lowton."

"I was raised in Old Trafford. Not so far from you." Like she couldn't tell from the accent. "I sense a warmth from you." That gesture again, this time from her heart to his. "You're a carer. You come here with a wonderful presence guarding you." He smiled beyond her shoulder. She quelled the urge to turn around. "I'll tell you more of that later. So what kind of caring do you do?"

Keep it vague. Don't help him.

"I work with people."

"You're good at reading people, situations." She refused to look away. "I'd like you to take these." He placed the pebbles in her hand and closed her fingers over them, watching her face. "Throw them."

She rolled them on the table like dice. The curtain cloth dulled their rattle. When they came to rest, she saw silver symbols painted on their brown surfaces.

"First, I want to talk about your health." He made that gesture of giving. "You're strong. Vigorous. But your personality is connected with the moon, like my own. For most of the moon cycle you're outgoing, confident. When there's no moon you close in on yourself, become full of melancholy." Where was the moon up to now? "But you need that, sister. Allow yourself that space to mourn."

She stared. How did he know?

He smiled, swept up the runes and gave them to her. "Throw again." She threw. "Tell me about your children. Ages, gender?" She told him. He nodded to one side as if listening to someone. "Your son is strong, like you. He attracts followers. A leader. He'll rise to the top of his chosen profession." Despite her scepticism, she puffed up a little. "Your daughter will choose a career that takes her abroad. She will struggle, but ultimately succeed."

So far, so predictable.

He hesitated. Held her gaze for longer than felt comfortable. "Throw, please." She threw. "This is my message for you, sister. There's an older man here." Again he looked over her shoulder. Her spine went cold. He cocked his head to one side, listening. "Thank you. He wants to be remembered to you. He's a warm presence. Attractive. People loved him. A lovely twinkle in his eye."

Could be anyone's granddad.

"He's with a young female. Someone who never grew to adulthood?" His fishing gentle but obvious.

"Can't think who that would be."

"Throw again, please. This is your year starting now. They've given me a flower for you. It will open as the year goes on and its perfume will grow ever stronger." He paused for a reaction. She gave him nothing. "Throw again? Your career is going well. I see a change coming from abroad. And a significant woman." All the time he watched her, checking if she was buying it. She wasn't. "Throw please. You want to travel." She allowed him a smile. "There's a place that will - already has - captured your heart." He frowned. "And there's a place you'll never return to. It haunts your dreams. Throw, please." Dazed, she threw. "I see you want to move house. You will. You haven't been happy in your home. Something holds you there. But you will move. A new place will draw you to it. You will want to be there. Away from… ah, it eludes me, but it deeply troubles you."

This is stupid. "That's probably £10 up, isn't it, Eldred? I don't want to hog your time."

"I sense strength in you, but deep conflict also. Stay a while, sister. We want to share with you the truth of the wonderful presence guarding you." She'd forgotten about that. "She's a water goddess, known by different names in different cultures. When you need to recharge and centre yourself, you must seek out water. Don't go to tarot readers when you need guidance and solace. You need only water. Walk by it, sit by it, bathe. You will come away refreshed and refocused."

This must be the spiel for anyone who doesn't want to talk to their dead Aunt Betty.

"Would sitting with my feet in a bucket do the trick?"

He ignored the jibe. "The water goddess is always with you." Clearly a wrapping-up statement. He made to stand, but sank back in his chair, as if pushed. He stared over her shoulder again, frowning. This time she couldn't resist the urge to glance behind her. He leaned across the table, whispering now. Urgent. "This from my heart to yours, sister. Truly. Be careful. There *is* a presence with you. Not the water goddess, that was filler." He tilted his head to one side for longer this time. Listening. "Thank you. It's a strong presence, strange. I can't tell, but my guides are afraid of it. You must be careful."

She stood and turned to go. He stood, too. He gripped her shoulder, made her turn back. The softly-softly patter gone now, he was just a rough-looking bloke from Old Trafford who'd dared lay hands on her. "I know you don't believe, Isobel, but please, *please* take care. There's something with you. I don't understand it, but it seems angry, confused. Try not to be alone, yeah? They say... they say it doesn't know itself."

She was back at the car, breathless from running, before she remembered what she hadn't told him.

How did he know her name?

Chapter 52

"I'm home!" She pushed open the door with her foot and staggered in with the shopping bags. "Ben, can you come and -?"

She'd forgotten. The dog greeted her, wagging his tail. He missed them, too.

"How are you at unpacking, boy? Come on, let's find us both a treat."

She dumped the bags in the kitchen and made a pot of tea. She rummaged in the shopping until she found the chocolate; the rest could wait. She got the dog a chew stick and hauled her carcass back to the living room. No rush to get a meal ready.

"There you go. Good boy." He took the stick from her and lay down to devour it. That would keep him occupied for half an hour or so. She unwrapped the Mars Bar. She hadn't eaten one of these for years. She opened her mouth to bite into it.

What's that smell?

Sweet, sticky. It took her back to university, to that ethnic shop where she bought those ridiculous floaty kaftans. *Bringing It All Back Home,* that was it. Impossibly exotic, with its reek of patchouli…

Who's been wearing that in here?

She sniffed about. Strongest here in the living room. And fresh. She hadn't noticed it this morning. She pinched her work tunic to her nose. Eau de care home.

She flopped on the sofa, avoiding the haunted chair, and resumed the Mars Bar. She was sick of trying to work out what it all meant.

So it likes patchouli. Who gives a shit?

She washed down a mouthful of gloopy chocolate with a gulp of tea.

A knock. She looked over to the door. A shadow. Small, twitchy: Belinda.

"It's open!" Isobel wiped the corners of her mouth with finger and thumb, and sat straighter.

Belinda bustled in. "Only me! Don't you keep your door locked now? You should."

"Bit late for that. There's tea in the pot if you want one."

Belinda perched on the edge of the haunted chair. "I need to discuss something with you, Iz. I think you're not going to like it, but please hear me out."

"Not this again. I told you I don't want to talk about it."

"It's not the doctor. It's everything that's happened, everything you're going through. Don't give me that look. We have to do something. You can't live with this," she made a vague gesture that took in the room, or maybe the whole house, "blighting your life. You've already lost the kids."

"I have not! They need a break, that's all."

"And you don't? For God's sake, Iz, look at you!"

Isobel crammed the remains of the Mars Bar in her mouth, dropping bits of chocolate onto her tunic, and chewed, defiant.

"We need help. So I... Iz, don't be angry with me. Promise?"

"What've you done?"

"I knew you wouldn't do anything about it for yourself."

"What have you done?"

"I found this man, Ernie, he's really sweet. He can sense things, presences. He's a medium, and he's good. He's on Facebook."

"Why didn't you say? If he's on Facebook, he must be - hang on. Ernie: isn't he the one on Melissa's Facebook, the one who was hassling her about that video? For god's sake, Belinda."

"I know how it looks, but -"

"No way! I'm not having any lunatic séances in my house."

"He's not like that. He can sense trouble, tell you what's causing things like Melissa's video. But there's other stuff, I know there is. You won't tell me, but I've seen the lights going on and off in the night. I've seen the shadows at the windows. And Joe's heard things through the wall, music, a woman laughing."

Isobel stood. "I've got a load of shopping to unpack, I need to get changed and I haven't eaten yet, so…"

Belinda didn't move. "Thing is..." She shook her head and went on in a rush: "The thing is I asked him round this morning while you were at work."

It took Isobel a moment to catch up. "You asked him round? What, you mean *here*?"

She nodded. "I know. Don't be cross."

"But I wasn't in. What was the point of that? Bet he wasn't too chuffed you wasted his time."

"I let him in with your spare key."

"You let him into my house when I wasn't here?"

Belinda stood now. "I knew you wouldn't agree, but he can help. I was with him. I didn't let him wander about on his own. And he did sense something, Iz. I need to tell you -"

"Give me your key." Isobel held out her hand.

"But -"

"Give me that bloody key!"

Belinda dipped into her pocket and took out a single Yale key. She put it into Isobel's hand.

"Now get out."

"Iz, please -"

"Get out of my house!"

How dare she?

Isobel paced the living room, fists clenched.

Who does she think she is?

A bang resonated upstairs, like the doors of some great hall slamming shut. She flinched, covered her head. *What the hell?* The TV blurted on full volume, jarring, demanding. She whirled to face it. Gurning masks, jostling close-ups, screeching voices competing for screen time.

You're doing this, you know you are. You need to calm down.

But she didn't want to, she wanted to charge across the road and scream at Belinda some more.

The dog cowered as the cuckoo clock set off cheeping insanely. That was too much. She couldn't bear to see Brodie scared, and she couldn't risk hearing that rasping voice again. She scooped him up and ran into the back garden.

Safer here. To quell her shaking, she knelt at a small patch of border she'd cleared yesterday. She bent her head, and tears dropped, moistening the dry soil. She dug her fingers into it and squeezed. Why was this happening to her, blighting her life? What the fuck had she done to deserve it?

She brushed her hands together, picked up a trowel, dug a hole, tapped a pot base, and pressed the basil into its new home. Soil crumbled between her fingers: warm, real, earthly. She lifted it to her nose: wholesome, untainted. She rocked back on her haunches, lifted her face to the sun, closed her eyes, listened to a warbler in the wood across the field.

"Hiya! Sorry, didn't mean to make you jump."

"Eamee! How lovely to see you." Isobel scrambled to her feet, and brushed mud from her knees.

"I knocked, but you didn't answer. I saw your car so I thought you might be out here. I know how you like your gardening."

Isobel unlocked the gate. "Good to see you, love." They hugged. She breathed in Eamee's lovely cheap perfume. Could she risk taking her inside? Brodie seemed to think so. He was at the door, waiting to be let back in. "Come on in."

Her eyes must have lingered on the lane because Eamee said: "I'm on my own. Ben doesn't know I've come."

Isobel arranged her face. "That's fine. You're always welcome, you know that."

They went inside, dark after the bright sunshine. Isobel switched on the light, scanned the kitchen furtively. "Will you stick the kettle on while I get cleaned up?" She held up her soily hands and gestured to the bathroom.

Eamee's look of horror cut deep. Why hadn't she noticed how edgy the kids were? What kind of mother can't see her children are afraid? "Or I'll use this sink. Have you got time for a brew?"

Drinks made, they sat at the table. "So, how are you?"

Eamee swirled her coffee. "Me, I'm fine, but you lot are wrecking my head. I wish you hadn't fallen out."

"We haven't. Ben and Melissa, they need some space, that's all."

"Have you even spoken to them, though? It's been two weeks. They're in bits."

Why on earth hadn't *she tried to talk to them?* "I didn't want to mither. Are they all right? What have they said?"

"Nothing. They haven't sent me or anything. I decided to come on my own."

"Ok."

"I'm proper gutted. You're all so unhappy. Why don't you just talk about it?"

"About what?"

Eamee shrugged: "Whatever you fell out about."

"We didn't fall out."

"You must have. Your Ben loves you. He's always on about you. Or he was. Now he only talks about the mad shit - sorry - going on here. You being weird, and that."

"I've made banana bread."

"Isobel…"

"It needs eating."

Isobel walked over to the counter, keeping her back to Eamee. "Tell me what he's been saying."

"It's not just Ben. Melissa's in bits. And she doesn't say much, but I can tell Sula's worried too."

Isobel put the cake on the table. "Maybe you could take some back with you."

"I'm not being funny, but you're not getting it. They don't want cake, they want you! They thought you were ill, but not now. That video's changed everything. They realise it wasn't you doing all that stuff."

"Video?"

"Belinda told them you've seen it." Eamee glanced over her shoulder at the living room, lowered her voice: "Until they saw him, they really thought you'd lost it. Who *is* that on the film?"

Isobel traced the rim of her mug. "I don't know. But I do know you're safe. It's not interested in you."

"So who *is* it interested in? Can you hear yourself? You *do* know what's going on. No wonder you drove Ben crazy."

They held each other's gaze. Isobel looked away first.

Eamee pressed her advantage: "To be honest, they thought you were attention-seeking. I know I did, until we saw. Ben doesn't understand why you haven't been in touch. They were sure you would be once you saw it. They're frightened for you, on your own here with that... They want to help you but they're afraid of this house. You can understand that, can't you? Why don't you grab a bag, and come with me?"

It would be so easy to walk out, join them at Ursula's. But she couldn't. What if it wasn't this house? What if it was her?

It doesn't know itself.

She couldn't say this to Eamee. So she sent her home loaded with cake and cash, and a promise she'd call.

She closed the front door and leaned against it, badly wanting her kids.

She ran to the kitchen, found her purse, tipped out the contents. It was in here somewhere. She spread out the cards. There, hiding under her cash card. She peered at the number and picked up the phone.

Chapter 53

PC Dyson assured her this priest was the real deal. Isobel had only the vaguest notion what that might mean, based mainly on the corny horror films Richard relished.

"He's helped a couple of families we were involved with. I'm not an expert, Mrs Hickey. I don't know what he does, or how he does it. All I can say is, after he gave them support, things began to sort themselves out. Those families were happier and we stopped getting calls. Best to talk to him directly. Maybe start by telling him what happened the day I was with you?"

But lovely, kind PC Dyson had no idea of her whole appalling mess. Could a priest really help her? She'd phoned him straightaway, before she lost her nerve. He sounded nice enough, down to earth. That was the day before yesterday and she'd picked up the phone to cancel twice since, but something told her not to. She had to put this right, for the children's sake. And more than that, she was weary. She couldn't carry on. She'd driven away the only person who believed her: Belinda hadn't been in touch since she gave back her key. Isobel needed someone on her side. If she had to go on alone like this… well, she wouldn't. She'd had enough.

He knocked on the door as the cuckoo sang eleven.

The dog barked.

"In your crate, Brodie."

Isobel smoothed her hair and opened the door.

He doffed his tweed trilby, an actual trilby. "Mrs Hickey? Ellis Worrall. We spoke on the phone."

"Please, come in."

He smiled. Sun glinted in his brylcreamed hair. He stepped inside.

"Do sit down."

He scanned the available seating and chose the haunted armchair. She sat opposite. On the doorstep, she'd seen a short middle-aged man, but he was much younger than her first impression, only in his mid-thirties. So why did he dress straight out of the fifties? He even wore an overcoat, despite the warm day. She should have offered to take it. He turned the trilby in his hands. A vague memory of her long-dead grandfather wearing one like it. And his hair: it seemed naturally curly, dark turning a premature, distinguished grey, but he'd disciplined it with the cream, creating kinks across its sheen like ripples in wet sand.

"Oh, gosh." She stood. "I haven't offered you a drink. Coffee? Tea?"

In the kitchen, she clattered mugs and broke several of the posh biscuits she'd bought in specially. "Shit."

He called from his seat. “Can I help?”
“I’m fine.” She flapped.
He mustn’t come in here.
What was she thinking? How could she tell a stranger what she was going through? But he seemed grounded, sensible. He wore a trilby, for god’s sake. She fixed a smile, and rejoined him. “Here we are.” She offered the biscuits.
“Not for me, thanks.” He patted his non-existent stomach. “I’ve not been managing my run as often as I’d like.”
An image of him in Roger Bannister-style shorts rose before her. Her smile blossomed. “Very wise.”
“Hello, who’s this little fellow?” The dog trotted in to accept some fuss. The priest - *or is he a vicar? vicar suits him better* - the vicar stroked him, and Brodie took that as permission to jump into his lap.
“Brodie, off!”
“I don’t mind, if you don’t. I had a Westie. You miss having one around.” He sat back, adjusted Brodie’s weight on his knee. “So, let’s set the ball rolling. How do you think the Church ministry can help you?”
“The church? I hadn’t thought…”
“I’m a minister of the Anglican Church.”
“Of course. It’s just I’m not a member.”
He smiled. “That’s all right. You don’t need a club card to benefit.”
“Oh no, I didn’t mean -”
“I’m sorry, that was flippant. I’m embarrassing you. Let me explain: the Church extends its ministry to all who need it, whatever your faith or lack of it. Now, would you like to tell me what’s

been happening, Mrs Hickey? I take it your experiences are based here, in this house?"

Why would he assume that? What about Dorothy, the Elms, the Flash? Was she abnormal, then, even for exorcists?

"Please, call me Isobel."

"In that case, I'm Ellis."

That was the whole Reverend thing neatly swerved.

She perched on her seat. "I'm not sure where to start. I've gone through it so many times in my head, you'd think I'd have it all ready for you. But it's confusing, I don't know what's real, or if you can even help. I think I might be going a bit mad, and -"

He stilled her with a gentle movement of his hand. "I understand you got my number from a local police officer? Why don't you start with why he gave it to you, and we'll take it from there?"

That she could do. He listened while she recounted that visit, nodding when she needed him to, stroking the dog asleep in his lap. When she'd done, he was silent for a long time.

He didn't believe her.

"That sounds distressing, Isobel. Was it an isolated incident or have there been more?"

She was alarmed to hear herself laugh. "How long have you got?"

He opened his hands. "As long as you need."

That felt like a cool draught of water in a hot desert.

She told him some, but not about Dorothy or Zag's owner: they'd already been placed outside the norm. He'd arrived with certain expectations, and she was too damn polite to confound them.

She couldn't talk about the doctor, either: too dangerous, too close.

He listened, didn't interrupt. The cuckoo sang twelve.

"The clock seems to be working all right now?"

"I knew you wouldn't believe me." She got up. "Of course you don't. What sane person would? I'm sorry I wasted your time. Thank you for coming. Can I make a donation to the church?" She was at the front door.

He remained in the armchair. "Please, Isobel, sit with me." He gestured to her seat as if this was his house, and she the guest. Deflated, she came back. "I believe you. And I want to hear the rest. I can see there's more you need to say. I understand this is difficult, painful, but I hope you'll feel able to share with me the weight of what you're carrying. Not all today. I'll be visiting you until we get this sorted out, with the Lord's help."

"But I don't go to church. I'm atheist." She dipped her head to hide her jutting chin.

"He doesn't discriminate."

She struggled to lower her hackles: after all, he was offering to help. "So how does it work? Do you do, I don't know, an exorcism?"

He smiled. "I think not, at this stage. There's a lot of misunderstanding around exorcism. That involves banishment of malevolent influence - evil, if you will. From what you've told me so far, I don't think that's what we're dealing with here."

"I guess I should be relieved. So what *are* we dealing with?"

"As yet I'm unsure. I need more information before I can come to any answers that might help us."

"But what do you *think* it might be?"

"There can be a number of causes for the events you've described. The obvious one would be an unquiet spirit, the spirit of one who's passed. This is why I need to know more about you and your family, before I can say."

"What else?"

"We don't want to get ahead of ourselves. I'd rather not rush to conclusions."

"Let's talk possibilities."

She was persuasive when she needed to be and, sure enough, Ellis wavered. "Some of this sounds like poltergeist activity in which case it might emanate from a living family member. I need more information before I can say."

"So, not the devil, then?"

"I'd be inclined to think not, but we'll say some cleansing prayers before I leave to be on the safe side. How's that?"

What had she come to when the thought of prayers to protect her was reassuring? "What do we do now?"

"That depends on what's causing the events. If there is an unquiet spirit with us, my ministry and pastoral care extends to them also. I'd want to perform a requiem Eucharist to help them find peace. We'd do that in church and you and your family would be most welcome to attend. In fact, I'd encourage you to. And rest assured that I, and my congregation, will be praying for you and yours from now on. If a poltergeist *is* indicated, that can be more complicated to deal with."

She folded her arms. "Why?"

"We don't understand the mechanism, but mental distress can sometimes trigger energy events external to the distressed mind." He was getting into this, like it was a game, a puzzle to be solved. Like it wasn't the tattered wreck of her life. "Sometimes an unquiet spirit's presence causes distress that, in turn, sparks poltergeist occurrences. Then the two, very different, phenomena, conflate into one challenging experience. If this is poltergeist in nature, my aim will be to restore peace, normality and tranquillity in your home." He leaned forward to take her hand. Brodie jumped off his lap with a resentful grunt. "You don't have to do this alone, Isobel. You have our Lord Jesus on your side. And me, for what that's worth."

Chapter 54

The prayer Ellis left with her the other day - "Think of it simply as a beautiful poem for now" - had comforted her. She read it again while she waited for him.

Christ be with me, Christ within me,
Christ behind me, Christ before me,
Christ to comfort and restore me...

It soothed like a nursery rhyme, but she couldn't bring herself to endorse it with an *Amen.*

He'd stayed hours last time, talking about all sorts of irrelevant stuff. He was a good listener and, before long, she told him about her parents. He didn't write anything down. He looked relaxed and at home in that bloody chair, even when she showed him Melissa's video on her phone. He'd muttered something about "place memory", but offered no further explanation.

The clock sang eleven as he knocked.

He sat in the armchair again. Maybe that was to remind her it *was* only a chair. Brodie ambled over, jumped in his lap.

"Cheeky little blighter. Do you mind?"

He laughed. "Not at all. We're firm friends now."

Brodie cast her a smug look.

She laughed, too. "Tea?"

"You read my mind. I'm parched."

From the kitchen, she called: "Did you manage to get hold of Ben and Melissa?"

"I did. I've got a clearer picture of what you're all experiencing, now. I'd like to talk to your friend Belinda too, if you don't object? I understand you've had words, but I got the impression, from what your children said, that she's been a tremendous support. She may be able to shed some light for me? I won't, if you don't want me to, of course."

Isobel brought the drinks through. "I wouldn't blame her if she wants nothing to do with me, but, yes, talk to her, if she'll agree."

He sipped his tea. "That's good. How have you been over the weekend? We covered a lot of ground last time. Sometimes that can take it out of a person."

"There's more I need to tell you."

"No rush. Let's take it as it comes. I'm building a good picture of events, as it is, and we're praying for you, so the healing has started, be assured of that. Would you like to say more about Richard today?"

"Is he our unquiet spirit?"

How had she dared say that out loud?

"If that is what we're dealing with here, and it's a big 'if', then it's possible. But there may be other candidates. We have to be sure."

Those cold spiders up and down her spine. "Other candidates?"

"Your parents? The poor little girl you found in the woods?" *Oh God, in my house?* "I'm sorry to be so blunt, Isobel, but you're an intelligent person. I don't want to soft-soap you."

The other day, at the stove, she'd seen Melissa standing behind her, reflected in the cooker hood. She'd turned to welcome her, but of course she'd gone. It hadn't occurred to her that it may not have been Melissa.

"Isobel? I'm sorry, perhaps that was too much, too soon. How did you get on with the prayer? Shall we say it together now?"

They did. She felt better.

"Tell me about Richard. His children adored him, I know that much already."

She looked up at the space where Richard's image had hung. She'd taken down all the photos after they turned their backs. "He was a force of nature. A one-off. I loved him. He loved us. He never wanted to leave us."

"'Where your treasure is, there will your heart be also.'"

"That's nice. What is it?"

"Matthew's Gospel. Have you been offered bereavement counselling?"

She dipped her head.

"Your GP should be able to refer you, or I can put you in touch with a voluntary organisation that offers it? It's possible some of your experiences are pure manifestations of grief."

"Let me think about it."

"Of course." He'd been leaning forward, and now he sat back. "So, you were saying Richard was a one-off. Tell me more."

She found herself recounting the day Richard bought...

"A *boat*?" This she wasn't expecting. "What kind of boat?" Not that it mattered.

Richard paced the kitchen, shaking his arms at his sides, like a boxer. Her heart sank. His voice high, staccato: "Speed. Speed boat. It's a speed boat. It's a Mariah Cuddy Power Boat 5 litre Volvo Penta engine with double axle trailer."

She dropped into a chair at the table. "I don't need the advert, love."

"It's red and white. You'll love it. Seven seats. Plenty of room. We can sleep on it, like a caravan, only two-berth, but still. Oh, and there's a toilet. How cool is that? Cruising speed of thirty knots."

She clasped her hands tightly in her lap. "How fast is that in real money?"

"It's, I don't know, fast. Ryan said it's a great spec for the price. Ryan helped me choose. It's fast. Well, it's a speed boat."

He spread his arms as he said "speed", as if this explained everything. Ryan must be someone he met at the pub.

"How much did you pay?"

"Bargain. That's why I had to go for it. Ryan said it was too good to pass up. Ryan said -"

"How much, Richard?"

"Cheap as chips. The guy's retiring. Selling up. Taking up caravanning. He didn't want to make a big profit, just wanted to see it go to a good home." He caught her eye and seemed to deflate a little. "Six and a half thousand."

Dear God. "Have you actually bought it yet?"

"Yep. All done and dusted. Even got the insurance. But Ryan says that'll come down when we do all the courses."

"Richard, sit down a minute, will you?"

He sat opposite her, and immediately stood again. "They have rallies. Gatherings. Like a regatta? It'll be great for summer holidays."

"Where is it?"

"We're going to berth it at the marina in Padstowe. That's where Ryan's got his boat."

"Padstowe? Richard, we've never been to Padstowe."

"No. Yeah. I know. But we will now, won't we! It'll be great. The kids'll love it. We can go all over with it." He looked at her again. "You don't like Padstowe? We can move it. We can take it anywhere you like. Doesn't have to be Padstowe. We could take it up to Shetland. Remember that marina at Brae? Where we hired that boat? The salmon farm? You remember. That would be amazing!" He was striding about again.

"It's not Padstowe, love. It's the boat. Where is it now?"

He had to think. "London. Camden, I think he said."

"But you've paid marina fees at Padstowe?"

"It's fine, chick. You worry too much." He tickled her under the chin. She pulled away. "It's got a trailer thrown in free! Like I said, it was a bargain."

"So with the insurance and marina, how much have you paid?"

"Oh, Bel. You know I'm not great with figures. And anyway, we can afford it. We're loaded. Everyone has a boat."

"I need to know."

He thought about it. "Insurance was six thou, the mooring was five, oh and the application fee's one hundred. So that's… seventeen thousand six hundred. Jesus. Mounts up, doesn't it? We didn't need to pay the full year, but I thought…"

That was one busy night at the pub. Smart phones had a lot to answer for.

"Richard." She patted the chair next to her and reached for the shopping pad. He grabbed the chair, turned it round and straddled it. He rested his chin on his hands on the chair-back, and watched her open the pad. "Who did you buy it from? Which card did you use?" She thought she'd stopped them all.

He jumped to his feet. "No! You're not doing *that* again. You'll make me look a mug. I've bought it, and that's that. Anyway, I got it on HP, so." *How the hell did he manage that?* "It's fine. Really, Bel, don't worry." He bent to kiss the top of her head. "I've got it all under control this time. You'll love it. You'll absolutely love it, I promise." His mobile rang. He turned from her to answer it. "Ryan, you bastard! Yes, she's thrilled! Can't wait to get out in it." He laughed. Caught her eye. Turned away again. "Yeah, that's right." He put a placatory hand up to her and walked out, laughing and talking.

She sat back. She hadn't asked exactly when he'd bought it. Last night, probably. He couldn't have kept it to himself longer than that. So they should have a cooling-off period, still. She hoped. She picked up the landline and dialled.

"It's me."

"Hello, you. What's wrong?" Ursula always knew.

"He's done it again."

"Hell. Shall I come round?"

"I can't get him to think straight. *I* can't think straight."

"I've a nice Laphroaig. I'll bring it. That should get his attention."

"I don't want to give you the wrong impression, Ellis. Perhaps that wasn't the best story. He was ill and he struggled with it. He was so brave, and strong. I mean, how do you live with something like that?"

"Did he have a formal diagnosis? The children weren't sure."

"Bi-polar disorder. But he was proud, didn't want anyone to know, not even the kids."

"That must have been hard, keeping it to yourself."

"I don't know what easy means any more. Haven't had a full night's sleep since he... I couldn't hold down my old job, so I'm working for minimum wage now. Since we had to sell the house, everything's gone to shit."

Her brain felt fit to burst. She started plumping cushions. The dog leapt from Ellis' knee, and barked at her.

"Quiet!"

She plumped harder. *Why are you telling him this? He can't help you. Nobody can.*

The TV switched on at top volume. Ellis spilled his tea.

"Oh, sorry. I'll -" He gestured to the kitchen, but before he could get up, another racket broke in.

Music from upstairs, loud, discordant. "I didn't realise the children were home."

"They're not." She looked up at the ceiling.

Ellis made for the stairs.

"Don't. There's no one up there."

"But the music?"

"It's Richard's."

"Did you leave a cd on?" She didn't answer. No point. "I'll check it out."

"Be careful, he won't ..." She followed him.

Ellis started up the stairs three at a time, caught his toe, stumbled. She gripped the newel post. At her heel, the dog growled softly. "Felt like someone grabbed my ankle. Interesting." He continued up, more cautiously.

Over *This Morning* on TV and Nick Cave upstairs, she heard plugs being pulled out and replaced. Then Ellis declaimed a prayer, some sort of blessing. The song grew louder in response:

he's a ghost, he's a god, he's a man, he's a guru.

Ellis reappeared at the top of the stairs. She caught his look of fear before he managed to smooth it over. He descended slowly, resisting the push of the music.

"I can't turn it off. You knew that? There's no cd playing. No ipods."

"I tried to warn you."

They had to shout over the tumult. A stray curl escaped his hair oil and drooped on his forehead.

"Let's try this." He strode to the TV, pulled the plug. Silence from upstairs, too. "Ok." His breathing ragged. "Good."

"Are you all right, Ellis?"

"Don't worry about me. This is why I'm here. Will you join me in a prayer?"

She held his hand, shut her eyes tight, bowed her head.

"Lord God, bless and sanctify this house that in it there may be joy and gladness, peace and love, health and goodness, and thanksgiving always to you, Father, Son and Holy Spirit; and let your blessing rest upon this house and those who dwell in it, now and forever. Amen."

"Amen."

"Let's sit." They resumed their places. Brodie remained at the bottom of the stairs, hackles up. "Listen, Isobel. You're safe, do you understand? You've asked for the help of our Lord Jesus Christ, and He *will* give it." Ellis smiled, eyes bright. "He's got our backs, all right?" She nodded. She did feel safer. "Now, that was valuable for me to witness. How typical was it of what you've been experiencing?"

"I haven't had it exactly like that before. I mean, the music, yes. I thought it was Ben at first, playing his Dad's cds. I was angry. I didn't want him handling his Dad's things, I don't know why. Stupid. We argued about it, and I got rid of the cds, gave them to a charity shop with some of Richard's clothes. But…"

"It didn't stop?"

"It's always the same: *Red Right Hand.*" She laughed. "I used to love that song. Can't imagine why, now."

"Did Richard know you liked it?"

"Of course he did. He - oh."

Why had that not occurred to her*?*

"Does the telly often switch itself on like that?"

"Melissa accused me of doing it. She said I was hiding the remote, switching it on and off from the kitchen. She thought I was trying to freak her out. That's why she went to my sister's."

"Your children love you, you know that, don't you? They're desperately worried for you."

"They thought I was mad until they saw that video. Now I think they believe I've drawn this thing to me, that it's my fault this is happening."

"They think you're grieving. They wish they could ease your pain."

"It's their pain, too. He was their daddy."

He leaned over, patted her hand. "Shall I make us another cuppa?"

Chapter 55

Ellis phoned next morning and asked her to meet him "on neutral ground". He suggested the Robin Hood. When she arrived at two, he was waiting. He looked more relaxed here. Was he afraid of the house? Not a comforting thought.

He ordered sparkling water for her, a pint for him, and chose a table away in a corner of the empty Lounge.

"Tell me more about Richard."

"What is there to say? He was mad, and he made me love him." She sipped her drink.

"Does that make you angry?"

"I don't think so."

"Only you sound like you're accusing him."

"Of what?"

"Being mad?"

"He was ill. It wasn't his fault."

"Do you feel it was *someone's* fault?"

"No." She traced an old glass-ring on the table. "Yes. But only, you know, in the scheme of things."

"So whose fault was it?"

"God's?" She smiled.

He didn't react. He hadn't touched his pint. Irritation overcame Isobel: "What do you want me to say? That it was *my* fault? Ok, it was. Because I didn't see what was happening to him, did I? I was so wrapped up in my own world, my oh-so-important work, I didn't see."

"You were working full-time in a high-pressure job, and raising two young children."

He was right. She knew he was, but she couldn't seem to *feel* he was. "He struggled. He tried to stay on his medication, but then he'd hit a high and be convinced he was cured. He used to flush the lithium down the toilet until I caught him at it one day. He'd been doing that for ages, apparently. What kind of wife does that make me?"

Ellis shrugged. "He was an adult. He made decisions. You can't blame yourself for those."

"And the children, I had to protect them, especially when he got mixed up with…a bad crowd. I thought I'd kept them safe from all that, but turns out Ben knew all along. It was all round school. So I didn't protect them." A chair, behind her, scraped on the flagged floor. Ellis looked past her, eyes wide. She lowered her voice. "I was a bad wife, and now I'm a useless mother."

"That's not what I see."

"With respect, Ellis, all you see is a woman going a bit loopy because she let her husband die and drove her children away."

"With respect, Isobel, I can decide for myself what I see. And that's someone who's hurting, desperate to sort out her life so she can be reunited with her children, both of whom love her dearly and are equally keen to be back with her."

She gulped her drink, glared at him. He held her gaze. She put down her glass. "I keep thinking about something that happened a long time ago. Before Ben was born. Before we were married, even."

"Do you want to tell me?"

"Don't you have somewhere to be? No other ghosts that need busting?"

"You're trying to change the subject. Shall we stick with what you were saying? Before you were married?" He sat back and picked up his pint.

"Richard had been excited for days. Things were going well at work. He'd closed a couple of good deals on his own. He was an estate agent, did I tell you? Due a lot of commission. I assumed he was pumped up from that. He kept bringing me presents, flowers, chocolates. It was lovely, but I didn't like him spending money he hadn't yet been paid. Then, one day, I got home and there was this filthy old tramp at our table having tea with him. Fish and chips, and Newcastle Brown. I remember that, because Rich never drank Newcastle Brown. I could smell the old guy as soon as I walked in the door. He stank like a men's toilet. Our flat was over a parade of shops that had a chippy and an off-licence, and he'd been in the offy when Richard nipped down for a bottle of wine. They'd got chatting and Richard invited him up. They were both pissed. The guy had a bottle of vodka or gin or something in his pocket and kept offering it. Of course, I refused, but Richard was happy to share. I got him on one side, told him to get rid. We argued, but the man took the hint, and shuffled off. Richard went ballistic. Ranting, accusing me of scaring off his friends, being a poor hostess. Then he left, said he was going after him to apologise." She sipped her water. "He didn't come back for three days, Ellis."

"What did you do?"

"Tried to find him. I went to his office. He'd phoned in sick. I called his friends, went round all the pubs. No one had seen him. I reported it to the police but they said they couldn't do anything."

"Where did he go?"

"I never found out, but he turned up in a terrible mess. Cuts and bruises all over him. Two black eyes. Cut lips. Like he'd been beaten up. He wouldn't go to A and E. He denied it, but I'm sure he'd been sleeping in his car. He was so apologetic, and so sad, somehow. He went to bed and slept round the clock. After that he was fine. Back to normal. I should have known right then, shouldn't I?"

"There's no *should* about it. You didn't know."

"And then there was all the dreaming."

Ellis leaned forward. "Dreaming?"

"Have you ever heard that saying: When you can't sleep at night, it's because you're awake in someone else's dream?"

He gave a mock shiver. "Creepy."

She laughed. "Don't be soft. You're an exorcist, for goodness sake!"

"Deliverance counsellor."

"Same thing."

"Not strictly speaking. I think I explained." His smile crinkled those grey eyes, made them sparkle. "So tell me about the dreaming."

"I shouldn't have... I'm sorry I brought it up."

"Whenever you're ready, I'll listen."

She swirled the water in her glass. Bubbles fizzed. "It was inheriting all that damn money that did the damage. When he gave up his job, he had no structure to his days. I should have realised it wouldn't be good for him."

"There's that *should* again. Listen out for that, Isobel. It can be insidious. Another drink?"

"No, I should be getting back."

"There you go again. Try to be easier on yourself."

"You're a really kind man, Reverend Ellis Worrall, d'you know that?"

"I'm your friend, Isobel. You don't have to face this alone."

He reached across to touch her hand.

And I dropped down and down

She snatched it away. "What if I *want* to face it alone? What if I *need* to? This is my husband we're talking about."

"Why did you ask for my help?"

She stood. "Thanks for the drink."

Ellis rose too, flustered. "Let me run you home."

"I'll walk. It's not far."

"But, Isobel -"

"I *said* no!"

Her chair tipped back, hit the floor with a crack. She had to get away, to be alone. She needed the red pen-knife.

Chapter 56

She woke to Richard's laugh, deep, appreciative, infectious. She joined in, turned to him.

"What's so funny?"

He wasn't there, would never be there. She rolled back to the clock: 03.14. The dog whimpered in his sleep, snuggled closer.

She gazed into darkness, and it came to her, what had been staring her in the face. These weird events, this *haunting*, were nothing to do with the doctor calling. They'd started long before she invited him in. Of course they had. And that poem, it had been pecking at her head for ages, well before she'd found the books in Richard's bureau, and definitely before she'd even heard of the doctor. She'd started to think of the doctor as some strange essence of Richard, let loose from the man she'd loved. Perhaps changed, embittered. And Zag's owner? He'd been kind, like the part of Richard who'd loved her.

But what if she was wrong?

She should feel comforted to know Richard was close, so why was she constantly afraid? Maybe because she couldn't get that note she'd found in the bureau out of her head. *Deofol*? And maybe because she'd started to remember Richard's dreams.

His laugh again. No longer infectious. Sinister. She pulled the duvet up around her chin. He'd laughed that way when he told her what he'd done that night.

Richard bounced into the kitchen, swung a chair round and sat across it. He beat a tattoo on the back of it.

Isobel poured him some tea. "Sleep well?"

He stretched. "I did, petal. Can't remember the last time I slept that well." He slurped his tea, and laughed. "God, what a night!"

She put toast on the table and sat down with him. "Last night?"

He layered on butter and honey. "Yeah! My God, I've not had so much fun in ages."

"Oh?" She scrolled back through the previous evening: tea, argument, bit of telly, then bed.

He ate, looking way too pleased with himself. Not internet gambling again? Please not that. But she couldn't help smiling with him. He was happy, relaxed, so beautiful.

"They really had it coming."

A fight, then. But when? She'd been with him all night. His face wasn't marked, his knuckles unscathed.

"Tell me. You know you're dying to."

He sprang from the chair and started his caged lion walk, to and fro. Isobel stood. Never sit down with a lion.

"It was amazing! A brilliant laugh! I felt like a five-year-old, but you should have seen their faces."

"Who are we talking about?"

He paused in his patrol. He focused on her with some effort, it seemed. "Andy and Dave. Who else would I be talking about? They thought they could go off like that, and leave me out of it? Well, think again, you pair of losers. You'll not get one over on me."

"They didn't leave you out. You told them you couldn't fly on your medication."

"Bollocks!" He slammed his hand on the counter. She winced. "Lying scumbags." He made a visible effort to control his temper. "But I fixed them. They won't forget this weekend in a hurry."

He was making no sense. "D'you want cereal?"

"Do you not want to know what I did, then? Jesus, woman! Have you no curiosity in that boring little skull of yours?" He tapped her head with his fist, not gently.

She ducked away. "Please don't talk to me like that."

He sat, patted the chair next to him. "If you're good, I'll tell you." She walked around the table and sat beside him. She didn't want him kicking off with the children in the house. "Good girl." He put an arm around her shoulder, hugged her tight, kissed her head where he'd just hit it. "If you're sitting comfortably, then I'll begin." Another slurp of tea. "I got in their room."

"But they're in Majorca."

"I *know* they're in Majorca, love. That's why I'm pissed off with them. Try to keep up."

"So how did you -?"

"In my dream! I know. Crazy, huh? But I was there, Bel, I'm telling you. I could hear Dave snoring. I could feel the air conditioning. Smell the hotel shower gel, even. I was right there. Dreamed myself there." He was so sure, she hadn't the heart to disabuse him. He'd been on a new tablet only a couple of weeks. Something the psychiatrist was experimenting with. Could it be having side effects? "And there they were, the bastards, fast asleep. Twin beds. Nice room. Nicer than what we got last time. I had a good snoop around, could go anywhere I wanted. I opened the wardrobe. Looks like Dave's bought all that twatty Pringle gear. But here's the thing: while I was going through their stuff, I think I made some noise - with the coat hangers? - because Andy started muttering in his sleep. I think he heard me! How mad is that?"

"That's - yep, that's up there."

"I know, right? So I bang the wardrobe closed and Andy wakes up. Who's that? he says. I freeze. He's bound to see me. But, no! He rubs his eyes and sits there, listening. Doesn't see me standing right there at the end of his bed. I mean, it's dark, but not that dark. I can see *him*. So I stay dead still and quiet. Eventually he mutters again and lies down. It's priceless, Bel, can you imagine?" He started pacing again. "So I go into the en-suite. One of the dirty sods has pissed on the toilet seat so I slam the lid down. Bam!" He slapped the counter again. "This time it's Dave that wakes up and he's out of bed like a shot. What the fuck? he's yelling. Andy wakes up, too. I'm stood in the doorway of the bog and I lean in and flush the toilet. Andy, that you? says Dave, all bold and brave. Not me, pal, says Andy from under his duvet. He's pulled it right up over his head like a little kid. Tosser! So Dave's standing there by his bed, all confused and I go over to the bottom of Andy's bed and pull the cover off him. Dave goes ape-shit now, because he's seen the cover come off. Fuck me, Andy, how did you do that? And Andy's there in his nasty grey keks shivering in bed. *Shivering*, Bel! It was sweet. Next, I spot Andy's golf bag, so I lift it up and take out a wood. I let the bag fall and try a swing. Well, there's not much room in there. You should have seen the two of them flinch. Cower, they did! Andy leaps over onto Dave's bed, and Dave sidles along the wall to the door. Like he's on a skyscraper ledge or something! I take another swing and Andy's off after him. Both of them were out of that door in a New York minute. I nearly pissed myself laughing." Sweating, red, he kept pacing, wiped his mouth. "You don't believe me. I can see you don't."

"I don't know what you're trying to tell me, love. It was a dream, yes?"

"Yes, a dream. The most vivid I've ever had." He rubbed his eyes as if he had a headache. "But it was more than a dream. I was *there.* And they felt me there. I scared the living shit out of them."

"But, Richard, how could -?"

"I don't fucking know!" He clutched a clump of his hair and pulled. "There's something in here. It's got me and it won't let go."

Isobel didn't like to run in the heat of the day, but she needed to burn off energy. She tugged at her tee-shirt, clinging with sweat. She was mad at Belinda for sticking her nose in, mad at the kids for sending Eamee to do their dirty work, and mad at Ellis for she didn't know what. Why couldn't they all leave her alone?

"Brodie, get here now!"

Clouds of midges everywhere. She'd forgotten her hat so the sun slammed down on her head. Bernard had been on the field but she had no patience for his tittle-tattle. A couple of women she usually chatted to were strolling up ahead, so she diverged off the path and rejoined it as a young guy whipped past on his bike. She stepped back, cooled by the rushing breeze of his speed, then traipsed after him. He was stripped to the waist, top tied around his middle, back glistening. He disappeared round the bend. She slowed. Brodie walked at heel, panting, uninterested in his surroundings. Grasshoppers sang above languid bird calls. Her scalp itched.

When did she last wash her hair? She couldn't even remember her last shower.

The lad on the bike reappeared ahead.

They meant well, Belinda, Eamee, even Ellis, they just needed to butt the hell out. She didn't want their sympathy or their understanding. What was there to understand, anyway? None of it made sense. Some things shouldn't happen in the real world.

The cyclist slowed, weaved his way towards her, wobbling a little, holding onto the handlebar with only one hand, his other hidden. The dog barked and ran at him.

"Brodie, get back here!"

The lad aimed the bike right at him.

"Hey! Watch what you're doing!"

Brodie dodged, snapped at the wheels. The lad kicked out, uselessly. His bike tipped, but he righted it and came on, fixing her with an odd grin. Brodie went mad, tried to bite his foot, intent on damage. Then she saw that the boy, he couldn't have been more than eighteen, had his shorts pulled down, exposing his hard-on. And he was determined she'd see, because Brodie jumped up and bit his calf, and he cried out, but still he came on past her. She gawped, all the clever, acid comments she'd imagined she would spit out in such a circumstance dried on her tongue. He leered at her over his shoulder.

Brodie squeaked a stifled bark, as if someone had clamped his jaws shut, and peeled off to one side. Before Isobel could fully take in what was happening, a man stepped onto the path ahead and blocked the flasher's way. It was Zag's owner. The boy, still ogling back at her, didn't see him.

"Look out!" She wasn't sure which of them she was warning. The lad leaned into his pedals to pick up speed, and turned to face the way ahead. He shouted in alarm, lost control, nearly went over, skidded, then stopped suddenly, as if he'd hit an invisible wall. Only there was no wall. But that didn't stop the impact throwing him from the bike. He slid painfully along the gravel away from her towards...

She shaded her eyes against the sun: Zag's owner was gone.

She hoped the lad was badly hurt, but she didn't wait to see.

She ran.

Ellis called up the street: "Hello! Glad I caught you."

Bloody hell. Isobel was about to lock the front door. If she'd left earlier, instead of gazing gormlessly into space, she would have missed him. He drew level with her garden path, breathless, perspiring in the beating Indian summer heat.

"I'm just on my way out."

"I don't suppose you could give me half an hour of your time?"

She couldn't think of an excuse fast enough to say no. He followed her into the kitchen. She poured him a tall glass of water which he emptied almost in one swallow.

"Get that coat off. I don't want you collapsing with heatstroke. I've had enough of that at work these past few days."

He handed back the glass. "I can't ever remember heat like this in September, can you?"

He shrugged off the coat, threw it over the back of a chair.

"Not there!" She grabbed it. "I'll hang it up."

"It was good to see you at the service yesterday."

She reached in the fridge for orange juice, lingered in the cooling draught.

"I was sorry you didn't stick around afterwards to say hello."

"I had to get back for the dog."

She offered him some juice.

He took it, raising a hand to his mouth to suppress a yawn.

"Sorry. Didn't get much sleep last night. This guy kept knocking on my door. I went to answer it several times, thought it was a parishioner, but he'd scarpered every time I opened the door. Irritating. He was a bit old for knock and run, and it's not even Halloween. Anyway, that's the price of being available 24/7, I suppose. Enough of me." He gestured for her to lead the way into the living room.

She tried not to gape. "What did he look like?"

"Sorry?"

"The man, what did he look like?"

"Isobel, are you all right?"

"What did he look like, Ellis?"

"I don't know. Does it matter? I only saw him from my bedroom window. He was wearing black. Tall, I think. Just a Halloween prankster. Wretched festival. The Americans have a lot to answer for. Don't worry about it. I only mentioned it to explain my tiredness today. Shall we?"

What could she say? They sat in their usual seats.

"So." Ellis pulled at the creases in his trousers. "How have you been this week?"

"How have *I* been? I'm not sure that's the right question."

"How have you been feeling?"

"There's not been much activity, if that's what you mean."

"I'm asking how you are, Isobel, that's all. You seem on edge."

She heard a dry, joyless bark: her own laugh. "You'd be on edge in my situation. I thought things would get better. I thought he'd gone."

Her words hung in the air between them. He fixed her with that patient gaze, his eyes clear as mountain pools. Now she'd have to tell him.

But he didn't ask. Instead, he said: "Have you been involved with spiritualism recently? Through a church, or more informally? A medium, perhaps, or tarot cards, that sort of thing?"

"Why?"

"Because something's bothering me." He smoothed a hand over his unruffled hair. "There's a presence here that's - I can't rightly describe it. I suppose 'mischievous' gets closest to what I mean." He talked fast, softly, almost to himself, those eyes looking inward now. "It's not an energy I've experienced before. It's full of confusion and... *life*. So much life. And spiky. It has," he made an odd plucking gesture with his fingers, "sharp edges. At times, it's almost as if it's coming from..." He cast her a strange, wary glance.

kept treading treading

"I need to pin this down, to eliminate anything that doesn't come directly from this house and the people attached to it."

Isobel shrank into the sofa. She'd felt safe with Ellis, he was so assured, so contained, so absolutely normal. He hadn't run when things kicked off; he'd coped. But now he believed there was something in this house beyond his control, and she realised, with profound shock, that she already knew.

"Ellis, please speak plainly. What have I done?"

That strange look again. Then he leaned forward, held his hands together, prayerfully, between his knees. "Sometimes in bereavement, people, feeling desperate I'm sure, turn the wrong way for help. If you *have* experimented with anything occult -" *Occult, oh my god.* "Mediums, fortune-tellers, Ouija boards? - I need to know. It's vital, for all our sakes, that you tell me. Otherwise, I don't know what I'm up against, and I can't shield you or myself. Does that make sense?"

She went to the window. Maud tottered past and waved.

It doesn't know itself.

What if all this had nothing to do with her loss, her grief, her Richard? What if something else was haunting her?

She turned back to the room. "I saw a fortune-teller a few weeks ago. I didn't mean to. It was an accident."

Ellis tamped down a look of alarm. "Ok." He made a small soothing gesture. Eldred had done the same. "Let's take a breath and try to stay calm. Why don't you sit with me?"

"But if there's something here, if it's not... we have to get rid of it."

"And we will when we work out what it is. Tell me what happened with this fortune-teller. I need to know everything. Leave nothing out."

He looked grim, drained, the fifty-something she'd originally thought him.

"I'm so sorry, Ellis."

"Don't be sorry. Be accurate. I need you to focus now. Remember every detail. What he said, what you said. What he *did,* what you did. Let's start with the room. Give me everything you can recall. It's all important."

He made her go over and over it. Then he went into the garden to make a call. When he came back, a good ten minutes later, he hurried from room to room repeating the blessing he'd done before.

“That should do it, for now. I’ve got to go, but I’ll be back, all right?” He took her hands. His were cold, and slick with sweat. “Forgive me. I can’t stay. Will you be ok?”

“I -”

“I’m sorry. I’ll be back soon.”

He almost ran from the house.

She waited all afternoon on a kitchen chair she’d pulled up to the wall to feel solid brick against her back.

He didn’t return.

Isobel sought the safety of her bed early, but couldn’t sleep. The hostile house lurked empty outside her door. She hugged Brodie close, listened to strident silence.

When Richard had dreamed about that hotel room, it wasn’t the craziest he’d been, but it wasn’t far off. The next day, she’d got a call from Annette, Dave’s wife.

“Can’t do lunch tomorrow, Iz. Sorry. He’s home.”

Isobel’s stomach had filled with ice. “I thought they were staying the whole weekend.”

“So did I. Thought I’d have some peace. But no, they flew back last night.”

“He’s not ill?”

“Some problem with the hotel.”

Isobel’s throat tightened. “What kind of problem?”

“Not sure, exactly. He’s been unusually cagey about it. Something about the plumbing, the toilet not fitting properly. The loo seat kept slamming down and catching the flush handle? I don’t know. Seems a daft reason to come home. I said why didn't they just change rooms, but he said they'd had enough."

Isobel never told Richard about that phone call. She couldn't risk reinforcing his delusions. Really, though, *was* he deluded? At the time, back when life was still worth living, she'd put the incident behind her. She'd filed it away in some recess of her mind marked: *to be sorted.* But now, in this malevolent house, she had to confront it.

She must warn Ellis what Richard had been capable of.

Chapter 57

Ellis knocked two days later, without warning or apology, and before Isobel had summoned the courage to phone him. The weather had finally broken. Fat rain dashed the windows. His overcoat brought in damp autumn smell, welcome contrast to the unwashed fug surrounding, no, emanating from her. He shook the coat, folded it and placed it on the floor by his accustomed chair. The dog promptly lay on it. Ellis waved away offers of tea - she had none, anyway - and sat.

"I felt vulnerable the other day, exposed. I had to remove myself for both our sakes. And I couldn't share my thoughts with you until I'd discussed it with my colleagues. Isobel? You don't look well."

"You've told other people?"

"No priest does this alone. We're supported in prayer by our congregations and everything we do is supervised by more senior priests. I did tell you. Now. This is what I think we have here. It's complicated, so speak up if I say anything you don't understand, all right?"

She clasped her hands. "Ok."

"Let's start with the easy stuff: place memory. These houses are old. According to my research, they were built at the turn of the last century for farm labourers, or possibly miners' families. Think of all that's happened in this house over all those years. Think of the families who've lived here, loved and died here. Yes?"

"Yes."

"We -" He waved his hand, impatient with himself. "The Anglican Church often gets called to deal with instances that can only be described as replays of history. Events, seen by several people, sometimes at the same time, that never change from occurrence to occurrence. Do you follow?"

How many people had *died in this house?*

"They're literally watching history repeat itself. We believe certain events hold such powerful emotion that they're imprinted on the place they happen, for all time. You've surely heard stories of Roman legionnaires appearing to march through walls, their legs cut off at the knee? We would call that place memory, do you see? The event occurs nowhere else. In layman's terms, it's not haunting the person, it's haunting the place. Are you with me?"

She nodded.

"Can you see what parts of your experience might be place memory?"

"When I saw Brodie under the bathroom door, and he wasn't there?"

Ellis clapped his hands. "Bingo! You've got it. Think how many dogs must have lived here down the years. And what about the video? The man in the chair? Place memory."

"But Brodie reacted to him."

"If *we* can perceive the memory, why shouldn't dogs? Their senses are so much sharper than ours."

"But the kids didn't see that man. And I've never seen him in the flesh, even when the dog's reacted to something in the chair. Melissa caught it on camera. It's only through the video that we saw him."

"Good point. I need to give that a little more thought. But, still, do you accept the principle?"

What about that spiky energy he'd got all in a lather over? What about her dabbles with the occult? The poor guy was way out of his depth, and she'd still not mentioned the doctor.

So tell him, you idiot. Tell him everything now, before he fits the rest into neat little boxes.

Ellis looked at his hands. "We've talked about unquiet spirits, and I know you have your suspicions. I think this is going to be tough for you. Shall we get the kettle on?"

"Just get on with it." She hadn't meant to snap.

He held up that soothing hand. "You've told me a lot about your husband and what he, what you all went through with his illness. After much thought and prayer, we believe Richard is not yet at rest. And I think you believe that, too."

She clamped a hand over her mouth, but the moan escaped.

"I'm sorry, Isobel. I should have arranged for someone to be with you. This must be so hard to hear, but we need to do it now. We can't stop. I'm phoning Belinda. Is she in, d'you know?"

She shook her head. He had the number in his mobile. He walked through to the kitchen, talked in whispers. Suddenly she was shaking like she had a fever. What the hell was happening? A knock at the door, Belinda burst in with a gust of rain, and ran into her open arms. Isobel clung to her.

"Blin, I was such a bitch."

"Oh, honey, it doesn't matter." She pressed Isobel's head to her chest. "I know, sweetheart. Let it out."

It started quietly, that song, almost gently, but rose to a roar all around them:

he'll appear out of nowhere but he ain't what he seems.

Belinda held her tighter. Ellis answered with an authoritative incantation, not a blessing, this time. The music screeched to a stop as if a record player needle had scraped across it.

Still, Belinda held her. Isobel burrowed into her dark, scented warmth, and cried herself stupid.

Ellis brought in a tray of tea and sandwiches. Isobel sat up, wiped her eyes. He must have nipped out for them; she had nothing in.

He offered her a sandwich. He'd cut off the crusts. "Eat something. You'll feel better."

The three of them sat, politely chewing.

"Tea?"

"Ellis, let me."

"You need to eat, drink, and try to relax, Isobel. We have much yet to discuss."

Belinda squeezed her hand. "D'you feel up to this, honey? Say if you don't."

"I need to know."

Ellis nodded, swallowed a mouthful of sandwich and gulped his tea. "We've talked before about how different phenomena can trigger each other, become confused and conflated into one event? Do you remember I mentioned poltergeists? My hunch is Richard's presence has created such stress for you that a poltergeist has manifested."

"The music?"

"That's right, Belinda. As Isobel's distress built, her emotions burst into poltergeist activity, causing that music. Music she associates with Richard."

"I could understand that, just about, if there was a cd or iPod or something, that my *emotions*," Isobel made air quotes, "could switch on, but where's the music coming from? I got rid of the cd player."

Ellis spread his hands. "We can't say how it happens. That remains a mystery as yet, but your situation here is far from unique. And rest assured, a poltergeist can't harm you spiritually. There's nothing demonic about it." *So she should be afraid of demons.* "It's possible the poltergeist triggered place memory events. But listen Isobel, I say again, a poltergeist cannot harm you. It thrives on tension and fear, and never survives once that fear is conquered."

And hit a World at every plunge

Was she really having this mad conversation with these seemingly sane people as she barely held on to the frayed threads of her own sanity? And who made this mumbo-jumbo vicar the expert, anyway? She should kick him out.

But he hadn't finished: "The cuckoo clock, your lost keys, coats moved about, all these might be explained by a poltergeist."

"You think Richard's here?" She was *not* going to cry again. "So why can't I see him? Why is he trying to frighten me? Why can't he talk to me, *be* with me? Why can't I have him back?"

"Richard died, Isobel. Nothing can change that. What I meant was his *spirit* may not be at rest. His spirit is very different from Richard, the man. Spirit is the eternal part of us, not human in an earthly way."

"Why is he here, if it isn't my Richard?"

"He was ill. His poor mental health may have damaged his psyche. That might explain these irrational explosions of activity, these seemingly vindictive acts." Ellis shrugged. "How can we describe the ineffable? He was taken from you so suddenly and, forgive me, so violently; he didn't have time to prepare himself. He couldn't say goodbye. That can be enough to disturb eternal rest. And it could account for the sense of confusion that pervades this house."

"Stop it. I don't want to hear." That terrifying, dizzying sensation again of her atoms dispersing, of her body dissolving, and snapping back into solidity just as her hand made contact with Ellis' shocked face in a smart slap. Belinda, small as she was, wrapped her arms about Isobel and held on tight.

"Don't, Iz. It's all right."

"But it's not. It's all wrong. All spoiled."

They tottered together, an ungainly dance of grief.

Ellis' voice seemed to come from far off: "Look at me, Isobel."

Belinda's grip loosened, but Isobel wouldn't look.

"Do you remember that saying from the Bible I shared with you? *Where your treasure is, there will your heart be also*? The power of love can be so strong it holds the spirit of the departed to the object of their love. Do you see?"

That wasn't what he'd said just now, but she should accept his tacit offer of a gentler way to bear this. She wiped her face. "That's kind of beautiful, I guess. If he wasn't suffering, unquiet, it would be beautiful."

"Thank the Lord for helping you see that."

"Amen." Belinda fought back tears. Isobel squeezed her hand.

"I think you've known in your heart Richard was at the bottom of all this. Our duty now is to help him find rest, and I promise you we can do that. We'll pray together now, and we'll hold a special requiem for him in church very soon. It'll be important for you and your children to be at that service."

She nodded.

"For now, let's say the Lord's Prayer together."

Strange how these things stay with you from childhood. The familiar rhythm comforted her. At the end, she opened her eyes, but he wasn't done:

"Protect us, Lord Jesus. Send your holy angels to guard and defend us. Be with us, Lord, for you have cast down Satan by your death and have risen in triumph. Amen."

Poor Ellis, trying to convince her he had it all worked out. She'd still not told him about Zag's owner, or the doctor, and she couldn't now.

Belinda cleared her throat. "Can I ask a question? Where does the doctor fit into all this?"

"What doctor?"

Watching Ellis warily, she told him how they'd contrived to invite the doctor into the house.

Ellis put his head in his hands. "Damn it, Isobel, I *knew* you were hiding something! Did I not make this clear? I can't help you if you won't tell me everything. This presence - if I don't have all the facts - sweet Jesus!"

He worried his fingers through slicked hair.

"I'm sure Isobel didn't mean to hold back."

Ellis raised a hand. "Please, Belinda, you're not helping. Don't you see, either of you, how much danger we're in right now? I told you I needed to know everything, but you've been leading me into God only knows what! I've been preparing, praying, for one situation, all the while we're deep into something else entirely. For God's sake, woman, what's the matter with you?" He glared at them, breathing hard.

Belinda laid a hand on his arm. "We all need to take a breath. It can't be as bad as all that, surely?"

He turned on her. "Can't it? It's simply a matter of a few prayers, is that what you think? A sprinkle of holy water and all will be right with the world? You have no idea what's happening here." He stooped to pick up his coat, and said, quieter but no less angry: "I can't stay."

The front door slammed behind him. Isobel winced. "Has he gone? He's not left us? He can't do that, can he?"

Belinda went to see. "I think he has."

"Are you sure he's not just nipped out for a cig?" She joined Belinda at the rain-lashed window, peered over her shoulder into the premature dark.

"Did he look like he was nipping out? Does he even smoke? Gosh, I didn't realise he was so…"

"Volatile?"

"Passionate. It suits him." Belinda flicked her hair in that insouciant way she had.

"You are unbelievable."

"Just saying. He came off a bit unstable, though, didn't he?"

"He was scared. Don't you get it? Something here's got to him."

Belinda stared around the room. "Shit."

"*Yes*, shit."

"But he'll come back, won't he? He wouldn't leave us?" She opened the door a crack, peeped out. "He's definitely gone."

"Blin, I don't feel safe. Can you feel it?"

"Now you're scaring me."

"There's something in the air. Like a vibration. Like electricity. Don't tell me you can't feel it. It prickles. Like pins and needles."

Belinda's eyes stretched wider. She held out her arm. "Look, the hairs are standing up."

"That's it! That's the feeling. Someone's here. Could it be Richard?"

A sudden voice, male, angry: "One two three four!"

They flew into each other's arms.

"Fucking Ramones! That's your phone, Iz. Answer it."

Isobel let it ring. The room zipped with crackling vitality. "Richard?"

"Don't talk to it."

"Richard, love? It's me. It's Bel."

"Isobel, I mean it. Don't."

Belinda's mobile rang now. She reached into her pocket for it. "Hello? ... Oh my God, thank you … Please hurry." She hung up. "He's coming back.

He got as far as the bus stop. He said we're to get out of the house."

"I'm not leaving him."

Belinda grabbed her. She tried to snatch her arm back, but Belinda was stronger, dug fingers into her flesh. "You're coming with me, lady." She dragged Isobel through the door. "Brodie, come on, with us."

He didn't need telling twice, and skittered ahead. Belinda pulled the door shut behind them. Isobel reached for the handle to go back. As she touched it, all the lights came on inside. *Red Right Hand* blurted out, louder than ever.

"Come *on*, Isobel. What if it's *not* Richard?"

They'd only got to Belinda's front door when Ellis arrived at the gate, soaked and out of breath.

"Get inside, quickly. We need to regroup."

Chapter 58

Crockery rattled as Belinda made coffee. In the cosy, jasmine-scented confines of this cluttered living room, that charged, opaque atmosphere across the road seemed unreal, imagined. Yet Belinda had felt it, too.

"Forgive me, Isobel. I shouldn't have left like that. I need to be honest with you. I was afraid, and I still am. This situation's new to me." He pulled aside Belinda's gold voile curtain. From where she sat, Isobel saw lights blazing in her house with a wattage she'd never installed. Ellis' shoulders sagged. He dropped the curtain, turned to her. "Tell me everything. No holding back this time. Tell it all, so I can decide what help we need."

"I should move. Take the children. Find somewhere new."

"You're not *listening.* It's not the house, it's *you*. It's been you all along. You can't run from it. It will follow you."

"No."

"*Yes*." He gripped her elbows, shook her. "Wake up! You *know* what's going on here."

"No!"

"Things happened in your old house, didn't they? *Didn't* they?"

She nodded.

"And elsewhere? Tell me!"

"I'm making this happen? Putting my children in danger? Please, I don't understand."

"Come, sit down. What I need now, above all, is for you to stay calm, ok?" He knelt before her, held her hands. "No, Isobel, look at *me*. Whatever this is, is feeding off your emotional state, that's clear. Now calmly, I want you to tell me what's occurred away from the house. Try not to remember your feelings, only the events themselves. Can you do that? I need all the things you haven't told me. Everything."

So she told him about Zag's owner, how he'd been lovely at first but then sinister, how he'd appeared again when she felt threatened by the flasher. Between nervous sips of espresso, Belinda described the doctor's visits. Then Isobel told him Zag's owner seemed to drop out of her life only once the doctor started calling. The horror of that evening when she'd invited the doctor in, and something had seemed to invade her, rushed back, raw and menacing: "We didn't know." She couldn't muster the energy to speak above a whisper.

"It's not your fault, either of you." Ellis held his tiny cup out for more coffee. Belinda poured. He sat back on his haunches and drank slowly. "I'm going across there to try to calm things down for the moment. I want you two to stay here." He stood and handed Belinda his cup.

"No!" Isobel ran to the door. "You mustn't!"

"Isobel, I can't let you go back in there until we know more about what we're facing. Don't you see you're influencing it?"

"But you can't go alone."

Belinda placed the coffee pot on her messy desk. "I'll go with you."

"Neither of you are coming. And I'm not alone, Isobel." He dipped into his pocket and brought out a plain silver crucifix that filled his palm. He wrapped his hand around it. His knuckles whitened. "Won't be long."

He tried to smile, a ghastly twist of his mouth, and walked out.

Their silence reached after him into the relentless rain.

Isobel struggled for breath. "I can't let him."

"Are you mad? You heard what he said. Stay here. I mean it. You're going nowhere."

Belinda blocked the door, but Isobel had to stop him. What if it was only Richard, after all? She couldn't let Ellis drive him out. Couldn't lose him, not again. She wrenched Belinda aside, pushed through the door.

And now she was running as she did in her dreams, her front door receding as through the wrong end of a telescope, her peripheral vision blurred. She sensed red, in sharp focus, ahead. She knew what it was, somewhere deep within. She had to get to that red. She had to find Richard. She tensed against the arm that always grabbed - and ran straight into number sixty's closed door. She staggered back, surprised to feel rain. Where had the sun gone? She shook her head, cleared wet hair from her eyes, grabbed the door handle.

"Aargh!"

She snatched her hand from the white-hot metal.

The pain's not real. Ignore it.

She grabbed again, gasped, turned the handle and pushed. The door banged against the wall with a wrong, deadened thud. Blazing light. Blearing beat of music. In the dazzle, blue tendrils tentacled from the walls, groping for her.

"Lord have mercy. Christ have mercy. In the faith of Jesus Christ, we claim this place for God, Father -" His back to her, Ellis held the cross high before him.

"Stop! Ellis, please don't!"

He faced her, blinked as if rising from a dream himself. "Isobel, it's not what you think. Not anymore." He turned from her: "Deliver us, merciful Lord, from all evils past, present and to come!"

He wasn't going to stop. She flew at him, tried to snatch the crucifix. Searing heat burned into her flesh. He held the cross higher, eyes fixed on it, face etched with pain.

"Isobel, for the love of God and your family, you have to make this stop."

"I can't, I -"

And then a Plank in Reason broke

Enough. She needed Richard. She *wanted* him, and she would have him. No one was taking him from her, not this time. Charged ions prickled and pranced about her. Alive. Bright. Knowing. They invaded her mouth, her ears, they pierced her skin, burrowed deep, grew her taller. She stepped in front of Ellis, electricity surging through her, sparking from her fingers.

"Look at me." Her voice was not her own, and she was glad.

He kept his eyes on the crucifix, sweat pouring from his brow. Blue tendrils reached, lassoing for his neck.

"*Look* at me!" Deep, sonorous, unhuman.

"Lord have mercy. Christ have mercy." Something behind her dragged his attention against his will. His eyes widened. He ducked. The cuckoo clock caught him a glancing blow to the temple. He fell to his knees, but still held up the crucifix.

"Lord have Mercy. Christ have mercy."

"I don't want to hurt you, Ellis. Leave us be."

"In the faith of Jesus Christ we claim -"

"Leave us be!" Rasping. Death-drooling. She held her throat.

The TV blasted on, shrieked: "Leave us be!" Through grey-green static, a dark-distant figure emerged on the screen, strode toward them, small, looming larger, larger, until its hooded face filled the frame. And still it didn't stop. Skeletal, dead-green, its head broke through, plunged into the room's chaos. Mouth yawned open. "She's mine!" The dead scream penetrated her, wrapped around and grasped her in its stranglehold. It melded with her, inescapable.

She stared into Ellis' pleading, melted-steel eyes, into his unbearable pain, and sank to the floor, bleeding hope.

"Richard?" she whispered. "You have to make this stop. You brought this with you. You have to take it back." Ellis shuffled to her side, held her tight with one arm, and raised the crucifix in defence. “I’m sorry, Richard, I can’t save you. I love you. I always will. I love you, I love you. I love you…”

The TV snapped off. Nick Cave faded to nothing. Lights dimmed, guttered, snuffed. They sat in daytime-dark.

But still the air crackled.

Chapter 59

She drifts. All is silent in grey cloud. Damp fog fills her nostrils, ears, mouth. She is unempty, unfull. Wet air draws in, invades deep in her lungs. Chill-choke cough. It's in her head, this fog. Not fog, more solid, like spun sugar. And cloying, but not sweet. Not sweet at all.

She shakes her head, almost wakes.

It won't dislodge, it's staying put. Clinging. Clawing. Chiselling? Intent. Invidious. She rubs her forehead. It doesn't belong, this... this... , but it's inside her and it won't let her go. Her brain…

wrecked, solitary, here

…throbs, pulses with its own heartbeat. Pushing her, squeezing, expanding, filling. She's pressed against the fragile bone of her skull. It hurts, and it won't stop.

It has her.

Chapter 60

Isobel sits alone on a hard chair in a narrow grey corridor. Too much silence. An odd chemical smell. Her hands in her lap are strange, like small furless rodents huddling together for safety. She watches them for movement.

"Mrs Hickey?"

They cling to each other, poor things.

"Mrs Hickey?" A shadow blocks the overhead light. She looks up. "Good afternoon. I'm Adam Harris-Marsh. From the consulate? We met yesterday."

"Yes." The small creatures clutch tight together.

"May I join you?" The young man points to the next chair. She nods. "Is your sister not with you?"

This question is more challenging. The little animals twitch. "She - she stayed at the hotel - with the children."

"Ah, I see. And that's why I'm here? Yes, of course, it is." His hands appear in his lap next to hers. They hide, palms together, between his thighs. "Have you been waiting long?"

"I'm not sure."

"Have they said how long this will take? Have they explained what will happen?"

"I…"

"Not to worry. I'll nip and see if I can find out what's going on. Back in a jiffy, all right?" His white shirt sleeves are rolled to his elbows. His neat tie looks like it isn't used to being around his neck. He is earnest and he has kind eyes. "All right, Mrs Hickey?"

She can't remember what the question is. She nods. She watches him walk down the corridor and turn at the end. The skinny creatures pinch and claw. She watches them.

"Mrs Hickey, this is Inspector Almonte from Mossos d'Esquadra, the Barcelona police. He's investigating - He's trying to find out how…"

A tall man. Thin. Eagle nose. "How do you do. I am sorry you are made to wait. We are ready for you now. Please come with me." She doesn't want to. No, she doesn't want to go with them. She's fine right here. Here is good. She hides her hands between her legs. "Señora, if you please." He clicks his heels. She's only ever seen that in films.

"It's all right, Mrs Hickey, I'll come with you. Shall we?" She stands and the young Englishman takes her arm which is good because she finds her legs won't hold her. "Steady! All right? I've got you." He links her arm through his and squeezes it to his side. Is she trembling, or is it him? "Shall we go?"

The policeman makes what might be an impatient click in his throat and leads the way. The young man exerts pressure on her arm, gentle, pulls her forward. She wants to snatch it back and run the other way. She allows herself to be lead. A grey door with a small frosted window. She stops. If she goes through this door everything will change. There'll be no going back. It will all be true, and her future amputated.

The policeman turns the handle, and walks through as if this is any ordinary door. The sweet chemical smell almost finishes her. Adam draws a sharp breath, takes her free hand. She squeezes hard. The room is small and white. There's a metal trolley. No viewing window like she's seen on TV. Just a plain hospital trolley, nothing special, here in the room with them.

There's something on the trolley, a green sheet over it. She pulls back, feels for the door. This can't be right. This is not how she feels when he's around her. She doesn't want to see what's under that sheet. It's got nothing to do with her.

Adam crowds her into a corner, blocking her from the policeman. "Isobel? Look at me. That's it. Shall we try to get this over with? The police need the identification, and we need to get you all home. So let's do this, yes? Two minutes and it'll all be over, I promise." He takes both her hands and shakes them. "You've been so brave. Come on."

He leads her back to the trolley where the policeman stands.

"Are you prepared, señora?"

Adam grips her hand. She nods, swallows the bile rising in her throat.

A small man, in dark green overalls, appears and folds back the sheet.

The policeman watches her with greedy eyes. She looks at him and back at what's on the trolley. Adam coughs, looks away.

"Mrs Hickey?"

He wants her to confirm that this is Richard, but she's not sure. He's different. His skin is grey. His poor eyes bruised, sunken. Richard's eyes were laughing when she last saw him. He has a beautiful golden tan. This man is dead, for heaven's sake. They've got mixed up. This man isn't even wearing Richard's clothes. Where's his linen suit? Why has he got that thing on his head? Green, like the sheet and the orderly's overalls. A surgical drape wrapped around his face like a hijab, a tight hood, hiding his forehead, his sunlight hair. More ugly green cotton wadded and packed around his head. Is that supposed to be a pillow? The green makes him deathly pale. Dark stains have seeped into the wadding. He looks uncomfortable. She can't see his hair. She steps forward.

"*¡Dejalo!* No touch!" The inspector slaps down her reaching hand.

"Hey! You can't do that!" Adam puts himself between them.

She hugs her hand to her. Her legs give way. Adam holds her. Muttered Spanish. A chair is placed under her. The policeman kneels before her. "Forgive me, señora. I did not mean to distress you. If you please, can you confirm that this is your husband?" Her hands are balls of skin and gristle, white at the knuckles. She nods. "Say it, please."

"Yes, this is my husband. This is Richard Hickey."

Chapter 61

Isobel vacuumed the bedrooms, immersed in Melissa's mess, Ben's earthy boy-scent. How she'd missed them. How she wished them back safe with Ursula. But how could she push them away when they'd returned all brave and determined? She struggled downstairs with the full laundry basket. She had just enough time to get this load in before work, and then - stomach lurched - she missed her footing, grabbed the banister, dropped the basket. It thudded down the remaining stairs, shedding clothes, as she regained her balance. God, that was close. Ben could have carried this down for her before he went out. But she was so used to him not being around, she'd not thought to ask. She gathered the spilled load, trying to dismiss the impression that something had clutched her ankle to make her stumble. She tipped the clothes onto the kitchen floor and started sorting. Easier without Brodie trying to run off with her knickers. She straightened, rubbed the small of her back. Where was he, anyway?

He'd been in the garden, sunbathing in sudden autumn warmth. She'd closed the back door before she went upstairs, hadn't heard him bark to be let in. Must be enjoying himself.

She flicked the washing machine on, tidied breakfast things, sang along to *Mister Blue Sky* on the radio, whistling in the dark. Did she have time to throw a stew together, leave it in the slow-cooker? She glanced at the clock: god, no, she'd be late as it was. Got to get moving.

She reached to open the back door, but her hand leaked strength, seemed to pale and fade, as she tried to press the handle. She snatched it back. *Not this, not now.* She rubbed her hands together, tried again. This time, the door opened as normal.

She stepped outside: "Brodie, time to come in."

Nothing.

"Brodie!"

There was nowhere to hide in this tiny garden. Damn, he'd not gone behind the shed again? Just what she didn't need. She fetched treats and a torch, then crouched at the gap between shed and garden wall, and shone the light.

"Brodie?"

He'd have barked like crazy if he was stuck. Where the hell was he? She walked to the gate: the padlock was still secure. What about the gap underneath? Could he have squeezed through that? Surely not. But he wasn't in the garden, so he must have.

She tamped down simmering panic, and called to him over the fence. She scanned the field. No sign. How long had he been gone? She was upstairs for half an hour, or so. He could be anywhere by now.

She ran inside to the phone: “Blin, I’ve lost the dog.”

Chapter 62

Ellis asked to meet on neutral ground, again. She'd avoided speaking to him at the hastily-arranged Eucharist service. How could she have put into words what had passed between them? So she'd kept the children close, left the talking to Ursula.

Now she needed to get out on the street with the *Lost Dog* posters Ben had made. She never wanted to see Ellis again, in truth, but she owed him this last conversation.

They met at the new café in Leigh. Tea in flowery china pot, daintily decorated cup cakes. They were alone, apart from the waitress, engrossed with her mobile. This café, the deserted rainy street, more surreal than anything they'd experienced together. Nothing felt real, anymore. Even the kids' homecoming had provided only temporary respite from hopeless dislocation. Now she'd lost Brodie, she existed veiled from life, ungrounded, unattached. Unhinged.

"How have you all been since the service?"

She didn't need to ask how he was. Fresh blood seeped through the dressing on his temple. Surely that should have healed by now? He poured her tea with a marked tremor.

"I suppose you know why I wanted to meet?" She held his once-steady gaze. "I feel we need closure, both of us. I feared you'd never contact me, and I wouldn't blame you, so I'm reaching out to you." She bit into her cake. "We didn't get chance to talk at the end, did we? To work out what it was we went through? It all happened so fast. Would it help to discuss it?"

She shook her head.

"I can understand your reluctance, but I want to make sure you see the full picture, how this whole experience has affected you."

What does he know about it? Hasn't he meddled enough?

"I've watched you, Isobel, over these weeks I've had the privilege to know you. Hard to believe it *is* only a few weeks, isn't it?" The hope in his eyes, as he sought a response, almost hurt her. "Feels like a lifetime." He said this more to himself than to her. "I've talked with Belinda and Ursula. They tell me you're doing better, that you're moving on. Would you agree?"

Where's all this leading? She could no longer look him in the eye: all she saw was the pain she'd inflicted that day.

"I remember you saying you'd got Richard's bird-watching gear out because - because that man got you interested again. Yes?" She stared at her plate. "And you decided to stop wearing your wedding ring. Wasn't that after a conversation with him, too? You've given away most of

Richard's possessions now, his clothes, his music. The hostel was grateful, by the way." He drank, watched her over the rim of his cup. "What prompted you to part with them?"

"What d'you want me to say?"

"It's not a test. What I'm trying to get at is this experience, it's helped you let go of the past, yes? You're beginning to move on with your life, to rise from your mourning."

Is he so *deluded?*

Her mourning, her loss, was part of her, had shaped her. Just like this tightly-curled parasite nestled inside her, armoured, grey as a wood louse, spikes sheathed, listening, biding. A sharp pain beneath her sternum reminded her it slept restless, ready to fog-wrap and bring her down.

Ellis wasn't finished. "It seems to me this man at the Flash, this presence, had a positive effect. Watching over you, nudging you toward acceptance?" He sat back, pathetic, clearly desperate not to acknowledge what they both knew happened that last day. "Does none of this chime with you?"

"I haven't thought of it like that, no."

He reached across, took her hand. "But do you think you might begin to see it that way?"

Gently, she pulled away. "Why's this so important to you?"

"I want you to heal. I want you to move forward, not cling to the past. I want you to find peace."

She sipped her tea. "That's sweet of you."

"Damn it, Isobel, I'm not trying to be sweet. You can be so obtuse, do you know that? Tell me you'll think about what I've said."

She had more to worry about than massaging his ego.

"I know you don't believe in Our Lord."

Oh, here we go.

"And possibly you never will, but I have a book I feel can speak to you." He reached into his pocket, pulled out a tattered paperback. CS Lewis. "I hope it will help you make sense of your loss. He says grief is part of our experience of love. We can't have one without the other. Do you see?"

She took the book. "Thank you."

"I'm not reaching you, am I? I've failed you."

She pushed her cup away, and picked up her bag. "Don't worry about me, Ellis. You did your best. No one could have done more."

"But it wasn't enough."

What could she say?

She roamed the town centre, handing out a hundred leaflets to anyone who'd accept one, then walked the three miles home, looking in every garden, down every drive and passageway. She stopped to talk to every dog walker, describing Brodie, asking for sightings, giving her mobile number. She had no umbrella. Rain dripped from her dipped head.

It wasn't enough. Poor Ellis.

Horn-blare.

"Dozy mare!"

She staggered back. Pushed wet hair from her face, raised an apologetic hand. Plodded on.

Bodden Street was quiet. She walked past the Hares' house, immune to vindictive eyes. Fiddled with her keys, hands slippery, and pushed open the door. No mad tail-wagging. No needy whining. The house had never felt so empty.

She shambled into the kitchen. The children would need to eat, even if she didn't. She checked in the fridge for the makings of a meal. Scrabble letters messed up, mixed in with postcards, shopping vouchers, all the other crap that adorned her fridge. But no cryptic words. She sighed. Maybe it *was* ending. Then she noticed a couple of adjoining letters peeping out from under the milkman's invoice: *EN.*

She didn't want to, she really didn't, but she lifted the invoice: *LISTEN.*

Chapter 63

Toby invited himself for lunch. He phoned at ten, wanting to arrive at noon.

"It'll be lovely to catch up. Only it'll just be soup and sandwiches. If you can come later in the week, give me chance to shop, I can feed you properly."

"What an ungallant wretch you must think me to foist myself upon you, virtually unannounced, like this."

"Don't be daft. You're welcome always. You know that."

"Will the sprogs be around?"

"Both out, as usual."

"Well, although I'm keen to see them, and it's been too long, that's perhaps no bad thing."

Ice in her stomach's pit. "Why?"

"Don't be alarmed, my love, but I don't want to do this over the phone. See you shortly. Ciao for now."

She opened the door bang on twelve. He was walking through the gate, punctual as ever. They laughed, and hugged.

"You know me too well, Isobel Hickey." He gazed up at her. "My God, you're beautiful."

"Flatterer. And get you, in your pin-stripe suit."

He did a theatrical, surprisingly Gene Kelly-esque twirl.

She laughed. "Are you ready to eat?"

"Something smells divine."

"Afraid it's just tomato soup, bit of basil, garlic bread. Come through."

He looked around the kitchen. "No Brodie?"

She told him, fighting back the panic that rose when she thought of her Brodie lost and alone. It had been a week now.

"Have you tried searching online?"

"The kids are on it. But there have been travellers in the area. I'm beginning to think they took him. If he'd wandered off on his own, he'd have come home by now."

"My love, I'm so sorry."

"Can we talk about something else?"

Obediently, Toby delivered bullet points of his life since they'd last met. He'd been on a blind date. This revelation had Isobel spluttering into her soup. A man less likely to blind-date, you could not meet. He made her laugh with his punctilious account of exactly why it hadn't worked out.

He seemed to know about the children leaving, and coming back. If he knew the reason, he didn't let on.

He mopped up the last traces of soup, pushed his bowl away, and patted his round belly.

"Just what the doctor ordered."

She couldn't return his smile, and gathered up the dishes to cover her distress. "Coffee?"

He placed a hand on hers. "Can that wait, do you think? You're probably wondering why I so rudely insisted on coming today." He fumbled in his inside pocket, produced an envelope. "I wanted to hand this to you in person. I've let you down, Isobel. I've let you down badly."

She kept her eye on the envelope. "What d'you mean?"

"This is from Richard. It was with his papers, his will and other documents he lodged with us."

She drew back her hand. "What is it?"

"A personal letter, nothing to do with the estate as such. Have no fear, my love. This isn't about finances or property. We settled all that when you moved in here. No more unpleasant surprises on that front. This is simply a letter. He wanted you to have it in the event of his death." Still, he held on to the envelope. "I'm ashamed I've fallen short of his expectations. He trusted me. I'm so sorry."

"But where was it?" She daren't ask what she really wanted to know: *what's in it?*

"The safe where we keep our clients' wills. We're required to keep them in a secure place, you understand. That safe had become outmoded, and we've just replaced it. When we cleared the old one, we found this." He looked at the letter in his hand. "I'm mortified. I've failed you both. When I ordered up his documents after he died, it wasn't on the checklist. An oversight. And I, fool that I am, had clean forgotten about it. It seems it was caught on the inside rim, hidden under a stack of another client's documents. That's why the… do you see?" He held it out to her. One corner was chewed. “I don’t think the contents will be damaged. I sincerely hope not.”

She took it from him. Large and white with a typed reference number, it read: “To be given to Isobel Hickey in the event of the death of Richard Hickey.”

“I shan’t blame you if you never want to set eyes on me again after this. I’ll go now, and let you…”

He gestured to the envelope.

She held a letter from Richard. Richard’s words were here in her hand. Toby was saying something. She stroked the envelope.

The front door closed softly.

Richard. Her idea of him had become so distorted over the past months it seemed impossible he could ever have done something so mundane as write a letter. She carried it into the living room, holding it at arm’s length, as if it might explode in her hand. She looked at the wall that no longer displayed his face. For the first time in weeks, she could picture him. His wide amused eyes, tilted smile, teasing her.

Her hands began to shake. She held a letter from a ghost.

She took it back to the kitchen, put it on the table. After everything, after all he’d put her through, now he sent a letter. The bastard had been driving her mad all summer when he could simply have done this all along.

Don’t be foolish. This letter came from the solicitor’s office. Toby, solid, real Toby, had put it into her hand. It was nothing to do with this summer.

She folded her arms. It lay there, ordinary, waiting. The fridge ticked. The distant donkey brayed, a dog barked. If she opened the letter, this might all end. She'd be able to rest, and she so wanted to sleep through the night. She could let go, float away, leave it all behind.

But why would she want to do that?

She didn't want to let him go. She wouldn't let him go. If she opened that letter, she'd hear Richard. And that might be the last of him.

Open the damn letter.

She ripped the envelope. Inside was another, expensive, pale blue. Richard's large, black handwriting: "My Isobel".

She opened this one carefully. Two sheets of matching notepaper, handwritten, with the letterhead she'd seen before. She pictured him, seated at the bureau in his study, with newly-acquired stationery and that fountain pen, imagining himself lord of the manor.

She sat. A block of hurried scrawl scattered about with shouty capitals. She heard Richard's voice racing, breathless:

"Isobel,

Now I sit down to write this I feel a bit daft, melodramatic. But it's been on my mind, stressing me, so here goes. We both know this won't end well for me. I try to control this craziness, but it's so hard. Here's the thing. I want you to know that inside, deep down, I'm still here, still caring, still clinging on, because my Bel, my beautiful, dutiful, noble Bel, I LOVE YOU. There, that's what I wanted to say. I LOVE YOU. I always have. I always will, through all eternity. I'm afraid the end might be sudden and I won't have time to tell you I LOVE YOU. If it's bad, the end, if it's hard for you, I'm sorry. Christ, I only hope I don't drag you down with me. If it's messy, painful, please, please remember my head is more than I can stand sometimes (see poem enclosed). Try to understand and forgive me. But most important, never, never forget that I LOVE YOU. I know you're strong. I know you'll cope. I know you can be happy again. You have so much love, and talent, and kindness, and beauty. Use them! After me, BE HAPPY. That's what I wanted to tell you more than anything. BE HAPPY. There, I've said it, and I feel better already.

BE HAPPY, my Bel.

My undying love, always and forever,

Richard."

She placed the letter on the table, and smoothed it. She put a finger to her lips, kissed it and pressed the kiss on his name. She went to the fridge, pushed aside appointment cards and, from the scattered scrabble, created her own message: *I LOVE YOU TOO.*

She stood back and gazed at it.

Hang on. What about the second page?

She picked up the letter. The second sheet was arranged in verse.

When did he start writing poetry?

There'd been none amongst his papers, not that she'd found so far. Only those books. Then the lines hit her with a force of recognition like a punch in the mouth. Richard's handwriting, but not his words. The dashes, the strange, airy spaces, they belonged to Emily Dickinson and they'd echoed in her head for months now, ricocheting back and forth, tormenting her at night, in a voice she didn't want to know...

I felt a Funeral, in my Brain

A voice that wasn't Richard's.

Chapter 64

Isobel walked up Sandy Lane, scanning gardens, looking through windows, checking posters were still on lampposts. She crossed the main road, entered the gates, then on past the war memorial and around the back of the little church to an area hidden from the road. Belinda had mentioned Greyfriars Bobby. Crazy to think Brodie would be here, guarding his dead master's grave, but worth checking, surely, and anyway Isobel had unfinished business.

The churchyard wasn't how she remembered. Had she taken a wrong turn? She searched the ground, a strange tugging sensation wanting her to look away.

There it was, hemmed in, surrounded by newer stones, more recent disasters.

Life goes on. And out.

Some plots were overgrown, adorned with dead flowers, but not his. The polished granite shone as if newly washed, and in a little stone flute, a single red rose, fresh and dewy.

Ursula.

Birdsong, and children singing sweetly in the school next door.

She'd passed the churchyard most days of the last two years but had never once returned to this spot, only round the corner from Bodden Street. It had become a beacon, a fixed point she preferred to leave undisturbed. Often, she'd drawn comfort from eternal flames on graves near the road as she walked by with the dog.

She sighed, fought back tears: *Oh god, Brodie, where are you?*

This not-knowing was killing her. Had someone taken him in, were they caring for him? Or was he alone, afraid, needing her, searching, waiting for her to come? Maybe he was dead, knocked over by a car, thrown over some hedge. She'd covered every inch of the Flash and surrounding fields over the past days, shouting herself hoarse. All the dog-walkers knew to watch out for him. A woman down the road had told Ben she'd heard a dog whimpering out the back, so they'd searched every shed and garage they could get access to. Twice.

She was beginning to believe they'd never find him. She was beginning to believe he was gone, and she could feel something congealing inside her. It felt like something essential.

She knelt heavily on the cold grass before the small flat slab. What if he never came back? What if they never found out what had happened to him? Could she survive that? She doubted it.

Wrecked, solitary, here...

She emerged from bleak reverie, hunched, cold, last night's rain soaking through her jeans. She straightened her back. Neck and shoulders creaked their complaints. She picked needlessly at the neatly-trimmed grass along the slab's edges.

"Good morning."

She craned her neck. An older man, well in his eighties. He read the stone over her shoulder.

"He was young. Sad, that. You didn't have much time, the pair of you."

She should have stood for him but somehow the moment passed, and anyway, she probably couldn't. Not just now.

"I wondered when we'd finally meet you. I'm pleased you've managed it, love. Some never do, and that's a fact. That's me and Connie there, see? I've just brought her chrysanths. The yellow ones. Connie loves her chrysanths. Always did."

Isobel doubted that.

"Anyway, lovie, it's grand to meet you. I'm Clive."

He held out his soft-wrinkled hand. She twisted awkwardly to shake it. "Isobel."

"Beautiful name for a beautiful lady. I hope to see you again, Isobel."

He touched his hand to his head to tip a cap he wasn't wearing, and shuffled away, weaving through the stones, pausing every now and then as if to chat with old friends. Did that make her want to smile, or scream?

She stared at the slab, forcing herself not to look away.

He was under there.

"I'm not going, Ursula. I don't know where he is, but he's definitely not *there*."

"Some would say that's the only place he definitely *is*. And what about the children? They need to visit. It'll help."

"You take them if you think it's so important."

He was under there. In a heavy wooden casket just large enough for a pair of his walking boots. There'd been a polished brass plate with his name and dates. She pushed from her mind an image of what it might look like now. They'd followed the solemn curate who carried it from the vestry to this spot on a warm, windy July morning, two years ago. They'd watched it placed in the shallow hole. Then they'd stepped forward in turn and dropped a white rose on the lid. She'd refused the handful of earth. She couldn't do that.

She'd come back alone the next day to find the gravedigger had removed the roses before filling in the hole. He'd arranged them carefully on the freshly-dug earth. Such a simple, kind gesture had thrown her into a frenzy of anger. She'd started digging with her bare hands until someone rushed to restrain her. She'd kicked up a huge fuss. When she calmed down, she insisted on a meeting in that officious way she used to have. The poor gravedigger's bewildered face when she demanded disciplinary action and retraining in bereavement awareness. Ursula had intervened to put a stop to her nonsense, thank goodness.

Ever since, Ursula had been the one who came to remember and care.

It should have been her.

She traced his name with her finger. "I loved you. Why are you doing this to me?"

She leaned forward to touch her cheek to the cold stone, then tilted her head to the sky. Red and gold leaves of the shading cherry tree shimmered against infinite blue.

"That's not a bad view you've got there, mister."

She stayed like that a long time. Where else would she want to be?

Chapter 65

They strolled about la Boqueria market. Colourful, deliciously-scented fruits dazzled like the sun while the indoor cool stroked away the street's hot glare. Richard bought a bagful of pomegranates. Melissa spent too much of her pocket money on neon-coloured sweets. Ben kept picking up strange-looking fruit and sniffing, before replacing it with disdain. Back out in the relentless heat, they wandered on up La Rambla towards Placa de Catalunya. They were ready for lunch. Melissa spotted a café on the left with a hand-written sign in the window: "Tortillas". She would eat only tortillas, potato omelettes, as she called them.

If that sign hadn't been there…

"I'll check it out." Richard nipped inside. He emerged from the deep shade a moment later. "We're in business. Potato omelettes all round." Ben groaned. "Let's sit out here. Bit dim in there."

They huddled about a small round table crammed, with several others, on the pavement in front of the café, in the way of passing tourists, ramblistas and pickpockets. Isobel placed her bag firmly in her lap. When she'd asked around her friends about Barcelona, several had warned against pickpockets on La Rambla (or was it Las Ramblas? She wasn't sure). But she loved it: the markets, the street-sellers and entertainers, all these people. Traffic roared in two streams separated by a central tree-lined promenade, but the chatter of voices was nearly as loud. People strolled along, taking in the sights, bargaining for tat with traders, relaxing. Incredible that such a bustling place could feel so chilled. Movement above the tree tops, high in a building across the street, caught her eye. A woman, dressed in black, had opened a shutter and was shaking out a bright red cloth. They must be apartments. She'd assumed they would all be hotels above the shops. What must it be like to live here? Most of the shutters were closed against the afternoon heat. Washing hung on a couple of wrought-iron balconies, splashes of colour in the sun-bleached scene.

A canvas canopy sheltered their table from the intense sun. It was good to sit in its shade a while. She'd feared, when they arrived four days ago, she'd made a mistake. She couldn't cope with this heat. They should have come later in the year. But then the kids would have missed school, and this was Ben's GCSE year coming up. Also, it was supposed be her birthday treat. Forty. She'd argued it was Richard's fortieth celebration, too, so they could have come earlier, in February. But he had a big target to hit in spring, so here they were, in the middle of July.

Despite the heat, she was having a ball. She loved the crazy Gaudi architecture, her main reason for choosing Barcelona. They'd visited Gaudi's yet-to-be-finished Sagrada Familia yesterday. In the glorious forest interior, they'd watched as a great gnarly capital was raised into place atop a huge tree-like column. Stained-glass colours painted patterns on white stone within. That bold, clear red moved her to tears, the way it dripped onto pale surfaces. She wasn't religious, but she saw Gaudi's vision was genius.

The others were enjoying themselves, too. For Ben, they'd done the FC Barcelona tour. He'd bought his Barca strip, leaving himself skint, and was now content to be dragged around the Picasso and Miro galleries Melissa was avid for. She loved her art. Isobel swelled with surprised pride that her thirteen-year-old could identify Picassos without reading the cards beside them. Richard was all over the shopping, as ever. He'd foregone Picasso for the Passeig de Gracia, and met them back at the hotel, laden with the usual designer bags. He'd probably maxed out the credit card already. But if she challenged him, he'd say it was only money. They all enjoyed the beach, a few minutes' walk from the city centre. They would definitely be coming again.

Tortillas arrived along with a bottle of local cava.

"Rich, it's the middle of the day."

"We're on holiday."

Ben held out a glass. "Can I have some?"

"Why not?"

"He's fifteen."

"Let him have some, Bel. Just half a glass. Both of them. We're celebrating."

"Don't want any. Can I have a coke?"

"Course you can, Mellymoo."

He attracted the waiter's attention. "Two cokes, please."

"You said I could have wine."

"Your Mum says no. And what your Mum says goes."

Ben muttered under his breath. Melissa, next to him, laughed. Isobel thought he'd said: "Grow a pair."

She let it lie.

The food was good, cava great, kids talkative and funny. She was happy.

For the last time.

They sat watching the world go by.

"There's a Santander across the road, see? I'll nip in now for some cash, shall I?

"We're ok for cash, aren't we? Get it later."

But Richard was already walking away. "No time like the present. Won't be long."

Ben stood. "I'll come with you."

"I'll only be a sec. Keep an eye on your Mum. You know what she's like when she's had a drink."

He winked at the kids. They laughed. He darted out into the traffic, over to the central promenade where she lost sight of him among trees and people.

He'd been gone no more than a couple of minutes when bangs ricocheted off the walls. Like a car backfiring, but three - four - five in quick succession.

"Fucking hell!" Ben was on his feet.

An old lady, walking by, stopped, held her hand to her heart.

A young man dropped to the pavement, pulling his girlfriend down with him.

"Mum?" Melissa grabbed her arm.

Staff from the café ran into the street. More loud cracks.

What the hell?

Isobel jumped up, pulled Melissa to her.

One of the waiters waved her to get down. He dropped to his knees behind a table. "¡Abajo! ¡Abajo! Shooting!"

"Mummy, what's happening?"

"Get under the table, Lissa. Ben, you too." More bangs. This time it did sound like gunshots. She pushed Melissa to the floor. The waiter put a protective arm about her. "Ben, get under the table. Now!"

Ben glared at her, scared but defiant.

"Do it!"

Clatter of percussive claps. He dropped down next to Melissa. "Mum, get down. It's terrorists!"

Terrorists?

She looked around wildly. That table wouldn't protect them. Where could she take the kids?

Think.

Sudden sirens. Blue lights. Street empty, but for that flashing blue.

Where did all the people go?

Police cars stopped across the road outside the bank. Outside Santander where Richard had gone.

No.

She started running.

"Señora, acá. They're shooting. Not safe!" The waiter sounded scared.

Ben caught up with her, grabbed her arm. He was strong. "Mum! What are you doing?"

"Stay with your sister. Keep her there, d'you hear me?" His eyes were pure panic. She fought to make her voice calm. "It's ok, love. I'm going to get your Dad. Stay with Lissa. Take her in the café. Look after her for me."

He seemed to nod. She pulled away, and ran across that endless promenade. The sirens had stopped. Quiet. Still. No cars, except police barricading the bank. No people. Just her, and her gasping breath, running to the bank. Her peripheral vision blurred.

No way was she going to faint.

She staggered on. The Santander logo blazed red in sharp focus. She had to get there. She had to find Richard.

Something hooked about her waist, swung her around. "¡Tranquila! ¡Tranquila. Es peligroso!" A policeman.

More gunshots. Rapid. Like a machine gun.

She hit out. The stubble on his face grazed her hand. He pulled her to the ground and covered her head with his free arm. Smell of sweat.

"Let me go! Richard! Let go, you bastard!"

She wriggled, scratched, kicked. Her knee made contact with his groin. She scrambled to her feet. Ran again. Straight into another fucking policeman.

"Por favor. My husband's in there. He's in the bank. Richard! He's in the bank." He held her, arms pinned to her sides. Her panic fizzed: "Marido. Banco. English. Inglés! Please help me. Socorro!"

"¡Quédate allé!"

She screamed at him: "I don't understand. Por favor. Speak English. Inglés. What's happening? Where's Richard?"

The officer held on to her. She kicked him. Another arrived, and held her, too. Then Ben was there, shouting at the policemen, pushing them.

"Get off her! Leave her alone! Leave my Mum alone!"

"¡Abajo! ¡Ahora!" They put him on the ground. "Las manos - atras." They wrenched his arms behind his back. The handcuffs were on him in a moment. "¡Tranquilo!"

"What are you doing? That's my son. You're hurting him. He's just a boy. English. Somos ingleses."

"Mummy! Mummy!"

"¡Aios mio! ¡Saquenlos de aquí!

"Melissa! Por favor! Don't hurt her!"

One of them picked up Melissa, who seemed too stunned to protest, and ran with her, crouched, to a nearby police car. Isobel was dragged after them. The policemen bundled them inside the car, and left. She tried the door. Locked. She banged on the window.

"Where's Ben? Where's my son?"

There he was! Only metres from them. An officer pulled him to his feet, hustled him roughly into a van close to them.

She slammed the window. "Ben!"

So many policemen, all crouched behind cars parked in a semi-circle around the bank.

Melissa tugged her tee-shirt. "Where's Daddy?"

"I'm not sure, sweetie."

Isobel put an arm around her, yanked the door handle again. Still it wouldn't open. She hammered on the window with her fist.

"Hey! Let me out! Let me out, you bastards!"

An officer, crouched behind one of the barricading cars, glared at her over his shoulder. He put a finger to his lips: *Shush.* Then he held up something for her to see. Not threatening, but to show her what was happening. It was a gun. A big gun.

He turned from her, and pointed it at the bank.

She punched her pillow. She mustn't look at the clock: that way time dragged. Still dark outside. She played it over and over. Boqueria: if they'd just stayed there five minutes longer. Tortillas: if Melissa hadn't spied that crappy little sign. Santander: if Richard hadn't spent up earlier. If, if, if. When she closed her eyes, she saw red and flashing blue, heard sirens, stuttering shots. She smelt hot dry pavement, as if her face was still pressed against it.

She flung back the duvet and got up. Too early, but she couldn't bear lying there. She opened the window. A faint autumnal scent of decay came in with the breeze. How cold would it have been out there in the night? She shrugged on the ratty dressing gown. Eau de Brodie. She'd been going to wash it, but couldn't now.

Chapter 66

She pulled up outside the house. Joe Jessop stood on his doorstep.

"Isobel, have you got a minute?"

What's Melissa been up to now?

"Sure." She grabbed her handbag and locked the car. "Everything ok?"

"No, I'm sorry, love, I have to show you, I wish I didn't but I couldn't just…could I?"

"Joe, are you all right?"

"In here. Come in."

He steered her into his front room, held her elbow as if he expected her to drop. "I'm sorry."

On the worn settee lay a little bundle wrapped in a tartan rug. She glanced back at Joe. He didn't meet her eye. She approached the bundle, the Border Terrier sized bundle.

"Joe, tell me it isn't. Please, it isn't, is it?"

He coughed. "I'm so sorry, love."

She did drop to her knees before the settee.

"Brodie?" She reached out and placed her hand on it. So slight, so still. And, even through the blanket, cold. "Where did you find him?"

"I couldn't leave him there like that. Thought I'd best bring him in. Hope I did the right thing. Wrapped him, nice and gentle, like."

"Run over? Where was he?"

Joe still couldn't meet her eye. He reddened. "On your front wall."

"Front wall?" She stroked the thing under the blanket. It didn't wriggle for a tickle, didn't whinny with pleasure, didn't thump its tail or lick her hand. Didn't move at all. She untucked the blanket.

"Wait up, Isobel. I should tell you. His neck's been broken." She snatched her hand back. "Clean, like. He wouldn't have suffered."

"Broken? Oh, my little Brodie. He was always running in the road. I should have trained him."

Joe shrugged. "Don't think he was knocked down. Looks deliberate to me, what with where he was left. And the state he's in."

She couldn't keep up. Was he saying someone *killed* her Brodie? She pulled away the blanket.

Stench of shit and vomit billowed at her. Both were caked about his snarling mouth and dull, matted fur. His eyes stared open but clouded, like the little girl's. His ears flat, unhearing. Tail inert.

It had only been a week but he seemed smaller, shrunken. His little head lolled back at an impossible angle.

"No, please no. Brodie?" She stroked him, shook him. "Come on, little one, wake up now. I'm here. I've got you." She picked him up, cradled him, but he was cold, empty. Gone. "No, no, no…"

"I'll get Belinda. Or, or Maud, or ... Back in a sec."

She buried her face in Brodie's poor, violated neck.

She got back in the car to fetch Melissa from Bernadette's. She couldn't tell her over the phone. Ben had bathed the tiny abused body, so gently it broke her heart. Now he sat on the living room floor, in front of the fire, Brodie swaddled in a towel on his knee. He refused to give him up, whispered endearments through dripping tears. Belinda would have gone for Melissa, but Isobel couldn't bear to watch Ben a moment longer.

"You go, Iz. I'll sit with him."

Ben had found a rope burn on Brodie's neck, as if he'd struggled against a cruel tether. Who could have done this to him, to them? She'd report it to the police. She'd put up a reward for information. She'd find them. And when she did...

She gripped the steering wheel; invading dream-fog uncurled, welled up, threatening to unravel her. That voice, spiky, unhuman, no longer hiding:

And I dropped down and down - and hit a World at every plunge

Hands hot. Burning heat spread to cool plastic, building, building - She wrenched away, rubbed her palms: *What the hell was that?*

She glanced at the ruffled, muddy rug on the back seat, breathed in the dog scent.

She switched on the engine, pulled out and set off down the street. Yvonne and Carl Hare stood outside their house, watching her. She slowed. As she passed, Carl raised his chin and let out a plaintive howl, like a dog in pain. Yvonne nudged him, said something behind her hand and smirked at her.

That sealed it.

Half an hour later, Isobel turned back onto Bodden Street. She glanced at Melissa in the passenger seat. She hadn't cried yet, but it wouldn't be long. Isobel had hoped never to break such news to her daughter again. Someone should pay for that alone. And they would. She could see the horror sinking in as emotions swept across that sweet face. Melissa stared sightlessly at mayhem in the road ahead.

What on earth...? Isobel stopped the car

She got out and took a moment to absorb the bizarre scene before her. Ben had Carl Hare on the ground, kicking him. Looked like he was aiming for the head, but the little scrote had curled into a tight ball, shielding his skull with his arms. Yvonne had Belinda in a head-lock, a rope of soft blonde hair wrapped around her meaty paw. Belinda was screaming, more in rage than pain, as she squirmed to get loose. Ricky, the ex-con boyfriend, stood at the Hares' door, laughing. As Isobel took all this in, Joe Jessop burst from his gate and thundered into the fray. His energy infused her with action:

"Ben, stop that!"

Joe reached Yvonne, grabbed her arm. Isobel yanked Ben by his collar. He whirled at her, fists raised, grit glistening in an oozing graze on his brow. She flinched.

"Shit, Mum. What're you playing at? Get back." He turned on his victim: "I'm going to fucking kill you." He leapt on the motionless heap.

"Ben, enough!" But she didn't try again to stop him. He seized the kid's ears, banged his head against the tarmac with a satisfying smack.

Then Joe Jessop dragged him off. Isobel turned to Belinda. Ricky was hauling Yvonne by the elbow, none too gently, both of them shouting insults at the street. He shoved her inside the house, slammed the door behind them. Belinda looked ready to faint. Isobel ran to her, offered a steadying arm: "You ok? What happened?"

Belinda sobbed: "She's an animal."

"She's gone. Come inside, hon."

Isobel glanced back. Ben stood eyeball to eyeball with Joe, flexing his fists. Beyond them, her Micra blocked the road. Melissa sat inside it, still staring vacantly. Carl Hare was picking himself up, keeping his eyes on Ben.

She took Belinda in the house. "Sit."

The towel-wrapped bundle lay in the armchair, carefully placed in his favourite spot.

She reached in the fridge for wine, poured a glass: "Drink."

Belinda swigged it in too few draughts. "That little shit started taunting Ben. He came right up to the window, cheeky sod, saw him crying with Brodie. So Ben goes out and tackles him. I tried to stop them, but that bitch grabbed me, choked me. Iz, she tried to kill me."

Isobel hugged her. "My poor love. You were brave to get involved. Thank you."

"Didn't need any help, did he?"

"Didn't look like it to me."

Belinda laughed, feebly. "God, those Hares are a nightmare. They need sorting out."

Ben burst in, followed closely by Joe Jessop. "He's a dead man."

"Ben -"

"They killed Brodie. He told me. Said his fat twat of a mother had him tied up in their shed all the time. The bastards didn't even feed him." He punched the wall. "Aargh!" Dropped to his knees and sobbed.

Isobel hadn't seen Melissa follow them in. Now she knelt beside her brother, rubbed his back. Then she lowered her head to his and cried with him.

They buried Brodie the next day in the back garden, under the flowering currant. Now she could never leave Bodden Street.

Chapter 67

Belinda had tried to persuade her to take time off work, but what would be the point?

Sickly-sweet death filled the unventilated room. The poor wasted body under its thin sheet clung to life stubbornly, but the man inside had slipped away hours ago. Wilfred had smiled his thanks, squeezed her hand feebly, and given himself up. Isobel's bedside vigil was now for the absent family's sake alone.

The grandson was due to arrive in an hour or so. She checked the pulse, smoothed the sparse hair, straightened the sheet across the valiantly rising chest. Nothing to do now but wait. She drew the chair closer to the bed so she could reach the parchment-dry hand without stretching, then rested her head against the high chair-back, closed her eyes.

She walks possessed, cold rising through feet, chilling legs then belly to nestle around her beatless heart.

She's not alone. Cloud-grey, unsoft, mucous-sticky, spiked with intent, it slinks inside her. Nudges, squeezes, jostles, swells. She's pressed against cranium's porcelain curves, and still she plods, her footsteps unsettling soundless ground, her body unwieldy, careering.

She staggers in numb-dark, eyes seeking light comfort; mind, what scrap remains in that skull's tight corner, knowing there is none.

Cruel-cold, sound-starved, dead-dark.

She walks in void, out of context, out of time.

And stops outside a gate.

Knocking.

beating beating

"You can't come in, you don't belong. Leave me alone."

Isobel woke with a start. Feverish. A dream. Just another stupid dream.

Hammering now. Flat of a big hand on her front door. She sprang out of bed. Ben ran ahead of her down the stairs.

"Stay there, Mum."

He opened the door and stood back. "It's the police."

Points of light pierce darkness, rip and tear, but still she cannot see. Air, solid as soft flesh, sliced by light. Sparkles dance about her: *look here, no here, too late.* She whirls as tricksy light tickles and teases. She whirls and jabs. Solid light spears from her fingertips. She whirls and jabs and stabs. Echoes bounce and prance, deceiving. Ululating voices conflict, compete, conjoin in terror.

Metallic, glooping steam floods her nostrils. She tastes. Gags.

Her hands slip and slime.

She'd been seen, they said, standing outside the house the night it happened. At the exact time it happened, she was seen standing at the gate, staring intently, angrily, at the front door while behind it…

"It's complete nonsense and they know it, Isobel. Do not worry about this, my love. It will all go away. They have absolutely nothing. Your manager's confirmed you were in work at that time, as have your colleagues. You were nursing a dying man, for God's sake! How they had the temerity to question you is beyond me. It's utter tosh." Toby, pink, perspiring, paced the living room watched by Ursula and Belinda. "As if you haven't suffered enough. If you hear any more about this, and I mean phone call, email, *anything*, you're to tell me *immediately*. I'll wipe the thrice-damned floor with them."

He was sweet.

She wandered into the kitchen, away from all the outrage, picked up a tea towel and started to dry the pots. She gazed out at the little cross the kids had made, at the cut flowers already fading, ruffling in the breeze.

So who had seen her?

No, she didn't want to know. Safer that way.

Chapter 68

Belinda watched her over chunky red knitting. They were always watching her now, Belinda, Ursula, the kids. Eyes forever following her.

Belinda fiddled cluelessly with the wool: "Did you hear they've arrested that Ricky? I knew it had to be him. Remember the broken arm?"

Isobel looked up from her own, neater stitches. *Is she serious? She knows who broke Yvonne's arm.*

Belinda went on: "They had young Carl in yesterday. Can you imagine? Her own son! But they're saying all the doors were locked, no sign of a break-in, so they're bound to suspect the family, I guess. Damn, I've dropped another."

"Give it here."

"What's this going to be, anyway?"

Isobel straightened her stitches, retrieved the lost one, handed it back. "That's entirely up to you."

"Scarf?"

"It certainly has that potential."

"Sarky cat." Belinda chucked the knitting to the floor beside her. "I can't be arsed with this, Iz. Not with everything that's going on. How can you concentrate on knitting, for heaven's sake?"

Isobel needed something to focus on, to keep her mind from wandering, because when it wandered... She put her needles aside. "Shall I stick the kettle on, then?"

Belinda followed her into the kitchen. "No wonder the police were so cagey with you. It's like something out of a horror. Now they're saying -"

"Who's this *they*? The police?"

"No. You know, they, people, word on the street etcetera. They're saying -" Isobel shot her a look "- ok, Phyllis told me -"

"Oh, right. *Phyllis*."

"She's seriously shaken up, Iz. It's horrible. Not the sort of thing an old lady needs to know."

"And yet you insisted she tell you." She handed Belinda a coffee.

"She wanted to, she needed to tell me. I was doing her a favour listening to that stuff. It's just too awful."

Isobel heard the catch in her voice. Sweat prickled from her pores, trickled down her back. "Who told her?"

"Don't you want to know what she said?"

"Who told her?"

"She got it from a woman on Sandy Lane who knows one of the forensic guys who went in. D'you want to hear this, or not?"

No, she really didn't.

"It was carnage. Blood everywhere. Splattered all up the walls, the ceiling, pooling on the floor. They found her in the kitchen. Carl found her. I'd never have thought I could feel sorry for that boy. Her own knives, Iz, out of a block on the worktop. Can you imagine? Stabbed repeatedly with her own knives. And not just one, all of them. Strewn over the floor all around her body, the CSI guy said. Hundreds of cuts and slashes, poor cow. He reckoned she put up a fight. Loads of what he called defensive wounds on her arms, so they know she tried to protect herself, that she was alive through most of it."

"Blin, please..." Isobel gripped the edge of the counter.

"A sustained and frenzied attack, they said on the news. Did you see it? Have those reporters knocked on your door, yet?"

She straightened. "Why would they?"

"Don't get all aeriated. They're pestering everyone, that's all. I couldn't sleep last night for them gabbing away right under my window. They were even talking to kids on the playground at the back of me, yesterday. Trying to get stories about Carl, I suppose. I guess this is what they mean by media circus. Anyway, CSI, he said what finished her off wasn't her throat being cut like they said on the telly. That wound was superficial. No, it was four deep slices on the inside of her elbows. Just here, see?" Belinda put down her mug, pulled up her sleeve and drew her finger across soft, vulnerable skin. "Imagine." Isobel swallowed hard. "Apparently, there's veins or arteries or whatever, close to the surface here. It's where they take blood from, isn't it? But, see: whoever did it must have grabbed her arms -" She grasped her own, yanked it round to present the inner elbow. Isobel winced. "That wasn't mindless slashing, was it? They knew what they were doing, and the poor cow bled to death in a pool of her own blood."

"Enough! I get the picture."

"But the weird thing is the locked doors. How did they get in? And not just that. There was no blood anywhere else in the house. He said the killer would have been covered in it, but it was like they'd teleported into the kitchen and out again afterwards. You know, like in Star Trek? It must have been the family, d'you reckon? I mean they're saying we've no reason to be afraid. That must mean they think she knew her killer, that it wasn't random, d'you think? Iz, are you ok?"

"Can we please talk about something else? I've got the kids to worry about. Melissa's frantic over all this. She's terrified. Once the police have cleared off, I'll not convince her to stay. She'll go back to Ursula's."

"But we're all scared. I know I am. Aren't you?"

Isobel dropped onto a chair. Scared didn't begin to describe how she felt right now. Did she honestly believe she could keep it at bay by *knitting*? She must leave. The children weren't safe with her in the house. She had to get away from them, as far away as she could. And then she must make it stop. Any way she could.

Chapter 69

She didn't go to bed. She couldn't risk sleeping. She lay on the sofa with the lights out, TV volume low enough not to disturb the kids, high enough to keep her eyes open. After three episodes of *Come Dine With Me*, she flicked to the BBC iplayer, scanned the documentaries. She needed something to hold her attention, stop her thoughts drifting. Drifting thoughts were dangerous. *Horizon*: that would do. Something about a lunar eclipse, a big deal, talk of a blood moon. She yawned, snuggled deeper into the sofa. Earnest analysis, pointless graphics. She was floating off, losing track …

"Super moon…magnificent views for the UK…northern Scotland…farther north the better. Northern Scotland…"

Fitful Head.

She sat up. Somewhere far away. Somewhere she knew. Blood moon, how appropriate. And Fitful Head, where Richard had joked about haunting her. She leaned forward, turned up the volume.

Now they were on the relationship between solar and lunar events.

"Never mind that. When's it happening?"

"Mum?" Melissa. "Aren't you coming to bed? Who are you talking to?"

"No one, sweetie. Just watching telly. Go on back to bed. I'll come up soon."

She listened. A bedroom door closed softly.

More waffle. Rounding up.

But when is it?

She'd missed it. They'd said already, and she'd bloody missed it.

"Mum? You said you were coming up."

"I am, sweetie. Just a sec."

"So it seems the weather's set fair for some extraordinary views of this once-in-a-lifetime event next Monday."

Monday! Thursday today. She could do it.

Hang on, when was this programme aired?

She checked the *date first shown*. Last night. She could still do it.

"Mum, I can't sleep."

Isobel clicked off the TV. At the bottom of the stairs, she peered up into darkness, made out Melissa sitting on the top step, cuddling a long-discarded teddy. She joined her. "Shove up."

Melissa shuffled to make room.

"Can't sleep?" She brushed Melissa's hair from her eyes.

"Can't stop thinking about Brodie."

Isobel put an arm around her. "Don't do this to yourself, love. Try not to think about it."

"But he was all alone." Melissa started to cry. "He must've been scared, mustn't he, all on his own? D'you think he was crying for me?"

"Liss -"

"But Mrs Proctor said she heard a dog crying."

"I know, sweetheart, but we didn't find anything when we looked, did we? So I don't think it was him."

Melissa shrugged off her arm. "Yeah, but those bastard Hares killed him. We didn't look in *their* shed, did we!"

No one would answer the door whenever they'd knocked. Isobel should have realised.

"It was him crying, I know it. He was frightened and he needed me, and I didn't come."

"Sweetie, how were you to know?" Isobel hugged her again, squeezed tight, then released her, fearing she might go too far. "Would Brodie want you to be all upset like this? He wouldn't. Remember how he'd come and snuggle up with you in bed when you were sad?" She stroked Melissa's hot cheek. "Try to think about those times, ok? You loved him, he knew that." That past tense tore at her, but she tried not to show it. "He was a happy little thing, and he's had a lovely life. Remember that. Now, let's get you into bed."

Melissa got up, turned her face to her bedroom door. Her voice had shrunk to venom. "I'm glad that bitch is dead, and I'm glad she died so horribly. I hope she was scared. I hope she screamed for help."

"Melissa, you don't mean that."

"I do, though!"

They stared at each other.

"Get into bed. You'll feel better in the morning."

Melissa cast her a strange glance: "Weird though, isn't it, what's happened? So soon after what they did. Everyone's talking about it. Supposed to be a secret how she died, but everyone knows her boyfriend slashed her to ribbons. D'you think he was punishing her for Brodie?"

"We don't know what happened, Melissa, and I don't want you thinking about it."

"I hope that's why he did it. I hope he really hurt her."

"Bed."

Melissa blew her a sad little kiss and slipped into her room.

Isobel ran down to the kitchen, switched on her laptop. She was panting like a spooked rabbit.

Buffering. *Come on!*

What if Melissa worked it out? What if she knew already? She couldn't bear for her children to know what she'd become. *Just calm down.* She breathed deeply. *Don't be an idiot, how could she possibly know?*

Still, she had to get away.

She clicked to book a Shetland flight. One way.

Chapter 70

How had she forgotten this tangle of masts, this low, intrusive building? In her heart, Fitful Head rose empty, desolate, haunted. She gazed up at the strangest mast, a giant's golf ball set atop its scaffolded tee. She wandered, fighting disappointment and biting cold. She'd forgotten, too, this perpetual Shetland wind. She'd romanticised it all out of the picture, airbrushed her memory. Not deliberately. Through the intervening years, she'd had eyes only for Richard. All else blurred to vision's edge. Richard was all she wanted, all she'd expected. She shoved her hands deep into her, Richard's, parka pockets. She raised the fur-lined hood against gusts blustering at her ears. The wind had gained force as she trekked the undemanding tarmac across bleak, boggy moor. She'd abandoned the hire car at the track's start. She could have driven most of the way up here, another fact she'd forgotten, or maybe never knew, but she wanted to walk. Just in case he… By the time she arrived at the abandoned listening station, she was sound-wrapped: buffeting gusts, tramping boots, ragged breathing. And she stank of sheep shit.

The guy at the bed and breakfast had pressed to find out where she intended to view the eclipse. A sensible man, full of warming kindness. She told him Sumburgh Head, an easy lie. He'd offered his garden instead. Blankets, single malt, company. She said she was tempted, to save his feelings, but that she had her heart set on Sumburgh. Then he offered to accompany her, his solicitude becoming an irritation. She could see his concern mounting: single woman, long way from home, air of batty distraction, turns up on spec, no booking, only luggage a small rucksack. So she told a partial truth to allay his suspicion. People always stepped back from bereavement, lest they be contaminated. She'd learned she could rely on that. She was finally allowed to leave at midnight with a promise she'd be back by dawn and, yes, she'd phone if she needed anything.

She left the phone in the car at the bottom of the track.

She wanted to be close to Richard now, at the end. She hoped he could find a way back to give her the strength she needed to go through with this. The backdrop of cosmic disruption pleased her in a perverse way, but wasn't important. She'd always known she would return to Fitful Head. It had called her in her dreams.

She walked south along the cliff edge, watching the moon unspool across agitated ocean. Foula crouched black on distant water, like a panther stalking. She climbed over a low warning fence. Surely, that was new? Inched to the brink and looked down, expecting blackness, but the supermoon lent a silver-tinged monochrome to unquiet sea, islands, layering coastline, and she saw clearly wave-washed rocks two hundred and fifty metres below. No sheer cliffs as she'd made them in memory, but grassy flanks sloping steeply, before dropping to welcoming teeth below. The fall wouldn't be through clean air, but a battering, breaking descent.

She edged forward.

It lay curled at her core, this spiky, murderous intruder. Deofol: powerful, frightening, biding its time. If she could only unlock herself, unfurl, soften...but it was too late. It would break her, unless she broke it first.

She must destroy it.

She held out her arms to let the wind nudge her closer. She leaned back, only a metre from the verge. The wind buoyed her. If a sudden, contrary gust should push, it would be easy, and not her doing.

But the wind was not so murderous. It dropped. She staggered back, glanced around, embarrassed, but no one saw. She was alone, completely. She had to seize this chance.

Go on. Finish it now. You can do it. You want to. Just one step and it'll all be over.

Creeping forward. Racing heart pushing her on. Heavy limbs pulling her back. Head

beating, beating and then a plank in reason broke and I dropped down and down

She lifted her foot to step into empty air.

Isobel, no! Think of the kids. Richard's voice, distraught.

She teetered on the edge. He was close, and he didn't want her to do this. It wasn't *him* goading her on with strange poetry.

She swayed, stepped back into a wave of relief and love. Her legs gave way, she sank to her knees, stones stabbing into bone. But then her shoulders sagged. She'd fired herself with the crazy idea that she would exchange this brutal invader for Richard. She'd believed that if *she* died, the thing would die with her, and she could rest with Richard. But he'd stopped her, didn't want her, after all.

She climbed back over the pointless fence to official safety, knowing there was no such thing.

She trudged to the low building, its masts reaching to grab the moon. And the moon seemed bigger now as if muted wind, not wanted here, had shimmied skyward to balloon it. She opened her rucksack, pulled out the sleeping bag. The flask fell out and rolled from her. She dipped to catch her caffeine fix before it got going for the edge. She shook out the bag, an old one of Ben's, stepped into it, pulled it up over her shoulders, buried her face in it. Warm fug of teenage boy. She squirmed with shame: she'd given her children not a thought, moments earlier. She sat carefully on damp ground, leaned her back against the brick wall, and faced a moon so bright she was surprised it didn't warm her skin. Head against cold bricks, she closed her eyes.

Why had she come?

To get rid of her parasite, that spiky, uncoiling fog. To kill it before it hurt anyone she loved.

And because she believed Richard would be here, waiting for her. When her mind tormented her with that metal trolley, she'd picture him here, windswept, pissed off, alive. She wiped her streaming nose on his parka sleeve.

You do know I'm going to come back and haunt you.

At Fitful Head, he'd promised. So where was he?

In that sad little plot not half a mile from her own front door.

She hit her head hard against the wall behind her. Once, twice, three times. Satiating hollow thwacks, rattled teeth, release.

Go home, you fool.

She opened her eyes to the blood moon, rich rust red. The eclipse was almost complete. She gazed long at the beauty, close enough to touch, until at last cold bit through. She stretched through stiff neck and tight shoulders to touch the back of her head, gingerly. It felt wet. She rubbed her fingers together: blood. No matter. She clambered to her feet, let the sleeping bag fall around her knees, then stepped out of it, catching her boot, nearly overbalancing. She poured a cup of tepid coffee, gulped it down; wretched investment in continuing existence. She packed up her little encampment, and walked back to the cliff edge.

She was sick of being manipulated. She wanted peace. On her own terms.

The earth's shadow slinked across the moon, like a thing ashamed. She looked north to seascape of silhouetted land and water. No shame in such beauty. No shame in any of this.

She raised her face to chilling light. Long-forgotten lines came, unbidden:

I left him behind me throwing his shade
My head unturned lest my dream should fade.

Wasn't that what she'd been doing all summer?

uncurling unfurling

Perhaps she could find a way to live with this possession.

Wind played about her neck like winter breath. She dipped her cheek to the corpse-cold hand upon her shoulder.

As long as she never looked back.

Acknowledgements

Thanks to Sue O'Connell, Susan Johnson, Joe J-H and Jonathan Lord for sharing their professional expertise. Accuracies are down to them. Any inaccuracies are mine alone.

I'm grateful to the members of South Manchester Writers' Workshop for their constructive criticism. Special mention to Boz Masters and David Beckler for their detailed critiques which made this a better novel.

I'd also like to thank Wigan Novel Writing Group for its support in the early stages of developing this story.

Thanks again to Mike Martin of **www.redherringcg.com** for another fabulous cover design.

My friend Eamee Boden generously allowed me to use her unique name. Thanks, Eamee.

Harry Harter has my huge thanks and undying love for putting up with all my dramas, and for being my first reader.

I want to thank the people of Lowton for their forbearance as I've taken fictional liberties with their village. In particular, Bodden Street is real but has only two terraced blocks of houses. The events of the story take place in a fictional third block. None of my characters bear any resemblance to real residents of Bodden Street and none of the houses are haunted… as far as I know.

And finally...

If you've enjoyed *Fitful Head: A Ghost Story*, I would be so grateful if you could tell your reading friends, recommend it to your book group or leave a review on Amazon.com, Amazon.co.uk, Goodreads, indeed anywhere you get your book reviews. Great reviews really do help authors sell their books and that in turn means they can continue to write the stories you enjoy.

Here is the web address to find the book on Amazon.

getbook.at/FitfulHead

Just type it into Google.

Thank you.

I love to hear from my readers. Keep in touch with me via:
my website **www.cjharterbooks.co.uk**
Facebook **www.facebook.com/cjharterbooks**
Twitter **@cj_harter**

And if you'd like to read my first novel, psychological suspense *Rowan's Well,* you can find it here:

myBook.to/RowansWell

Great reviews always make my day.

Here's the opening of *Rowan's Well* to whet your appetite, with my compliments.

ROWAN'S WELL

Chapter 1

2003: Ten Years After

"Can I tell you one more story before we finish?"

In his head, Dutton punched the air. "Yes, of course."

Mark Strachan remained where he was, looking out of the window at the upper floors of the high-security wing opposite. He thrust his hands into his pockets.

"This happened a long time ago. I must have been about five or six. I hadn't been in school long, anyway. We made these autumn collages. With leaves and twigs and stuff. We walked to some woods to collect things. It was cold. My fingers all red and tingly. I remember running, looking for the most colourful leaves. Then we brought them back to school, and we put them in a big pile on the teacher's desk. It looked like a great big bonfire. God, I can smell it now, all damp and earthy. We got to choose what colour paper we wanted for our pictures. I chose this rich shade of green. I could picture my bonfire burning all bright and fiery on that green. I picked leaves, beech nuts, acorns, all that, and I built this amazing bonfire. I stuck it all down with that white glue we used back then. Smelled rank. Like fish?"

He cast Dutton a quick glance.

"Yes, that's right."

"You had to apply the glue with those little plastic spatulas and it got all over your hands and your jumper, everywhere. I remember thinking my mum would be cross about that. But then I thought, no, she wouldn't be because I was going to give her my picture, my beautiful bonfire. She'd be so pleased she couldn't be cross."

He bowed his head. Dutton held his breath.

"The teacher - Miss Pickmere? Pickford? something like that - she was thrilled when she saw what I'd done. She helped me make flames out of red, orange and yellow cellophane - her idea - and I stuck them on. It looked all shimmery and fiery. And nobody else got to use the cellophane that day, because my picture was special. Miss Pickmere told me to take it home to show my mum but to bring it back tomorrow because she wanted to put it up on the wall for our autumn display. God, I was so proud."

Another pause.

"I ran out of school with my picture. I had to hold tight to it because it was windy, and the picture was big. I was scared it would fly out of my grasp. I ran to my mum. She was standing further up the road. She never stood with the other mums. I showed her the picture and she took it from me and she said - she said: 'I don't have time for this nonsense. I'm late for work. Hurry up.' And she shoved my picture into her bag. Not carefully. No. She scrunched it in her hand and she shoved it, all screwed up, into her bag. She grabbed me by the wrist. And - and I don't remember any more after that."

Want to read on? Find the rest here:

myBook.to/RowansWell

Happy reading!

CJ Harter